―――――――― ★ ――――――――

A THOUGHT STRUCK HIM

Professor Kaa had said this device would be developed by others to become a doorway into the future and the past. If so, Patch reasoned, there would surely be movement through it both ways, and probably not just within the present limits of eighty years or so.

In that event, why had nobody ever met anyone who had come back on a visit through Professor Kaa's doorway? Why had it never happened? Or why would it *never* happen?

Patch was so immersed in speculation that he scarcely felt the long tremor that ran through the ship as an iceberg tore a three-hundred-foot gash in the starboard hull of the *Titanic*.

―――――――― ★ ――――――――

"There's something for everyone in the British Crime Writers' Association's second annual collection..."

—*Kirkus Reviews*

"It is the lesser-known writers whose snippets are the most appealing."

—*St. Petersburg Times*, FL

WAIT! I THINK THE DOG KNOWS SOMETHING!

2ND CULPRIT

AN ANNUAL OF CRIME STORIES

edited by

LIZA CODY AND MICHAEL Z LEWIN

WORLDWIDE®

TORONTO • NEW YORK • LONDON
AMSTERDAM • PARIS • SYDNEY • HAMBURG
STOCKHOLM • ATHENS • TOKYO • MILAN
MADRID • WARSAW • BUDAPEST • AUCKLAND

2ND CULPRIT: A CRIME WRITERS' ASSOCIATION ANNUAL

A Worldwide Mystery/June 1995

First published by St. Martin's Press, Incorporated.

ISBN 0-373-15280-9

CONTENTS
THE ANNUAL ANTHOLOGY OF THE CRIME WRITERS' ASSOCIATION

2ND CULPRIT

BETTER TO FORGET

★

SUSAN MOODY

SHE FLITS LIKE A MOTH behind the windows, pulling the shutters closed in the green dusk. From my chair under the walnut tree, I watch the flutter of her progress, room by room, from the big *salle de séjour*, through the kitchen and dining-room, then, one after the other, the seven bedrooms.

Who is she?
Who am I?
Why are we here?
This not remembering is terrible to me.

She says I have lost my memory but if that is truly so, how can I remember that I have forgotten? How can I be aware of my past, waiting, weighted, full of incidents, happenings, memories, all the separate pieces of time which make up the me-ness of me? How can I find it again, that past? Why did I lose it?

She is on the top floor now, in the long low attic room which stretches across the top of the house, just as the *séjour* stretches across the ground floor. The attic lies under curving beams which hold up the roof, arching across the pale plaster. The interstices where wood meets wood, touches, intersects and continues, are netted with cobwebs. Not the intricate circular miracles I remember (I *remember*) from another time, but sticky, clinging to the fingers, decorated with the fragile wings of insects: moth, butterfly, bee, even a dragon fly which hangs suspended, its long body somehow enlarged by the perpetual twilight under that sounding roof.

As the last shutter encloses the room behind it, the house stands neatly packaged, pink and grey in the dusk, safe for one more night. But am I safe?

Why am I here?

Who is she?

She moves between the rooms, touching tables, the backs of chairs, the brass locks on the wardrobes. Her long fingers move over dried grasses, tall vases, bowls. Her dresses are pale, gauzy, the colours of insect wings. When I ask why we are here she smiles at me, she puts her head, clouded with rich dark hair, on one side and shakes it gently. She rarely speaks. Sometimes she passes my chair and lays a hand on my shoulder softly, as though anxious not to disturb my passage from the now we currently occupy to the past I cannot recall.

I am obsessed by that lost distance. I hover in the present, robbed of dimension. I have no past because I have, somehow, mislaid it, no future because I have no experience on which to build one. Yet as I think this, I wonder how I can make use of words like dimension, future, distance, if my memory has gone.

Her hair hangs around her face like a cloud of dark butterflies. It is the most stated thing about her, the most positive. Is she guardian, gaoler, nurse, companion? Is she mother, sister, daughter, wife? Because I have asked her before, I know that if I asked again she would say she was self, *her* self; she would say she is no longer attached to others, she would say that was why we are here.

But you are attached to me, I cry, you must be, and she smiles at me, head inclined. I sit under the walnut tree and watch the land beyond the river curve gently out of the earth to meet copse, wood, lines of upright poplars. The fields are yellow, furred with the brown silk of maize or burned with dying, drying sunflowers which hang their scorched faces to the dry earth. The heat is intense. We sweat, our faces damp, the skin at wrist and knee shining with moisture. It is shimmeringly hot so that the tall poplars, the willows, the laden fruit trees, move behind a haze, not quite defined. At the end of the garden the river runs, flat and brown, flat and green. On

ne opposite bank the poplars stand reflected, reaching to-
vards me.

LIE ON THE FLOOR of the second *chambre*. It is situated above
he living-room and there are gaps between the floorboards. I
an see her down there, seated at the table, her head resting on
er hand. She is reading a newspaper. She sighs, lifting the
eavy hair from her neck. If I could only read the words I
now I would find my past and thus regain my future, but
rom here I can see nothing and when I go downstairs there is
o newspaper, no rescue.
Who am I?
I want myself back. I am foetal, marooned in the present,
astless and futureless. Unmarked, and yet marked. I look into
he dim green mirrors in the seven *chambres* and see that the
ast has written itself on my face. If only I could read what it
ays.
She calls me softly, through the twilight. At the top of the
neven steps of slippery cream stone which climb the side of
he house to the first floor, she stands waiting, gauzed in ice-
ream colours: white cotton, pink lawn, green silk. I can
ardly see her sometimes as she waits for me to cross the warm
rass—and then she touches a switch and the lamp above the
oor comes on to illuminate her strong black hair. I imagine
ometimes, as I lie in bed in the hot nights while the insects
ance unseen about me, that her hair is like a cobweb, full of
truggling wings.
Above us, as we drink soup, cut meat, pass vegetables, nip
t cheeses or bread, I can hear the rooms settling and sighing,
heir wooden floors creaking under the weightless feet of
hosts.
But whose ghosts?
Whose house is this?
Why are we here?
Tonight the soup is made from tomatoes. I picked them for
er earlier, liking the feel of the plump fruit in my hand, the
ontrast between their fleshy redness and the yellowed leaves
mong which they hang. Yet now, looking down at the bowl,
cannot eat. The soup reminds me—if I can use a word for

something of which I cannot have a concept since I have n
memories to recall—of something I do not wish to remember
It sits in front of me like—like . . .

I raise my eyes and she is looking at me, head on one side
smiling. She tells me to eat and I put my spoon into the re
liquid. There are circles of oil on the surface, golden in th
light from the lamp. I can see onion floating under the su
face, liked peeled skin, translucent, softly ribbed the way in
sect wings are ribbed.

Eat, she tells me. Eat. It's good.

*What language are we speaking? Is it my own or one whic
is so familiar to me that it seems my own?*

Is it hers?

Eat, she says again, but I cannot. I push the bowl away fro
me.

She brings meat, the lines of the grill black across its su
face. She brings a flat dish of wax-coloured beans with butte
melting into the nest of their intersecting lengths. Red sou
yellow beans, the charred animal flesh—I stare at her. Am
child or adult? How can I know that such states as childhoo
or maturity exist if I have no past? How can I have retained
vocabulary? How can I have kept the skeleton of words, con
cepts, yet lost the images which flesh them out and turn then
into memories?

I must retrieve my past.

I STAND SOMETIMES in the attic room and look out at the gar
den. It runs down to the river past trees, bushes, a vegetabl
patch. She walks between raspberry canes, wearing a flat stra
hat. She carries a basket in which to imprison the beans, th
tomatoes, the plums with which the garden is so bountiful
There is a greengage tree at the edge of the grass, its frui
mothed with grey bloom. The fruit is the colour of the river i
the morning, the colour of her dress at night. There is yellov
under the plumped-out skin, and when I bite into it, the ston
at its heart is red.

SHE IS FALLING, the cream steps slippery under her sandals. She looks up at me as I hurry across the grass to help her to her feet.

My ankle, she says, leaning on me. The shopping. You will have to go into the village, she says. The *boulangerie*. The butcher.

Butcher, butcher—the word clangs in my head like a bell, resounding through the cobwebbed caverns of my brain.

Butcher.

I take a basket and walk down the white road. The word hangs in front of me as though I am reading it from a newspaper headline. A plump word, rounded, full of blood.

Butcher.

Butchered.

I buy sticks of bread, a plum tart, milk and cream. I buy onions. I stand waiting in a queue in front of a glass counter. Behind it are steel dishes of organs: livers, kidneys, sweetbreads. Yellow fat. Dark blood. Cobwebs of white tissue. I push my way out of the shop and stand trembling on the narrow pavement. They remind me of—of...

You forgot to go to the butcher, she says, when I reach the house again. She puts her head on one side and smiles at me. I stare at her and after a while she looks away.

This evening there is more soup made from the last of the tomatoes, but this time she has disguised it with cream. I spoon it into my mouth and think: we have done this before, she and I: this house, these rooms, are not just the present but the past as well.

THE LAMP in the living-room is on but she has forgotten to close the shutters. Tonight she is wearing a dress the colour of air. Moths flutter round the circle of light, their wings bumping softly against the shade. I lie on the floor in the greengage twilight and spy on her from above. She is reading. Another newspaper. Different words. She moves her clouded hair and I read HUNT SHIFTS TO. What does it mean? My foot scrapes across the dusty boards and she looks up sharply, her face white. She calls my name but I do not answer and after a while

she stands and limps across to the hearth where she strikes a
match and sets fire to the paper.

I WATCH HER from the window of the attic. She lies in the garden under the trees. Her eyes are closed. Softly I walk down
the creaking wooden stairs and into the kitchen. She has been
preparing more of the yellow beans. They lie drowning in a
pan. Beside the chopping board waits a knife with a black
handle. I pick it up, hold it in my hand and feel the weight of
it, the balance. Light gleams along the blade and the present
dissolves for a moment into the past.

Where?
Why?

I stab the knife into the table. If only I could remember. If
only I could bring it back. When I turn, she is standing in the
doorway, watching me. She does not smile.

SHE SAYS THERE WILL BE rain tonight. Behind the poplar trees
the sky is the colour of greengages. Wind rattles among the
stalks of maize. Under the plum tree the ground is purple with
fallen fruit. She moves between the raspberry canes, picking
the last of the berries. Brown leaves fly about her head like
moths and I know, without knowing how I know, that the
summer is ending, that it has ended in this house, this garden,
many times before, that I have been here, part of it.

Tyres crunch behind the house. People. Go inside, she says.
Go upstairs. Her voice is not quite calm.

I feel my heart begin to pump. In the room above the *séjour* I lie and listen. I can see them between the floorboards.
Two men, both wearing white shirts and jackets, although heat
still hangs heavy in the house. I can see sweat on their fore-
heads; their wrists shine with it.

They speak in low voices, as though they do not wish to be
overheard.

Caught up with you at last, they say. Cooperation. French
police. Afraid we shall have to.

She says: you didn't know him. What he did to us. What he
did. You don't understand.

Tell us, they say.

This house was the only place, she says. He tried to destroy it, to destroy everything. She begins to weep. You don't know what it was like. I'm not excusing anything, she says and tears drop on to the backs of her sunburned hands. Her hair droops darkly over her face.

That room, one of them says. A slaughterhouse. Butchered. Like an animal.

That's what he was, she says. It's what he deserved.

Blood, one of them says. Everywhere. And...other things. Butchered.

This house, she says. My refuge. It was all I had. I didn't know what to do, she says.

She is lying. All my life she has known what to do.

Who did it? they say. Who used the knife?

She shakes her head. What it was like, she says.

You'll both have to come, they say. Back with us. Home to England.

She says: It's not our home. It never was.

They stand. They look up at the ceiling. I hear them slowly climbing the stairs and think that if I could only get back my past, I would be able to change the future. But I am caught in the overwhelming present. As the feet come nearer to where I lie beneath the cobwebs and the trapped insects, rain begins to fall. I hear it beating on the roof and against the shutters. I hear it falling down the chimney on to the hearth. Outside, the leaves of the plum tree and the greengage clatter against each other and the sunflowers clash like cymbals. Footsteps boom along the passage.

PERHAPS IT WOULD BE better not to remember.

THE FRUSTRATION DREAM

★

ELLIS PETERS

HAVE YOU EVER had the frustration dream? I wouldn't mind betting that you have, I fancy few people escape it all their lives. But you might not recognise it, let alone call it by that name. I have a tendency to categorise dream patterns, a hangover, perhaps, from my abortive studies in philosophy, which never came to anything. There is, for instance, the flying dream, in which you tire of such tedious means of progression as walking, and take off from the ground, or sail comfortably from a cliff-edge without so much as thinking about it beforehand, or realising that it is not the usual prerogative of humanity. Natural optimists regularly fly in their sleep. Pessimists fall into pits instead.

The frustration dream comes in several variations. The most frequent, perhaps, is of setting out to go somewhere, and finding that roads shrivel into narrow lanes before you, and narrow lanes into paths blocked by bushes and briars, rocks, stones, fetid puddles and even nastier obstacles. A slightly different form of the same type is of looking forward eagerly to some particular treat, and rising to dress for the occasion with special care. Whereupon everything you attempt to put on, even supposing you can find it at all, is either crumpled in the laundry-bin, or tears at a touch, or suddenly develops foul stains. Women must go through legions of laddered tights if they suffer from the frustration dream.

Another kind is the dream of being just settled in a hotel somewhere, going out for a walk, and finding that you either can't find your way back to the hotel and can't even rememer its name to ask someone, or if you do rediscover the place, you can't recall the number of your room, and can't find any spot in miles of corridors that even looks like the right door, or any person around to ask.

Another familiar version is of falling in front of a moving vehicle—mine was usually a steamroller—and being quite unable to move hand or foot to get up and evade it. For hours you watch the approach which seems to cross only about one yard of road surface.

Yet another is of being with a companion, on some business absolutely vital—in any surroundings, the locale doesn't matter, though usually indoors, and in a fairly complex building. Your companion goes away for some innocent purpose demanding only a few moments. And never comes back. And because this is important and must be completed, you go looking for him. The building about you does as the roads do, folds up in dark passages and gloomy corners, empty rooms vary the monotony, your search becomes ever more frantic.

Well, you get the idea. And the really absolute law that applies to all these dreams is that they never have any ending, never a solution. When you set out to go somewhere, you never arrive. If it's the variation where you're dressing for a ball, you never even set out. You never find your lost hotel or your vanished room. You never get run over by the steamroller, though you never get to your feet and run, either. And whatever you're searching for, you never find it. The frustration dream never has any conclusion. You just wake up out of it, still lost, still half-dressed, still yelling for help, still desperately hunting for what is lost. Lost for good. Balked and exasperated and aggrieved, you start off on the wrong foot for the day, even though you thought you were glad and relieved to find it was a dream. You're still cheated of a solution.

You never get used to it. But you can, I think, develop a kind of internal defence that can wake you out of it before it gets too maddening to endure. Or so I thought, until the time when it happened to me while I was wide awake, and I couldn't break out of it, and it did have an ending.

It's several years back now, before I was married. Indeed, I hadn't been thinking of marriage, and working up the

courage to broach the subject with Laura, it might never hav
happened to me. I was working with a firm of architects out
side town then, before I joined up with Martin in Bir
mingham, and we set up the partnership. I had a small flat i
the conversion of some old minor spa buildings, and once
month half a dozen of us who had been juniors together fo
the New Town Development Corporation used to meet i
Breybourne for a meal or a pint or two. I didn't run a car then
more because the buses were frequent and convenient tha
because I couldn't afford it. I was being canny with my sav
ings with a view to matrimony and house purchase, an
somewhere ahead, a family.

So on this particular autumn evening we'd been dining a
our favourite place, a crumbling old pub on the edges of ol
Breybourne, which had the best food in the town. A little late
in the transformation of Breybourne, we suspected, th
Golden Spur was pretty certain to go the way of many othe
fine buildings left over from the old town and in the way c
profitable development. It wasn't listed, though it probabl
should have been, and it wasn't really so outstanding as t
arouse protests, so we made the most of its cuisine while
lasted.

We ate early, because two or three of the bunch had lon
drives, and it looked as if it might turn foggy with the dark. W
broke up about nine, since mist was hazing all the street ligh
already, and it looked as if the forecast would be accurate; an
I walked towards the bus stop intending to take an earlier bus
but in no hurry, since I didn't have to drive. There was some
thing curiously Dickensian in strolling the streets of the ol
town under those haloed lights, even if they weren't ga
lamps, and that surviving quarter was a maze of narrow lane
sudden corners, and narrow Victorian shopfronts, some sti
lit even below, some gleaming above through drawn curtain
for here small dealers and craftsmen lived above their shop
The few people I met could have belonged in Dickens, to
going hurriedly home, almost furtively because of the wind
less silence and the gathering fog, shadows in a shadow
world.

I had plenty of time, or thought I had, and had never really explored this quarter, so I was tempted to turn aside and take a more leisurely look at it now, the narrow frontages that ran back and back into remote and complex rears, built over and built on over centuries, huddles of invisible, complicated chimneys up there on top, sudden extensions skyward of the cramped house-fronts that sported below such unexpected and secretive show-windows, one here and there still lit at this hour. The highly professional enclaves of very old towns, where the jewellers and gem-cutters and locksmiths and pawnbrokers and money-lenders operated, kept no closing hours against customers of substance. Much of their business was done in the twilight, not by reason of any dishonesty, but because it was personal, private and vulnerable. Something of that era— how far back? Back, certainly, to before the expulsion of the Jews—lingered here in this autumnal and half-obliterated evening.

One of the alleys actually still had its medieval cobbles, and deep-rutted stone laid for where the cart-wheels would have run. And there was a small rounded bay window in one of the narrow frontages, a Victorian modernisation that had probably replaced stone mullions. It was still lighted, a solitary gleam in the dark, and it caught my eye by the glitter of cut stones within. Of all shop windows to leave lighted after closing, a jeweller's, I thought, and stopped to examine what was on show. No great value at risk, probably, except that most of it was antique, some Victorian jet and onyx, and some semi-precious stones of the more modest kind, in older settings, and period pieces have become fashionable again lately, far beyond their value in commercial terms. But there was one quite lovely amethyst pendant, five stones of excellent colour and finely cut, in delicate silver filigree. Without a chain, but most women have an assortment of chains to suit all occasions.

I like amethysts, and by that time I had discovered that Laura liked them, too, and frequently wore shades of iris and lavender that cried out for this kind of embellishment. A pity it was well past any closing time, and would it be there if I dropped in here next time?

I don't know why I tried the door, since I knew it would be locked.

Only it wasn't. It gave at once, and the attached bell rang loudly and clearly, startling me into stepping back instead of forward. But what was the good of retreating, now? People here lived over the shop. Better go in and at least warn the jeweller that he'd left his wares open—some of them, at least— to any opportunist who happened to come along and try his luck. And in any case, waiting within for attention would prove I was no such raider. And who knows, if the boss was actually working late in his back room he might not be averse to making a late sale. He might even knock a bit off the price in gratitude for the warning.

And Laura's birthday was only three weeks away. I went in and closed the door behind me to produce another alerting peal.

The shop was lighted only by the incongruous fluorescent strip in the window, and its corners retreated into obscurity even though it was small and as much workshop as sales depot. A curtained door sealed it off from the back premises; there were closed cupboards built in behind the single counter, the glass showcase which had been emptied, evidently the more valuable pieces put into a safe for the night, I thought. Clean, worn and bare, totally without glitter, the kind of shop where a man could reasonably look for a fair bargain.

A woman came in through the rear door, drawing the curtain aside with a rustle of rings and folds, and releasing a faint odour of dust. The sort of woman who went well with that sort of shop, fairly tall, erect, in forgettable black, possibly forty years old, and not at all bad looking in a severe way, her face oval, and looking pale in the dimness. She did not switch on another light. Nor did she seem surprised at seeing a customer at this hour. The bell had called, and she came in response to it. And sparing of words, too, for she left it to me to open contact, merely standing before me with her head inclined and a faint smile, inviting approach.

'Good evening,' I said. 'I was surprised to find the shop open at this hour. Did you know the door was still unlocked?'

'I worked late,' she said. Her voice was very quiet, low-pitched and without resonances. 'But I had forgotten. Thank you for reminding me.'

Well, since I was there, and she was there, I might as well ask.

'I just happened to be passing, but there is an item in your window I should like to buy, if the price is right. And if you'd be kind enough to make a concession for me, even at this hour, I may not be this way again for some time.'

She came forward then, and turned towards the window. 'I have cashed up. But of course... Open is open for business!' She had a smile as distant as her voice. Her short, straight hair was dark, maybe black, her eyes large and dark. She looked her years, but she was still handsome. 'Which piece is it you liked?'

I told her, and she lifted it out, and stood for a moment cupping it in one palm. Then she looked up directly at me, and really smiled, a momentary warmth shining through her tiredness. She had worked late, and it showed.

'It is for a gift?' she said, very softly.

'If I can afford it,' I said cautiously.

She priced it at £60, her eyes steady on me, and I knew by the workmanship in the filigree setting it was worth more, possibly a great deal more. I had that much cash on me, and no card, as it happened, and in any case this was a curious, once-only transaction between us two, to be sealed and shaken hands on here and now. It was almost as if she and the shop itself would have vanished utterly if ever I came that way again. Outside, the fog was thick. Even here within, outlines seemed to have softened and melted in mist.

I gave her the money, and she checked it into tomorrow's takings in the empty till.

'I'll find a lined box for it,' she said. 'Wait just a moment. I'll be back.' She went away through the curtained door, and I heard her footsteps diminuendo along a paved passage, but only for a few paces. And I waited. The earlier bus would have gone by that time, but I had plenty of time before my usual one, even allowing for delays due to the fog. So I ranged about the little shop and looked at the other bits in the window, and

the empty velvet pad that lined the showcase, and the array of
cupboard doors in the panelling, and the swirls of shifting fog
outside in the alley. And listened to the silence. And waited.

But she didn't come back. It took me a long time to begin to
feel uneasy, because it had all been so ordinary, after all, a
fortuitous find and an unexpected sale. Nothing to write home
about. But I'm not a very patient person, and there was little
entertainment there to keep me interested, and I began to be
irritated first, then uneasy, and then so annoyed that I might
have walked out and shrugged off the whole thing, but for the
fact that my £60 was shut into the till, and she had gone away
with Laura's amethyst pendant in her hand. Reasonably
enough if she had a selection of boxes from which to choose,
and wanted the most suitable one; but I wanted that pendant.
So I couldn't leave. And time ran on, and I began to think of
my bus.

In the end I opened the door through which she had vanished, and called through it, rather tentatively: 'Are you there?
I have to go!' I didn't know a name for her. 'Please hurry! The
box doesn't matter, I'll find one.'

I was looking into a stony passage, unlit, with the shadows
of doorways deepening the dark on one side, and beyond,
what seemed to be the foot of a staircase. Absolute silence beyond there. I called again, and the shaken air lay like a faintly
stirred blanket heavy over me. Groping, I opened the nearer
door, and found a light switch on the wall inside. A shabby,
ordinary living-room, furniture old but once good, everything neat and clean but somehow impersonal. The second
door was a jeweller's workroom, with a large, solid bench,
tools, a little furnace, an air of having been quitted for the day
some hours ago, with everything austerely put away until tomorrow.

Under the stairs a dusty cupboard with a vacuum cleaner,
brooms, all the paraphernalia of a modest household; no way
of lighting it, I identified the nature of what it held by falling
over and into the various traps. Close to it, working backwards through a convoluted and bewildering depth of house,
two empty closets and a small, bleak kitchen. This place was

ery old, and I was falling backwards through history in plumbing its depths.

And there was no one there, and in every corner the dank feeling that there had never been anyone, or not for centuries. And no amount of exasperated calling raised any answer but a hollow echo that went batting back and forth from every wall ahead of me, apparently into infinity.

I don't even know why I went on, except that the impetus of setting out on such a search makes it difficult to slow down, and almost impossible to stop. And I wanted my property. But perhaps even more, by that time, I wanted to set eyes once again on that quiet woman, and see for myself that she did exist, and that she was just as material and practical as she had been in the shop. Whatever the reason, I went on up the stairs. The first room there was a double bedroom, quite well furnished, but with wardrobe doors hanging open. After that the usual disintegration of the frustration dream set in, through rooms shrinking in size, ever more deserted and dusty, and at last narrow and empty. The house was very, very old. Floors swayed up and down, and creaked. There were tiny windows which had been sealed shut for centuries.

I came back to the stairhead, and peered again into the bedroom, where I had done no more than look in, and see that it was empty. This time I went in, switching on the light, and advanced to the bed. And beyond it, on the flowered carpet between bed and window, there she was, the vanished lady in black. She lay contorted, limbs tossed wide, as if she had been seized by the throat and flung down forcibly. Her head was turned a little aside, on her right cheek. Her face was suffused and discoloured, her throat bruised. Every detail leaped into my eyes stunningly in the sharp light, and I knew she was dead. While I waited below, she had been dying above. From here not a sound would carry below. So short a time it takes to end a life.

I say I knew she was dead, and I did, but it took an age to believe what I knew. And while I was staring helplessly at what I had been searching for, and wishing I had awakened before I ever found it, the door closed behind me, and I heard the key turn in the lock.

And while I was wrenching the handle and refusing to be
lieve it wouldn't turn and let me out, the light went out. I wa
left alone with a murdered woman, unable to get to a tele
phone, unable to break out of this room and this dream an
run for it back to reality. The frustration dream had broken a
the rules by arriving at last, by finding what was lost, and wit
all my appalled senses and soul I wished it had not.

IT MUST HAVE BEEN a couple of hours before they came; an
they were the police. All that time I'd been trying to pick tha
lock, with every possible thing I had about me that resemble
a tool, but without success. There had to be a telephor
somewhere downstairs, if only I could get to it. But it seeme
someone else had used another telephone to warn the loc
constabulary that lights had been going on and off in the Ame
house in a somewhat suspect way, and the caller thought the
might have been a break-in.

So they told me, when they had forced the lock of that be
room door, and firmly, but with the sort of gentleness (
caution?) you use towards a case of precarious mental stabi
ity, escorted me downstairs to await transfer to the local p
lice station. Held on suspicion of murder. What else could
expect? Alone in that huge, rambling labyrinth with the dea
woman—a natural suspect if ever there was. The fact that v
were locked in, and the key was certainly not in there with
or I would have used it, did not prove that I had not killed he
merely that someone else, offered the opportunity, had turne
the key to make sure I stayed to be arrested. Though I wasn
actually arrested, merely held for questioning.

I told them the whole story, not being sure what to tell an
what to leave out if I hedged. The entire progression of n
evening, complete with times, when I had left the Golden Spu
the names of all my friends who would confirm it, and so
the shop and the pendant. Yes, the pendant—where was it?
hadn't seen it since, and I remembered to tell them that my fe
in the till would speak for me. I checked and signed a lor
statement before they locked me in a cell, still uncharged. The
let me call my boss. At that time of night he couldn't have be

very grateful, but he came up trumps and promised police bail next morning if they'd allow it.

Then they locked me in. I didn't have any dreams that night, but then I didn't have much sleep either.

THE BOSS WAS as good as his word, and bailed me out next morning. To tell the truth, I was surprised they let me out so complacently, seeing the state of the case, but they weren't giving anything away, just turning me loose with the request-cum-warning that I should remain at their disposal while enquiries continued.

TWO DAYS LATER Detective-Sergeant Sharp came to see me at my flat, after office hours. I'd got used to his poker face by then, and didn't want to jump to any too hopeful conclusions.

'It's all right,' he said, 'you're off the hook. We've got our man. Picked him up at Heathrow, with all the good stuff and all the cash from the safe in his luggage. Her husband! He was still in the house when you barged in, of course, he's the one who locked you in, he's the one who telephoned us to go and get you an hour and more later, when he was well on his way south. The business was hers, you see, came of generations of jewellers in that house. Seems things had been going awry between them. Anyhow, she seems to have had reason not to put much trust in him, for she'd changed the combination of the safe. You should see that safe. Built into the panelling feet deep, super job. It took him ages to break into it after he'd killed her, or he'd have been away before ever you blew in and spoiled things.'

I mulled that over, and objected suddenly: 'Wait a minute! How *could* he have been off the scene before I came? She was alive then, she was in the shop with me. She answered the bell.'

He didn't answer at once, he was looking at me as though I'd said something at once pertinent and lunatic. 'Well,' he said then, 'as a matter of fact, we didn't really think much of you as a suspect after that first night. If then! But certainly not after that. There was the fact that someone had been there to lock you in with her, and who was it likely to be but the husband who just didn't seem to be around any more from then on? Then next day, when we went over the house, sure enough we found your notes in the till, the safe cleaned out, the best of the male clothes from the wardrobe gone. And this—' He took from his pocket and laid before me the amethyst pendant, opening out the tissue paper in which he had wrapped it. 'This we found about seven yards along the downstairs corridor from the shop.'

It didn't make sense. None of it made sense.

'I can't hand it over,' said Sharp, 'Not yet, anyhow, but I rather think by rights this is yours. You paid the price tag.'

I said that I didn't think she would want it, now. I'd have to buy her something else.

'Perhaps you're right,' he said. 'But of course, it was after the post-mortem that we knew you were out of the picture. By all the signs, she was dead by nine o'clock at the latest, probably before. About the time you and your mates were coming out of the Golden Spur, Ames was strangling his wife in the bedroom over the shop.'

He didn't wait to reason, or listen to reason, he got up and made for the door. There he looked back to where I sat struck dumb. 'I shouldn't even try,' he said kindly. 'Just be thankful.'

So there you are, and make what you can of it. I don't know! The bell rang, and she came to serve a customer, just as she must have done for years. Do you suppose that they have, for a limited time, like an echo that sounds quite realistically but then dies away, the faculty of lingering on in a corporeal echo? Just for a brief while only, before they make sense of death, and leave? She only got a few yards along the passage before she dropped the pendant. And it was a long stone passage, and I only heard the first seven or eight footsteps, before they died away. Well . . .

WOMEN ARE STRANGE. I didn't tell Laura the whole story, I left out all about the time of death, but she read the reports at the police-court hearing, so she knew. And when I said I hadn't wanted to accept the pendant because of its associations, she said, why not?

'You did her no wrong,' she said. 'You helped to get justice or her, if that was what she wanted. And there was a moment f contact, remember what you told me. When she looked at ou, and asked: Is it a gift?, and went off to find a pretty box o put it in. She saw a young man buying a present for his girl, nd just for a moment it gave her pleasure. In a way,' said aura, 'you were the last person to see her alive.'

THE DUKE

★

ERIC WRIGHT

IN A STORY LIKE THIS, you have to get the hero right. Every
thing else—plot, conflict, resolution—will all grow out of him
or not. This is enough of a task for one story, and I can assu
the reader that the 'I' in the story is a thoroughly reliable na
rator; there is no need to go behind him. This said, I've mad
a start.

After half a lifetime of not being very much at home in th
world, Duke Luscombe had finally found exactly the right job
He was a cook, trained in Montreal by a catering company t
run the kitchen of a construction camp. The training could ne
have been very extensive: the Duke could cook about twent
different menus, though the same vegetables appeared on mo
of them, but because some of the items, like steaks and chop
were offered at least once a week, and because there was
roast or a boiled ham every Sunday, some of the menus, lik
pork tenderloin, appeared only once a month, giving th
Duke's repertoire an appearance of being much bigger than
really was. But his skills matched the needs of the men. The
wanted soup, and then meat, in some form, every night, an
while they were prepared to eat canned fruit for dessert occa
sionally, most nights they wanted pie, with ice-cream. Th
soups were shipped in from Montreal, in drums, and the pi
were made from dough prepared in Montreal and from hug
cans of pie filling. The Duke had printed instructions for th
preparation of every meat dish, so the best test of his skill can
at breakfast, where his bacon was crisp and his eggs done t
order.

By the time I came to the camp the Duke was well established. He had command of a dining-room serving the foremen, of whom there were about twenty, including the timekeepers, the men who recorded the labour and materials used on each contract. Even a kitchen this small called for two cooks, but the Duke did it all with some help from a couple of Ojibway girls who came in from the Indian camp down by the railway tracks. There had once been another cook before I arrived, but he had only stayed a month. The Duke had complained in head-shaking fashion from the day he arrived about the 'goddam useless bum' that Montreal had sent him, and at the end of the month the new man was gone. When the foremen appeared for breakfast one morning the Duke told them he had put his assistant on the train and told him not to stop until he got to Montreal. 'He was just under my feet all the time,' the Duke said. 'Help like that I don't need. And if the Montreal office don't like it, they can find someone else to replace me.'

The new man had tried to get the foremen to hear his side of the story when it became obvious that the Duke intended to get rid of him, but the prime concern of the men in the dining-room was that the Duke not be upset. All of them had worked on jobs where one day the cook had been too drunk to make breakfast, or had gone berserk with a knife, and they could tolerate the knowledge of the Duke's unfairness for the sake of their food. No one was surprised when the assistant left. And presumably the Montreal office was happy with the saving in wages.

The Duke got up at five to pick up the Indian girls. Breakfast had to be ready by seven for a work crew who started at seven-thirty. Lunch was soup, cold cuts with some kind of vegetables, and pie. Around three, the Duke began on the supper which had to be ready at five-thirty. He closed the dining-room at seven-thirty and ate his own supper—usually a steak—and the girls helped themselves to what was left over from the night's menu. He waited, then, until they had cleaned up the kitchen, and drove them back to town. The Duke took responsibility for more than their transportation. While they worked in his kitchen they might as well have been in a con-

vent. There were very few women around that far north and
inevitably, since all the foremen had pickup trucks, someone
would have offered them a ride home, but the Duke watched
closely for any suggestion of that and cut it off immediately.
One of the men said that he got the impression that the chief
sin that the short-lived assistant had committed was nothing
to do with the work, but that he had cast his eye on one of the
girls, and perhaps even made a suggestive remark to the Duke.

When he returned from driving the girls to their camp, the
Duke went to the beer parlour, drank two beers, and went to
bed by ten. On Sundays, he cooked a big meal at noon, usually a roast, or—a speciality of the catering company—a New
England Boiled Dinner, the only place I have ever seen it on a
menu, then, at five, laid out a cold supper of platters of boiled
eggs, cold meats, pickles and canned salmon, which the girls
served while he looked on, dressed in his best clothes, thus
proclaiming that he was not there to work, although there was
no question of absenting himself while anyone was in the dining-room. He worked six fourteen-hour days, and on Sundays he worked for six hours and watched for three. On
Sunday afternoons, before the supper buffet was set out, he
joined in the poker game that had been going since Friday
night, dropping out when he had won or lost $10, about a
day's pay at that time. He usually lost, and seemed in this way
to be paying his dues. Apart from the weekly poker game, he
relaxed by sitting at the foremen's table in the beer parlour
listening to the talk and contributing only confirmatory re-
marks; he went to the army cinema two days a week, and spent
a lot of time looking after his clothes. He was not a dandy, but
he prided himself on his ironing, even doing a shirt for one of
the rest of us for a special reason, to have a clean one to get off
the train with when we went to Winnipeg, for example. The
Duke never went to town: we understood he preferred to save
up his leave and take it in one lump when the contract was
finished, but I believe that more important was his distaste for
having anyone in his kitchen.

He had no friends. He referred occasionally to a sister in
Montreal to whom he sent money to spend on her children, but
he never seemed to hear from her. He avoided intimacy

eeming to require only as much companionship as he found
at the foremen's table. At first I thought him simply intellec-
ually disadvantaged, as they say now. His obsessive behav-
our was something I had come across before when a simple
erson has been given a responsibility that exactly suits his
apabilities—running a dishwasher, say—and blossoms in
ride and then becomes fiercely protective of the area he has
earned to control. Then I realised that this was an arid understanding of him, and I thought then that he was by nature
a monk, a monk who had found his work and his monastery.
He burned with a low flame in all other areas; as far as we
new he was uninterested in sexual matters except to under-
tand that his girls had to be protected. In his spare time he
ead—westerns, hundreds of them, again and again as if the
West was the paradise it seems to a ten-year-old, and yet, I
hink, he had already found his Eden in the place where the
est of us saved up to escape. He was a happy man.

Until Paddy Vernon came along.

Vernon was a plumbing foreman who took over in the mid-
le of the job from a man who refused to come back off leave.
He was a gregarious fellow who made it clear immediately that
he was used to being regarded as the life of the party. Always
oking, he was, mostly practical. I didn't know so clearly then
hat teasing is a form of cruelty. Vernon was a born tease, and
nyone could see right away that the Duke was a natural butt
or someone like Paddy Vernon.

The Duke was very vulnerable, of course. He took pride not
a being a chef, but in being able to do his job exactly as he had
een taught. If anyone complained, he would taste a morsel of
whatever they found fault with, nod and say, 'That's the way
's supposed to taste. Take your complaint to Montreal.' Very
ccasionally, he would acknowledge a problem for which he
as responsible. Then he would shake his head. 'That's not the
vay it's supposed to taste,' he would say, not apologetically,
ut in a puzzled way, and offer to cook something else to make
p. For the rest of the meal he would try to think his way back
ver the course of the preparation until he found the point,
here, say, too much salt had been added, questioning the In-
ian girls, solving the puzzle then and reporting back to the

diner, who had by now lost interest, 'I'd put the salt in, bu
there was a power failure this morning, remember, when th
digger cut the cable, so when the lights came back on I saw th
salt still out—I always put it away right after I use it—and
must have thought I hadn't put it in yet. That was what it was

Such an error was rare, and always caused by an outsid
factor. By never allowing anyone into his kitchen space, th
Duke kept such factors to a minimum. After the departure o
the sole assistant cook, no one was ever allowed into th
kitchen area except the two Indian girls to stand behind th
steam table and serve. When the place was cleaned up after
meal, the Duke snapped the locks—he kept locks on all th
cupboards including the walk-in freezer. It *was* obsessive be
haviour, of course: he guarded his territory with the passion c
a man who had never owned a territory before.

In the way of such things, we affected a pride in him, gav
him an 'interesting' status. 'Old Duke doesn't allow anyon
behind that counter,' we would tell the surprised newcome
who had found his way barred wordlessly by the Duke. We di
the same thing with the secret that everyone felt must lie at th
centre of his life. The Duke gave us no context in which to u
derstand him, no past, no family history, no existence outsid
the camp, and the men used to wonder what he was concea
ing. On the whole the reasons men went that far north to wor
were easy to find. For most, in those days, it was money, be
cause the skilled tradesmen could earn three times what the
earned in town, and keep most of it. Alcoholism was anothe
big reason; the north was the last stop for men who had use
up their welcome in town. There were several men on the ru
from alimony payments, there were a handful of romantic
and there was at least one with a broken heart. The Duke f
none of these categories: he wasn't saving to go back home, c
on the run. He *was* home, but not seeing this we assumed h
had an interesting secret. 'People don't come up to a place lik
this to cook without some good reason,' Tiny Williams, th
general superintendent said, and we nodded solemnly until th
Duke began to acquire a touch of Conradian mystery whic
satisfied our need to mythicise him by failing to answer ov
questions. Personally, even at the time I was sceptical of th

nlargement of the Duke's mysteriousness, seeing it as spring-
ng more from his customers' desire to make him interesting
han from anything in him, but I knew better than to say so.

Paddy Vernon didn't. He was looking for a target as soon as
ie arrived. He began with a young timekeeper from New-
oundland, telling him tall stories to test his credulity in front
)f the other foremen. He also constructed an elaborate run-
iing joke at the boy's expense, pretending the boy was meet-
ng civilisation for the first time, though there can be nothing
n Newfoundland as barren as that construction camp. 'Pass
ne the marmalade, Hector,' he would say. 'That's the orange
tuff in the jar there.' It was mild and feeble stuff, and Hector
iccepted it mildly as the proper due of the youngest man in the
oom, but it only lasted until Vernon saw that his real target
iad to be the Duke.

He started with a string of jokes about camp cooks—the
nanure-in-the-pumpkin-pie joke was typical. The Duke lis-
ened carefully, not to the words, it seemed to me, but to the
:adences of Vernon's sentences. I think he had no sense of
iumour whatever, but he had watched and listened to men
naking jokes, and laughing at them, and learned to chime in
vith a smile to avoid being noticed. If the joke was genuinely
'unny, enough to catch the other listeners by surprise, then the
)uke would come in late with his response, as if he had just
een it. Usually, though, he could time his laugh to respond to
he climax he could feel in the rhythm of the speaker's words.
Ha!' he would bark, once, loudly, then, 'You want beans?' or
nore eggs, or toast.

Vernon made me nervous when he started to tease the Duke,
>ecause none of us was sure then what lay behind the cook's
içade, what sensitive area might not explode into violence, a
iot uncommon occurrence in that place. Fights happened for
rivial reasons. But Vernon found the Duke irresistible and
oretty soon he had progressed from jokes about cooks to more
ictive horseplay. Very early the two men had a small confron-
ation over territory. Vernon wandered behind the steam table
or the first time to help himself to some corn, but as he dipped
iis spoon into the well, the Duke pushed the lid across to close
iff the reservoir, trapping Vernon's spoon against the edge.

Vernon looked up, genuinely surprised, as the Duke pointe
to the notice prohibiting non-authorised personnel (everyon
except the Duke and his girls) behind the counter. He lifted th
lid of the well so that Vernon could retrieve the spoon, an
Paddy looked around at us to see if we found it as ridiculou
as he was beginning to, but so sacred was the Duke's area b
now that I think we were shocked to find Vernon in it, an
waited for him to come away. Vernon saw that it was some
thing he didn't understand, and decided to try it for laughs. H
read the notice again, jumped back in alarm, and made
business of running out of the Duke's area before he could b
caught, one hand behind him to protect him from spanking
Some of the men smiled politely, but Vernon was left lookin
foolish by the lack of a real supporting laugh. I could see h
didn't like that.

So he tried to find a space on the edge of the Duke's terri
tory where he could mock the very idea of a territory sacred t
the cook. He would keep his eye on the Duke, and when th
cook disappeared for a few minutes, as he did occasionally t
fetch supplies, Vernon would race round the counter and hel
himself to something he didn't want, then run back before, o
as, the Duke reappeared. The point, of course, was to get al
most caught by the Duke.

The Duke appeared to understand what Vernon was up tc
and rather neatly, I thought, turned the joke against Vernon
Now and again he would return immediately, before the doc
had swung closed, making Vernon hurl himself across the en
of the counter to get back without being 'caught.' 'Ha!' th
Duke said, thus turning Vernon's tease into a kind of 'What'
the time Mr Wolf' game for grown-ups, and Vernon had to tr
something else. Once he took our breath away by locking th
Duke in his own freezer, a large walk-in locker by the exi
where the cook kept all the meat and fresh (frozen) milk, an
bread. It was hardly necessary for eight months of the year; fo
part of that time it was probably warmer in the freezer than i
was outside, but its main function was security. It was one o
the Duke's two lockable storage areas; the other held all th
canned goods. They were locked, not simply because the Duk
was responsible for the inventory but because they were his

We had a little hot-plate in the bunkhouse, a fry-pan, a kettle and a coffee-pot, and we could make ourselves a fried egg sandwich late at night, during the poker game. The Duke supplied us with everything we needed; we only had to ask. But we did have to ask, because he would hand over the key to the stores to no one. The Duke fetched what we wanted.

One day at suppertime, Paddy Vernon asked if for once he could have a little fresh milk in his coffee. Normally the fresh (frozen) milk was kept for special purposes because it was expensive to ship and bulky to store, and we regularly drank Carnation in our coffee. But this time the Duke looked at the ceiling for advice, nodded, unlocked the freezer and disappeared inside. Vernon was over the counter in one jump and had the door slammed in a second. The idea, I guess, was to wait until the cook was good and chilly, then let him out, but the Duke was out before Vernon got back to his chair. There's a safety lock on those doors; you can't get locked in accidentally, and once more the joke was on Vernon as the Duke shouted 'Ha!' and went back to work.

After that Vernon seemed more or less to give up on the Duke, concentrating on leaving two-dollar bills in the urinals to see who would pick them up, that kind of thing. I say 'seemed' because in fact he was working on a major joke.

ALL THE ELEMENTS are now in place; you can write the rest of the story yourself. You must know what comes next. Inevitably Paddy Vernon will have to construct a practical joke involving the Duke's territory, and the heart of that territory, the freezer. Inevitably, too, given the safety mechanism of the freezer door, Paddy Vernon will have the bright idea of getting inside the freezer to surprise the hell out of the Duke when he opens the door. How Vernon does it is irrelevant. Say he goes to town and gets hold of some duplicate freezer keys from a pal in Winnipeg. Anything will do. Now you have to think of a way to give Vernon an audience when he leaps out on the Duke. Make it Sunday at suppertime when the Duke will not have had to use the freezer for an hour or two. Then set up one of the men to suggest to the Duke that he check his freezer because there was a power failure that afternoon. Will that do?

The important thing is to get all the men assembled in th dining-room waiting for the Duke to arrive and open the door And, of course, the other important thing is so to manage th story that sophisticated readers will know that this is going t turn out badly for Paddy Vernon, but exactly why will not b seen until the last paragraph.

Make the Duke disappear after lunch, forgoing the poke game. At this point, you will have to put in the information that one of the timekeepers who prefers the Duke to Vernor has tipped off the cook. Probably the boy from Newfound land. At any rate, at suppertime after they have waited long enough, the timekeeper tells them that the Duke knows abou the joke and is probably not coming. But why hasn't Vernor already let himself out? Because, someone points out, there i a three-inch nail threaded through the flange of the handl making it impossible to turn. Is Vernon dead, if not of cold then of suffocation? Is this going to be the Duke's revenge? don't think it will do. He's only been inside a couple of hour at most and there's plenty of air for that long.

Someone pulls out the nail, but the door is still locked, so they smash the lock and the door swings slowly open and a frozen, much chastened Vernon stumbles out. Or better, he faints. Yes, because then he has to be taken to the camp hos pital, giving time to discover that the Duke left on the after noon train. This seems excessive behaviour. Was the violatior of his territory that important?

This seems to be the case until Vernon recovers and leads them back to the freezer where he spent two hours in the com pany of that other cook who had been there for three months.

Leave the rest to the reader.

THE CURIOUS COMPUTER

★

PETER LOVESEY

IT WAS ALREADY 4 a.m.

George Harmer, better known as 'Grievous', was having a sleepless night in his penthouse suite in Belgravia. His brain had been working like a teleprinter for the last two hours. He was in despair.

So he tossed and turned: tossed caution to the winds and turned to the naked blonde who lay beside him. She was Silicon Lil, a stripper of manifest charms who performed nightly in his chain of night-clubs and afterwards by special arrangement.

'Lil.'

She barely stirred.

'Lil.'

She stirred barely.

'Lil, are you awake?'

'Tie a knot in it, Grievous.'

'I want to talk to you. I've got something . . .'

'What?' She snatched at the light switch and sat up. 'What did you say?'

'. . . something on my mind. I can't think of anything else.'

'Don't you ever give up?' Lil flicked off the light and resumed the attitude of slumber. 'What you want is a cold shower.'

If anyone had spoken to Grievous like that in daylight they wouldn't have lasted long enough to complete the sentence. He was the undisputed boss of organised crime in Britain. Undisputed and unforgiving. But at four in the morning he was pathetic. He said in a voice like a choked-up waste disposal unit. 'Lil, I just want to bend your ear.'

She sighed, rolled over and said, 'You must be desperate. What's bugging you, then?'

'Holmes.'

There was a pause.

'What sort of homes? Stately or mental?'

'Holmes with an "l", Lil.'

'As in Sherlock?'

'Right.'

Lil smiled to herself in the dark. 'Him with the deerstalker, Grievous?'

'Not him exactly.' Grievous flicked on the light again, hopped out of bed, switched on the TV and slammed a cassette into the video.

'Give me a break, Grievous,' Lil protested. 'I'm not watching some old detective movie at four in the morning.'

'Shut your mouth, bint!' said Grievous savagely. He was becoming his normal, psychotic self. 'This ain't Peter Cushing. This is a top secret video that was smuggled out of Scotland Yard for me. It's being shown to every chief constable in the country.'

The TV screen flickered. A countdown of numbers appeared, then a famous head in profile, with pipe and deerstalker.

'That's no secret. That's in the tube at Baker Street,' Lil commented.

Grievous silenced her with a growl.

The title of the video was superimposed.

Introducing Holmes...

A voice-over spoke in the ponderous tones peculiar to documentary films: 'Everyone has heard of Mr Sherlock Holmes, the world's greatest consulting detective. In his day, if Sir Arthur Conan Doyle is to be believed, this celebrated sleuth consistently outwitted everyone, including the police. He was streets ahead of the best brains at Scotland Yard.'

Stills of wooden-faced Victorian policemen were superimposed over Old Scotland Yard. A hansom cab stood waiting.

'In the modern police, it's another story.'

A clip of New Scotland Yard, with buses and cars cruising ast.

'Holmes is working for the police. Holmes is a computer ystem for use in large-scale enquiries. Home Office Large lajor Enquiry System.'

The words appeared on the screen with the initials blown up o triple size.

'They've got to be joking,' said Lil.

The commentary continued, 'Holmes is the most valuable id to the detection of crime since fingerprints were classified. Iolmes will range beyond the boundaries of the police forces, roviding instant information on suspicious persons and ehicles. Through free text retrieval, it will provide data on, ay, all bald-headed men on record over forty owning -registration Rolls-Royces.'

'My God, that's you,' said Lil.

Grievous fumbled for a cigar.

The screen was filled by a close-up of the computer's inte-or.

'Holmes is more powerful and more flexible than the Po-ce National Computer,' the commentary continued as the amera panned over crowded logic boards. 'It is a means of nking different forces engaged on similar investigations. Iolmes can issue descriptions of persons interviewed or no-ced, listing their previous convictions, addresses, telephone umbers and vehicles. It can collect information received from ny source, whether it amounts to a verifiable fact or a mere pinion. No member of the criminal fraternity can sleep eas-y now that Holmes is working for the Yard. The game's foot!'

The screen went blank. Grievous had pressed the 'stop' utton.

He said in a voice laden with doom, 'This is the end of crime s we know it.'

'Come off it!' piped up Lil. 'It's only a computer, for cry-1g out loud. You wouldn't let a piece of hardware get you own, would you?'

'It isn't just me,' moaned Grievous. 'It's the movement I present. It's employment for thousands of skilled profes-

sionals. It's generations of experience and hard graft. It's ma
jor industries like prostitution and drugs and pornography
Nothing's sacred no more, Lil. We're all under threat.'

'Strippers?' enquired Lil, betraying some concern.

'With Holmes on the trail? I wouldn't care to be caught i
a G-string.'

Lil gave a shudder, and the motion had the effect of di
tracting Grievous. He enfolded her in a sudden clinch.

'Grievous, my love, you've got to think big,' Lil panted.

'You're big enough for me,' came his muffled reply.

'This is just a cop-out. You must call a secret meeting of th
crime bosses from all over Britain and tell them abo
Holmes.'

He drew away from her. 'I can't do that. They'll go be
serk.'

'And if you *don't* tell them . . . ?'

'They'll roast me,' Grievous admitted. 'You're right, Li
I've got to face it.'

'I'll help.'

'I wouldn't let you within a mile of that lot.'

'No,' Lil explained. 'I'll get to work on Holmes.'

'You?' he sneered. 'What do you know about computers?

She puffed out her chest provocatively. 'Why do you su
pose I'm known as Silicon Lil?'

Grievous grinned. 'It stands out, don't it?'

'Are you talking about my figure?'

'I'm talking about a silicone job.'

She slapped his face. 'Bloody cheek. There's nothing fals
about these. Silicon without an "e", get it? Ever heard of si
icon chips?'

'Naturally, Lil.'

'So?'

He stared at her, open-mouthed. His face was giving hi
gyp. 'You're a computer freak?'

'In my spare time,' she admitted casually. 'More to th
point, I have some helpful contacts in the electronics worl
Give me a week or two and I might be in a position to sav
your bacon, Grievous Harmer.'

So a meeting was convened at a secret location in the capital. They were the top men in their respective fields: terrorism, drugs, armed robbery, protection and vice. Grievous ran the video and the air was thick with denunciations and obscenities. They denounced and swore for two days and well into a second night before deciding on the proper response of organised crime to this vile threat to its very foundations: they formed a sub-committee.

Within a week, one of the sub-committee was caught red-handed tunnelling into the Bank of England, and the word got round that Holmes was responsible.

'Already they're pointing the finger at *me*,' Grievous told Silicon Lil. 'They want action. What am I going to do?'

She gave him a serene smile. 'Don't panic, sweetheart. If they want action, they can have it. I've found the only guy in the world who is capable of helping you.'

'Thank God for that! Who is he?'

'Hold it a minute. What's in it for me?'

Grievous said cautiously, 'What have you got in mind, Lil?'

'A trifling consideration. Six months' paid leave at the Palm Beach Hotel in the Bahamas.'

'You sure this fellow can nobble Holmes?'

'Nothing is certain, darling, but you won't find a better hacker than this one. He's a professor.'

'Fair enough. You've got your holiday. Now introduce me to this genius.'

The safest place in the world for a secret rendezvous is a metropolitan railway terminus, so Grievous and Lil made an assignation the same day with the Professor under the station clock at Victoria.

To be truthful, the Professor on first acquaintance was a disappointment, if not an affront. He shuffles into our story in decrepit shoes, a shabby raincoat with the buttons missing, a battered violin case under his arm and an ancient bowler on his head. He is obviously very old indeed, desperately thin, tall, but round-shouldered, with deeply sunken, puckered eyes. Around his neck on a piece of string hangs a notice with the words *Accident Victim*.

'He's a common busker!' said Grievous in disgust.

'Possessed of extraordinary mental powers,' murmured Lil.
'He's as old as the hills!'

'"...from whence cometh my help,"' said Lil opportunely. She wasn't religious; some previous inmate had inscribed the psalm on the door of the cell she had occupied last time she was in Holloway.

And helpful the Professor proved. Over a couple of beers in the station bar, he enlightened them both as to how he could outwit Holmes. In a soft, precise fashion of speech that produced a conviction of sincerity, he said that he regarded the prospect as an intellectual treat. 'I was endowed by Nature with an exceptional, not to say phenomenal, faculty for mathematics,' he informed them. 'At twenty-one, I wrote a treatise upon the Binomial Theorem which earned me a European reputation. I was offered, and accepted, the Chair of Mathematics at one of the better provincial universities. Later, I was obliged to be attached to the military, but I retained my grasp of numerical analysis.'

'What about computers?' put in Grievous anxiously. The old man was rabbiting on too much for his liking.

The Professor gave him a withering stare, and continued to rabbit on. 'In middle age, I had the singular misfortune to suffer a climbing accident in Switzerland. I might easily have perished, for the drop was sheer and I struck a rock in the descent, but I fell into water, which saved me. I was carried downstream by the force of the torrent and deposited in the shallows, where I was ultimately found by a Swiss youth. I spent some weeks in a coma. The Swiss doctors were beginning to despair of me when I opened my eyes one morning and asked where I was. Happily, none of my faculties was impaired. I recovered all my powers.'

'Luckily for us,' said Lil.

'If we ever get to the point,' said Grievous.

The old man appeared to sense that some acceleration was necessary. He made a leap of many years. 'With the advent of computers, I rediscovered all my old zest for numerical analysis. Are you familiar with the terminology? Have you heard of hacking?'

'Breaking into computers?' said Grievous with enthusiasm.

'Crudely expressed, yes. It is an activity peculiarly suited to my present capacities. Physically, I am not so active now. Mentally, I am as alert as ever. Hacking is my chief joy in life. No computer has yet been invented that is proof against my ingenuity. The Bank of England, the Stock Exchange—'

'But have you heard of Holmes?' asked Grievous.

'The name is not unknown to me,' answered the Professor with a strange curl of the lip.

'The police computer—can you nobble it?'

'Give me a month,' said the Professor, adding, with a fine grasp of modern vernacular, 'So long as the bread is up front.'

In the next weeks there was astonishing activity. With Lil acting as the Professor's buyer, vast sums were invested in computer hardware. Such was the drain on resources that Grievous had to order a million-pound bank job to finance the operation.

'He must be knee-deep in chips by now,' Grievous commented.

'It's a mammoth assignment, sweetheart,' Lil told him, 'but progress is spectacular.'

They installed the machinery in a Surrey mansion owned by a forger who was unavoidably detained elsewhere. In this secret location, the Professor worked undisturbed apart from occasional visits from Lil. After three weeks, word came through that he had succeeded in getting a line into Holmes.

Grievous lost no time in summoning the underworld bosses for a demonstration. One month to the day that the Professor had agreed to help, a stream of limousines with dark-tinted windows arrived at the Surrey mansion. The mobsters and villains hurried inside and stood uneasily in the ornate pillared entrance hall muttering obscenities and dropping cigarash on the Persian carpet.

Grievous let them wait a full twenty minutes before making his entrance down the marble staircase. So that there should be no confusion about who took the credit for outwitting Holmes, he was alone. Silicon Lil was already on her flight to the Bahamas and the Professor had been given his fee and shown the door. This was the moment of triumph for Grievous, his confirmation as the Godfather of British crime.

'Today, gentlemen,' he announced, 'I will show you wh[y]
Holmes is no longer a threat. Come this way.'

He led them into a vast room as cluttered with compute[r]
hardware as the last reel of a James Bond movie. 'Take you[r]
seats,' he said in a voice resonant with authority. 'There shoul[d]
be a VDU for each of you.'

Porno Sullivan, the vice king, gave him a filthy look. '[I]
didn't come here to be insulted.'

'A visual display unit,' Grievous explained. 'A box with [a]
glass front just like the telly, right? Now, comrades in crime[,]
don't touch the keyboards yet. What you have at your finger[-]
tips is the underworld's answer to Holmes. Let's face it, [a]
month ago we were in dead lumber. Holmes could have put u[s]
all away for the rest of our naturals. Holmes—don't let th[e]
name worry you—that was just a public relations exercise[.]
Sherlock Holmes was said to be infallible, but we know he wa[s]
just a work of fiction. Some nutters believe he really existe[d]
and that he's still living in retirement somewhere on the Sus[-]
sex Downs keeping bees. He'd be over 130 by now. I've hear[d]
of honey being good for your health, but that's ridiculous.' H[e]
paused to let the audience appreciate his wit, but nobod[y]
laughed.

'Get on with it,' Porno urged.

'All right. When I heard about Holmes, I didn't panic. [I]
happen to know a little about computers, gentlemen. I've bee[n]
working on the problem, and I'm glad to say I've cracked i[t.]
What you see in front of you is our own computer, plugge[d]
into the private circuit out of Scotland Yard. I call it Mo[r]
iarty.'

'Morrie who?'

'Moriarty, Sherlock Holmes's greatest enemy.'

'Professor Moriarty, the Napoleon of crime,' said Porn[o]
who had done some reading in his youth. 'Not the happiest [of]
choices, Grievous. He came to a nasty end, didn't he? G[ot]
pushed off a ledge by Holmes.'

This came as a shock to Grievous. He was less familiar wit[h]
the works of Sir Arthur Conan Doyle than he made out. H[e]
hadn't known, until Porno spoke up, that Moriarty had bee[n]
a professor. Was it possible . . . ? For one distracting momen[t]

he remembered the *Accident Victim* notice around his saviour the Professor's neck. He pulled himself together. 'Never mind about him. This computer is known as Moriarty, and you want to know why? Listen: Microcomputer Output Rendered Impotent And Rot The Yard.'

A burst of spontaneous applause greeted this popular sentiment.

Grievous basked in their approval a moment and then went on, 'To keep it simple, Moriarty gives us total access to Holmes. By using the password, we can call up our own police records and examine them. Better still, we can alter them, erase them—'

'Or give them to some other bleeder?' suggested Porno.

Grievous gave him a withering look. 'That wouldn't be comradely, would it? Now I shall key in the password and you can type out your names on the keyboards and examine your form.'

It worked like a dream. The coos and whistles that presently ensued were music to Grievous's ears. The delegates were like kids on Christmas morning. For a happy hour or more, Grievous went from one to another giving instruction and encouragement as they learned how to make their criminal records unintelligible.

It was 'Hash' Brown, the drugs supremo, who had the gentlemanly idea of calling up Silicon Lil's record and erasing it for her. After all, she wasn't there to do it for herself.

He entered her name.

Instead of a criminal record, there flashed on to the screen a quaintly worded instruction:

PRAY BE PRECISE AS TO DETAILS.

With a frown, Hash cleared the screen. He called out to Grievous, 'What's Lil's full name?'

'Lilian Norton.' Grievous spelt it for him.

This time, Hash got the following:

NORTON, LILIAN
A.K.A. SILICON LIL. BORN 1.4.54, KNIGHTSBRIDGE. PAR-

ENTS: JAMES & MARY NORTON. NIGHT CLUB PERFORMER &
ASSOCIATE OF GEORGE 'GRIEVOUS' HARMER (SEE FILE).
PRISON RECORD: MAY, 1985, 1 MONTH, DRUNK AND DISOR-
DERLY; DEC, 1986, 3 MONTHS, HARBOURING A KNOWN
CRIMINAL. NOTE: GREAT-GRANDFATHER RUMOURED TO
HAVE BEEN CHILD OF GODFREY NORTON & IRENE ADLER.
SEE: A SCANDAL IN BOHEMIA.

'What's this about a scandal in Bohemia?' said Hash.
'One of the Sherlock Holmes stories,' said Porno. '"To
Sherlock Holmes she is always *the* woman."'
'Who?'
'Irene Adler.'
'Let me look at that,' said Grievous. 'Move aside a min-
ute.'
He keyed in the name Irene Adler and got the following re-
sponse:

NOW, WATSON, THE FAIR SEX IS YOUR DEPARTMENT.

'Who the hell is Watson?' asked Hash.
Grievous was already tapping out another message:

AM I IN COMMUNICATION WITH MR SHERLOCK HOLMES?

Instantly come the response:

IT IS AN OLD MAXIM OF MINE THAT WHEN YOU HAVE EX-
CLUDED THE IMPOSSIBLE, WHATEVER REMAINS, HOW-
EVER IMPROBABLE, MUST BE THE TRUTH.

'Well, that beats everything,' said Grievous.
All the others had left their VDUs to see what was happening. They watched in fascination as Grievous typed in:

ARE YOU REALLY WORKING FOR SCOTLAND YARD?

Holmes responded:

I SHALL BE MY OWN POLICE. WHEN I HAVE SPUN THE WEB,
THEY MAY TAKE THE FLIES, BUT NOT BEFORE.

'I don't like this,' said Porno. 'I don't like it at all.'

Precisely at that instant the screen went blank as if the power
supply had been cut. Every other machine in the room behaved likewise.

Then a voice announced over an amplifier, 'This is the police. We are armed, and we have the building surrounded.
Listen carefully to these instructions.'

Grievous rushed to the window. The drive was cluttered with
police vans. He could see the marksmen and the dogs. Resistance would be pointless.

That, in short, was how the entire leadership of the underworld was taken into custody. While they were sitting in the
van on their way to be questioned, Grievous blurted out the
whole extraordinary story to Porno, and then asked, 'Where
did I go wrong?'

'You trusted Lil. She was working for Holmes.'

'The computer?'

'No, the guy who fancied her great-grandmother.'

'Come off it, Porno. He isn't still around.'

Porno gave him an old-fashioned look. 'I've been thinking
about this Professor of yours. Holmes was a master of disguise and he played the violin. He retired to Sussex, which
happens to connect with Victoria Station.'

Grievous was wide-eyed. 'Still alive? And into computers?
Unbelievable!'

'Elementary,' said Porno dismally.

THE LAST RESORT

★

MARGARET YORKE

MRS ROBINSON dressed carefully for the journey up the Rhine.
Setting off from Heathrow, she wore her brown and navy
check tweed skirt—not an expensive one, although when he
gave her the money for it, she had told Roderick that it cost
over a hundred pounds. The truth was that she had bought it
at a chain store. Roderick liked her to be well dressed; it was
part of her image as his chattel. She understood her role. With
the skirt, she wore what looked like a silk blouse, and her
pearls. These were genuine, left her by her mother, but now
worth very little. A camel-hair jacket covered all these items.

She had to admit that Roderick had never been mean, as
long as what was bought could be appreciated by others. For
many years he had worked for an organisation with offices in
West Africa, Mexico and the Far East, and had spent more
time abroad than at home. He had been well paid for his labours, and enjoyed a good pension. While he was away, Mrs
Robinson—Lois—had raised two sons and a much younger
daughter, Angela, who was now attached, without benefit of
marriage, to a guitarist named Barry. They travelled around
with other musicians performing in clubs or wherever they
could get engagements, to the horror of Angela's father, who
condemned her domestic situation as immoral. Angela, re-
named Cat, sang with the group, and a photograph of her,
wearing a leopard-like catsuit, ornamented their posters and
the sleeves of the few records they had made. Roderick had
convinced himself that drink or drugs, probably both, provoked the group's noisy energy; he had disowned Angela. Mrs

Robinson knew that cheap wine was Barry and Angela's only stimulation, and that in modest amounts. Using cunning, she had visited them in Paris.

After Roderick retired, the Robinsons began travelling in Europe, which he had seldom visited, his business trips taking him much further afield. A habit of restlessness had developed within him, and after a few weeks of playing golf and studying the Stock Exchange, he would fret until he could pack and be off. Now, with no business associates, he required company, and his wife must provide it: who else? They had been to Spain, to Germany, and several times to France, but after a few journeys on their own, they joined escorted tours where ill-chosen hotels or disappointing excursions could be blamed on the organisers, not on Roderick's selection. And there were people to impress, new audiences for his opinions on the day's events or anything else he wished to talk about.

Last year in Paris, Mrs Robinson had found Angela and Barry living in an attic in a cheap area, where they had an outlook across the roofs towards the towers of Notre Dame. The Robinsons' programme for the day had included a visit to Fontainebleau, and that morning Lois had said she felt unwell. Roderick, as she had known he would, went off without her, and she had won her chance to visit Angela.

When she arrived at the flat, she was warmly welcomed by Barry, who had three days' growth of stubble on his chin, but that, Mrs Robinson knew, was current fashion. Nevertheless, it prickled her cheek when he kissed her, and she wondered briefly how Angela felt about it. Her first impression of their one room was of colour: bright cushions, a vivid bedspread thrown over the divan; next, she noticed the cheap furniture, the damp walls. They had rented it from another musician now in America, and would be there for a further fortnight. They had some other bookings, but it was clear that their future was insecure. When they had enough put by, they said, they wanted to open a guest-house of their own in Spain, where Barry would entertain the visitors with songs. Would it ever happen? Mrs Robinson looked at Barry, with his tangled mane of rich brown curls, and saw the kindness in his eyes and their soft expression when he glanced at Angela, whose own blonde

hair was cropped to fit like a skull-cup round her small head
Barry's real name was Bartholomew and he was a vicar's son
Mrs Robinson knew that they lived in the hope of realising
dream, but what was wrong with that? Maybe they woul
achieve it; in the meantime, they had love.

There was no love between her and Roderick; she knew tha
now, knew also that the illusion of it years ago had been jus
that: a fantasy. But she had not missed the experience, for sh
had been married before. Her first husband had been killed
soon after the invasion of Normandy. He had stepped on
mine and was blown to pieces. Lois had loved Teddy deeply
but they had had only a week's leave together, which had lef
her pregnant with Thomas, who was now a plumber in Aus
tralia. Occasionally, when subjected to a particularly sever
reproof from Roderick about her failure to fulfil one or an
other of his requirements, Lois would wonder what life wit
Teddy would have been like. They had scarcely known eacl
other, meeting at a dance in the town where she lived. At th
time, she had been a clerk in the local office of the Ministry o
Food; it was essential work and exempted her from bein
called up so that she could live at home and look after her fa
ther. Her parents' house had been hit by a bomb in 1942, an
her mother was killed. Her father had been badly injured an
had lost a leg. The house itself had been shored up and mad
habitable, and here she had remained, her circumstances littl
altered until Thomas was born. Her father had made no ob
jections to her hasty marriage; he had married his own wif
during the First World War and understood the need to clutcl
at happiness. It had worked out for them; why should it no
work out also for their daughter?

The young widow, her father, and the baby Thomas wer
happy enough for more than a year, and then Lois's fathe
died suddenly in his sleep. There was not much money left, bu
mother and baby had a home. After a while, Lois found worl
at a nearby hospital where there was a crèche arrangement, an
there she met the convalescent Roderick, who had had pneu
monia. Years later, during a quarrel, she discovered that a gir
to whom he had been engaged had married someone else b
whom she was already pregnant; at least she hadn't foiste

nother man's child on him, the furious Roderick had said, when revealing this history.

'I didn't foist Tom on you. You said he was a dear little hap,' wept Lois, but even as she spoke, she recalled how Roderick had laid out Tom's precious little cars—bought second-hand because there were few new toys in those days—in regimented rows for the child to play with. Only with hindsight did she realise that Tom had not been allowed to let them range freely about or be used as tanks and lorries.

'No. They are cars, and must be parked so,' Roderick would say, disciplining Thomas before he was three years old. 'A boy needs a father,' he had declared, offering his hand but never, as she later understood, his heart.

He had assessed the potential value of the property she owned, the bomb-damaged, temporarily repaired small house on the fringe of a south coast town. When they sold it, the money went into Roderick's account and was used to buy another in his name, in a Midland suburb near his new firm's offices. That had appreciated and they had moved again, to a bigger place appropriate to their improved status, and so it had gone on but she was now dependent on Roderick for every penny.

No longer, however, for she had been cheating him for years, building up a nest egg by fraudulent accounting for her clothes and other expenses, and by economical housekeeping. She had milked Roderick of many hundreds of pounds, planning her escape, and she meant to achieve it on this holiday which, after the flight from Heathrow and a night in Cologne, would continue with a trip up the Rhine. Somewhere on the journey she would have an opportunity, and when it came, she must seize it bravely or it would be too late; she was getting old.

Had he been different when he was young, she wondered, watching him across the table in the ship's restaurant. They were travelling with a group of people professing interest in ancient buildings, and they had disembarked to visit cathedrals, churches and occasional castles in the towns through which they passed. With them was their courier, Kay, a trim woman, no longer young, who was adept at defusing friction

among her small group. At intervals she also took on the bur
den of plain Miss Smythe and blowsy Miss Howard, who were
each travelling alone and unfortunately had not taken to one
another. Roderick ignored them, apart from ostentatiously
allowing them to precede him through any doorway. He did
not ignore pretty Mrs Clifford, just over five feet tall and as
slim as a twelve-year-old girl; he supervised the loading and
unloading of her baggage, and nightly included her in the
Robinsons' bottle of wine. She lapped all this attention up a
though accustomed to it, as, indeed, she was. She had been
married three times, divorced once and widowed twice. Now
she was looking for someone new, but had not found him on
this holiday, for all the men were married and she preferred the
unattached. Mrs Robinson could see, in Roderick's manner
towards Mrs Clifford, traces of his short-lived concern for her
and Thomas; it was all false. Meanwhile, his preoccupation
gave her breathing space and she could concentrate on strat
egy.

Mrs Robinson had been told that Strasbourg would be
spectacular, the pierced spires of the cathedral a marvel to be
hold. Her chance might come there, she thought; she knew
they had some distance to walk from their parked coach
Roderick would sit with her in the coach, his bulk uncomfort
ably close, but he would be watching for Mrs Clifford, wait
ing to hand her down. Lois would be prepared to slip away, i
she could.

That morning, he questioned why she carried her small
zipped holdall when the day was warm and dry, but she did no
answer. In the bag was a change of underwear, spare tights, a
toothbrush, and a fat bundle of travellers' cheques which rep
resented all her savings.

She watched Roderick and Mrs Clifford walking ahead o
her along the narrow street towards the cathedral. They had
driven round the town, admired the buildings used by the
European Parliament, and stood gazing at the timbered
houses, so ancient and historic, in the centre of the city. The
guide had said that Strasbourg was spared destruction in the
war because the United States Command had already decided

to have its headquarters there. Forward planning, thought Mrs Robinson, just like Roderick's. And now, her own.

After their marriage, he had not been demobilized for some time and was stationed in Germany, where it was never suggested that she should join him. She and Thomas carried on as before, but she was no longer a widow and there was more money. Soon there was also Julian, now an accountant in Manchester. Mrs Robinson did not like to remember her honeymoon with Roderick, so different from her few nights with Teddy; Julian was the result of that experience.

He's like a tank, running over everything that's in his way, regardless, she thought in the years that followed, and was thankful for his frequent absences overseas. Sometimes he was gone for months, and though wives and families could accompany their husbands on some postings, Roderick, to her great relief, never proposed that his should do so. She was happy while he was away, but when he returned he cross-examined Thomas and Julian about the details of their lives since last he saw them. Thomas never said a lot, but Julian could be led into revelations of maternal mismanagement—running out of eggs, failure to equip him with the right sort of shoes for school, seeing too much of neighbours whom, he sensed, his father disapproved of. Tiny betrayals were easily contrived.

She could not leave Roderick, for she had no money of her own, and there were the two boys to support; in those days, separated mothers were not assured of maintenance or state aid.

The birth of Angela put an end to dreams of a different life, and Mrs Robinson developed a protective shell against the hurts administered verbally by her husband, though she could not always avoid his physical assaults. She had not anticipated having more children, had taken steps to prevent it happening, but had been defeated by Roderick's impatience after a spell overseas. At first the notion of a daughter had intrigued him, but Angela had always been a rebel and she was often in disgrace; small wonder that she, like Thomas, left home as soon as she was old enough.

Thomas had gone to Australia. In those days you could
emigrate for very little outlay, and he soon earned enough. In
Sydney, he had his own plumbing business which was pros-
pering. He had married, and his daughter Sally, a nurse, had
been to England on holiday—a period of delirious joy for the
English grandmother whom she had never met before. Her
visit coincided with a spell abroad for Roderick; it was easy to
pretend that all was well.

Roderick's retirement had meant constant fear, sometimes
real terror when he struck her. How many other wives lived in
similar dread, she wondered? She had noticed that some wid-
ows, after a few months' bereavement, shed years and thrived
on their new freedom.

She would not wait till she was widowed. She might have to
wait too long; indeed, the time might never come.

The Robinsons now lived in Devon, by the coast, near where
they had taken the children for seaside holidays. Mrs Robinson had expected grandchildren to visit them there, but Julian
and his smart, sophisticated wife, who was a banker, had no
children. Roderick had taken up golf, which kept him out all
day; he lunched at the club with his cronies after their morning round, and allegedly played another in the afternoons. On
fine days, he did; if it was wet the men sat round drinking, or
played snooker. While this went on, Mrs Robinson built up a
small network of local activities so that she could escape for at
least some evenings in the week. She studied history, she
learned to weave, she took up painting. Roderick always made
her late for her classes, insisting on her serving dinner first, and
he never let her take the car, so she cycled, until people realised what she was doing and began giving her lifts.

Did they suspect anything? Did Elsie Burton, whose husband was one of Roderick's golf partners, notice Lois's
bruised cheek, the burn on her hand? No one ever said a word.

Mrs Robinson had known her break must be made while
they were away from home, otherwise Roderick would find her
before she had properly escaped. Besides, at home she would
lack the courage to choose a date and stick to it; on holiday
she briefly bloomed, for Roderick, wanting to impress their
fellow travellers with his generosity, would tell her to go off

...d buy herself a pair of shoes or some trifle, and sit back as ...to say she must be indulged. When she returned with her ...urchase, he would belittle her choice to the company.

Because he already had a passport when they took up trav...ling, she had obtained her own, though he had intended ...utting her on his. Foreseeing this, she had already applied. ...he had decided to visit Tom and her grandchildren in Aus...alia. Roderick had never allowed her to do this; they were not ...s grandchildren, he had pointed out, so he had no interest in ...em, and it was her duty to stay at home and look after him.

Mrs Robinson had not planned what would happen when ...er money ran out. Tom might understand, might suggest she ...ould stay in Sydney, might find her accommodation—she ...ould not live with him and his family, even if they suggested ... She supposed she was too old to find work, though she ...uld cook and clean, and did so every day at home. Perhaps ...meone would employ her as a housekeeper; latterly, such ...reams had given her hope.

She did not know that you had to have a visa for Australia. ...On the river cruise, their cabin was small, the space be...ween their beds less than three feet. At home they no longer ...ared a bedroom; she had moved her things into the small ...ack bedroom when she had a cold, with the excuse of not ...anting to infect him, and had never returned. There was a ...olt on the door, but so far her privacy had not been chal...nged. On the boat she lay wakeful, waiting until Roderick's ...ores began before relaxing. After a few hours he would ...ave himself out of bed and visit the small closet which held ...e shower and toilet. He was often noisy in there, but the trip ...as only for four days; she could endure that. She turned her ...ce to the wall and pulled the duvet round her ears. He left her ...one.

Leaving Strasbourg cathedral after admiring the amazing ...ock, she had begun to walk away from the group when Mrs ...lifford called her.

'Lois, we're going to have a cup of tea. Come along,' she ...ied, in her high, light voice.

She'd left it too late, and next day the voyage, but not the ...oliday, would end.

After disembarking, they were to travel by coach to a Swiss
lakeside hotel for the final two days and nights. Here, the
Robinsons had a large room, almost a suite, with a spacious
lobby separating the bathroom from the bedroom. There was
a balcony overlooking the lake and the mountains, which unfortunately, when they arrived, were shrouded in mist.
would clear by morning, Kay, the courier, said encouragingly
telling them what time dinner would be served in the hotel
restaurant.

Mrs Robinson decided to leave the next day. An excursion
by steamer on the lake was planned; she would say she was
tired of the water and wanted to see the churches in the town
choosing her moment, speaking in front of witnesses so that
although Roderick would chide her, he would do it in the win-
some manner he adopted in front of other people, as much as
to say, look what I have to put up with, with this silly woman
but he would enjoy escorting Mrs Clifford. Mrs Robinson
would go to the station, which was near the hotel, and catch
train to Geneva airport, then buy a ticket to Australia. That
night she hardly slept for excitement, and in the morning, she
woke early, needing the bathroom.

She padded quietly out of the bedroom, a thin figure in her
long cotton nightgown, and crossed the carpeted lobby to the
bathroom. She did not see the soap on the shiny tiled floor
where Roderick had dropped it the night before, and she
slipped, striking her head on the side of the bath. She gave no
cry as she fell.

An hour later Roderick found her. Her face was pale and her
limbs cold, but she was breathing. He stepped across her to
reach the lavatory, relieved himself, washed his hands carefully, rinsed out his mouth and spat, then stepped over her
again to return to the bedroom where he crossed to the window and gave himself up to ten minutes' hard thought. After
this he picked her up—she was surprisingly heavy—and put
her back in her bed, covering her up. She made no sound at all.
He was thinking that she must have had a stroke or a heart attack: then, returning to the bathroom, he saw the soap and
decided that she was probably concussed. He uncovered her
again and opened the window while he bathed and shaved

then dressed, spraying himself with eau-de-Cologne, which he had bought at the start of the holiday. Crisp and brisk, he went down to breakfast, nodding across the dining-room at the rest of the group. Mrs Clifford was sitting with Kay, the courier, and he asked if he might join them.

'My wife has a headache,' he told Kay. 'She doesn't want any breakfast, and she won't come on the excursion today. She's best left. I'll take her up some tea and toast.'

Giving a good performance as a devouted spouse, he poured out the tea, spread butter and marmalade on a slice of toast, and bore it upstairs. He would eat the toast himself and drink the tea instead of having a second cup downstairs. This would indicate that Lois had consumed the light meal before her death.

For the chances were that she would die, if left long enough without treatment. If she were to recover consciousness, she would be confused and would accept as the truth his version of events. He left her exposed to the chill air coming through the balcony window until the last moment before setting off, in his raincoat, and with a scarf wound round his neck, into the sharp October day.

The sky was clear and in the distance the mountains sparkled under a covering of snow. It boded well for the trip, and he would devote himself to entertaining Mrs Clifford; he fancied she enjoyed his tales of life in the Far East.

Before departing, he pulled the covers up over Mrs Robinson as far as her waist, leaving one arm out as if she had fallen asleep in that posture, and in the bathroom he rescued the errant soap, put it in the rack at the side of the bath, and wiped the slippery place on the floor. He hung on the bedroom door the red notice indicating that the occupants did not wish to be disturbed, walked down the passage and rang for the lift.

Mrs Robinson was dead when, in the late afternoon, the housekeeper entered after tapping and tapping on the door with no response, and after reception had telephoned the room several times to ask when it could be cleaned.

Roderick, returning with his travelling companions after an enjoyable outing, was greeted by the anxious face of the hotel manager and by two policemen. When the news was broken, he went into his rehearsed speech about how his wife had felt unwell. He was told there was a bruise on her head and that she could either have fallen or been struck down. He said that must have happened after he left; no doubt she went into the bathroom; perhaps she fell there; the floor was dangerously slippery, he added, frowning, the word *damages* hovering in the air, unspoken. She'd had tea and a piece of toast before he left, he said.

It was Mrs Clifford who said she thought it was odd that he had spread marmalade on his wife's toast, for she knew that Lois Robinson preferred honey or jam, and, indeed, on the boat had said that she never ate marmalade, nor did she take sugar in her tea, yet her husband had put two spoonfuls in her cup. He, however, did take sugar, she had noticed; he liked marmalade, too, and had several times asked for it on the river boat when it was absent from the breakfast table.

'The autopsy will show if she ate the toast and drank the tea,' said the police officer.

He already knew that Mrs Robinson's holdall contained over £3,000 in travellers' cheques, an address in Sydney written on luggage labels, and a timetable of flights from various cities to Australia, as well as her passport. If she had drunk the tea, her lips would have marked the cup and her fingerprints would be on the handle. Tests would prove if this was so. Meanwhile, it was a suspicious death, as she had been dead for hours.

Roderick, demanding to see the British Consul, was taken off to the police station.

Mrs Clifford was glad she had been so observant. This characteristic had prevented her from making serious mistakes in the past.

CLEWSEY'S CLICHÉS

LAVERTON-WEST GAVE HIM A FISH-LIKE STARE.

EXQUISITELY GOWNED—REVISING MY FIRST NOVEL FIFTY YEARS ON

★

ERIC AMBLER

Eric Ambler's first novel, The Dark Frontier, *published in the UK in 1936, was not published in America until 1989. With pleasure we reprint Ambler's introduction to the belated American edition. His observations and notes are those of a master reviewing his craft.*

LC & MZI

THE AGEING thriller writer who makes prefatorial apologies for the shortcomings of his early work also makes a fool of himself. The fact that, although once young and inexperienced, he has learned much about his craft over the years is of no interest to new readers. They are looking for entertainment, not excuses.

They may, however, be entitled to explanations, especially of what may appear to be gross anachronisms. *The Dark Frontier* was my first published novel and I wrote it in 1935. What, it may be asked fifty years later, was I doing in those far-off early thirties, using the term 'atomic bomb' so familiarly and describing the effects of an atomic explosion as if the hideous thing already existed?

I lay no claim to special prescience. Having had a scientific education and through it gained access to academic journals, I had read about the early work of Rutherford, Cockcroft and Chadwick in the field, and understood some of its implications. How superficial that understanding was will be apparent now to any 'A' level student. The atomic bomb that I deduced was the work of a small team directed by one exceptional man of talent with a chip on his shoulder and grudges to bear. The difficulties of producing substances like enriched uranium, and the enormous resources, economic and industrial, that would be needed to overcome them, were factors I was able to ignore because I was only dimly aware of their existence.

My estimate of the critical mass likely to bring the bombmaker to the threshold of a fission chain reaction was more cagily vague. 'A little larger than a Mills grenade' was my 1935 guess and I allowed its explosive force to shift a thousand tons of rock. In 1935 I knew theoretically, that E probably equalled Mc^2, but could not quite accept the numerically awesome consequences of the equation. I mean, c^2 was such a huge and weird multiplier. And in some ways I was handicapped by my own experience of explosives. I knew what it felt like to throw a Mills grenade thirty yards and the way the burst clouted your ears if you threw short or were slow getting your head down. I knew because while a college student I had been in the Territorial Army. Multiplying the violence of an infantry weapon out of all proportion to its size and normal destructive power seemed a dramatically acceptable device. With TNT I felt that I was on even surer ground. One evening in January 1917, when I was nearly eight and living in London not far from Greenwich, there had been an accident at a munitions plant two miles away across the river. They were processing TNT there; something went wrong and over fifty tons of the stuff blew up. Not even on the Western Front had there been such an explosion. It killed and wounded hundreds and flattened an entire factory area. The blast wave hit our street with great force and broke a lot of windows. I remembered the feel and sound of it. The idea of using a kiloton of TNT as a measure of explosive violence, even for a fictional nightmare bomb, seemed far-fetched and possibly absurd. In the welter of impulses, literary, political and commercial, that drove me to start writing *The Dark Frontier*, the wish to parody was, at first, central. I intended to make fun of the old secret service adventure thriller written by E. Phillips Oppenheim, John

Buchan, Dornford Yates and their cruder imitators; and I meant to do it by placing some of their antique fantasies in the context of a contemporary reality. For plot purposes, the reality I thought I needed was one of those unexpected threats to world peace, one of those dark conspiracies of evil men, that will succeed unless our hero can brave all dangers and arrive in the nick of time to foil the wicked in their devilish moment of near triumph. The development of an atomic bomb in a small Balkan state ruled by a corrupt Fascist-style oligarchy was likely, I thought, to yield an interesting crop of villains. The real, though maybe not immediately present, danger of the atomic bomb was surely a convincing threat to world peace. After all, it had convinced me. Quite so. But this was parody. Were there not unities to be observed? Don Quixote should not be expected to tilt at windmills defended by machine guns. I should have threatened the world with something more obviously far-fetched—a secret army of robots, say, or a polar submarine base sited over a volcanic thermal spring. Or, if I were going to fool with matters that should be taken seriously, perhaps I should think again and discard the idea of parody. But I was halfway through the book by then and reluctant to admit to myself the size of the mistake I was making. Besides, I felt committed to my folly. For the young, for new writers, parody can seem like a safety precaution, a form of insurance against adverse criticism.

It brings with it other handicaps and illusions. The matter of size and scale must be understood. Max Beerbohm, perhaps the century's master parodist, was always brief. With Max's help Henry James, G. K. Chesterton and Rudyard Kipling are each brought to judgement and petrified, temporarily at least, in a few short pages. Max's four acts of 'Savonarola' Brown's great poetic tragedy may be read aloud with stage directions, and to hilarious effect if well read, in less than thirty minutes. But Max was wise not to find the missing fifth act himself. The joke is over at the end of the fourth. Satire can be sustained by a single comedic idea and the wit to pursue it. Parody requires an established root system of critical insight and the constant nourishment of humour. Max could not have written *The Battle of the Books* and Jonathan Swift could not have trifled so engagingly with Joseph Conrad's heart of darkness. Parody can be the expression of literary dandyism.

Why then, it may be asked, if I were so alive to the difficulties of parody, especially those of sustaining it at length, did I take the risk? It is a fair question, so I will skip the nonsense about youth being a time for risk-taking, rule-breaking and experiment. Instead, I will try to give what I believe to be the answer.

When the English novelist Mary Webb died in 1927 not much notice was taken of the event. Her five or six novels, though of the earthy primitive, regional romantic school then in vogue, had not been popular. The circulating library public, while not averse to purple prose, tended to prefer the less fervid tone of others working in the genre, of healthier ladies like Sheila Kaye-Smith. The *Oxford Companion*'s summing up of Webb as 'passionate, morbid and frequently naive' still holds good. Perhaps she had been too close to the rustic quiddities and bucolic squalor about which she wrote. She was a country schoolteacher who married another teacher, worked in the country as a market gardener and died wretchedly, after a long struggle with exophthalmic goitre, at the age of forty-five. A year later she was made famous and two of her novels, *Precious Bane* and *Gone to Earth*, hastily retrieved from oblivion, had become bestsellers. It could have happened only in England, but even there it was remarkable. British politicians have often declared their love of literature and even quoted the Latin poets in their speeches, but few have been prepared to praise the work of a particular novelist. One sees the difficulty, of course; the kind of fiction a politician enjoys, or pretends to enjoy, will tell the voters more about the man's true disposition than may be good for his political health. Prime Minister Disraeli, himself a novelist, had a short, impudent answer for those who sought to probe his literary taste buds—'When I want to read a novel I write one.' In 1928 Prime Minister Stanley Baldwin, the trusty pipe-smoking, true blue Tory statesman who had seen England safely through the General Strike and whose safe hands were later to accept the abdication of King Edward VIII, threw caution to the winds. He praised a novelist publicly. True, she was a woman and dead; there would be no political mileage in it for anyone except her publishers; but the event was still extraordinary. The occasion Baldwin chose for the delivery of his eulogy was the annual dinner of the Royal Literary Fund, an old and honourable charity. He praised her lyrical intensity and evocation of the Shropshire landscape. The speech was widely reported in the better newspapers and the Mary Webb bandwagon began to roll. Mr Baldwin gave it a final shove by writing an introduction for a new edition of *Precious Bane* and the other novels soon began to appear in a collected edition. As Britain sank deeper into the Great Depression, Mary Webb's purple prose, 'blending human passion with the fields and skies', according to Baldwin, penetrated the circulating libraries and lingered about the shelves like the after-smell of a cheap air freshener. This was true artistry. Mr Baldwin had said so.

At the time my literary tastes were those of any other guilt-ridden young man who had rejected all orthodox religious texts in favour of the teachings of C. G. Jung, G. I. Gurdjieff and Oswald Spengler. The novels of Dostoevsky and the plays of Ibsen were my bedside books. I wallowed in the nether worlds of George Gissing and Knut Hamsun and mooned with George Moore over the fate of *Esther Waters*. For me in those days misery and madness were the stuff of dreams, even when the dreamer was as troubled as Strindberg or as haunted as Kafka. Why, then, did I find *Precious Bane* so insufferable?

Mainly, I think, because of its pretentious breast-beating. All that blending of human passion with the fields and skies that Mr Baldwin so admired was for me no more than an untimely and artless revival of the Victorian poets' pathetic fallacy by an author writing beyond her means. The incidence of psychoneuroses and violent crime among Shropshire yokels may have been exceptional at the time, but the attempt to render it as high tragedy was a mistake. Mrs Webb's adolescent insights stimulated by overdoses of schoolroom Wordsworth could produce nothing more tragic than high-sounding gush. I hated it, and in doing so failed to appreciate the rich splendour of its absurdity.

Cold Comfort Farm was published in 1932 and was an immediate success. The author, Stella Gibbons, was thirty at the time, and although she had published a book of poetry and worked as a magazine journalist, this was her first novel. As parody it was and remains unique. Who could resist her brisk way of explaining primal scene trauma as 'saw something nasty in the wood shed' or the aura of dignity with which she invested Big Business, the bull, and the herd of wayward cows she served so faithfully? Their very names—Graceless, Pointless, Feckless, Aimless—brought a gust of fresh air to the milking shed. *Cold Comfort Farm* followed the narrative pattern of the genre it was to destroy by describing in rather too much detail the history of a family. Mary Webb's hare-lipped heroine had been Prudence Sarn. The Cold Comfort family are Seth, Elfine and Aunt Ada Doom. But the book has long ceased to depend on its elements of parody. In 1933 France took the unusual step of awarding Stella Gibbons, an Englishwoman, with the important Fémina Vie Heureuse Prize for literature. *Cold Comfort Farm* is a wittily conceived and beautifully written comic novel. The French were recognising it as a work of art.

Stella Gibbons seems never to have quite recovered from this early success. None of the good novels she wrote later was nearly as good as the first, and her only sequels to it were short stories. She has always thought of herself as a poet, and more interested in the nature of God than in human beings. Well, it must be an eerie moment when one finds oneself in one's eighties and still the only novel-length parodist to be published in the twentieth century. Mine cannot have been the only prentice hand to have been tempted by the brilliance of her achievement.

A revised edition, then, presents the failed parodist with a chance to tidy up. What came out of the defective parody was a thriller with a difference. True, it invited some suspension of disbelief, but it did not expect the reader to swallow nonsense or to tolerate really bad writing. However, one of the hidden dangers of parody is that one may find oneself actually enjoying the process of writing 'in the manner of' some excruciatingly awful stylists. I recall, in particular, E. Phillips Oppenheim. The Prince of Storytellers his publishers used to call him. He made a fortune which ran to a yacht on the French

Riviera. Some of his novels had such good stories to tell that for his teenage readers, of whom I was one, the rococo style seemed part of the entertainment. I was a teenage smoker too. These bad juvenile habits catch up with the sinner later in life. Thirty years or more after *The Dark Frontier* was published, a respected and, at that time, greatly feared critic named Clive James made my work the subject of an essay in a literary magazine. He had his reputation as a killer to sustain, of course, but I escaped with only a few bruises and one bad cut. The cut was deep. In his piece he used a sentence from my first novel to demonstrate that I had improved slightly as a writer over the years. The middle-aged Ambler, he assured us with a smirk, would never think of describing a well-dressed woman as 'exquisitely gowned'. The young Ambler hadn't even hesitated.

I was appalled. How was I to explain that it had been the young Ambler parodying the euphuistic Oppenheim who was to blame? He was supposed to be a critic. Why hadn't he seen that the phrase 'exquisitely gowned' was pure Oppenheim? It ought not to have been there, of course. The fault was mine. Back in those days young authors, and old, were expected, rightly in my opinion, to be their own editors. There were house styles in punctuation and in euphemism for the coarse or blasphemous—'beggar' for 'bugger', 'crikey' for 'Christ' and so on—which one accepted uncomplainingly because one was told that irritating or giving offence to book-buying librarians and strait-laced readers was not the best way to sell books. In those days readers were more touchy and often wrote pedantic letters of complaint to publishing houses or, worse, to the big book wholesalers who could refuse to stock a book and distribute it. They had copy-editors who read books in proof for them. That was to protect themselves against the absurd libel laws of England, as well as to report on dirty words. None of them would have bothered with 'exquisitely gowned'. That was left to me, and I had missed it. I worked on those revisions at night. I must have nodded.

Well, the blot has gone at last. However, there are, I find, limits to what may legitimately be done by way of revision. For instance, quite early in the story our amnesiac hero finds himself in Paris and committed to a dangerous Balkan adventure. Feeling that he may be called upon to defend himself, he goes into a gunsmith's in the boulevard St Michel and buys a Browning automatic and ammunition for it.

When I first reread this I laughed aloud. A gunsmith in the old Boule' Miche'? I ask you. As every old Paris hand will recall, the lower end runs through the heart of the Latin Quarter and along one side of the Sorbonne. In the early thirties it was the cheap and noisy sections of an *arrondissement* which included the Luxembourg Gardens, the boulevard St Germain, much of the University of Paris and most of the attractions of what was then understood by the phrase Left Bank. The river end of the Boule' Miche', however, had big, impersonal cafés and their patrons did not include Sartre and Picasso. Their customers were mostly office workers who lived in the suburbs and students, students of all ages and levels of poverty. The goods in the stores were shoddy and those who sold them spry. There was a ready-to-wear men's tailor who exploited the fad for jackets without lapels—'*très chic, très sport, presque cad.*' Prix CHOC 28off.—and a milliner who pirated scarf designs from the Right Bank couturiers and sold reproductions printed on art silk with dyes that ran. In the narrow side streets there were dismal apartment buildings, *prix-fixe* restaurants and small hotels where, on at least one floor, bedrooms were available by the hour. It was a quarter in which one might find a place to pawn a revolver but would not expect to buy one.

In my time as a writer I have committed a few solecisms and made some silly mistakes, but I have not, on the whole, been careless. When unsure of facts and unable to verify guesses, I have gone warily. I was especially careful with what used to be called 'local colour'. I could not really believe that I would have placed a gunsmith in the boulevard St Michel unless I had known for certain that there was one there. Memory had to be assisted. I thought myself back into one of those small hotels behind the Sorbonne—in the rue Victor Cousin, since we are recalling the irrelevant—where one could live so cheaply when the French franc was eighty to the pound sterling. How did one

get there? One walked from the métro station, Luxembourg.
Ah, yes. That was it.

In the early thirties it became a habit with me to go as often
as I could to France. I had to travel cheaply: never first class
and second only when there was no third available. This was
usually on international trains or on fast night services between cities. My fellow travellers on these second-class journeys were mostly French of the middle bourgeoisie of small
business, travelling salesmen and the like. Unaccompanied
women would most likely have sleeping car reservations. The
characters I studied most attentively were the travelling salesmen. I knew something of the ways of their English counter-
parts, and the mere fact of one of these prosperous knights of
the road denying himself the comfort of a *couchette* in a
sleeping car meant to me that he was almost certainly fiddling
his expense account. Of course, those were the golden days
before credit card billing made false expenses less easy to
claim.

Preparations for dozing the night away tended to have a ritual quality. First, there would be the stroll along the corridor
to check that the sample cases were safe in the baggage racks,
then a visit to the WC. Outside in the corridor again a cigarette would be smoked. Back in the compartment there would
be the loosening of the collar stud, the unlacing, or unbutton-
ing, of ankle boots and, finally, the application of scent. This
was eau-de-Cologne or a similar lavender water, and it was
sprinkled liberally on a handkerchief which was then used to
wipe the face and hands. The whole compartment benefited,
of course. Ventilation was poor and we were a smelly lot in
those days. Middle-class townsmen might change their underwear twice a week if they were single or if they had married
money, but for most once a week was customary. A daily
change was for the rich or the depraved. A sprinkling of cologne was evidence of a respectable upbringing, as was the
possession of a clean white handkerchief. For those allergic to
lavender, the alternative defence against the smells of confined humanity was tobacco, and there were always plenty of
compartments for smokers on the trains. Nights spent in them,
however, invariably seemed much longer. In the small hours

there would be noisy disputes about window-opening and *courants d'air*. The *non-fumeurs* were more restful.

And probably still are. The intention behind this thick slice of European social history was not to encourage non-smokers or to sell deodorants but to explain how I came to know that in France in those days a great many travelling men used to carry guns. They carried them in their overnight bags along with the bottle of cologne, the flask of rum or brandy and yesterday's newspaper. The bag was of the satchel, briefcase type—the French called it a *serviette*—and when it was open, the contents were clearly visible. Not that there was ever any attempt at concealing them. The first time I saw one of these guns was when its owner put it on the seat beside him while he rummaged in the bag for a box of toothpicks. It was a .25 single-action revolver, made in Belgium and, I found later, popular because cheap.

How cheap I never discovered. The French friends whose views I sought thought strongly about guns. The husband said that in town only jewellers needed guns. The wife said that women of a certain age should have pistols to protect their honour or to take their revenge on faithless men. I asked if it were true about *crimes passionelles* going unpunished in France. 'The little guns women keep in their purses never do much harm,' she said with a shrug. 'If the man is unlucky the law is reasonable.'

But that was in the towns. What about the country? Ah, said the man, there one needed a heavier weapon. Every peasant and all his kids had shotguns and would mistake a man for a rabbit if given half a chance. In the Dordogne and parts of Provence it was still bandit country, as bad as Corsica. Here in France those at greatest risk were the *automobilistes*. In bandit country the possession of a private car was sufficient evidence of personal wealth, and highway robbery was all too easy. All drivers with any sense went armed. When driving, he kept his gun, an excellent Czech automatic, wrapped in greaseproof paper, in the door cavity pocket on the driver's side. At other times he kept it locked in the toolbox with the spare inner tube and first aid kit. It was no trouble; border police and customs men expected drivers to be armed; the *gendarmerie* in some parts of the country counted on it.

I could not quite believe all this; I did not want to believe it. That French travelling salesmen should find it necessary to carry guns I was prepared to accept. French thieves went armed—*Paris Soir* said so—and it wasn't only jewellers who carried valuable samples. In the movies nervous householders kept revolvers in the drawers of bedside tables. Perhaps some French householders did so too. But in car-door pockets? Surely not. Door pockets were for maps and driving gauntlets and slim boxes of Balkan Sobranie cigarettes.

The girl with whom I had been sharing a bed had left me and gone off with rich Greek friends to Cannes. The following day I had to go back to London and my job in advertising. The idea of moping in a café did not appeal to me so I went in search of a puppet theatre I had heard about. It was in the Luxembourg Gardens. That was how I came to know that there was a gunsmith's in the boulevard St Michel. It was at the upper end near the Luxembourg, away from the Latin Quarter I now loathed, and was located in the ground-floor arcade of an office block. The display window was *très sport*—shotguns in blued steel and walnut, decoy birds and suede ammunition waistcoats—but in the showcases at the back of the store there were plenty of handguns.

I had decided to put the whole subject out of my mind; but on the cross-Channel steamer from Dieppe to Newhaven I got talking to a Frenchman in the bar. He was going to London for the first time and asked the barman how to get from Victoria to Belsize Park. The barman, a Brighton man, did not know for sure. I did. The Frenchman was going to work in an Oxford Street language school for six months to see if he liked the work. My guess was that he would not, but instead of saying so I asked if he drove a car. He did; at home he drove his father's. When he drove did he carry a revolver?

The gun, he explained somewhat sheepishly, was his father's. Old-fashioned men, men of a certain age, liked to carry a gun when they were driving.

This was Freudian country. I preferred to read Jung. Again I put the subject out of my mind, until, a couple of years later

I needed an approximate location for a gunsmith in Paris. I see no reason to revise it. Nowadays, I read neither Freud nor Jung.

I rest my case. However, for the ill-natured who like to poke at old scar tissue to see if wounds have really healed, the sentence, 'She was exquisitely gowned,' was part of a descriptive paragraph placed just before the electric power failure in the Zovgorod Opera House—the very page before.

London 1989

JEMIMA SHORE AND THE FRIGHTENED GIRL

★

ANTONIA FRASER

AT FIRST Jemima Shore did not understand what was happening. She had the impression of unease, then disturbance among her neighbours, the feeling that something troubling and even aggressive was about to take place. As in a nightmare, everyone knew what it was going to be—except her.

The hand was stuck out firmly in her direction. It was there waiting for her.

'Jemima,' whispered Mia, the child standing beside her. 'Take it. You've got to shake the hand. It's the sign of peace.'

The hand belonged to a dark-haired girl—wonderful tumbling jet-black hair—wearing a scarlet jacket. Large gold earrings were visible beneath the hair; like the jacket, they looked expensive. Altogether the girl had an elegant cared-for look as if maintenance of her charming appearance was her chief work in life. She was flanked by two male companions, both dark-haired and wearing suits: but somehow they did not convey the same air of studied chic.

Before Jemima could pull herself together, the scarlet-clad arm—also, she noted, bearing two gold bracelets—had been energetically pumped by her companion. The men did not appear to have made any such friendly move. Or maybe they had already done so and Jemima had missed it.

Startled and at the same time feeling slightly foolish, Jemima shook the next proffered hand. It belonged to a large middle-aged black lady in a navy blue and white spotted silk

ress. She also wore a navy blue straw hat and carried a sub-
tantial navy blue leather handbag. In contrast to the girl in
ront—Spanish? South American?—the black lady's appear-
nce conveyed dignity rather than money.

The rest of the congregation were dressed more informally.
here were several Filipinos: young women in white blouses
nd black trousers. The Catholic Church of Saints Cosmas and
)amian was in an area which served a number of embassies;
emima judged these young women to be attached there.
emima herself was wearing jeans, as indeed was her god-
hild Mia O'Brien standing at her side.

'Peace be with you,' said the black lady. Her voice, like her
ppearance, was stately; it was also remarkably deep. Mia
rabbed this hand too and said loudly, as though to make up
or Jemima's lack of courtesy: 'And with you too.'

'And with you,' echoed Jemima. She then thought she had
etter shake Mia's hand. But even that did not go smoothly.

'You can *kiss* me. Jemima, because we *know* each other.'
fter dutifully kissing Mia, or at least the tip of her ear be-
eath the curly brown hair, Jemima turned to the others round
er. She must not let Mia down again by seeming to ignore any
utstretched—and peace-bearing—hand.

Jemima was not a Catholic, although she had been edu-
ated at a Catholic school. She retained both admiration and
ffection for the nuns who had taught her there: old-fashioned
uns as they now seemed. She also retained—or had thought
e retained—a knowledge of Catholic ritual from her con-
ent days. But the truth was that Jemima had not really at-
nded Mass for years except for the weddings of schoolfriends
ike Mia's mother for example). She had forgotten how many
hanges had taken place in the traditional ordering of the Mass
recent years. She had certainly forgotten, or expunged from
er memory, the existence of the sign of peace.

'Lord Jesus Christ, you said to your apostles "I leave you
eace, my peace I give you"...' the priest had intoned in his
ft Irish accent a short while after the consecration. Later,
ou may now offer each other the sign of peace.'

Peace! How could anyone really give anyone else peace,
ought Jemima. And what sort of peace was intended? Par-

ticularly something offered to a total stranger. Peace of mind!
How could she presume to know what was troubling he[r]
neighbours? The dark-haired girl had certainly looked trou[bled]
bled enough when Jemima stared at her with her outstretche[d]
arm. But that might have been the effect of Jemima's inept[i]
tude. At least Mia, in the energetic fashion of an unselfcon[-]
scious seven-year-old had done her bit in welcoming th[e]
braceleted arm before it was withdrawn. You could go furthe[r]
and say that the dark-haired girl had actually looked frigh[t]
ened: but that was surely over-fanciful.

Jemima studied the girl's scarlet back, high, narrow wais[t]
standing up, she was not very tall. Did the girl love one or oth[er]
of the men who flanked her? Did the wrong one perhaps wa[nt]
to marry her? Were they linked in some jealous triangle? O[n]
the other hand they might simply be her two protective brot[h]
ers. No, Jemima could never have any idea of what was trou[-]
bling—or frightening—such a total stranger. As for th[e]
dignified black lady beside her, one could fantasise too abo[ut]
a vanished husband, unsatisfactory grandchildren (she wa[s]
that kind of age, the neatly cut hair beneath the hat quite gre[y]
and a lifetime of toil... On the other hand, her troubles mig[ht]
be absolutely different, to do with the accounting system of [a]
string of businesses which she ran.

It occurred to Jemima that inquisitive little Mia probably d[id]
know who her neighbours were since she came to this parti[c]
ular Mass every Sunday. Hence Jemima's presence with h[er]
today: Helena O'Brien had gone on holiday with Charles, t[he]
man she hoped to marry after her divorce from Gerry cam[e]
through. Talk about a vanished husband! Jemima herse[lf]
thought that Helena had been loyal to the memory of Gerry f[or]
far too long, considering that he had in effect disappeared [to]
the United States after she became pregnant with Mia.

Of course Jemima had theoretically understood Helena[']
reluctance, as a Catholic, to call an official halt to her ma[r]
riage. Yet surely it had been a sham from the start: Jemima d[id]
not believe that unreliable Gerry had ever intended to hono[ur]
the vows he had breathed at the altar. Maybe that lack [of]
commitment would enable Helena to get an annulment o[ne]
day: Jemima was hazy about the Catholic rules and did n[ot]

care to probe Helena. She was simply glad her friend had found someone better in Charles.

In the circumstances it was also perhaps natural that Helena should be so determined to plant Catholicism in her child. She once told Jemima that she did not want Mia to suffer for 'the sins of her parents'.

'What parents' sins?' asked Jemima rashly. 'What are you trying to lay on Mia? Sins of the father, more likely.' Helena looked hurt. The upshot of this was that Jemima, to atone, agreed to take Mia to Mass on the three Sundays Helena was away with Charles.

'And besides, Jemima, you're almost a Catholic,' ended Helena.

'You mean, once at a Catholic school, always a Catholic... No, I'm not, darling. No way. Look at how you're stuck, for one thing... But of course I'll take Mia to Mass. Brunch afterwards at the Halcyon. Pleasure to follow piety.'

Now the congregation was going up to Communion. Letting the black lady pass, and seeing Mia make her way forward, Jemima had leisure to look around again. She studied the back of the trio ahead. There was no move here to the Communion rails. As she gazed, Jemima was aware of something quite surprising about the little group. The two men were pressed so closely to the girl that they might have been guarding her... They *were* guarding her. Suddenly Jemima was convinced of it. In the last episode of her most recent television series, *Jemima Shore Investigator*, she had become involved with a Middle Eastern princess, who needed constant security. The stance of the princess's guards had been exactly the same. If Jemima's previous experience was any guide, there would be another guard posted behind them in the church.

The shorter of the two men, as if in response to her gaze on his shoulderblades, turned round and stared back at her. His expression was not particularly benevolent: no sign of peace here. But then why should there be? Unless you really thought that all members of a given religious congregation lived in harmony with each other. As if on cue, another man who looked to be of similar nationality appeared from somewhere behind her, taking advantage of the general disruption caused

by people going up to Communion, and whispered something
in the short man's ear.

The short 'guard' turned round again. Mia was now back a
her side kneeling, her face buried in her hands. The black lady
eased herself gracefully past once more and knelt down. Je
mima noticed Mia toying with something in her hands as she
prayed. When the little girl looked up, she looked rather pink
The black lady continued to pray, her face buried in her prayer
book as she leafed it over. A piece of paper fluttered to the
ground. Instinctively, Jemima went to pick it up for her. Be
fore she could do so, the short 'guard' ahead swooped down.

The Sacred Heart of Jesus: Christ with his hands wide and
a red heart, surmounted by a crown and rays of light, showr
in the centre of his robe. Jemima recognised the image from
her convent days when the girls had collected such 'Holy Pic
tures'. There was some writing on the back. The 'guard' scru
tinised it long enough for the black lady to say in her deep
voice: 'I will thank you, sir.' Then the 'guard' handed it back

There was something vaguely disquieting about all this
Jemima trusted her instincts sufficiently to know that she wa
not imagining it. She would wait for brunch to question Mia
about their various neighbours. She might even get into con
versation—but as the priest announced, 'Go, the Mass i
ended', there was a stir head of them.

The trio, in advance of the general rush, were leaving thei
pew. The short man gave one more fixed stare in the directior
of the black lady. Then he started to hustle his charge—tha
was the language Jemima felt like using—away. Before h
could do so, the girl glanced briefly in their direction onc
more. The object of her gaze was not so much Jemima or Mi
as the black lady. She was biting her lip: she looked distinctl
frightened. A sign of fear not a sign of peace! Yes indeed. No
troubled but frightened. Furthermore, for the first time th
pretty, artfully made-up face looked familiar to Jemima. Di
she really know her or was it imagination? A frightened half
familiar girl...

By this time the Mass really was over. Mia was exiting from
the pew, with a big genuflection to the altar. Jemima followe
her, remembering to genuflect in her turn. The smell of in

cense, wafting in the half-empty church, filled her with sudden nostalgia for distant days. As a result it was not until emima was seated with Mia at the Halcyon that she realised her charge was still pink in the face. She was also clutching something tightly, in her hand.

'Can you keep a secret?' Mia asked in a voice which shook between nerves and excitement. Without waiting for an answer she went on: 'That lady gave me something. I thought it was chewing-gum, but it wasn't. She gave me a note. It's a secret.'

'What lady? The black lady?'

'No, that's Mrs Scotland. She used to work for Dad. She gives me sweets sometimes. She didn't today. No, the one in front of us. When you didn't shake her hand and I took it.'

Mia produced the tiny folded note from its encasing of chewing-gum. Secret was the only large word.

'Spotty. Don't look or give a sign. I've got to get out. It's all till SECRET. Come next week.' The rest of the writing was miniscule. It ended with a word that looked like 'Bailey'. But the second time Jemima read the note, she realised that it was 'Scotty' not Spotty. And the note was ended 'Baby', not Bailey.

'What are we going to do now?' asked Mia anxiously; she had the look of strain on her face that sometimes accompanied her attempts to explain where her dad was.

'We are going to eat brunch,' was the firm answer. 'And naturally we are going to keep all this a secret.' Jemima took the note and put it into her Filofax (where it stuck). It was only later that she began to question Mia—as casually as possible—about Mrs Scotland. Yes, she had worked for Mia's dad, not when he was married to her mum but a long time ago. She was quite old and very kind. She was a wonderful cook, she had been a chef somewhere in a white hat, Mrs Scotland was very clever, she could make dresses and things...

'And did you ever call her Scotty?'

Mia paused. 'Dad did, I think. Mum and I always called her Mrs Scotland. Mum says it's more polite.'

'And when she left working for you, where did she go?' Mia looked blank. 'I just know I see her every Sunday,' she said

after a while. 'Once she told me that she was praying for m'
dad, that he would come home safe to his family.' It was evi
dently an uncomfortable memory.

'So we'll see her next Sunday when I take you to Mas
again.'

Mia cheered up. 'She might have sweets.' Then she frowned
'Jemima, what about the lady in the red jacket and the se
cret?'

'Don't think about it, Mia. I'm not going to think about i
at all.'

That was not of course true. During the next six days Jemi
ma thought about the message quite a bit. And she did mor
than that. She also used the persuasive powers of television t·
have a conversation with Father Aloysius Rourke, parish pries
of Saints Cosmas and Damian. The excuse provided was
potential programme investigating the nature of Londo
Catholics and the proportion of foreigners among Londo
Catholics. Thin perhaps, but it certainly got Father Rourk
talking and he proved to be a splendidly loquacious man. Un
fortunately he could not help her about the trio in the pe·
ahead. As Jemima had noted for herself, there was a hig
proportion of foreigners in his parish and she was right to as
cribe this to the embassies in the district. Such people did nc
take part in community activities. On the subject of Mi
Scotland he was, however, a mine of information.

'Ah, Teresa Mary—and isn't that a grand name for a goo
Catholic woman, and she *is* a good Catholic woman too.' /
litany of praise followed about cakes for bazaars, and clothe
for fêtes, rather along the lines of Mia's own catalogue of M·
Scotland's virtues.

'So she's Teresa Mary Scotland.'

'She is. But of course most of us call her Scotty.'

'And did she ever . . . work or cook or housekeep, or what
ever, for any of these embassies? A friend of mine is trying t·
trace—' Father Rourke scarcely needed the prod.

'A terrible experience!' He repeated the words several time:
'God save us from such things. Those people: to treat her lik
that after so long. Foreigners, you know. She was thrown ou
Just like that. And they didn't even pay her. Then pressure wa

brought: our local MP, a very good man, not a Catholic, but sympathetic, a churchgoer, mercifully...'

Father Rourke seemed to recollect at this point that he was talking to a member of the press. 'But we must put all that behind us, as Scotty did, sufficient unto the day, as Our Lord said... Now about this programme on television—' In the end it was quite a long time before Jemima could question the priest further on the subject of Mrs Scotland. But she did discover that Mrs Scotland lived very near the church. After that the London telephone directory helped her to pinpoint 'T. M. Scotland' quite easily: she lived in a block called Duchess House, a stone's throw from the Church itself.

But Mrs Scotland's telephone was not answered. By now it was Thursday. And Jemima was due to take Mia to Mass again on Sunday. Something had to be done about the message-in-the-gum before that, since it had evidently been intended for Mrs Scotland, not Mia. Somehow Mia's quick intervention to save Jemima from disgrace had made the plan go wrong. Jemima was going to see a prize-winning Russian film at the Gate cinema; she would drop in on Mrs Scotland on the way.

At first there was no answer from the flat bell. Jemima rang again, waited and was about to depart, when that characteristic deep voice boomed out: it was so low and resonant that now, disembodied as it issued from the ansaphone beside her, it might have belonged to a man.

'Who is it and what is your business?'

'My name is Jemima Shore. I took Mia O'Brien to Mass last Sunday,' Jemima spoke as rapidly as possible. 'I think I have a message for you.'

There was a further silence, then: 'I remember you, Miss Jemima Shore. I recognised you on Sunday. Are you alone? Then enter.'

Mrs Scotland's flat was immaculately tidy, and like her hat and clothes at church, rather formal in an old-fashioned way. It was quite dark, not because the plate-glass windows of the modern block were inadequate but because velvet curtains, and further white lace curtains were masking them. There was more velvet, of a peculiarly sombre crimson, and more lace, on the sofa and chairs. Holy pictures in gold frames abounded and there was at least one crucifix, and a holy water stoup. As with the nostalgic smell of incense in the church, Jemima found herself transported back to her schooldays. Mrs Scotland had recreated the formality of a convent parlour, and with her dignity and politeness, would herself have made a most impressive Reverend Mother.

Perhaps it was the feeling of respect Jemima had entertained for her late headmistress Mother Ancilla which persuaded Jemima not to bother Mrs Scotland with any kind of false cover story. Jemima simply offered the note and asked: 'Could this be meant for you, Mrs Scotland? Mia O'Brien was given it. I think it was a mistake.'

Another longish silence, then: 'Miss Shore, I've seen you on television. You know important people. Can *you* help her? My Baby. I'm frightened for her and lately, the last few days, frightened for myself. I daren't—I haven't even dared answer the telephone since they started threatening me. And my poor Baby.'

It turned out that Mrs Scotland's 'Baby' and Jemima's glamorous stranger was actually called Rosario de Loreto Casares. She was the daughter of the Ambassador—the former Ambassador, rather—of Santangela. At this point Jemima suddenly realised why the face encased in its carapace of curling black hair was familiar. Jemima was far from being an expert on the intricacies of Latin American politics—she knew few people who were. But she was at least aware that there had been a recent rather bloody military coup in Santangela.

The United States was accused of condoning it for the sake of trade: she could visualise the placards of denunciation outside the American Embassy. Britain, she rather thought, had done nothing (having no trade interests there). The previous regime, which had at least aimed at being democratic, had called for international protest. One of the most vocal of these protesters had been Rosario de Loreto Casares. Jemima visualised her on the late night news; her pretty passionate face had been pictured on the front page of the *Guardian*. Then Rosario Casares had vanished from the public attention, together with the fate of Santangela itself.

'They're holding her. She's a hostage, Miss Shore. They grabbed her to stop her daddy speaking out about what's going on there. The killings and all those terrible things. The soldiers—they're even killing nuns—killing and worse. They're holding my Baby.'

'But surely in London—'

'You don't know, Miss Shore. These people have the Devil with them—'

'Then why do they bring her to Mass?' interrupted Jemima.

'Miss Shore, Santangela is a Catholic country; it used to be a good holy country, now they kill priests. They bring her to Mass to pretend they are good Catholics, but really to show her daddy they have got her. These people are dangerous. Two Sundays ago she managed to slip me the first message. I think they're beginning to suspect ... And now they are threatening me. On the telephone. "Leave her alone," they say. "Don't you dare be in contact. Don't think of helping her. You're rubbish. Just an ignorant old black woman. Remember, Scotty"—how dare these devils call me Scotty? Have they no respect—"Remember that we know where you live."'

'This new message: she wants to escape.'

'Yes.'

'I'll be there on Sunday,' Jemima promised. 'I'll sit by you. I'll help you. And her.'

Mrs Scotland's last words were: 'Take care: these are evil men. Angelo and Roderigo are evil, godless. They never pray, just sit there guarding her. Worst of all is the one who sits behind, Garcia. I don't know his first name.' Jemima said goodbye to Mrs Scotland as she stood at the top of her stairs, formidable and at the same time, like Rosario, frightened. Jemima hoped that her own presence, with Mia, on Sunday, would make her feel more secure.

But on Sunday morning there was no sign of Mrs Scotland at Saints Cosmas and Damian. Jemima tried to stop herself feeling apprehensive. The trio—short, broad Angelo, taller Roderigo, and Rosario in the same scarlet jacket—duly appeared slightly late which, like leaving early, was obviously the

agreed technique for both displaying and guarding Rosario.
Garcia was presumably somewhere behind them.

Jemima went into a kind of ruminative dream, the effect the
familiar words of the Mass had often had on her in her youth.
Part of her rumination was about contacting people to help
Rosario. A friend of hers—a Cambridge contemporary—in the
Foreign Office? Could the Foreign Office really help in such a
delicate situation? She was awakened from her dream by a
gasp from Mia. The child clutched her hand. There were tears
in her eyes, and she was beginning to sob as she said: 'Jemima! Don't you hear? It's awful, poor Mrs Scotland—'

The priest was still reading over the list of the recently dead:
'For their souls, and the souls of all the departed . . . may they
rest in peace.'

'Mrs Scotland! Oh, poor Mrs Scotland. She died in a road
accident.' For a London child, a road death was in a sense both
the most terrible and the most believable death, because it was
the constant peril against which such a child was warned.

At this moment Rosario Casares herself turned round, ignoring the heavy flanking shoulder of her guards and gazed in
anguish in Jemima's direction. Her dark eyes, like Mia's blue
eyes, were full of tears. She looked completely stricken.

Jemima took a decision. Under the cover of a particularly
deep prayer—as the priest moved to the Canon of the Mass—
she scribbled something in her ever-present Filofax. Her assumed piety did not however deceive Mia, whose sharp eyes
detected the surreptitious opening of her black leather book
(which to others, Jemima hoped, had the look of a leather-
bound missal: were Filofaxes the late twentieth-century pa-
gan prayer books?). Mia's expression had that special reproach
shown when a grown-up has been discovered behaving badly.
At least Jemima's action had distracted her, however temporarily, from the death of Mrs Scotland.

Mia would simply have to overlook Jemima's lapse. More
to the point was the reaction of the guard behind them—Garcia?—and whether he would have noticed Jemima's furtive
scribbling. He would not necessarily have figured Jemima as
a danger, given that she was merely escorting Mia, who came
to Mass regularly.

Nevertheless Jemima still felt extremely nervous when the priest addressed them—not Father Rourke this Sunday but another priest with a faintly Italianate accent in place of Father Rourke's Irish one.

'Lord Jesus Christ, you said to your apostles ... My peace I give you ... Will you now give each other the sign of peace,' he added in his liquid voice, 'according to the custom of the country.'

The custom of *this* country, thought Jemima, is to act swiftly and boldly. She ignored Mia's upturned face, expecting her kiss, grabbed Rosario's timidly outstretched hand, deposited the note, and turned back to kiss Mia at last. It seemed to work: especially since Mia herself tried to shake hands with 'Roderigo' ahead. She also looked genuinely affronted when he did not respond but shot her instead a look of downright hostility. Mia, like another little boy in a pew several rows ahead, continued to seek further prey around her to receive her sign of peace—or so it seemed to a Jemima breathing more easily now her ploy had worked.

Now she had to talk to Father Rourke. And also to Mia. And she had to think how next week the sign of Rosario's fear might be properly transformed into a sign of future peace for her. Then the convent training returned unbidden: she started to think of Mrs Scotland, wondering exactly how she had died, wishing her eternal rest, *requiescat in pace* ... Mother Ancilla had always maintained—most cheerfully—that the only true peace was in the grave: 'When we lose our earthly bodies and are gathered up in the arms of Our Dear Lord.' Did she, Jemima, now believe any of that?

There was a third person Jemima had to talk to, her old friend Detective Superintendent John 'Pompey' Portsmouth, now high up in the Diplomatic Protection Corps. That discussion was really the most urgent of the three: if her plan was to work.

Pompey ruminated, as he nursed the whisky with which Jemima had thoughtfully provided him.

'Nasty chaps, these. The new lot from Santangela, I mean. The old lot were rough and ready, finding their way if you like, often talked a lot of nonsense, left-wing rubbish, you know the sort of thing, but at least they never employed killers.' He hesitated. 'All the same we have to be very careful in our line of business. Are they diplomats or are they not? One false move and it's red noses all round, diplomatic protests, righteous indignation. Besides, you say the girl hasn't made any public move, just these messages—'

'She's a hostage, Pompey, it's a question of her father—'

'Father, or no father, we've still got to be very, very careful—'

'Exactly, Pompey. That's why my plan is worth a go: *you're* not involved. No official protest possible. No red noses. If it goes wrong, which it won't.'

'I'm providing you with a certain object, or rather objects, strictly off the record.'

Jemima smiled: 'I take it there will be no monograms or official markings on a certain object or objects!'

'But a church!' exclaimed Pompey. 'I realise that it's a *Catholic* church and that may be rather different.'

Jemima found herself nettled. 'It's only different because in a London Catholic church you get such a mixture of nationalities jostled together. You know, Pompey, the word Catholic means universal . . .'

Pompey ignored everything but the ominous word 'jostled'. 'There had better not be too much jostling . . .' he said.

Then he became more friendly. 'Thank you for the tip about the old woman. Sad business. Hit and run driver just outside her own block of flats. She always went to the 7 p.m. Mass in the week, regular as clockwork. It might have rested at that. No witnesses. Except that thanks to you, we've had a discreet examination of certain cars belonging to certain people attached to a certain Embassy . . . enough said for the time being.'

Two whiskies later, Pompey reverted to the subject of the church.

'You say the priest is with you? And the child?'

'They're both troupers. An old trouper and a young trouper. They both loved Mrs Scotland.'

Jemima did not want to confess to Pompey that while her conscience was clear where Father Rourke was concerned, she was much less happy about Mia. The case had begun with a frightened girl: she did not want to end with another much more frightened one. Mia was so dear to her, her confidence already so precarious in view of her family situation. Jemima wondered whether even the good-natured Charles would provide Mia with the rock-like solidity a child of her age really needed. She even debated leaving Mia behind on Sunday and somehow rewriting her plan. But at the mere mention of such a possibility, Mia became once again deeply upset—this time at the thought of a dereliction of duty.

'I *have* to go to Mass every Sunday. You promised Mum, Jemima, you did. It's the rule.'

Indeed, on the following Sunday—the third Sunday—Mia did radiate a remarkable confidence, far more confidence than Jemima herself was actually feeling. After entering the church, Mia lit a candle for Mrs Scotland at the altar of St Thérèse of Lisieux—'My favourite saint.' Then she knelt and said a short, silent prayer.

The arrival of 'the trio', slightly late as usual, was to Jemima on the one hand a relief—what if they had *not* come?—and on the other hand it filled her with a renewed dread. In Angelo and Roderigo—or perhaps in Garcia somewhere behind them—she was after all looking at murderers, the deliberate killers of Mrs Scotland.

After that, the Mass seemed to her to pass extremely swiftly. In an unreal manner, only Mia's small bell-like voice giving the responses with the rest of the congregation had any kind of normality about it. But Father Rourke's voice, when he came to call for the sign of peace, seemed both louder and more strained than usual, the Irish accent more pronounced. Father Rourke, unlike Mia, had an adult awareness of what was (or was not) about to happen.

'Now will you offer each other the sign of peace—'

As the trio ahead of Jemima did not stir, Mia leapt into action. 'Rosario!' she cried, quite loudly, and stuck out her hand.

Rosario Casares whipped round—and so did her guards. Tentatively, she went as though to respond to Mia—but her eyes, those huge imploring eyes, were fixed on Jemima.

Then with one swift movement—exactly as she had planned and indeed practised—Jemima took the handcuffs from her pocket. One link was already fastened round her own wrist. She snapped the second link round the wrist of Rosario Castares.

'*Now,*' said Jemima. Then she sat down sharply. That had the effect of both yanking Rosario towards her, and encouraging Rosario's own balletic movement as she clambered across the pew. It all happened so quickly that Rosario was sitting, panting slightly, her trembling body against that of Jemima before the guards had fully swivelled their attention in the right direction. The commotion around Jemima was just beginning. An American boy with fair hair and a brilliant turquoise T-shirt, pulled at his mother's sleeve:

'Mom, hey *Mom,*' he whispered. A prosperous-looking man in a blue blazer over an open-necked white shirt, started to protest more loudly:

'Look here, I say—'

It was to be Father Rourke's finest hour.

'Fellow parishioners,' he was saying at the altar. 'We have just offered each other the sign of peace. I want therefore everyone in this church to remain calm and peaceful, as Our Lord would wish. Everything which is taking place in this church at this moment is happening with the knowledge and consent of your parish priest . . .'

Then Father Rourke moved back to a more familiar invocation: 'Lamb of God, who takes away the sins of the world' repeated three times, with the final plea: 'Give us peace.'

It was at this point that Mia, amazing child, actually went up to the Communion rails and received the sacrament. Nor did she show any signs of agitation. In short, here was no frightened little girl. Afterwards Mia explained it all to Jemima, still herself in turmoil although trying to conceal it.

'You know that I lit that candle when we came in. I used my own pocket money for it. I prayed so hard then,' said Mia, 'prayed to Little St Thérèse, then I tried the Infant of Prague, Our Lady too of course, and a go at Mum's patron saint, St Helena, who found the True Cross . . . So I was never frightened. Not for a minute. I knew it was all going to be all right

Seeing that Jemima still looked uncertain, Mia added in a kindly tone, a parody of the tone grown-ups must have used to her: 'You've just got to have Faith, Jemima, Faith that everything will turn out all right.'

How could Jemima then say that she did indeed have faith—but in the handcuffs slipped to her by Pompey? For that matter, she had faith in Pompey's men, discreetly stationed at the back of the church. These were the men who had moved in on Garcia—wanted in connection with the death of Mrs Scotland—and then removed Angelo and Roderigo during the general disruption of the administration of Communion. There had been hugs and kisses with Rosario—and tears as the name of Scotty was invoked. No longer a frightened girl, Rosario was now free to join her father in New York. Soon, discreetly aided by shadowy authorities, she would be on her way there.

Yet, thinking it over, who was Jemima to say that Mia was wrong? In the church at least, before the altar of St Thérèse, Mia had found peace of mind. And somewhere, Jemima hoped that Mrs Scotland too had found peace.

TRUE THOMAS

★

REGINALD HILL

It was mirk, mirk night, there was nae starlight.
They waded thro' red blude to the knee;
For a' the blude that's shed on earth
Rins through the springs o' that countrie.

'NOT GUILTY!'

Disbelief. Shock. Anger. The need for a drink.

DI Tom Tyler was heading for the court exit before the judge had pronounced the dismissal. But quick as he was, Chuck Orgill was even quicker, bounding out of the dock to ignore Miss bloody Morphet QC's congratulatory hand and crush her instead in a joyous bear-hug.

Over the lawyer's skewed wig, his gaze met Tom's. For a second his lips pursed in a derisive moue. Then, which was worse, they spread in an almost sympathetic smile and his left eyelid drooped knowingly, ironically, conspiratorially.

Scotch became essential to sanity. Tom shouldered his way to the exit till he met a body too solid to be shouldered.

'Lost it then, did you?' said Superintendent Missendon. 'I got here in time to see little Miss Muffet take you to the cleaners.'

'Sodding lawyers. I hate them!'

'We had one on our side too, remember?'

'That prancing ponce! If he pissed in a snowdrift, he'd miss.'

He tried to resume his progress but Missendon caught his arm.

'Smithson's here from the Prosecutor's office. He's got a spare hour and would like to go over the Bryden case with us. And Tom, do me a favour. Go easy on the prancing ponce line, eh?'

It was a quarter to two before Tom made it into the murk masquerading as afternoon in wintry Lancashire. On the law court steps Missendon said 'Fancy a drink? We can make the Sailors before closing.'

Tom hesitated. The need was still strong, but not for the company of colleagues he'd find in the Sailors.

He said, 'I'll pass if you don't mind, sir. I ought to get down to South to check those points Smithson brought up.'

'Such devotion to duty. I'm impressed,' said Missendon unconvincingly. 'Catch you later then.'

He strode away. Tom watched him out of sight then headed over the road to the Green Tree.

The Tree had its disadvantages too. The nearest pub to the law courts, it was the traditional trough of sodding lawyers. Sodden lawyers, too. Despite the lateness of the hour, it was still crowded with the bastards, red in tooth and glass. Using his shoulder as a ram, Tom took a direct line to the bar, filling the air with protest and claret.

He was served quickly. Studying himself in the bar mirror, he understood why. A stocky, muscular thirty-year-old with a lowering, truculent expression, he looked the kind of trouble-maker the police warned the public against approaching.

He raised his drink in a mock toast. 'Long life,' he said. 'And up yours, Miss Muffet.'

He drank, and as if by magic, his image vanished to be replaced by a view of the woman he was so abusively toasting.

The door linking the saloon with the small bar serving the dining-room had swung open. Miss Morphet, brandy balloon before her, was shaking hands with a man Tom recognised as Orgill's brief, Walter Lime, 'Harry' to his friends. 'Slime' to the constabulatory. They'd probably just finished a celebratory lunch and Slime was oozing off to keep another of his crooked clients out of jail. Miss bloody Muffet on the other hand didn't need to rush her cognac. Crooks were dusted down and cleaned up before being ushered into her hygienic presence.

She was laughing now at some farewell pleasantry, probably some crack about how easy it was to stuff the police.

Tom turned from the bar with an abruptness which set the
claret flying once more and headed purposefully for the dining-room.

The brief had gone. Miss Morphet looked up at him with the
expression of interested puzzlement she'd worn as she insinuated that most of the police evidence was pathetic forgery.

Tom said, 'I'd like a word.'

She said, 'I'm sorry, I know we've met, but I can't just place
you...'

'No? You don't look at people you call liars then?'

'Ah,' she said. 'Inspector Tyler, isn't it? I don't believe that
in fact I used that term...'

'Of course you didn't. A bit too plain for a lawyer. What
was it you said? Oh yes. My notes had clearly been composed
so long after the event that, like Shakespeare's *Richard the
Third*, they might be great entertainment, but they were hardly
history.'

'Did I say that?' she said with amused complacency. 'Oh
dear. Though I'm sure it sounds far worse with a strong masculine delivery. Now I really ought to get back to chambers, so
perhaps if there were anything else...'

'I just wanted to know what it feels like to put a dangerous
criminal back on the streets.'

She pursed her ripe cherry lips and said, 'I don't know, Inspector. Perhaps you can tell me. Keeping people on or off our
streets is more in your line, I believe.'

'That's right,' he said. 'You just stand up in court, play with
words, never give a damn for the consequences of what you're
saying...'

She was gathering her bag from under her chair and her
jacket from its back.

'I think it best if I didn't hear this, Inspector,' she said. 'And
to tell the truth—'

'What the hell do you know about telling the truth?' he exploded. 'Before you rush off to make your official complaint why don't you try it, just for once in your life. Is Orgill guilty? Yes or no?'

'The jury found him Not Guilty, don't you recall?'

'Sod the jury! That's a verdict, not a fact. In truth, in honest simple truth, is Orgill guilty? Did he do it? Yes or no?'

For a brief moment he thought he saw the professional mask of that narrow, fine-boned, Siamese-cat-like face fracture.

Then she said, 'Won't you sit down, Inspector?'

Tom's anger, though still strong, had lost its head of steam and he was aware that other eyes in the dining-room were watching the encounter with undisguised interest. He sat.

She said, 'You clearly pride yourself on plain speaking, so why not say exactly what you've got on your mind.'

He took a deep breath and said, 'All right I will. I believe— I *know* there's a dangerous man roaming free because he didn't get sent down for a crime I *know* he committed. I reckon you're far too bright not to know that he did it too. But this didn't stop you asserting as true things you knew were lies, and smearing as lies things you knew were true. OK. I've heard all that garbage you people trot out about everyone being entitled under law to a defence. I just want to know how you as an individual human being can live with twisting the truth like this.'

He fell silent and sipped his whisky.

She toyed with her brandy balloon then said, 'My trouble is, I don't really know you, Inspector. I mean, I don't know enough about you to help me decide whether I should just tell you to go screw yourself, or whether I should simply get on the phone to the Chief.'

'And how much would you need to know to make you try to answer my question honestly?' he sneered.

'Oh, very little,' she said. 'I'd just need to be persuaded it was the question of an honest man. Are you that rare creature, Inspector?'

'I'm on the side of truth,' he growled, annoyed with himself now because it sounded pompous. 'And I don't believe you can get there through lies.'

'A real True Thomas,' she said, smiling as though at a secret joke.

'Sorry?'

'Thomas the Rhymer in the old ballad who went to Elflan
and when he came back he could never tell a lie.'

'Look, I'm not saying I've never told a lie, but...'

'But they are not necessary for your way of life whereas the
are for mine?'

'Something like that.'

'So you wouldn't find it difficult to manage, say, twenty
four hours telling nothing but the truth? What's up, Inspec
tor? You look disconcerted. You want to condemn me fo
allegedly doing something you couldn't avoid yourself for
mere day? Surely not?'

'Of course I could but—'

'Then that's my best offer. You go twenty-four hours with
out telling a lie and I'm yours to do with as you wish.'

She saw his eyes widen slightly at her choice of phrase an
gave a wicked smile.

'I mean, *morally*, of course, Inspector. So what do you say?

He looked at her, trying to show his scorn for such a daf
idea. She had green eyes, and those lips which in court ha
lured him into so many damning uncertainties and qualifica
tions were full and moist. As he hesitated she picked a Cox'
pippin from the bowl of fruit in front of her, polished it agains
her breast and offered it to him.

'What's this for?' he asked.

'In the ballad, the Queen of Elfland gives Thomas a magi
apple which makes him incapable of telling a lie,' she said
'I'm beginning to wonder if you don't need a bit of magic too
Inspector.'

The mockery stung. She'd done the same in court, provok
ing him into responses he knew were unwise. But even as h
recalled his resolve never to be so provoked again, he hear
himself saying, 'Not tell a lie for a day? No problem.'

'Oh good.' She nibbled a tiny edge out of the apple, the
offered it to him once more. 'A bargain, then?'

He took the fruit, said, 'A bargain,' and sank his teeth dee
into the incision she'd made, filling his mouth with the cris
juicy flesh.

'That's fine. What's the time?' As if at command, the old
all clock above the kitchen door began to chime. 'Two
clock. You've started. See you here in the Tree tomorrow. Or
rhaps I should say under the Tree.'
The secret mocking smile again.
'Suits me,' he said trying to sound indifferent as he watched
r wriggle her supple, slender arms into the sleeves of her
cket.
She caught his eyes and suddenly looked serious.
'One thing more, Tom. I may call you Tom? And you must
ll me Sylvie. Tell me, Tom, are you happily married?'
'Yes,' he said. 'I mean, most of the time, we have our ups
d downs but...'
He stopped, not just because of the tangles his search for the
ecise truthful answer was leading him on to, but also be-
use she had brought her face so close that he could feel the
armth of her five-star scented breath while under the table
r long, red-nailed fingers gently caressed the inside of his
igh.
'But would you fancy sleeping with me, Tom?' she whis-
red.
'What?' He pushed back his chair in confusion.
She stood up, laughing.
'No need to answer, Tom. Dirty trick, you reckon? I think
u may be surprised just how many dirty tricks twenty-fours
n play on a man devoted to the truth. See you tomorrow. Or,
not, I'll know why.'
He watched her go then he picked up the whisky glass he had
t on the table. He still needed a drink but it was no longer to
ed his anger.

E SPENT THE AFTERNOON at his desk catching up with pa-
rwork. Scrupulously, he applied as strict a regulation here
he knew he'd need when speaking, and the truth cost him
equent revisions and would probably cost him even more
equent rebukes when his reports were read.
But by six o'clock he felt satisfied he'd made an excellent
art to his twenty-four hours. Now with a bit of luck he'd have
l eight-thirty the next morning, safe from the testing pres-

sures of the job. Not that he doubted his ability to meet Mi
bloody Muffet's challenge, but he knew that his working li
offered all kinds of traps to the unwary.

One of them was coming along the corridor as he came o
of his room.

'Tom, just off?' said Missendon. 'You got things sorted wi
South did you?'

'Sorry?'

'You said you were heading off to South to tidy up sor
loose ends on the Bryden case.'

'That's right. I did.'

'Did sort things out, you mean?'

'Did say I was going,' said Tom.

'Ah.' Missendon was looking nonplussed. 'And did y
go?'

'No,' said Tom.

'Oh,' said Missendon. 'Why not?'

'Because,' said Tom carefully, 'I'd already got everythir
sorted that needed sorting.'

He smiled in valediction as he spoke and started to mo
towards the stairs. Missendon fell into step beside him.

'So why did you say you were going?' he persisted.

Tom sighed inwardly and said, 'It was an excuse.'

'For what?'

'For not going to the Sailors with you, sir.'

'You mean you didn't fancy a drink? Why not say so?'

'That's not what I meant, sir.'

'What then?'

'I didn't fancy a drink with you, sir, at the Sailors.'

Missendon was looking at him very strangely.

'Are you feeling all right, Tom?' he asked. 'You've be
acting a bit odd lately.'

'Yes, sir. I feel fine.'

'That's all right then. I'll see you in the morning. Go
night.'

'Good night, sir,' said Tom.

He heaved a sigh of relief as he made it to his car witho
further encounters. This truth business wasn't quite
straightforward as he'd asserted. Of course, the kind of lie he

old Missendon at the law court was pure white, a bit of that social mortar which holds the fabric of relationships together. But it made him aware that perhaps simply being away from his work wasn't going to give him the easy ride he'd hoped.

His fears were confirmed almost as soon as he entered his house.

Mavis appeared at the head of the stairs dressed only in her underwear, but not to offer him the soldier's welcome after a long campaign.

'Tom, there you are! Get a move on. We're due there at seven.'

It came to him instantly. It was a Very Special Day, to wit, his parents-in-law's wedding anniversary, and the whole Masserman family were going out to dinner.

'What kept you so late? You didn't forget, did you?'

This was a form of reproach rather than a serious accusation. Mavis didn't believe it was humanly possible for anyone to forget so important an occasion. The correct answer was something on the lines of, 'Of course not, darling. It was just that Missendon wanted to chat and with my promotion board coming up, you know I've got to keep on the right side of the old sod.'

Tonight was different.

He said, 'Yes. I forgot.'

Fortunately she hadn't stayed for an answer but turned back into the bedroom. He watched her heavy buttocks wobble away. He didn't mind that she had started putting on weight, in fact he found the extra pounds in most places a real turn-on. But he wished that she would acknowledge the change in her choice of clothes. The fact that her skimpy silk pants now almost disappeared into her rear cleavage affected only her own personal comfort, but when he came out of the shower and saw her struggling into the kind of figure-hugging dress she'd once looked so devastating in, his heart sank.

'There,' she said, pirouetting. 'What do you think?'

'Oh yes,' he said, nodding vigorously and smacking his lips. 'I'd better get a move on. Mustn't be late.'

'You mean, oh yes, you like it?' she said, unhappy as always with anything less than hyperbole.

He said, 'It's a very nice dress. Super. Shall I wear my plai
blue shirt?'

He knew she hated the blue shirt because it looked like of
ficial police issue, but even this provocation only provided
temporary diversion.

As he buttoned up the pearl grey pinstripe which nipped hir
under the arms but which Mavis thought made him look dis
tinguished (i.e. not like a policeman) she said, 'You don't lik
it, do you?'

He sought for further evasion, saw how close he was skirt
ing the boundaries of truth, and said, 'No, not really. The dres
is all right but . . .'

'But not on me, you mean? Why? What's wrong with me?'

'It looks a bit tight, that's all. Perhaps you got the wron
size . . .'

'No, I didn't. I got the size I always get. What you mean i
I'm fat, that's it, isn't it?'

She was glaring at him angrily, waiting for the reassurance
the explanation, the full frontal flattery.

He sighed and said, 'Yes.'

Only the fact that her parents were waiting to be picked u
and must on no account be kept waiting on this Very Specia
Day saved him. Nothing must be allowed to interfere with th
smooth running of a Masterman VSD. He'd long since give
up the attempt to count exactly how many VSDs Mavis's fam
ily celebrated per year, but he was pretty certain if they were al
made public holidays, it would solve the unemploymen
problem at a stroke.

They drove to his in-laws' house in a frost of silence be
yond the reach of the car's heating system. Mummy and Dad
dy's presence warmed things up superficially with Mavi
exuding enough heat for two, but his in-laws' attempts to brin
him into the conversation created more problems.

'So how's work, Tom?' asked Father Masterman in hi
hearty down-to-earth, am-I-right-or-am-I-right, self-mad
Northerner's voice.

'Much the same.'

'And your promotion board, is that looking hopeful?'

'There's always hope,' said Tom.

'Well, don't forget our little agreement. The moment you feel things have stopped moving for you in the police, there's that nice comfortable seat waiting for you at Masterman's.'

Father Masterman was a builder, one of the biggest in Lancashire, and for years now he and his daughter had been urging Tom to take charge of the firm's security. So long as Tom could imply that he was moving steadily onwards and upwards towards the socially acceptable level of Chief Constable, he could fend them off. But somehow a purely unilateral agreement' had evolved whereby they understood that any hiatus in his upward progress meant he would resign and join the firm.

Tom grunted unintelligibly.

From the rear seat Mother Masterman piped up, 'I dare say Tom's secretly hoping he doesn't get his promotion so's he can leave and join Father. Isn't that right, Tom?'

He didn't reply.

Mavis said sweetly, 'Tom, Mummy asked you a question, didn't you hear?'

'Yes, I heard,' said Tom.

'So why don't you answer? Polite people reply when they're asked civil questions.'

'What was the civil question again?' asked Tom.

'Wouldn't you rather give up this awful tying police work and take a nice nine-to-five job with Father,' said his mother-in-law, choosing a bad moment for one of her rare excursions into precision.

Tom considered, then said, 'No. I think I'd rather pick cotton.'

There was a long silence, ended when his father-in-law began to laugh.

'*Pick cotton!* That's a good 'un, Mother. Pick cotton! They're too sharp for us, these youngsters. *I'd rather pick cotton*. I'll have to remember that one.'

That got them over that hurdle without much immediate pain. But as they got out of the car and he gave Mavis a ruefully apologetic smile, all he got in return was a cold stare which promised payment deferred with interest.

He sighed deeply. He hadn't been lying to Miss Muffet whe
he said his marriage was generally speaking a happy one. H
and Mavis shared far more than they were divided by. Unhap
pily, Mavis's family was one of the divisors, and various gui
feelings of her own meant that no compromises were permi
ted here.

The rest of the family were already waiting in the restau
rant. There was his brother-in-law, Trevor, weak son of
strong father who tried to compensate by eschewing charm an
embracing fascism. With him was his wife, Joanna, whose a
coholism might be either a cause or an effect of her hus
band's growing impotence. Tom quite liked her, but he ha
never been able to grow fond of his sister-in-law, Trudi, wh
spoke as rarely as she bathed, which was not often. And t
make up the party there was Trudi's husband, Fred, sham
bling and uncoordinated, who had finally been found a job i
Accounts to keep him away from machinery and sharp edges

The meal followed much the usual pattern.

As their orders were being taken, Joanna announced wit
the piercing clarity of the chronically pissed, 'Spinach. M
husband will have spinach. They say it helps with erections.'

At the same time Fred, who despite his utter lack of physi
cal coordination, loved sport, was describing to Mavis hot
he'd built a break of six in his last game of snooker. Drawin
his right arm back to illustrate the shot, he drove his elbow int
the crotch of the wine waiter who was uncorking the manda
tory champagne. The man doubled up with a strangulate
scream, the cork blew off like a bullet and hit a woman at th
next table plumb between the eyes, while the jet of wine caugh
her dining companion on the back of his head with such forc
it removed his toupee.

What puzzled Tom on these occasions was the fact that n
matter what outrageous observations Joanna made, no mat
ter how much of the infrastructure Fred destroyed, their be
haviour never drew more than a resigned chuckle from hi
father-in-law, while he, Tom Tyler, who stayed stone-cold so
ber and could eat his prawn cocktail without breaking the dish
was clearly regarded as the disruptive member of the family.

Tonight, however, he at last caught up with his reputation

He kept out of trouble till well into the main course. Then:
'How's crime, Tom?' asked Trevor.

'There's a lot of it about.'

'You're telling me. It's the courts I blame. Too much wrist
slapping. It's time the legislature got its act together. Right?'

After his experience in court that morning, Tom couldn't
disagree.

'Right,' he said.

'Slap their wrists with a sharp axe if they're caught thieving, that's what they need,' continued Trevor, warming to his
thesis. 'The stuff we lose off our sites, you wouldn't believe it.
It's the Irish, too many bloody Irish, why we let them in I can't
fathom. And if we do catch them red-handed, what happens?
Nothing! They're off robbing some other poor devil the next
day. We need to make a few examples, encourage the others.
Am I right, Tom?'

Tom said judiciously, 'As a general principle, even-handedly
applied, I think a rational man might make a rational case for
that approach, Trev.'

It was, he felt, in the circumstances a rather good answer.
But the trouble with the Mastermans was, they didn't just want
a polite nod in the general direction of the family faith, they
needed you inside the temple, flat on your belly, kissing the
idol's big toe.

'So why don't you join us, Tom?' said father. 'Or if you're
not yet ready to do that, at least give us the benefit of your
expertise. Sort of consultant.'

'That's right, Tom,' said Trevor. 'Family's got to stick together, eh? So as an expert law man, where would you start to
clean up Masterman's?'

At the top, was the answer that rose in Tom's throat, but he
let it stick there.

'Look,' he said, 'the kind of petty thieving on the job you're
talking about, it sounds to me like it all comes down to how
much supervision you want to pay for.'

'Private security, you mean?' said Trevor. 'That's a bit rich,
coming from you.'

'Sorry?'

'Well, haven't I heard you going on about the evils of private education? And private medicine? And private every thing else? Why's it all right all of a sudden for your own family to be expected to pay for private security? What's happened to the forces of law and order, then? I mean, just because we're not the undeserving poor, aren't we entitled to the law's protection too? After all it's people like us who pay for it, isn't it? We're not on state benefits. We're paying our taxes. So shouldn't whoever pays the piper call the tune?'

'Depends.'

'On what?'

'On all kinds of things. Whether the piper's getting paid full whack for instance. Fred, could you pass me the horse-radish?'

His attempt at diversion failed. Fred performed the minor miracle of passing the dish without dropping it or knocking anything over with it. He looked hopefully at Joanna, but she seemed to have relapsed into a state of catatonia.

Father Masterman said slowly, 'Now I'm not sure I understand you, Tom. Let's get this straight. First off, the police is a public service, right?'

'Right.'

'That means it's funded from the public purse, right?'

'Right.'

'Which means taxes. And we pay our taxes, right?'

Tom didn't answer.

'Right, Tom?' insisted Father.

'To a certain extent,' said Tom.

'To a hell of an extent!' exploded Father. 'Have you ever seen our tax bill? Fred, you tell him. You know the figures. How much did we pay last year?'

For a moment panic pitted Fred's face like smallpox. Then he took a deep breath, let his lips move as though totting up columns of figures and said, 'A hell of a lot.'

'That's right,' said Father. 'A hell of a lot. So where's the problem, Tom?'

Time for evasion. Time to duck and weave. Time to kick Joanna under the table and hope she'd wake from some dream of Trevor's sexual inadequacy which she wished to share with the company.

But a vision of Miss bloody Muffet rose into his mind, the green-eyed Queen of Elfland offering him the apple with juice oozing out of the nick she'd made with those wicked white teeth.

He said, 'The problem's what you want those taxes to be spent on. The problem's the kind of people you vote into power to spend those taxes. The problem's that you might pay a hell of a lot, but you slide out of paying a hell of a lot too.'

'Tom!' exclaimed Mavis in outrage.

'No, let him speak,' said Father. 'What are you saying, Tom? That we cheat? Is that it?'

'Yes,' sighed Tom thinking with regret of the sherry trifle. They did a very nice sherry trifle here and he'd been looking forward to it. But he had the feeling that he would be heading for bed without any pudding tonight.

'You'd better explain yourself, I think, Tom,' said Trevor in his best senior management voice.

Tom pushed his plate away, saying goodbye to the rest of his roast beef too.

'All right,' he said. 'Take this dinner. You've got an arrangement with this restaurant, haven't you? They advertise Masterman's on the back of their menu. And the annual cost of that advert just happens to be whatever you spend on entertaining people here over the year. I've heard you boasting about the arrangement, Trev. So the cost of this meal will go down on your books as a tax-deductible advertising expense.'

'Aye, that's right,' said Father Masterman. 'I thought that one up myself when they stopped business entertainment except for foreigners. Nothing wrong with keeping one step ahead of the game, is there, Tom?'

He smiled proudly as he spoke, and lowered his left eyelid in a man-of-the-world's knowing, conspiratorial wink.

'Oh, no, nothing's wrong,' said Tom. 'Except that it's a tax fiddle! No. Hear me out. Let's take those building workers you're always complaining of, the ones who are robbing you rotten. How many of them are working on the lump through so called subcontractors that in fact you run yourselves? That way, there's no records to keep, no National Insurance to pay, and you can get away with paying them under the odds, 'cos

you know they need the work and they won't be filling in ta
returns anyway. In other words you and others like you ch
cane your way out of paying millions of pounds to the reve
nue every year, then you have the cheek to squeal, "We'
paying our taxes, aren't we?" The truth is, no, you're blood
well not! And until you do, you're not entitled to make crack
about an underfunded, overworked public service like the po
lice!'

It must have been building up for some time, the way
gushed out in a swift unstoppable flow.

Some similar process must have been taking place insi
Joanna, for suddenly she awoke, opened her eyes and he
mouth very wide, said, 'Oh dear,' then her half-digested di
ner gushed out in a swift unstoppable flow also.

Surely this would divert attention, if only temporarily, fro
his own disruptive outburst!

But no. Not even when Fred's attempt to dodge his sister-i
law's regurgitations sent him tumbling backwards in an e
plosion of splintering chair did the spotlight move from To

'Now see what you've done!' cried Mavis. 'You've ruine
everything!'

And Father said, 'You must hate us all very much, Tom,
go out of your way to destroy such a happy family occasion

It was his pulpiteeringly self-righteous tone that finishe
Tom off.

'Happy family?' he cried. 'Take a look at them. A lim
dick, a fall-about drunk, a shambling wreck, a smelly mut
and a Michelin tyre advert! Charles Manson had a happi
family than this!'

He headed for the door.

Mavis caught up with him as he paused to take in a dee
breath of car park air.

He was already regretting the Michelin tyre crack. Nothin
else, not yet. But that had been unforgivable.

He was right. She wasn't about to forgive him.

She said, 'You bastard. That's it. I won't be home tonigh
And when I do come, I don't want to find you there. I wa
you out, do you understand? Out! Or I'll get Daddy's solic
tor to throw you out!'

She could do it too. The house, a Masterman 'Georgian' villa, had been her father's wedding present and it was registered in her sole name.

He should have held out at the start, insisting that he didn't want a house he hadn't paid for. But he'd loved her too much then to believe it could be a problem. Loved her too much now to believe she meant what she was saying.

He said, 'Mavis, I'm—' but was prevented from further explanation or apology by a round arm blow that sent him reeling.

She really was putting on weight. Last time she'd hit him she hadn't got punching power like this!

He wiped the blood off his lip and drove home.

There he sat and slowly worked his way down a bottle of Scotch which seemed to have lost its anaesthetising power. Eventually the bottom came in sight, but he was still cold sober.

He knew this because when the phone rang he had no difficulty in getting up and going to answer it.

'Hello?'

'Tom? Missendon here. Listen, I was just driving home from a speaking engagement when I caught a shout on my car radio that there was a barney at the Dog and Duck. It sounded serious.'

Tom glanced at his watch. It was after midnight. It must have sounded very serious for the Chief Super to let a pub brawl keep him from his pit.

'You still there, Tom?'

'Yes sir.'

'Well, listen, you'll love this. You know what was going on at the Dog? A private party to celebrate the release from custody of your old chum, Chuck Orgill. There's been a ruckus. And there's been some serious injuries, maybe worse. I'm on my way there now, and I thought, seeing who it is, you might like to join me.'

Orgill. Where all this had started.

'Yes sir,' said Tom. 'Thank you, sir.'

He climbed into his car and found he was still carrying the whisky bottle. Carefully he laid it on the passenger seat. Was he fit to drive? Legally, of course not. But he felt he could have walked a high wire with no problem. He started up.

There were lots of police cars round the Dog and Duck. Lots of people, too, despite the hour. An ambulance came belling out of the forecourt and there was another one gently pulsating by the main door.

'Tom. There you are.'

Missendon came towards him, smiling. He was still wearing his dinner jacket and looked like a head waiter welcoming a high-tipping diner.

Tom said, 'Hello sir. What's the score?'

'One dead, two critical, four or five badly cut, a lot more gently bleeding. About par for the course when you let a mob like this loose among the bubbly.'

'And Orgill?'

'The guest of honour? He's inside getting a couple of stitches in his face. He keeps shouting he wants to get off to the hospital but there's no way he's going out of my reach till I'm done with him.'

'So who's dead?'

'Orgill's cousin, Jeff.'

Tom whistled and said, 'Someone's done us a favour, then. What happened?'

'Power struggle, from the sound of it. You know Jeff's been the heir apparent in the Orgill family for a long time. And when it looked like Chuck was going down for a stretch, he must have reckoned his hour had come. But little Miss Muffet changed all that. My reading is that once the booze loosened him up, he couldn't hide that he was less than happy to be welcoming Chuck back. Perhaps he even suggested that it was time for a change in the pecking order. Only he got pecked.'

'By Chuck, you reckon? Now that would be nice. Got any witnesses?'

'Don't be silly, Tom,' said Missendon. 'In the first excitement, the barman rattled on about the two cousins having a bit of a barney, then all hell breaking loose. But once he had a chance to remember who he was talking about, he went amnesiac. The rest'll be the same, no matter whose side they were fighting on. There's only one boss now, and no one's going to risk crossing him.'

As he spoke he led the way into the pub. Through the saloon door Tom saw a mixed bunch of men and women, most of them walking wounded, accompanied by half a dozen policemen noting names and addresses. Then Missendon ushered him into the public bar and he didn't need to ask where the fight had taken place. There was literally blood on the walls and the room was in such a state of chaos that amidst the confusion of broken glass and shattered furniture it took the eye a few moments to pick out the one piece of human wreckage.

'Stabbed?' said Tom approaching carefully to avoid treading on the blood which had gushed copiously out of the dead man's wounds.

'Three times by the look of it, maybe more. I just let the doc close enough to confirm death. I don't want anything moved in here till Forensic have gone over it with a fine-tooth comb.'

'What're you hoping for?'

'Anything that will put Orgill in the dock for murder. He slipped away this morning, Tom. He's not going to do it again.'

'It's going to be hard without witnesses,' said Tom. 'The kind of ruck that obviously went on here, it could have been anyone.'

'You sound like Miss bloody Muffet. Look, there's a knife over there. Obviously got chucked when the first of our boys arrived. Could be the weapon. It'd be handy if it had Chuck's dabs on it. There's blood on Jeff's hand. With luck it'll match Chuck's that spurted out when Jeff shoved a glass in his face. And I've got Chuck's shirt. Covered in blood. I bet it'll turn out to be Jeff's group.'

It was an empty optimism, thought Tom, because even if justified, what did it prove? For a start Chuck Orgill was blood group 'O', the commonest. He knew this because he knew everything about the man. And chances were that Jeff was 'O' or 'A' like 90 per cent of the population. He could hear Sylvie Morphet's insidiously persuasive voice.

'How many people received injuries during this fracas, Inspector? Fifteen? Twenty? More? So there was a lot of blood

around. And how many of those bleeding were groups 'A' o
'O'? *That* many? In which case how can you be certain . . .'

And so on.

'What's up son? You don't look happy,' said Missendon
sharply. 'Spit it out. What's on your mind?'

'I was thinking you're clutching at straws, sir,' said To
baldly. 'If the blood's all you've got to pin this on Orgill, Mis
Muffet will have us dancing the polka. You'll need somethin
a lot stronger than that to make this a runner.'

'You think so, do you?' exclaimed Missendon angrily
'What's up, Tom? Miss Muffet got you scared?'

'You'd better believe it,' said Tom. 'Hello. What have w
here?'

He squatted down close to the body and peered at the floor

'What's up? You got something?'

'That shirt of Orgill's. Is there a button missing?'

Missendon joined him and peered down. About eightee
inches from the corpse's outstretched hand was a sma
mother-of-pearl button with thread and some fragments c
cloth still attached, as though it had been forcibly ripped fro
its place.

'Hold on,' said Missendon excitely. 'I'll take a look.'

He left the room and returned a few seconds later with
sealed plastic evidence bag. Carefully, without opening th
bag, he shook out the bloodstained shirt it contained.

'Tom, you're a genius,' he said squatting down and di
playing the garment.

The buttons were mother-of-pearl and the third one dow
in the shirt front had been ripped off.

'Now that could be the clincher,' said Missendon. 'Happ
now?'

'It'll help,' agreed Tom, rising. 'But it's just another pointe
How many more buttons and bits of cloth do you think F
rensic will find in this lot when they start looking? Now if
had been in Jeff's hand . . .'

'But it was,' said Missendon in a surprised tone. 'Don't yo
remember? Look.'

He too stood up and stepped aside. Tom looked down at t
corpse.

Almost concealed in the curled fingers of the outstretched right hand was the mother-of-pearl button.

'Grabbed the shirt as Orgill stabbed him, fell back and tore the button loose,' said Missendon. 'Even Forensic can't miss that.'

'No, it was on the floor,' said Tom stupidly.

'That's right. Jeff was on the floor and the button was in his hand,' said Missendon. 'You remember now, don't you?'

He was smiling, and as Tom met his gaze one eyelid dropped in a knowing, conspiratorial wink.

'You do remember, Tom, don't you?' repeated Missendon.

Tom didn't reply.

He thought of Orgill who, if there were justice in the world, should tonight have been starting a ten stretch.

He thought of Sylvia Morphet's secret smile, mocking his claim to be able to exist in a world of complete truthfulness.

He thought of the Mastermans' dinner and his ruined marriage.

He said, 'No.'

'Sorry?'

'No. I can't do that. I can't go along with a lie.'

Missendon's face set hard as iron.

'What are you saying, Inspector?'

'I'm saying that, if asked, I'll tell the truth about where I found the button.'

'Then it's just as well you never found it, isn't it? It's just as well you've no standing here. It's just as well you're going home now and your name's going to appear nowhere in this investigation. You've been working too hard, Tom. You've managed to cock up one case today from not being up to scratch . . .'

'That's bloody rubbish and you know it!' snarled Tom.

'Rubbish?' Missendon stepped up close to Tom and sniffed. 'You've been drinking. I thought you must have had something to make you speak to me like that. How much have you had?'

'A bottle, but I'm not . . .'

'A bottle!' Missendon was genuinely amazed. 'And you drove out here? Have you gone off your trolley or what? No

wonder you don't know what you're doing. Now listen to this.
You go near your car and I'll have you arrested, so help me
God. I'll get someone to drive you home. And you can stay at
home. Sick leave, till further notice, you understand me, Inspector?'

'Oh yes,' said Tom. 'I understand. But you'd better understand me, sir. If I'm asked . . .'

'If you're asked?' yelled Missendon. 'Who the bloody hell's
going to ask you anything?'

'I am!' cried Tom. 'I am.'

IT WAS TEN TO TWO by the old wall clock when Tom walked
into the dining-room of the Green Tree.

Sylvie Morphet was at the same table, talking earnestly with
Slime. Tom had no trouble guessing what they were talking
about.

He approached and stood by the table till they looked up at
him—the solicitor in surprise, the woman with that expression of secret amusement which was both irritating and be-
guiling.

'Inspector Tyler, you look tired,' she said. 'Burning the
midnight oil in pursuit of justice, perhaps?'

'Something like that.'

'But not very like it,' she chided. 'Mr Lime's been telling me
you've got poor Mr Orgill banged up again. You don't waste
time, do you?'

'Don't I?' he said. 'Look, sorry to interrupt, but you did say
two o'clock.'

She looked puzzled, then smiled and said, 'Of course. Ex
cuse us, Mr Lime, a little private wager. No, no need to go. I
won't take a minute. Well, Inspector, how did it go? Have you
come to tell me you've won and want to claim your prize?'

In fact, he didn't know why he had come, except that when
he woke up, out of all the confusion of a life which seemed as
complete a wreck as that bloodstained room in the Dog and
Duck, only this appointment at two o'clock had remained as
something solid to cling on to.

She was looking up at him expectantly, green eyes glinting
like raindrops on spring foliage. Little white teeth gleaming

behind soft red lips parted in a sympathetic smile, one blue veined eyelid drooping in a knowing, conspiratorial wink...

It came to him then that he had seen that expression before.

So Orgill had looked in his triumph at beating the rap. So Masterman had looked as he boasted of his tax fiddle. So Missendon had looked as he invited complicity in fixing the evidence.

Now here it was again, the same look, the same wink, on the face of the Queen of Elfland...

That was it! It came as no surprise. He'd known it all his adult life. These three—and God knows how many more like them—actually belonged together, not in the ordinary workaday human world, but in another shadowy country of hazy boundaries and shifting sands and swirling mists above rivers that ran red with blood...

And what did that make him?

Simple. He was a stranger in Elfland, and if he spoke out of turn, he might stay here for ever.

'Well?' she urged. 'Did you win?'

He laughed and shook his head. He didn't know much, but he knew there was no way a mere human won bets with the Queen of Elfland.

'Don't be silly,' he said easily. 'Of course I didn't win. No chance. You always knew that. Now if you'll excuse me, I've got to go and meet my wife.'

Oddly, that wasn't a lie. At least he hoped it wasn't.

The way he saw it was that by now Mavis would have had an evening of Tom-bashing with the whole family, carried on the good work over breakfast with her parents, sunk into soul-searching soliloquy during morning coffee with her silent sister, and was probably at this very moment having her future spelled out during the course of a long lunch with Trevor—on the firm, of course.

Now that, by the most conservative estimate, ought to be exposure enough. For Tom Tyler knew his wife's darkest secret.

Too much contact with her family got right up her nose. This was why the VSDs had to be so very perfect, to ease her guilt at neglecting them the rest of the time!

She would never admit it, of course, at least not more than the odd hint in those confidentially languorous moments which followed their lovemaking. But Tom felt sure that by the time lunch was over, Mavis would have had enough, and she'd make an excuse about needing to collect something, and head for home to get some time to herself.

Well, she was going to be out of luck. Or in it, depending how you looked at things. He would go a long way towards mending his bridges with the family. Not as far as working for them, no way! But a long way. And if she wanted evidence that he still loved her and found her irresistibly attractive, he didn't doubt he could supply testimony that would stand up to any examination.

As he reached the door, the clock began to strike two.

It occurred to him that this meant his lie about losing had fallen within the twenty-four hours, which meant he really had lost . . .

Except if he really had lost, then it wasn't a lie . . .

Which meant . . .

He shook his head ferociously. This was Elfland logic. He had done with all that.

Boldly he stepped out of the shadows of the Green Tree into the bright winter sunlight which had replaced yesterday's mists, and headed homeward to start reassembling the fragments of his truth-wrecked life.

BETRAYAL

★

NANCY LIVINGSTON

THE DOCUMENTARY production office high above Shepherd's Bush was stuffy. A fly tumbled feebly on to the sill. Jay felt equally lethargic. Her friend Susan, newly appointed producer in place of Mike, was being far too crisp and decisive.

'I'm sorry to rush you...' Susan checked her watch, also new. Whatever had happened to the Mickey Mouse one Mike had given her? Jay picked up the file.

'That's OK, Suse. I've got the picture.'

'Haven't you any questions? I don't want any slip-ups.' Jay swallowed irritation. She had *trained* Susie, for Chrissakes! The trouble was Jay had never had her ambition or the fabulous looks.

Mike's photograph, beaming and waving his BAFTA award, caught her eye. The only questions Jay wanted to ask concerned his disappearance—the company was buzzing with gossip. Instead she said briskly, 'You want everything double-checked. You want the usual permissions from local authorities to film in the area. Shooting will be spread over two weeks and you want a suitable derelict house as a location, right?'

'We didn't have the time to look around.'

'Which is why I'm on my way to Derbyshire. Relax, Susie. I know the sort of thing. I'll take photos, you should have them by Wednesday. Let me know your choice and I'll do the rest. Congratulations on the new job, by the way,' she added belatedly, 'and thanks for remembering me.'

'Yes, well...' Susan fiddled with the watch, 'You were Mike's researcher long before I knew him.'

The forbidden topic at last!

'You were invited to take over, I assume?'

'Don't be coy, Jay.' She sounded edgy. 'This was Mike's latest project, we were working on it together—I was the obvious person. In answer to your *real* question,' she added sarcastically, 'I have no idea what's happened to him, neither have the police. And if you imagine I *like* being made producer under those circumstances. . . .'

With so many envious eyes watching your every move? To lose your lover as well as your boss without knowing why must have been bloody. Jay realised she'd been crass. She was about to apologise when the communicating door opened and a glossy young man stood there. He acknowledged her briefly before transferring his whole attention to Susie.

'Sorry to interrupt. We were due to start five minutes ago.'

'Be right with you.'

Jay's eyebrows had risen of their own accord. As the door closed, Susan said defensively, 'Gerry's new. He's been allocated to the programme as assistant producer.'

'Does he always wear a suit?' Mike's baggy garb was legendary.

'Times have changed, Jay,' she said sharply. 'The image matters nowadays.'

Jay sighed. 'OK, but please don't ask me to wear a skirt when I'm about to look at rundown houses.' This was ignored. She probed, 'So, no further news of Mike?'

Susan's face clamped shut. 'Since he walked out five weeks ago, not a word.'

'I've been in Birmingham. I heard the rumours, of course. It must have been a dreadful shock.' Susie's lip quivered.

'The worst thing is not knowing *why*. Mike didn't leave a note. When I contacted the bank, I discovered half our money had been withdrawn on the day he disappeared. That *hurt*.'

It must have done, Jay thought wryly; Susie's tastes were expensive. All the same, she was surprised; Mike could be impulsive but that sounded like foresight. She asked cautiously, 'What do the police think?'

'That it happens every day of the week.' The voice was tight. 'I've been over and over it in my mind—I nearly went crazy.

There's just no logical explanation. None. The company believe Mike has been tempted to America by a new backer but that's plain stupid. He's always been perfectly happy here. However...' she shrugged. 'We have a transmission date, so find me the best location and sort out the problems, OK? Everything's in the file: briefing sheets, photos, Mike's notes, also a provisional shooting schedule. Gerry collected leaflets from estate agents—he knows the area—he's sorted out the most likely ones.'

Their former easy relationship had vanished and Jay had been given her marching orders. She said simply, 'Mike would be pleased you've taken over, Suse. He wouldn't have wanted his programme shelved. Good luck.'

'Thanks.'

In the outer office she watched as Gerry ushered the first applicant inside. Susie was interviewing for a personal assistant. Jay remembered her own disastrous attempt for the all-important researcher's job. She had been turned down. Mike Fortune had come across her weeping in the corridor and had immediately invited her to join his team. Too fraught to understand her luck, Jay blurted out, 'You don't want me, I'm a cripple!' He'd swept her off to a pub, bought her a hot-dog and forced her to abjure self-pity for ever. Jay would have gone through fire for him after that.

He'd been an eligible divorcee, a journalist from the provinces who'd shed a wife and children and was making his name fast. When Susie appeared everyone prophesied the affair wouldn't last; she was too young, too glamorous. Jay knew of her ambition and thought otherwise.

Mike had been apologetic when he'd called her into his office. 'You're established now, Jay, you can pick and choose. I'd like to give Susie her chance.'

No tears that time, at least not in public. He was right, too. Jay had never stopped working but she had remained a researcher and now Susie had reached the top. All the same, this first programme would be judged against Mike's record. She shivered, 'Rather you than me, Suse!' Emerging into the sunlight, she headed for her car.

SHE'D BEEN GIVEN the bare bones: the programme would fol
low two Derbyshire school-leavers from different social back
grounds in their search for work. Nothing original in that, bu
Mike rarely divulged his plans beforehand. His results cam
from imaginative editing, intercutting visual reality agains
pompous responses. Sound against picture; an extremely dif
ficult technique. She hoped Susie had learned the knack.

Jay traced the route to the small town where the two youth
lived. The first was a dropout, thrown out by his family an
sleeping rough, hence the need for a derelict house.

Arty shots framed through broken glass? Surely they weren'
going to use that old cliché? And what contribution woul
'Gerry the suit' make? His devotion to Susie was obvious; Ja
wondered if her friend was aware of it. He'd certainly found
comprehensive selection of houses. She emptied the content
of the file on to the passenger seat and examined the estat
agent's handouts. On the first Susie had scribbled, 'If this ha
been used by tramps, so much the better. I want it to feel ver
minous.' Jay grimaced.

'Why do I always get the glamorous locations?' Maybe sh
would leave the motorway and wind through country roads,
was too good a day to waste on the M1. Her spirits began t
rise.

The middle-class youth appeared to be another cliché: fa
ther in the CID, mother a librarian: Mr and Mrs Greenslade
solid and respectable. The boy, Terry, looked plump and dull
Jay read the bold scrawl on the back of the photograph. Mik
had written: 'dim enough to be a bank manager.'

She laughed aloud. Why on earth had Susie decided to us
him? Obviously he wasn't Mike's choice. She sighed: hers no
to reason why, just to find the locations and get the permis
sions. She checked the list of filming requirements: M
Greenslade in the police station, his wife cataloguing books i
the library. Routine stuff, it shouldn't be difficult.

She began to shove stuff back in the file. There was a col
lection of photos of other youths Mike had interviewed. Mos
looked more interesting than Terry. Should he prove too dull
they might need a substitute. Maybe she should study th
notes. Then she remembered: replacing either boy would b

Susie's decision. Mike would have invited her opinion but things were different now. Jay must learn to tread carefully.

Winding country lanes proved a snare. The humidity of London had disappeared and Derbyshire rain swept over the windscreen. The first two derelict houses proved useless: both were close to main roads and the level of noise was unacceptable. By the time Jay reached the third, she was damp and depressed.

According to the leaflet the key was under a plant pot. Beside it was a large spider. She yelped, cursed herself for being a fool and let herself into the cottage.

If Susie wanted dilapidation, this was definitely the place. It also had an unpleasant smell. Jay moved cautiously; rainclouds made everywhere dusk. The electricity had been disconnected, so she fished out her torch. Holding her breath, she limped through the two downstairs rooms.

From Susie's point of view, it was perfect. Jay took extra shots through broken windows of the wilderness beyond—everything as per specification, even evidence of a squatter. The remains of plastic-wrapped food were mixed with the ashes in the grate—and on the hearth beside them were rat droppings! Yuk!! Shuddering, Jay pulled her anorak closer, thankful for her wellies. Spiders she could cope with, mice even. Rats, never.

'Take pics of the upstairs rooms and call it a day. What you need, my girl, is a stiff cup of tea.'

The back bedroom was small with a garish wallpaper. There was a bedstead with an evil-looking mattress and a few scraps of rope. Imagination made Jay think she could hear a creaking noise. Dear God, let it not be the rat!

She took two views of the room. In the silence, even the hiss of prints emerging from the Polaroid sounded sinister. She pushed open the door to the front bedroom.

The man's feet were less than six inches from the floor. Perhaps the flex round his neck had stretched. The question came automatically as Jay's mind absorbed every detail, including the fallen armchair below the window. Here at last was the source of the stench. Blowflies had discovered it ages ago. She heard the wild scream of her own voice as her mind be-

gan to reel. She grabbed the door to stop herself falling and the
slight current of air caused the body to rotate.

Face to face with the blackened, swollen mask, she gagged.
Screams mixed with bile and threatened to choke her. Scrab-
bling desperately for the banister, she half fell down the stairs
and crawled outside. Sprawled on the grass she gulped in air,
waiting for hysteria to subside.

A mangy cat brought her to her senses. It emerged from the
bushes and tried to sidle through the open door. Jay scrambled to her feet. 'Oh no you don't!' There was a rain butt beside the porch. She splashed cold water over her face. Her
heart still thudded but her breathing was more or less under
control. It seemed impossible that birds should continue to
sing. For several minutes she stood, eyes closed, recovering her
wits.

There was no phone. She must drive to the nearest police
station. Before she did, however, she knew she had to go back
upstairs and gaze once more at that dreadful face.

It took every ounce of will. Bracing herself, Jay looked again
and knew she'd been right. She wanted to weep as well as
scream, but what good would that do? Instead, she forced her
hands to remain steady as she used up the remainder of the
film.

There was no police station on the map but there was a cross
marking the Greenslades' house. Jay remembered his rank,
Detective Inspector, CID.

Mrs Greenslade took one look and urged her pallid visitor
into the living-room. As soon as she'd understood the garbled
account, she ordered Jay not to try to speak, simply put her
head between her knees if she felt faint. Mrs Greenslade would
bring strong tea once she'd contacted her husband.

Jay listened to the guarded conversation in the hall. 'A body
in the front bedroom, she says . . . Suicide, I suppose—'

'It wasn't suicide!'

That brought Mrs Greenslade to the doorway. 'I thought
you said he was hanging from the light flex?'

'Yes . . .' but he couldn't have done that himself, Jay had seen
the evidence. Realising the implication, Mrs Greenslade

gasped. With a whispered, 'Jack will be here shortly,' she fled to the kitchen.

There would be questions, lots of them, once the police arrived. Jay had to focus her mind on the facts just as she would for any other job. She pushed emotion aside; this was not the time to weep. One fact was glaringly obvious: it had been deliberate that she should make that dreadful discovery.

Gerry had collected the leaflets from the estate agents, he had sorted them into order. He was the only one on the team who knew the area. Jay gave a brief thought to what Susie's reaction would be. Forget it, all that would come later. It was up to her to help the police to the best of her ability. She'd start with the file; there might be something in there which would tell her more about Gerry.

She tipped the contents on to a low glass-topped table. The Polaroid snapshots she had taken she'd give to the police. Feeling safer now, her strength was beginning to return and her wits were less chaotic. It had been murder most foul and by God she was going to find the killer!

Her hostess returned as Jay was examining the packet of photos. 'Were these the boys who were interviewed when Terry was selected? Could you tell me something about them?'

Mrs Greenslade was grateful for the diversion. 'They're all from the same sixth-form college. Mr Fortune and his assistant interviewed them.'

'Susie, you mean?'

Mrs Greenslade shook her head. 'We met Susie of course, but she was dealing with the dropouts. Gerry helped Mr Fortune choose Terry. We were very proud when we got the letter.'

'You must have been.' There hadn't been anything on Gerry in the file but there had to be a reason why he and Mike came here. Jay tried to put herself in Mike's shoes. What had he been looking for? 'Who else was on the short list?'

'Two other boys from Terry's class, Christopher and Peter. These are the ones.'

Jay gazed at their faces, one bland and solemn, the other lively. She turned the photos over. Mike had scribbled a rejec-

tion on the first, on the second there was only the name
Christopher, in a small neat hand.

'It's a good thing *he* wasn't picked,' Mrs Greenslade said
pointedly. 'Christopher's a problem boy, I'm afraid. He's
adopted, which could be one reason.'

Suddenly, Jay felt her throat constrict. 'Was it Mike who
told you Terry had been selected?'

'No. The letter was from Gerry, on Mr Fortune's behalf, of
course.' Mrs Greenslade had heard tyres on the gravel and
rose, 'There's Jack now.'

JAY CLOSED HER EYES to recall every detail of that small,
squalid bedroom. It was a terrible place to die. Whatever he'd
done, no one deserved that. She had the information now.
Could she fathom what it meant? She looked up to find a tall,
serious-faced man staring down. Behind him, Mrs Greenslade hovered.

'DI Greenslade, Miss Jenkins. How are you feeling?'

'Better, thanks.' Jay managed a faint smile. 'Recovering,
anyway.'

He nodded, noting the signs. She wasn't over it by a long
chalk. He murmured, 'More tea, Grace, with a drop of
brandy,' and Mrs Greenslade vanished. Facing Jay across the
low table, he indicated she should begin.

When the tale was told she handed him the Polaroid shots.
DI Greenslade examined each in turn. As he stared at the close-
up of the swollen face, she forced herself to say, 'It's definitely Mike Fortune...' but her control gave way to a sob.
Greenslade pretended not to notice.

'One of our cars was near the cottage when the message
came through,' he told her quietly. 'As soon as they found
him, our chaps recognised him. There's been a lot of excitement here because of the film. Mr Fortune is very well known.'
He snatched a quick glance at her. And you loved him, you
poor bitch, he thought. His grave face gave nothing away.

Jay handed him the estate agent's leaflet. 'According to that,
the front bedroom was twelve foot square. Mike was hanging
from the centre of the ceiling...the only piece of furniture, the

armchair, was against the wall. He couldn't have kicked it that far.'

'I doubt it.' A careless, botched business, Greenslade decided, done by amateurs. 'My men are still there. We'll soon have a few more details.' He looked again at the close-up Jay had taken of the dead man's wrist. The mark made by the rope was clearly visible.

'When I saw that I knew it had to be murder,' she said flatly.

Equally colourless, he responded, 'I believe you're right.' Shock made her look old. He said anxiously, 'There's a WPC on her way. Or we could arrange for you to see a doctor?'

'I'd rather get it over. Talking might help.'

'Fair enough.'

As he stared again at the dead face, Jay said, 'I tried to pretend it wasn't Mike. My mind refused to accept it at first. That's one reason I went back and took those shots.'

'He went missing immediately after his trip up here?'

'I believe so. I was in Birmingham, I only heard the rumours.'

Greenslade lodged that in his memory and asked, 'You've known Mr Fortune a long time?'

'I used to be his researcher before Susie took over.'

'Uh-huh. What about enemies?'

Jay pulled a face. 'When you're as successful as he was...mostly it's back-stabbing because of that. I've never heard anyone *threaten* him. It just doesn't make sense that it could be anyone in television.' He made no comment. She was fiddling with the picture of Christopher. 'I reckon there had to be a reason why Mike came to this particular town. Did he say something to you that might explain that?' she asked.

He considered. 'His assistant, Gerry, did most of the talking. I got the impression they were up here because *he* knew the area well.'

Jay tried to control rising excitement. She put the photograph on the table-top. 'Do you know anything about this boy, Christopher?'

Greenslade said promptly, 'I thought he'd be the one they'd choose. Mike Fortune interviewed him for quite a long time— Terry only got five minutes. Christopher got more than half an hour and when he came out he looked really pleased with himself. In fact, I warned Terry not to be too disappointed.'

Jay said quietly, 'And then the letter came, signed by Gerry.'

Greenslade stared.

'What's that supposed to mean?'

She indicated the rope burn on the wrist. 'Mike wouldn't have let that happen, it must have been someone he knew.'

'But what has that got to do with Christopher?'

'An adopted boy.'

'So?'

'It's the one thing I never could forgive Mike for. He kept it very quiet, but years ago when he divorced his wife she threatened to put their sons in a home and he did nothing to prevent it.'

It occurred to Jay suddenly that Mike Fortune had been just as ambitious as Susie. This made her defensive. She said angrily, 'He was young, making his way. The family were nothing but a hindrance.'

Greenslade demanded, 'Are you trying to suggest Christopher was his son?'

'It's possible.' Jay repeated his words, '"When he came out he looked really pleased with himself"—so why wasn't he chosen? Why Terry?'

Greenslade shrugged. 'God knows. It made his mother very happy, that's all I know. Look none of this is relevant—what's that?'

Jay had taken Gerry's security pass photo from the pile and placed it beside the shot of Christopher. 'There's Gerry's photo and signature...' she turned over Christopher's picture, 'and there's his writing again. Christopher's name. All the others have Mike's scribbles on them. This is the only one that's different. Look,' she leant forward, striving to make him understand, 'I'm not saying Christopher is Mike's son. It could simply be that Gerry suggested he was as a ploy to entice Mike up here—'

'Why?' Greenslade was exasperated. 'If he felt like that about him, would he really want to see him again? And why bring a man all this way to a secluded cottage simply to kill him?'

Jay sank back, defeated. 'I haven't worked that out.'

He looked at her sternly. 'Accusing people is a serious offence.'

'Mike died up here. There has to be a link. There was food in the room downstairs. I think they kept him tied up. Perhaps they were trying to persuade him to do something—'

Greenslade stretched out his hands. 'Like what?' he said irritably. Jay felt incredibly tired.

'I'm very sorry. I've no idea at all. Can I go?'

'We shall need a statement. And if I were you I'd confine myself to the facts.'

At the police station, the long wait began. Gerry and Susie were being brought to Derbyshire to make their statements and Jay decided she would drive Susie back to London.

'Susie was in love with Mike, she'll be terribly upset.'

Jack Greenslade shrugged and suggested she could rest in one of the cells.

The door was open. In the corridor beyond, Jay could see a clock. She lay on the bunk and closed her eyes but sleep eluded her. The image of the clock-face refused to disappear. She forced herself awake and began to re-examine the events of the day from the beginning. It was then that the WPC on duty heard her sigh.

'Oh, of course...' She saw Jay struggle to her feet.

'Anything wrong?' Jay's face was covered in tears; she shook her head.

'Can I speak to Detective Inspector Greenslade again?'

'He's outside. The car's just arrived from London.'

Jay limped out to the reception area. Under the fluorescent lights her face was taut with strain. The door opened and Susie hurried towards her. 'Jay—it can't be true. Please tell me there's been a mistake. Please, it isn't Mike?'

The blonde hair was tousled and she stretched out both hands imploringly. Behind her, alongside Gerry, stood Jack Greenslade. Jay spoke to him directly. 'Isn't it the law that when one person dies, a joint bank account is frozen?' He nodded. 'What happens if a person disappears?'

'Several years have to elapse before he can be presumed dead and his assets unfrozen. Sometimes a bank will agree to use its discretion . . .' Jay was shaking her head.

'Mike had to be found. Susie couldn't wait that long.' She stared at her friend. 'You had his job but that wasn't enough. You had to get hold of his money. I don't know what you promised Gerry but he must have helped you—'

'No!'

'I'll never forgive you for sending me up here to find him.'

Susie was weeping but Gerry shrieked at Greenslade, 'It was Jay, she was responsible. She couldn't stand it when Mike turned her down for Susie, she's been bottling it up for years. She was in Birmingham when we were in Derbyshire—she must have contacted Mike, arranged a meeting—'

Stunned though she was, Jay retaliated. 'That's a pretty dumb suggestion.' The movement was only slight but her limp was perceptive. 'How am I supposed to have murdered him?'

'You must have had an accomplice,' he yelled.

'*I* couldn't have done it, I loved him!' Susie looked round the circle in desperation, 'I had no reason to want him dead!'

Jay stared at the paler patch of skin against which the new watch sparkled. 'You couldn't bear to wear the watch Mike gave you because of what had happened. I wish you had loved him. He deserved that much.'

'YOU GOT IT ALL WRONG, you know.' DI Greenslade held open the car door as Jay fastened her seatbelt. 'Christopher wasn't involved. It was Gerry who was Mike Fortune's son. He had his eye on the main chance.'

Jay stared. She stammered, 'Mike had two boys.'

'Yes. The other works in a solicitor's office in Matlock. Gerry's in a blind panic because you guessed about the money. He's been on the phone, asking for his brother's help.' He saw her expression and said kindly, 'Time moves on, Miss Jenkins. Neither of Mike Fortune's boys would have been Christopher's age today.'

'Does the other one wear a suit?'

'I expect so. Why? Most men do.' He peered more closely. 'Are you sure you're fit enough to drive?'

'Yes.'

'It was one of my detectives who thought of it after he'd read your statement.' Jack Greenslade was increasingly cheerful. 'He realised you'd got the age gap wrong so we tried the suggestion out on Gerry. As soon as we told him why we wanted to see his birth certificate, he started to crumble. I've no idea which of the two of them planned it but there's no doubt he hated his father. *She*'s still blaming you, of course.' Greenslade made a mental note to double-check Jay's account of her stay in Birmingham before adding, 'But I don't think we need detain you at present.'

'At least I was right about the watch,' she said defiantly.

'I expect so, yes. Drive carefully.'

He watched the tail lights disappear. If it had been you, you'd never have taken the damn thing off for the rest of your life, he thought.

BOSS

★

MICHAEL Z LEWIN

ONCE ONLY, on the way to the funeral, I stopped to look at my breath and wondered that it didn't freeze and fall to earth. But as I watched what I had exhaled I began to shiver beneath my thin coat and then I cursed myself for wasting time on such impractical considerations as frozen breath.

As I walked on I turned my curses toward my dead boss. 'Cheapskate. Thatcherite. Exploiter.' No sorrow for his demise but anger at the memory of his clench-fisted running of the company. And anger that my need for a job, even this job, was so great that I felt obliged to be seen grieving at the funeral and at the widow's afterward.

If the dead man had paid me half what I was worth I would be driving to the funeral, or at least walking inside the skin of a warm coat.

'DEARLY BELOVED,' the cleric began, but that is what none of us from the company were. None the less we cried, because no one, not even the managers, knew who would take the business reins, who was favoured in the widow's mind.

'He was so young!' I cried when there was a lull. Several heads turned my way and I was satisfied.

AT HER HOUSE the widow wore dark rings around her eyes. She welcomed every one as we arrived, shook every hand. For just a moment I felt sad for her. It was not her fault that the dead man screwed every penny out of the factory that was his living and our existing.

Though I had not planned to do so, I said, 'It is such a tragedy, but worse for you than anyone.'

She said, 'Thank you,' but could not raise a smile.

BUT INSIDE THE HOUSE I grew angry again. Perhaps it was the widow's fault after all. The house she lived in, now owned, was as lavish as the factory was bare. No comfort spared, even the wallpaper was soft. She was the cause of our misery. The dead man drew our blood to transfuse her. No wonder her pampered grief was deep.

I ATE WHAT I COULD and then watched for ways to take home more. I stood aside to wait my chance. I hung in the shadow of velvet curtains. Having drawn the attention that would serve me, now I avoided eyes. It was a practised skill.

THE TIDE TURNED. Having completed obeisances, it came time for company employees to leave the widow to her darkness.

From my shade I saw the widow thank each in turn for coming. But I was not the only employee who lingered. A man I knew only by name held back too, but the feast he planned was not the same as mine.

The widow turned to him. Her black grief broke and she smiled with bright warm relief. He winked. They thought they were alone.

Then the widow saw me in the velvet ripples. I had to leave, without food in my pocket.

But I was no longer angry, for was I not the only witness to a murder?

CRYPTIC CRIME ACROSTIC

★

SARAH CAUDWELL & MICHAEL Z LEWIN

The diagram on the following page, when filled in, will read as a quotation from a book. All the letters appearing in this quotation have been used to make up a series of 26 words, phrases and names (some particularly familiar to readers of 2nd Culprit). These words, phrases and names are indicated by the numbered blanks beside cryptic clues A to Z on pages 120 and 121. The number beneath each blank shows where that letter fits in the diagram. In addition, the first letters of the answers to the clues spell out the name of the author and title of the book from which the quotation is taken. In each diagram square, the letter in the upper righthand corner shows which clue that square may be filled from.

1 C	2 K	3 J		4 Q	5 Z	6 C		7 S	8 C	9 K	10 D	11 Z	12 X	13 Q	14 B	15 H
	16 C	17 X	18 G	19 S		20 D	21 H	22 K		23 Z	24 V	25 M	26 F	27 L	
28 M	29 C	30 S	31 K	32 Y		33 U	34 S	35 R	36 X	37 Z	38 G		39 L	40 Y	41 D	42 F
	43 H	44 U	45 R		46 K	47 L	48 Z		49 W	50 X	51 Q	52 L	53 R		54 S	55 C
56 N	57 D		58 S	59 B	60 O		61 N	62 C		63 Q	64 H	65 U		66 X	67 B	68 L
69 Y	70 D	71 S		72 E	73 Q	74 P		75 J	76 Z	77 R	78 Y	79 C	80 M		81 X	82 Z
83 Y		84 D	85 H	86 R	87 K	88 C	89 T		90 D	91 W		92 S	93 K	94 J	95 R	96 V
97 Y	98 T		99 E	100 Q	101 J		102 O	103 S	104 N		105 U	106 J	107 I	108 N	109 C
110 F	111 Q	112 N	113 U		114 O	115 Z		116 Q	117 I	118 X	119 J		120 V	121 R	122 T
123 L	124 O		125 W	126 X		127 M	128 C	129 Z	130 X	131 D	132 S	133 Q	134 R	135 L		136 A
137 X		138 P		139 H	140 Y	141 Q	142 U	143 G	144 E	145 P		146 Z	147 F	148 K	149 I
150 O	151 L	152 Z	153 H	154 K	155 B	156 D	157 G		158 H	159 N		160 G		161 Z	162 N	163 S
164 E		165 B	166 C	167 W	168 N	169 R		170 G	171 C	172 M	173 S	174 W	175 X	176 L	
177 C	178 X		179 I	180 U	181 Y		182 P		183 N	184 C	185 H	186 M	187 K		188 Z	189 G
190 Y	191 F	192 Q		193 P	194 N	195 Z		196 A	197 U	198 V	199 P	200 C	201 N		202 F	203 H
204 S		205 C	206 S	207 Z		208 W	209 R	210 D	211 I	212 M	213 Y		214 T	215 U	216 N
217 A	218 X	219 Z	220 I	221 Q	222 G		223 B	224 T		225 A	226 N	227 Z		228 K	229 Z	230 S
231 I		232 C	233 X	234 D	235 N	236 Y	237 H	238 M	239 I

A ___ ___ ___ ___ Substance hidden by cop, I think.
   217 136 196 225

B ___ ___ ___ ___ ___ ___ Is he uncut? Not exactly—a bit missing.
   67 223 14 59 165 155

C ___ ___ ___ ___ ___ ___ ___ ___ ___ ___ ___ ___ ___ ___ ___ ___ ___ ___ Crook shot
   205 88 29 166 79 128 6 200 171 55 62 109 16 8 221 232 177 184 1
   wife's lover—fragments of steel in several places, but
   it could be worse.

D ___ ___ ___ ___ ___ ___ ___ ___ ___ ___ ___ Did she need only one note to
   41 84 234 90 210 10 156 20 57 70 131
   write St Giles leper mystery?

E ___ ___ ___ ___ Spots one dame leaving Madeira on the quiet.
   144 72 99 164

F ___ ___ ___ ___ ___ ___ May come to harm, having no ma, no pa.
   26 191 110 147 202 42

G ___ ___ ___ ___ ___ ___ ___ ___ Where Dr Spooner said little woman
   157 143 160 18 189 170 38 222
   had passed away.

H ___ ___ ___ ___ ___ ___ ___ ___ ___ ___ ___ Not U to panic—but time
   85 203 15 64 194 43 185 139 237 153 158 21
   to say your prayers.

I ___ ___ ___ ___ ___ ___ ___ ___ ___ Gnu's pique, we're told, was the talk
   231 239 179 211 149 107 117 220
   of 1984.

J ___ ___ ___ ___ ___ ___ Younger relative, when no end in trouble, first
   94 3 106 119 101 75
   to write back.

K ___ ___ ___ ___ ___ ___ ___ ___ ___ ___ Imitation gun part found in special
   187 87 46 148 154 2 93 9 228 22 31
   effects room.

L ___ ___ ___ ___ ___ ___ ___ ___ ___ Some tussle! Macho sportsman is
   176 123 68 135 52 151 27 47 39
   finally broken by it.

M ___ ___ ___ ___ ___ ___ ___ ___ ___ Which crime novelist has ordered one
   238 212 25 127 186 172 80 28
   dozen little lacy items?

N $\overline{56}\,\overline{159}\,\overline{104}\,\overline{235}\,\overline{168}$ $\overline{61}\,\overline{183}\,\overline{216}\,\overline{112}\,\overline{226}\,\overline{108}\,\overline{201}\,\overline{162}$ DA poisoned rum cocktail—crime method typical of Latin.

O $\overline{114}\,\overline{150}\,\overline{60}\,\overline{102}\,\overline{124}$ Bad language used in court.

P $\overline{74}\,\overline{182}\,\overline{193}\,\overline{138}\,\overline{145}\,\overline{199}$ American lawyer has disguise of luxury silk.

Q $\overline{116}\,\overline{133}\,\overline{141}\,\overline{63}\,\overline{100}\,\overline{192}\,\overline{73}\,\overline{4}\,\overline{111}\,\overline{51}\,\overline{13}$ Hear we aren't doing badly— making pots.

R $\overline{169}\,\overline{86}\,\overline{45}$ $\overline{95}\,\overline{77}\,\overline{121}\,\overline{35}\,\overline{53}\,\overline{209}\,\overline{134}$ 'Take action against corrupt practices! Forward!' she writes.

S $\overline{173}\,\overline{19}\,\overline{30}\,\overline{132}\,\overline{7}\,\overline{206}\,\overline{34}\,\overline{204}$ $\overline{54}\,\overline{58}\,\overline{71}\,\overline{92}\,\overline{103}\,\overline{163}\,\overline{230}$ That lousy cheat got a month inside—ridiculously little—in idyllic rustic setting.

T $\overline{122}\,\overline{224}\,\overline{98}\,\overline{89}\,\overline{214}$ Action scene: soldiers taken in by retreating spy.

U $\overline{33}\,\overline{180}\,\overline{113}\,\overline{215}\,\overline{105}\,\overline{44}\,\overline{65}\,\overline{142}\,\overline{197}$ Hardy girl given washing by woman graduate.

V $\overline{198}\,\overline{24}\,\overline{96}\,\overline{120}$ City where certain lawyers are just acting on basic urge to get bedded.

W $\overline{167}\,\overline{49}\,\overline{208}\,\overline{174}\,\overline{125}\,\overline{91}$ A fellow going home at night starts at appearance of enormous hound.

X $\overline{50}\,\overline{66}\,\overline{175}\,\overline{137}\,\overline{178}\,\overline{17}\,\overline{81}\,\overline{218}\,\overline{118}\,\overline{233}\,\overline{12}\,\overline{130}\,\overline{36}\,\overline{126}$ Object of parade if just one face in it I don't get wrong?

Y $\overline{32}\,\overline{40}\,\overline{140}\,\overline{78}\,\overline{97}\,\overline{181}\,\overline{213}\,\overline{69}\,\overline{236}\,\overline{83}\,\overline{190}$ Will of literary genius not to be disputed.

Z $\overline{11}\,\overline{48}\,\overline{188}\,\overline{5}\,\overline{23}\,\overline{227}$ $\overline{152}\,\overline{161}\,\overline{229}$ $\overline{219}\,\overline{82}\,\overline{195}\,\overline{115}\,\overline{207}\,\overline{129}\,\overline{146}\,\overline{76}\,\overline{37}$ 'I did it,' said the king.

THE IMAGE OF INNOCENCE

★

MADELAINE DUKE

SOMETHING HAD CHANGED. I put down the hoe I had been using on the hard soil and climbed the steps to the top of the garden. Something wrong? It looked normal enough; the slope of golden gorse blending into the spread of pastures and vineyards and beyond, in the far distance, the jagged red mountains of the Sierra. The sky a brilliant, un-English blue and immensely wide. The only living creatures in sight, village cows sheltering from the heat under the hand-shaped leaves of a fig tree.

No, the cows were not the only animal life after all. Foreigners were emerging from the gorse. They had to be strangers. None of Redondo's Spaniards would be wearing white trousers and purple shirts, the man and the woman in matching clothes. Something wrong? About them or me? No reason why the sight of them should make me feel uneasy. The couple had cleared the gorse and stopped on the lowest terrace of my garden. They seemed to have realised that they were on private property. That did not deter the woman. She climbed on, the man trailing behind her.

I retreated into the shade of the cloisters and was about to go into the house when the couple caught me up.

'Excuse me.' The woman had a foreign accent. 'Do you speak English?'

I was tempted to answer in Spanish but I said, 'Yes.'

'What are you doing here? You're not Spanish, are you?'

'Chantal! Don't question people.' The man *was* English. 'I apologise for my wife. She's sometimes too direct. Chantal and Peter Black... We're intruding, I'm afraid.'

'Not at all.' So my social reflexes were still working. I felt like laughing. 'Sit down.'

'Thank you.'

'Would you like a drink?'

'Oh yes.' Chantal took the stone seat facing the mountains. 'We looked for coffee in the village but we couldn't find anyplace. I'd like water.'

Looking at them through the kitchen window they seemed pleasant enough: Peter tall, lean and dark-haired, Chantal fair and pink. A handsome pair in their late thirties, neat in their resort clothes and universal running shoes, dressed fashionably but not aggressively so.

I took out jugs of water, local wine and a dish of olives. Peter looked at his watch before opting for the wine. Chantal kept her eyes on my face, ingenuous baby-blue eyes. 'I have seen you before.'

'I don't think so. Try the olives.'

'I'm sure I have,' she persisted. 'I didn't catch your name.'

'I didn't mention it. It's Anna.'

'Some time ago I saw a film about...'

'This view,' Peter broke in, 'it's magnificent. And the building... must be ancient.'

'It is.'

'We've decided,' said Chantal, 'haven't we Peter? We're going to buy your place.'

Now I knew what was wrong. I had worked hard to bring about such an event, yet the appearance of the strangers made me feel threatened.

IT WAS NOT MY HOUSE that was for sale, I told them, but its adjoining twin. Never mind, said Chantal, she knew she wanted the place as soon as she saw the board from the foot of the hill. She always got *these feelings* about places, and people too. She thought there was something about me... something special. She thought I was beautiful.

I laughed at her. Beautiful? An old woman like me?

Peter asked for the history of Redondo. He had an impression that it was an historic village built on the site of an even older town with a fort.

I found myself telling the story in Father Manuel's words as the priest had told it to Andrew and me on the day we had discovered Redondo.

Many centuries ago, when the Moors from Arabia had been the masters of Spain, the great Emir Ab-del-Aziz had built a citadel on the summit of Redondo, a fortified palace constructed with the local stone and marble. Because the Emir had ruled his Christian subjects with understanding and tolerance many of his builder-craftsmen, gardeners and farmers had settled on Redondo. In the shelter of the higher mountains they had created terraces of olives and almonds, a flourishing community which withstood the sporadic sieges by the Christian forces fighting Islamic rule. But in the final battles, when the native Spaniards were regaining control of their country in the thirteenth century, the citadel of Redondo had been destroyed. All that was left of it was the towering building, my house and the twin which was for sale.

In the sixteenth century monks had restored that Moorish legacy, turned it into a monastery and built a church from the surrounding ruins. It was a fine church that served a large self-sufficient population, the kin of the people who had come to Redondo with benevolent Emir Ab-del-Aziz.

And then *they* had come, in 1936, shortly after Father Manuel had returned to his native village as an ordained priest. *They* had told people that Spain was at war. With whom? With itself. Brother killing brother. It was madness, surely. If that was politics then politics was madness. If *they* were fighting for freedom how did destroying the church serve freedom? And when the people of Redondo tried to save church and monks *they* had mown them down with their guns. Whole families had been wiped out.

Among the few who survived was a group of children whom Father Manuel had taken to the mountains to see a nest of golden eagles. In time they formed the new community of Redondo, a people who shared the memories of the Civil War and the skills the practical and learned priest had taught them.

There had been one more loss by violence when a young Redondo couple had visited Barcelona and died in a terrorist car-bomb attack. Their only child, Gabriel, had been brought up by Father Manuel like his parents before him.

'He must have been a remarkable man,' said Peter.

'He still is,' I told him. 'If you decide to buy Monks' House, he is the man you'll be dealing with.'

FATHER MANUEL still cooks the chickpea soup because no one else can make it to his satisfaction. As he told Andrew and me that first time he invited us to share supper with him and Gabriel, the *garbanzos* should be cooked on charcoal. Too much trouble for people nowadays. Well, God knows, Father Manuel has every right to one or two eccentric ideas.

Walking down the hill I see the evidence of his planning and his labours all around me; the irrigation system channelling the water from the mountains, the deep litter for chickens, the generator and the road. The road is far from perfect. In places it still crumbles in the winter rains, but not so badly that it isolates Redondo from the coast. It can't be too bad now or Peter and Chantal couldn't have climbed up in their small hired car.

It had been a dirt track made by the donkeys when Andrew and I had found Redondo twenty years ago. In the five hours it had taken us to go up from the coast I'd have given up several times if Andrew had been less determined to make it to the pimple of a village on the mountain. Determined he was on discovering the real Spain, unsullied by surfaced roads, hotels, restaurants, English-speaking waiters or any other amenity that might attract tourists like us.

He'd persuaded me that we were searching for the true home of Yerma, the primeval woman of Lorca's play which he was to produce in London and in which I had been given my first great chance—the title role. Just theatre. A play audiences would see and, perhaps, ponder for a while. But how vital for Andrew and me. To us the unlocking of life itself as we touched the ancient stones of the Moorish citadel. Marble! Hundreds of thousands of years old. And what light! Andrew had remembered a poet's words, *an ancient and inno-*

cent light, sharp and clear on pastures and mountains. It mus
have been such on the day the world came alive. How to pro
duce the merest illusion of all this on stage?

All this. The child Gabriel, a man now, taking us to Fathe
Manuel's cottage. The sturdy priest allowing us to stay in th
citadel because we were the first foreigners to arrive since th
Civil War and because we were willing to make it habitable
And the chickpea soup when we were hungry and tired an
everything was good because we were monumentally in love.

What now? I am the only foreigner who lives here and Re
dondo is the only place where my past, present and future ar
one, where there are no divisions of time, just the elementa
changing of the seasons. Suddenly my hard-won continuum o
time is under threat. At an arranged hour Peter and Chanta
will return to see Father Manuel. I will have to act as inter
preter for him, at the bank and the lawyer's halfway down t
the coast. And when they have bought Monks' House as thei
holiday home they will come and go in their time, not mine.

I will have to change. What? my thinking? my inner resis
tance to the unknown? Yes, the resistance must be overcom
for Father Manuel's sake. The church he has been buildin
with stones resurrected from the ruins of a vicious war, th
church built with his own hands over more than fifty year
must be completed. Now that Father Manuel is too old an
frail for hard labour he will have to pay for the final work an
therefore he needs the strangers' money.

A HUNDRED PEOPLE or more have wandered up from the vil
lage this Sunday morning. When something concerns all o
Redondo the cloisters of my house are the natural meetin
place. Father Manuel and another old man have come on thei
donkeys, animals and people keeping cool under the arches.

Last night's April rain has washed the young leaves of vine
and fig trees and left a halo of haze above the red mountains
The cows are gorging on the moist grass, and egrets, th
graceful white birds riding on their backs, are finding minut
edible parasites. All share the contentment of the sun-drenche
day, a very special day if the completion of the church is in
deed in sight.

The Vaquero, owner of the cattle and a powerful voice, asks the first question. Would Father Manuel tell his people about the foreigners who have offered to buy Monks' House?

They are a young couple, says Father Manuel, in their thirties. They are English, though the wife was an Austrian before her marriage. How many children? None. There is a murmur of regret. Are they going to live in Redondo? No, but they are hoping to stay two or three times a year.

Carmen says that I have put a lot of work into the house, replaced broken tiles, varnished doors and windows and waterproofed the terrace. Can one be sure that the new people will keep the place in good repair? One cannot be sure, Father Manuel tells her, but Peter and Chantal seem orderly people. They are aware that Monks' House is unique. He believes Chantal will take pride in it and see to the maintenance such an ancient place requires.

The Vaquero asks what is happening about the parapet. There never has been a conventional wall on the edge of the roof-terraces. Instead the sixteenth-century monks had installed low wrought-iron screens which allowed an almost uninterrupted view of the valley and the mountains beyond. Over the years rust had eaten into the intricate pattern of the screens and Gabriel had taken them to his workshop for repair. He and I had worked on them on and off for the past five years. Gabriel tells the people that the *parapets* are finished and would be cemented in before the new owners take over.

Carmen raises the question of putting furniture into Monks' House; just the basics, a table and chairs and a bed. That is the custom when houses are sold on the coast.

We are not on the coast, says Gabriel.

In the end it was Gabriel who found the basic furniture and put it in without saying anything. Typical of him. Andrew had called him *El Callado*, the silent one. Silent he still is, except when something important has to be discussed. And the *rascacielos*, the tower on the terrace of Monks' House, does concern him.

The unknown sixteenth-century monk who had recorded the history of Redondo in wall paintings inside the Moorish towers of my house and the one next door was no Michelangelo but he had created vivid scenes of the Emir and his court, the craftsmen, the farmers and the clergy of his own time.

Gabriel has looked at the paintings as if he were seeing them for the last time. 'Anna, do the foreigners understand that the walls must be kept dry?'

'I explained about the roof, though there's been no leak for years.'

'It seems good at the moment but one can't tell what the winter storms might do.'

'We'll be able to take care of that. Peter said he'll leave me a set of keys.'

Gabriel takes my hand and studies it. He sees the broken thumbnail, the knuckle bruised when I painted the wrought-iron screens on the terrace. An old woman's hand. He touches it with his lips. 'You should be more careful.' So I know that he will come into my bed tonight.

That first time he just materialised like a sensuous dream. Later I'd laughed and said, 'And not a word spoken.' Since then he asks, *'Permiso?* Permission. I answer *si*, yes to living on borrowed youth.

'WHO'S THE YOUNG MAN watering your garden?' Chantal wants to know. 'I saw him . . .'

'I hope you don't mind,' Peter interrupts, 'she wants to take some indoor pictures to give her ideas.'

Chantal, camera in hand, is surveying my living-room. 'Anna, where can I buy curtains like these?'

'They're old. I brought them from England.'

'I want the same yellow. And your chairs . . . sort of X-shaped. I haven't seen this kind before. Where can one get them?'

'Could be difficult. They're Spanish. I found the frames in a junk shop in Barcelona. Father Manuel said they're antique.'

Chantal touches the nearest chair. 'The seats and backs . . . cowhide, isn't it?'

'Yes.'

'Is there anyone who could make copies?'

'I don't know. I did the leather work myself.'

'You?'

'I like doing things with my hands.'

Continuing the tour of my house Chantal spends two rolls
f film on the kitchen, bath and bedrooms and takes close-ups
f curtains, wall lights, bookshelves and wood carvings. She
eeps telling me that she wants her house to look like mine.
Vell, why not if it makes her happy.

In the tower room she asks why it is unfurnished. I explain
hat I don't want to obstruct the view of the wall paintings.

'Yes,' she agrees without conviction, 'but it would make
uch a pretty guest room. Don't you think so, Peter?'

'No way. You must think of somewhere else for guests. Just
:ave this room to the paintings.'

'I'm not sure that I like them.' She wanders to the window.
What's this building? The one halfway down the hill.'

'A workshop, for repairs, ironwork, all sorts of things.'

'It looks like a ruin.'

'That's what it was until it was roofed over.'

'They should pull it down.'

'Chantal,' Peter shakes his head. 'Mind your own busi-
ess.'

Chantal ignores him. 'It's where I first saw the man . . . the
ne who's been watering Anna's garden.'

I may as well satisfy her curiosity. 'The man is Gabriel.'
erhaps she has seen him go in and out of my house. Perhaps
he has noticed him because he is handsome. So was Andrew.
once told Andrew that he was beautiful. He didn't like it. At
est a man can be handsome, never beautiful, he'd insisted.
Iandsome? Something to do with one's desire to touch? 'The
orkshop,' I tell Chantal, 'belongs to Gabriel. Even if it does
ok like a broken tooth he's unlikely to pull it down.'

Those wide-open blue eyes of hers fix on my face. Am I
ughing at her? She's not sure. 'Anna, I know who you are.'

'Then you know more than I do.' Now I *am* laughing.

'You're Anne Tremaine. Peter, don't you remember?' she
ppeals to him. 'The film star, Anne Tremaine. The classic
lovie we saw on TV. She played the Spanish woman who kills
er husband.'

I STILL DON'T KNOW WHY Andrew chose me for the role o
Yerma, but the result proved him right. A triumph, no less, th
critics declared. More satisfying, the London audiences ke
filling the theatre until the final performance. Afterwards th
play went on tour abroad and beyond those engagements,
most two years ahead, a Hollywood company had given me
contract for a film of the play.

By then Redondo was in my blood. Though our visits ha
become shorter and infrequent Redondo was our homecon
ing. Redondo meant the big, almost empty house under th
wide sky, eating chickpea soup in Father Manuel's cottag
watching the shifting shadows of clouds on the red mountair
and seeing the child Gabriel change into a young male.

In April the gorse flared into golden yellow. In May camo
mile and thistles turned the meadows flamboyantly purple an
white and about the same time the bougainvillaea began t
climb the Moorish walls. Mornings and evenings tiny linnet
hidden in the claret-red sprays, sang for exactly half an hou
Other birds, crickets and frogs gave voice at unpredictabl
times but they too played their parts in the symphony o
sounds and colours that captivated our senses.

Fecundity, said Andrew, the key to it all is fecundity. Th
night, on the hard bed, he told me that he wanted us to have
child; no, a whole family of children. I pretended to be aslee
Oh, I understood. I too felt the enchantment of all that wa
around us, the inexorable resurrection of life surging out o
death.

Lying still beside Andrew, hour after sleepless hour,
thought of the play which had turned me from a little-know
actress into a star. I had not grasped entirely why Yerma kil
her impotent husband. Suddenly it became clear. Like Yerm
Andrew had come to feel the overwhelming need for a chil
for the palpable miracle of renewal. I sensed then that h
would not let anything stand in his way. Or anyone. He wa
twenty-five and I forty. He would find himself a woman in th
prime of her childbearing age.

THE PAIN OF LOSING HIM did not go away. It made me cry o
on stage. It made me search for him in the shadows of fil

sets. It drove me through foreign streets when I thought I was seeing him in the distance. In the end I returned to Redondo.

If it was nostalgia that made me go back it soon changed. My awareness of Andrew was as strong as ever but the pain receded, absorbed into the greater needs of Redondo. It was Father Manuel's idea that I should buy the Monks' House. The money was wanted for repairs to the water and electricity systems and for the road. Perhaps there would even be a little left over for the completion of the church. And there was a lot of work to be done on the two Moorish houses, especially on the badly rusted parapet screens.

'You have good hands,' Father Manuel told me, 'come and work with us.'

Faced again with the wall paintings in the towers, the images of Redondo's people in war and peace, looking at the fertile land they had created, I recognized that this was my place, the place I loved above all others. Here, as nowhere else, I felt the fusion of past and present. And Father Manuel's laborious rebuilding of the ancient church seemed yet another affirmation of continuing life.

'What can I do?' I asked him.

'You have the hands of a craftsman. We will teach you. And we'll have the money you'll pay for the house. Money,' he laughed, 'faith alone isn't enough. That's what they forgot to teach us in seminary.'

Gabriel gave me a glass of wine. 'Anna, Andrew is coming back?'

'No.'

'There's room for you in my workshop.'

FATHER MANUEL'S EYES are warm with excitement. He has come into the workshop with news. They have finished the building and he has just heard that the foundry is sending the bells this week. Everything is on time for the Bishop to consecrate the church for the harvest festival.

Gabriel has fetched a chair for the old man but he is too restless to sit down. He is running his hands over the tall figure of the Madonna which I have been carving for the past couple of years. 'No problems with the wood Anna? No splits?'

'None. This time the wood was well and truly seasoned.'

'She's beautiful, our Lady of Redondo.' He touches the face, a round, almost childlike one modelled in a picture salvaged from the original sixteenth-century church. 'Isn't it strange? The first time I saw our foreign couple the young woman looked familiar. Now I know why. She has the same features as our Lady of Redondo.'

Gabriel smiled. 'You're not wearing your spectacles, Father. The *virgen* Anna has carved is a woman who thinks.'

'That's beside the point. There is this . . . innocence. Chantal is the image of innocence.'

'Our Saint Manuel,' murmurs Gabriel.

As PETER SAID, Chantal is *into birds*. Two years ago she arrived with a pair of powerful fieldglasses and took to standing on the terrace watching egrets and linnets, finches and owls. Peter didn't think her new hobby would last. But she has persisted.

On their eighth visit she has made Peter assemble a do-it-yourself kit of a bird-table, something like an Austrian farm house complete with plastic flowers in the window-boxes. I can't fail to see it over the low wall between our terraces. Together with her tall potted plants it blocks out my view of the church and much of the village.

Peter has come into my kitchen and accepted a glass of wine. 'I tried to talk her out of it. I mean, that bird-table is an eye sore. What do you think of it, Anna?'

'It's your house.'

'My house? She didn't allow me to buy it. Now she reminds me that she paid for it with her money from Austria . . . The birds will make an awful mess on the terrace.'

I had not yet thought of that. Of course, a concentration of bird-shit will damage the marble floor unless she keeps washing it off, and that's unlikely.

Well, there's one answer. Just as Chantal keeps buying plants and asking me to look after them while she is in England—always a few minutes before her departure—she'll ask me to replenish the food in her birds' Ritz. I won't do it. It's not the birds that need the contraption.

'Don't worry,' I tell Peter. 'Chantal will probably get tired of her new toy.'

'Like a child? Some of our friends think she's a sweet innocent . . . a child. I wouldn't know. I haven't been allowed a family because Chantal doesn't like children. She thinks they're vicious and destructive.'

He is not normally a man who confides. Now his face has gone tense with embarrassment. How to help him over it. 'This isn't England, Peter.'

'True.' He has understood me. Abroad things can be said which an Englishman of his background wouldn't put into words at home. 'You've been kind to us. I don't know what Chantal and I would have done if you hadn't found us people to build in kitchen and bathrooms, supervised all the work, got us the telephone . . . and just about everything else.'

'It would have been difficult to do it from London.'

'Impossible without a knowledge of Spanish. But I've been learning. It's a beautiful language. I've tried to get Chantal to join the course. No luck. She says she can make herself understood if there's something she wants.'

CHANTAL HAS CIRCLED the figure of the Madonna on my workbench.

'Have you finished her?'

'Not quite. She has to be painted.'

'What'll be the colour of her gown?'

'Blue.'

'And the face?'

'As lifelike as I can make it.'

She stands back, head tilted to one side. 'I think she's gorgeous. But I'd prefer her gown in yellow. She'd look fantastic in my hall. How much do you want for her?'

'She's not for sale, Chantal.'

'Why not? You've got other figures in your house.'

'They're just different woods I tried out.'

'I like them too, but this is the one I want.'

'Sorry, this one is for the church.'

'Are you a Catholic, Anna?'

'No.'

'Then why? You know, I've seen a film about Easter i
Spain. People taking these saint figures out of the churches
walking them all over town. They're carried on platform
decorated with flowers and candles. It's really weird...as weir
as the wall paintings in my tower room. I don't know wha
you...oh, and Peter...see in them.'

'Has Peter not told you?'

'Sure. He says they're Spanish history. He says the picture
celebrate life going on despite wars and revolutions.'

'That's right. Chantal, why didn't you buy your holida
home in one of the new urbanisations on the coast?'

'Where all the tourists go? I'd hate it. These modern devel
opments could be anywhere in the world.'

'Then you did want a truly Spanish place?'

'Well, my house is a sort of castle. I wanted a castle in Spair
Nobody we know has anything like it, not even the chairma
of Peter's company.'

'Is that the main reason why you wanted Monks' House?'

'Well,' Chantal takes her time. 'I think it was you too.
mean, you're famous.'

'Not now.'

'Oh, but people remember you. Peter's chairman doe:
We've invited him here... There's something about you.
mean, you're over sixty but you're still beautiful and sexy..
You know, I hate the idea of having to do without sex. I'll b
forty next month. And yet, you...'

That's unexpected. Chantal not only wanted her house an
furnishings to be like mine but she wants to *be* whatever I an
It hadn't occurred to me that I came into her calculations.

GABRIEL, sitting on my bed, is gazing into the moonlight. Th
crickets are in full voice. A sleepless lizard is darting about m
ceiling.

'Alfonso came to see me,' says Gabriel. 'Chantal's aske
him to do some painting for her.'

'Peter interpreting?'

'No. It's odd; she was on her own, with a dictionary. Alfonso suspects she wants him to get rid of the wall paintings. Of course he doesn't want the job. But he didn't refuse, to give us time to do something about it. Doesn't the woman know how our people feel about the paintings?'

'Perhaps not. She mentioned making a guest room up there, but that's a long time ago. Peter was against it.'

'Anna, speak to him. He must stop her.'

'How?'

'So that's how it is. She listens to you, doesn't she?'

'This time she didn't even mention what she has in mind.'

'Then she does at least know that you wouldn't approve. Anna, please understand... my people have had violence enough.'

The word violence hangs between us in a silence neither of us can break.

CHANTAL IS STANDING on her terrace, fieldglasses to her eyes. I don't want to step over the dividing wall. I never do except when she is away and I water her plants. I have to call her twice before she turns.

'Hello Anna. There's a little owl on the workshop roof.'

'Yes, the owls have always been there.'

She holds out her glasses. 'Want a look?'

'No, I can see... Chantal, are you planning to paint over the murals in your tower?'

'How do you know?'

'Alfonso won't do it.'

'I see. So I'll have to find somebody else.'

'Nobody in Redondo will do it. The paintings are... In England they'd be regarded as *ancient monuments* protected by law.'

'This isn't England.'

'No, it's a small place and therefore everyone has a personal share in its past. The murals matter to all the people here. They matter very much.'

'To peasants like them? Anyway they never see the paintings.'

'Unimportant. They know the murals are there.'

'They won't be much longer.' Chantal has flushed. 'This is
my house. I'll make of it what I want. Tell that to your young
lover-boy. And if his friend won't paint over the *ancient mon-
ument*, I will.'

I COULD CRY ON STAGE, never in real life. And this is real life—
the shock of brutality, a loathing of vandalism, and the anger. It is the anger that calms me, that allows me to think
coldly of what has happened.

From the west window of my tower room I can see that
Chantal has returned to her bird-watching. As far as she is
concerned I had nothing more to say, therefore her opposi-
tion has collapsed. Too late today, but tomorrow she'll tell
Peter to do the job and if he refuses she'll get to work herself.

The clear night before sunset lifts details in the murals on my
walls that seem new. The monk who is digging among the vines
has tucked his cassock into a pair of patched trousers. The
verges of the path from the mountains are sprinkled with
flowers of every season, periwinkle and kings' candles, cam-
omile, poppies and meadowsweet. The blacksmith at his anvil
is gazing at the distant figure of a girl. His face reminds me of
Gabriel's.

One day Gabriel and a girl will find one another. It's something I expect and accept. I have been grateful from the beginning for having been allowed to live on borrowed youth. I
am grateful, and always will be, to Gabriel for turning me from
a mere interpreter of a dramatist's creation into a creator in
wood and stone. Many saint-figures of Spain have survived
hundreds of years. I believe that my Lady of Redondo will be
one of them, as much a heritage as the wall paintings are.

Chantal is still standing on the terrace, glasses at her eyes.
She is standing against the wrought-iron parapet, the upper
two-thirds of her body unsupported, below her the sharp
edged stone steps of the garden. A fall from this height would
kill her.

IT WAS A WAKEFUL NIGHT. Not surprising. Trying to be truthful about one's self is a brutal process. What was it that made
me want to kill Chantal? How comfortable for me if I could

have persuaded myself that I felt an overpowering desire to protect the people of Redondo from committing revenge or even from the sadness of losing something irreplaceable.

In the saffron light of early morning I was no nearer to understanding the violence of my feelings. Was I being hypocritical in trying to justify murder for the sake of the people I loved? Was I trying to deny that I hated Chantal? Had I forged Redondo into a spurious romantic ideal? I had killed on stage. I could do it as Yerma. Was that going to make it easier?

There was no time for me to indulge in the luxury of justifying the murder I meant to commit. Chantal was a creature of habit. Predictably, she would take her morning coffee on the terrace. There she would hear the larks and get up to watch them. And after that? I had no doubt that she meant to go ahead with her plan of destroying the murals.

When I got to my terrace she was already standing at her parapet, fieldglasses trained on the valley below. I made myself think of the mechanics of my action, nothing else. I'd kick off my sandals, step over the wall that divided our terraces and go up behind her. I worked out where I'd place my hands, the exact area on her back. A sudden hard push. While she was holding the glasses she wouldn't be able to save herself.

From the moment I moved forward on bare feet I felt as empty of thought as a robot programmed to do a simple chore.

I WAS ABOUT TO STEP across the wall when I saw Peter emerge from his tower. He made straight for Chantal, grasped her legs and heaved. Even if I had been nearer, even if I had been capable of making a move, I could not have stopped him. It happened so fast.

Chantal seemed to fly over the parapet. And then there was a single sound, like a full earthenware pot smashing on stone. She was lying on the steps below, her skull split down the middle as if it had been struck by a cleaver. The brain in its open shell looked like a carnivorous tropical flower.

Gabriel and I would have to find a way of restoring Father Manuel's *image of innocence*. Somehow we'd have to make Chantal look like a sleeper at peace.

CLEWSEY'S CLICHÉS

WHILE SHE WAITED FOR NICK TO COME ROUND, NORA REVIEWED THE FACTS OF THE CASE AS SHE UNDERSTOOD THEM.

FIRST LEAD GASSER

★

TONY HILLERMAN

AUTHOR'S NOTE:

As a short story, 'First Lead Gasser' is important to me. The incident it concerns happened (with 'only the names changed to protect the innocent') and it caused me to think seriously for the first time about writing fiction. The Thompson of the story was the late John Curtis of the Associated Press. I was Hardin, then New Mexico manager of the now defunct United Press. Toby Small, under another name but guilty of the same crime, did in fact inhale cyanide fumes at midnight in the basement gas chamber of the New Mexico State Prison. Thus 'First Lead Gasser' is more or less autobiographical.

What makes it important to me, and perhaps of interest to mystery readers, are two facts. First, my inability to deal with the 'truth' of the Toby Small tragedy in the 300 words allowed me by journalism stuck in my mind. How could I report the meaning of that execution with only objective facts? I played with it, and a sort of non-fiction short story evolved.

Second, Toby Small's hands on the bars, Toby Small's shy smile through the gas chamber window, and the story Toby Small told Curtis and me became part of those memories that a reporter can't shake.

Those who read my novel, People of Darkness, met Toby Small under the name of Colton Wolf, reincarnated as he might have evolved if fate had allowed him to live a few murders longer. The plot required a professional hit man. Since it seems incredible to me that anyone would kill for hire, I was finding it hard to conceive the character until the old memory of Small's yearning for his mother came to my rescue. The novel gave me more space to communicate the tragedy of Small. But I'm still not skilled enough to do full justice to that sad afternoon spent listening to a damaged man wondering what awaited him when he came out of the gas chamber.

JOHN HARDIN walked into the bureau, glanced at the wall clock (which told him it was 12.22 a.m.), laid his overcoat on a chair, flicked the switch on the teletype to 'ON', tapped on the button marked 'BELL' and then punched on the keys with a stiff forefinger:

    ALBUQUERQUE
        YOU TURNED ON?
           SANTA FE

He leant heavily on the casing of the machine, waiting, feeling the coolness under his palms, noticing the glass panel was dusty and hearing the words again in the high, soft voice of Toby Small. Then the teletype bumped tentatively and said:

    SANTA FE
        AYE AYE GO WITH IT
           ALBUQUERQUE

And John Hardin punched:

    ALBUQUERQUE
     WILL FILE LEAD SUBBING OUT GASSER STORY IN MINUTE.
    PLEASE SEND SCHEDULE FOR 300 WORDS TO DENVER
     SANTA FE

The teletype was silent as Hardin removed the cover from the typewriter and dropped it to the floor. Then the teletype carriage bumped twice and said:

SANTE FE
   NO RUSH DENVER UNTHINKS GASSER WORTH FILING ON
NATIONAL WIRE DIXIE TORNADOES JAMMING WIRE AND
HAVE DANDY HOTEL FIRE AT CHICAGO FOLKS OUTJUMPING
WINDOWS ETC HOWEVER STATE OVERNIGHT FILE LUKS LIKE
HOTBED OF TRANQUILLITY CAN USE LOTS OF GORY DETAILS
THERE.
   ALBUQUERQUE

Their footsteps had echoed down the long concrete tube,
passed the dark barred mouths of cell blocks. Thompson had
said is it always this goddam quiet, and the warden said the
cons are always quiet on one of these nights.

Hardin sighed, said something under his breath and
punched:

ALBUQUERQUE
   REMIND DENVER NITESIDE THAT DENVER DAYSIDE HAS
REQUEST FOR 300 WORDS TO BE FILED FOR OHIO PM POINTS.
   SANTA FE

He turned his back on the machine, put a carbon book in the
typewriter, hit the carriage return twice and stared at the clock
which now reported the time to be 12.26. While he stared, the
second-hand made the laborious climb towards 12. Something clicked and the clock said it was 12.27.

Hardin started typing, rapidly:

FIRST LEAD GASSER
   SANTA FE, N.M., MARCH 28—(UPI)—GEORGE TOBIAS
SMALL, 38, THE SLAYER OF A YOUNG OHIO COUPLE WHO
SOUGHT TO BEFRIEND HIM, DIED A MINUTE AFTER
MIDNIGHT TODAY IN THE GAS CHAMBER AT THE NEW
MEXICO STATE PENITENTIARY.

He examined the paragraph, pulled the paper from the typewriter and dropped it. It slid from the top of the desk and

planed to the floor, spilling its carbon insert. On a fresh carbon book Hardin typed:

FIRST LEAD GASSER

SANTA FE, N.M. MARCH 28—(UPI)—GEORGE TOBIAS SMALL, 38, WHO CLUBBED TO DEATH TWO YOUNG OHIO NEWLYWEDS LAST JULY 4, PAID FOR HIS CRIME WITH HIS LIFE EARLY TODAY IN THE NEW MEXICO STATE PRISON GAS CHAMBER.

THE HULKING KILLER SMILED NERVOUSLY AT EXECUTION WITNESSES AS THREE GUARDS PUSHED THREE UNMARKED BUTTONS, ONE OF WHICH DROPPED CYANIDE PILLS INTO A CONTAINER OF ACID UNDER THE CHAIR IN WHICH HE WAS STRAPPED.

Hulking? Maybe tall, stooped killer, maybe gangling. Not really nervously. Better timidly, smiled timidly. But actually it was an embarrassed smile. Shy. Stepping from the elevator into that too-bright basement room, Small had blinked against the glare and squinted at them lined by the railing—the press corps and the official creeps in the role of 'official witnesses'. He looked surprised and then embarrassed and looked away, then down at his feet, and the warden had one hand on his arm. The two of them walking fast towards the front of the chamber, hurrying, while a guard held the steel door open.

(And above their heads cell block eight was utterly silent.) Hardin hit the carriage return and typed again, rapidly.

THE END CAME QUICKLY FOR SMALL. HE APPEARED TO HOLD HIS BREATH FOR A MOMENT AND THEN BREATHED DEEPLY OF THE DEADLY FUMES. HIS HEAD FELL FORWARD AND HIS BODY SLUMPED IN DEATH.

The witness gallery had been hot. Stuffy. Smelling of cleaning fluid. But under his hand the steel railing behind which the reporters stood was cold. 'Wonder why they paint that gas chamber white,' Thompson said. 'It looks like a big incinerator. Or like one of those old wood stoves with the chimney out the top.' And the man from the *Albuquerque Journal* said the cons call it the space capsule.

'I wonder why they put windows in it,' Thompson said. 'There's not much to see.' And the man from the *Journal* said, with a sort of laugh, that it was the world's longest view. Then it was quiet. Father McKibbon had looked at them a long time when they came in, unsmiling, studying them. Then he had stood stiffly by the open hatch, looking at the floor.

Hardin took a deep breath and typed again:

SMALL, WHO SAID HE HAD COME TO NEW MEXICO FROM COLORADO IN SEARCH OF WORK, WAS SENTENCED TO DEATH LAST NOVEMBER AFTER A DISTRICT COURT JURY AT RATON FOUND HIM GUILTY OF MURDER IN THE DEATHS OF MR AND MRS ROBERT M MARTIN OF CLEVELAND. THE COUPLE HAD BEEN MARRIED ONLY TWO DAYS EARLIER AND WAS EN ROUTE TO CALIFORNIA ON A HONEYMOON TRIP.

You could see Father McKibbon saying something to Small—talking rapidly—and Small had nodded and then nodded again and then the warden said something and Small looked up and licked his lips. Then he stepped through the hatch. He tripped on the sill but McKibbon caught his arm and helped him sit in the little chair and Small had looked up at the priest. And smiled. How would you describe it? Smiled shyly, maybe, or gratefully. Or maybe sickly. Then the guard was reaching in, doing something out of sight. Buckling the straps, probably, buckling cold, stiff leather around a warm ankle and a warm forearm which had MOTHER tattooed on it, inside a heart.

SMALL HAS SERVED TWO PREVIOUS PRISON TERMS. HE HAD COMPILED A POLICE RECORD BEGINNING WITH A UTAH CAR THEFT WHEN HE WAS 15. ARRESTING OFFICERS TESTIFIED THAT HE CONFESSED KILLING THE TWO WITH A JACK HANDLE AFTER MARTIN RESISTED SMALL'S ATTEMPT AT ROBBERY. THEY SAID SMALL ADMITTED FLAGGING DOWN THE COUPLE'S CAR AFTER RAISING THE HOOD ON HIS OLD-MODEL TRUCK TO GIVE THE IMPRESSION HE WAS HAVING TROUBLE.

Should it be flagging down or just flagging? The wall clock inhaled electricity above Hardin's head with a brief buzzing sigh and signalled 12.32. How long had Small been dead now? Thirty minutes, probably, if cyanide worked as fast as they said. And how long had it been since yesterday when Thompson and he had stood outside Small's cell in death row? It was late afternoon, then. You could see the sunlight far down the corridor, slanting in and striped by the bars. Small had said, 'How much time have I got left?' and Thompson looked at his watch and said, 'Four-fifteen from midnight leaves seven hours and forty-five minutes,' and Small's bony hands clenched and unclenched on the bars. Then he said, 'Seven hours and forty-four minutes now,' and Thompson said, 'Well, my watch might be off a little.'

Behind Hardin the teletype said ding, ding, ding dingding and began typing:

SANTA FE
    DENVER NOW SEZ WILL CALL IN 300 WORDER FOR OHIO PM
WIRE SHORTLY. HOW BOUT LEADING SAD SLAYER SAMMY
SMALL TODAY GRIMLY GULPED,GAS, OR SOME SUCH????
    ALBUQUERQUE

The teletype lapsed into expectant silence, its electric motor purring. Outside, a car drove by with a rush of sound.
    Hardin typed:

SMALL REFUTED THE CONFESSION AT HIS TRIAL. HE
CLAIMED THAT AFTER MARTIN STOPPED TO ASSIST HIM THE
TWO MEN ARGUED AND THAT MARTIN HAD STRUCK HIM. HE
SAID HE THEN 'BLACKED OUT' AND COULD REMEMBER
NOTHING MORE OF THE INCIDENT. SMALL WAS ARRESTED
WHEN TWO STATE POLICEMEN WHO HAPPENED BY STOPPED
TO INVESTIGATE THE PARKED VEHICLES.

'The warden told me you are the two that work for the out-fits that put things in the papers all over and I thought maybe you could put something in about finding...about maybe...something about needing to know where my mother

is. You know, so they can get the word to her.' Then Small had
walked back to his bunk, back into the darkness, and sat down
and then got up again and walked back to the barred door,
three steps.

'It's about getting buried,' he said. 'I need someplace for
that,' and Thompson said, 'What's her name, your mother I
mean?' and Small looked down at the floor. 'That's part of the
trouble,' Small said, talking so low you could hardly hear him.
'You see this man she was living with when we were there in
Salt Lake well she and him . . .'

ARRESTING OFFICERS AND OTHER WITNESSES TESTIFIED
THERE WAS NOTHING MECHANICALLY WRONG WITH
SMALL'S TRUCK, THAT THERE WAS NO MARK ON SMALL TO
INDICATE HE HAD BEEN STRUCK BY MARTIN, AND THAT
MARTIN HAD BEEN SLAIN BY REPEATED BLOWS ON THE
BACK OF HIS HEAD.

Small was standing by the bars now, gripping them so that the
stub showed where the end of his ring finger had been cut off
a long time ago. Flexing his hands, talking fast. 'The warden,
well he told me they'd send me wherever I said after it's over.
They'd send me back home, he said. They'd pay for it. But I
won't know where to tell them unless somebody can find
Mama. There was a place we stayed for a long time before we
went to San Diego and I went to school there some but I don't
remember the name of it, and then we moved someplace up the
Coast where they grow figs and like that, and then I think it
was Oregon next and then I believe it was we moved on out to
Salt Lake.' Small stopped talking then, and let his hands rest
while he looked at them, at Thompson and him, and said, 'But
I bet Mama would remember where I'm supposed to go.'

MRS MARTIN'S BODY WAS FOUND IN A FIELD ABOUT 40
YARDS FROM THE HIGHWAY. OFFICERS SAID THE PRETTY
BRIDE HAD APPARENTLY ATTEMPTED TO FLEE, HAD
TRIPPED AND INJURED AN ANKLE, AND HAD THEN BEEN
BEATEN TO DEATH BY SMALL.

Subject: George Tobias Small, aka Toby Small, aka G. T. Small. White male, about 38 (birth date, place unknown), weight 188, height 6' 4"; eyes, brown; complexion, ruddy. Distinguishing characteristics: noticeable stoop, carries right shoulder higher than left; last two joints missing from left ring finger, deep scar on left upper lip, tattoo of heart with word MOTHER on inner right forearm.

Charge: Violation Section 12-2 (3) Criminal Code.

Disposition: Guilty of murder, Colfax County District Court.

Sentence: Execution in gas chamber.

Previous Record: 18 July 1941, sentenced Utah State Reformatory, car theft.

7 April, 1943, returned Utah State Reformatory, breaking and entering, parole violation.

14 February 1945, burglary, possession of stolen property, resisting arrest. Classified juvenile incorrigible.

3 August 1949, armed robbery, 5-7 years at

SMALL HAD BEEN IN TROUBLE WITH THE LAW SINCE BOYHOOD, STARTING HIS CAREER WITH A CAR THEFT AT 12, AND THEN VIOLATING REFORMATORY PAROLE WITH A BURGLARY. BEFORE HIS 21 BIRTHDAY HE WAS SERVING THE FIRST OF THREE PRISON TERMS.

Small had rested his hands on the brace between the bars but they wouldn't rest. The fingers twisted tirelessly among themselves. Blind snakes. Even the stub of the missing finger moving restlessly. 'Rock fell on it when I was little. Think it was that. The warden said he sent the word around about Mama but I guess nobody found her yet. Put it down that she might be living in Los Angeles. That man with us there in Salt Lake he wanted to go out to the Coast and maybe that's where they went.'

It was then Thompson stopped him. 'Wait a minute,' Thompson said. 'Where was she from, your mother? Why not...'

'I don't remember that,' Small said. He was looking down at the floor.

And Thompson asked, 'Didn't she tell you?' and Small said, still not looking at us, 'Sure, but I was little.'

'You don't remember the town, or anything? How little were you?' And Small sort of laughed and said, 'Just exactly twelve,' and laughed again, and said, 'That's why I thought maybe I could come home, it was my birthday. We was living in a trailer house then, and mama's man had been drinking. Her, too. When he did that, he'd whip me and run me off. So I'd been staying with a boy I knew there at school, in the garage, but his folks said I couldn't stay any more and it was my birthday so I thought I'd go by the trailer house and maybe it would be all right.'

Small had taken his hands off the bars then. He walked back to the bunk and sat down. And when he started talking again it was almost too low to hear it all.

'They was gone. The trailer was gone. The man at the rent office said they'd just took off in the night. Owed him rent, I guess,' Small said. He was quiet again.

Thompson said, 'Well,' and then he cleared his throat, said, 'Leave you a note or anything?'

And Small said, 'No, sir. No note.'

'That's when you stole the car, I guess,' Thompson said. 'The car theft you went to the reformatory for.'

'Yes sir,' Small said. 'I thought I'd go to California and find her. I thought she was going to Los Angeles but I never knowed no place to write. You could write all the letters you wanted to there at the reformatory but I never knowed the place to send it to.'

Thompson said, 'Oh,' and Small got up and came up to the bars and grabbed them.

'How much time have I got now?'

SMALL STEPPED THROUGH THE OVAL HATCH IN THE FRONT OF THE GAS CHAMBER AT TWO MINUTES BEFORE MIDNIGHT AND THE STEEL DOOR WAS SEALED BEHIND HIM TO PREVENT SEEPAGE OF THE DEADLY GAS. THE PRISON DOCTOR SAID THE FIRST WHIFF OF THE CYANIDE FUMES WOULD RENDER A HUMAN UNCONSCIOUS ALMOST INSTANTLY.

'WE BELIEVE MR SMALL'S DEATH WILL BE ALMOST PAINLESS,' HE SAID.

'The warden said they can keep my body a couple of days but then they'll just have to go ahead and bury me here at the pen unless somebody claims it. They don't have no place cold to keep it from spoiling on 'em. Anyway, I think a man oughta be put down around his kin if he has any. That's the way I feel about it.'

And Thompson started to say something and cleared his throat and said, 'How does it feel to...I mean, about tonight,' and Small's hands tightened on the bars. 'Oh I won't say I'm not scared. I never said that. They say it won't hurt but I been hurt before, cut and all, and I never been scared of that so much.' Small's words stopped coming and then they came loud and the guard reading at the door of the corridor looked around and then back at his book. 'It's the not knowing,' Small said, and his hands had disappeared from the bars and he walked back to the dark end of the cell and sat on the bunk and got up again and walked and said, 'Oh God, it's not knowing.'

SMALL COOPERATED WITH HIS EXECUTIONERS. WHILE THE EIGHT WITNESSES REQUIRED BY LAW WATCHED, THE SLAYER APPEARED TO BE HELPING A GUARD ATTACH THE STRAPS WHICH HELD HIS LEGS IN PLACE IN THE GAS CHAMBER. HE LEANED BACK WHILE HIS FOREARMS WERE BEING STRAPPED TO THE CHAIR.

The clock clicked and sighed and the minute hand pointed at the seven partly hidden behind a tear-shaped dribble of paint on the glass and the teletype, stirred by this, said ding, ding, ding.

SANTA FE
    DENVER WILL INCALL GASSER AFTER SPORTS ROUNDUP
NOW MOVING. YOU BOUT GOT SMALL WRAPPED UP?
    ALBUQUERQUE

Hardin pulled the carbon book from the typewriter and
marked out DOWN after the verb FLAGGING. He penciled a line
through GIVE THE IMPRESSION HE WAS and wrote in SIMULATE.
He clipped the copy to the holder above the teletype key
board, folding it to prevent obscuring the glass panel, and
switched the key from 'KEYBOARD' to 'TAPE' and began
punching. The thin yellow strip, lacy with perforations, looped
down towards the floor and built rapidly there into a loopy
pile.

HE HAD SEEN SMALL wiping the back of his hand across his
face. When he came back to the bars, he had looked away.
   'The padre's been talking to me about it every morning,'
Small had said. 'That's Father McKibbon. He told me a lot
never knew before, mostly about Jesus and I'd heard about
that, of course. It was back when I was in that place at Lo
gan, that chaplain there he talked about Jesus some and I re
membered some of it. But that one there at Logan he talked
mostly about sin and about hell and things like that and thi
McKibbon, the padre here, well, he talked different.' And
Small's hands had been busy on the bars again and then Smal
had looked directly at him, directly into his face, and then a
Thompson. He remembered the tense heavy face, sweaty, and
the words and the voice too soft and high for the size of the
man.
   'I wanted to ask you to do what you could about finding m
mama. I looked for her all the time. When they'd turn m
loose, I'd hunt for her. But maybe you could find her. With th
newspapers and all. And I want to hear what you think about
it all,' Small said. 'About what happens to me after they tak
me out of that gas chamber. I wanted to see what you say
about that.' And then Small said into the long silence: 'Well
whatever it's going to be it won't be any worse than it's been.'
And he had paused again, and looked back into the cell as i
he expected to see someone there, and then back at us.
   'But when I walk around in here and my foot hits the floo
I feel it, you know, and I think that's Toby Small I'm feeling
there with his foot on the cement, It's Me. And I guess tha
don't sound like much but after tonight I guess there won't b
that for one thing. And I hope there's somebody there wait
ing for me. I hope there's not just me.' And he sat down on th
bunk.

'I was wondering what you thought about this Jesus and what McKibbon has been telling me.' He had his head between his hands now, looking at the floor, and it made his voice muffled. 'You reckon he was lying about it. I don't see any cause for him to lie. Nothing to gain. But how can a man know all that and be sure about it.'

HARDIN PUSHED DOWN the 'TRANSMIT' key and the clatter of the transmission box joined the chatter of the perforator. He marked his place in the copy and leant over to fish a cigarette out of his overcoat. He lit it, took it out of his mouth, and turned back to the keyboard. Above him, above the duet chatter of tape and keyboard, he heard the clock strike again, and click, and when he looked up it was 12.33.

MCKIBBON HAD HIS HAND on Small's elbow, crushing the pressed prison jacket, talking to him, his face strained and fierce. Small had been listening, head cocked, intent. Then he nodded and nodded again and when he stepped through the hatch he bumped his head on the steel hard enough so you could hear it back at the railing. When Hardin could see his face through the round glass of the chamber it looked numb and pained.

McKibbon had stepped back and while the guard was working with the straps, he began reading from a book. Loud, wanting Small to hear. Maybe wanting all of them to hear.

'Have mercy on me, O Lord; for unto Thee have I cried all the day, for Thou, O Lord, art sweet and mild: and plenteous in mercy unto all that call upon thee. Incline thine ear, O Lord, and hear me: for I am needy and poor. Preserve my soul, for I am holy: O my God, save thy servant that trusteth in thee.'

THE PILE OF TAPE on the floor diminished and the final single loop climbed towards the stop bar and the machine was silent. Hardin looked through the dusty glass of the teletype, reading the last paragraph for errors.

There was Small's face, there through the round window, and his brown eyes unnaturally wide, looking at something or looking for something. He must have heard something, perhaps the cyanide capsule dropping into the container of acid under his seat. He looked out at them, directly at Hardin, and Hardin had seen he was pressing his lips tightly together. But just for a moment. Then his head dropped out of sight below the window, and there was the sound of the pump. The pump made a sucking noise, getting the gas out of the chamber and into the exhaust system and the warden came over and said, 'Well, I guess we can all go home now.'

Hardin switched the machine back from 'TAPE' to 'KEY BOARD' and punched:

> SMALL'S BODY WILL BE HELD UNTIL THURSDAY, THE WARDEN SAID, IN THE EVENT THE SLAYER'S MOTHER CAN BE LOCATED TO CLAIM IT. IF NOT IT WILL BE BURIED IN THE PRISON LOT.

He switched off the machine. And then in the room the only sound was the clock, which was buzzing again, and saying it was 12.34.

SISTER BRONA AND THE SACRED ALTAR CLOTHS

★

ALEX AUSWAKS

IT WAS BAD ENOUGH, Mother Superior used to say, to have tourists gaping and gawking at her sacred altar cloths. She wasn't having photographers and television cameras. It wasn't that her sacred altar cloths were the labour of generations of nuns. Mother Superior wasn't one to defend the labour of nuns even as a ritual acknowledgement of trendy populism. No, for Mother Superior prided herself that she was no politician to bend with every passing wind. She was there to uphold the faith. And the sisters who urged her to give way to cheap publicity methods had better remember that altar cloths were for the table on which the eucharist was celebrated. Had the sisters forgotten how Protestants had broken communion tables on the grounds of their association with the doctrine of the eucharistic sacrifice! It was because their own altar had been miraculously saved that the nuns had sworn to sew and embroider an altar cloth every year...which accounted for the famous collection. You could chart the rise and fall in the fortunes of the order from the quality of the altar cloth. But recently times had been hard. To sell the altar cloths on the antiques market was out of the question. Someone had suggested they should be displayed and admired...for a fee.

The very thought of men and boys in the place had driven Mother Superior to a frenzy. It was rumoured that one or two sisters had to work very hard (and be very cunning) to prevent

her discovering that Protestants came to admire altar cloths as
works of art.

Following the paying visitors had come the requests to pho
tograph the sacred altar cloths, first for the posh Sunday
newspapers, and then perhaps for a prestigious coffee-table
publication.

Now that sort of thing Mother Superior wasn't having.

She knew all about photographers and their immoral ways
They grew their hair long, smoked pot, wore jeans and slept
with their models. Heaven knows what effect this would have
on the younger novices who had come straight from convent
school! After all, most of the sacred altar cloths were not on
display in the long gallery, where a selection had been framed
for the public gaze. Most of them were well inside, where the
nuns ate, slept and washed. To allow photographers and tele
vision cameras there was out of the question.

It therefore came as a surprise when a photographer named
Paddy (for Patricia) Drew was given permission to photo
graph the entire collection: the lovely white altar cloths, of
which a new one was lovingly produced year after year, to be
just a little different from the previous one: exquisite altar
cloths hanging on the front, rich in needlework and art; and
the curtains or 'riddels' which hung on the north and south
ends and set off the other two.

Miss Drew (as she introduced herself) approached Mother
Superior quite cannily, saying what a shame that the holy
martyr, whose relics lay under the altar, had never been can
onised. Was there any chance that the publication of a book
of photographs of these altar cloths, these sacred altar cloths
would lead, she suggested tactfully, to a greater recognition of
the martyr in appropriate quarters? It was the right tack to take
with a Mother Superior who was no politician, but theolo
gian enough to work out the implications for herself. Besides,
Miss Drew wore very long skirts, which concealed what might
have been shoes rather than boots. Her blouse extended to her
chin. She wasn't the sort of young woman who flaunted her
body shamelessly. She wore only a hint of make-up, and, noted
Mother Superior with approval, gloves!

Miss Drew arrived every morning at a quarter to nine, to tart at nine, and dipped her fingers in holy water as she came n. She worked till twelve, when she left (fingertips delicately troking sacred liquid), returning at a quarter to two, to start t two. She left punctually at five. And, of course, she never vorked on Sunday.

Mother Superior spoke with approval of a professional voman unspoilt by success, who did not make a great show of eing Catholic (quite unlike some she could name), and noted vith approval how the photographer neither gushed nor apeared ill at ease with the sisters.

T SHOULD HAVE BEEN no surprise, in retrospect, that it was Sister Brona who foiled the attempt to steal the altar cloths. After all, her father was a member of the gardai back home in reland. He had even attended a course which stressed the imortance of crime prevention, a subject on which he was wont o dwell often and at length.

Sister Brona shared her misgivings with one of her superiors, who was quite shocked and reprimanded her for enteraining such a thought. After that, direct recourse to Mother Superior was unthought of.

We are not told how Sister Brona communicated her suspicions to DC Thomas Doherty (who had Anglicised his name rom the Donegal O Dochartaigh) known as Dots at the cophop, or how she managed to send him a number of the subtituted altar cloths which forensics established were not even kilful forgeries. Presumably, the forgeries were brought in nder the long skirt and the genuine ones smuggled out again n the same way.

DC Doherty followed the photographer, performed the earch and carried out the arrest. It is certain that he received nore recognition than did Sister Brona. After all, his superiors had to allocate credit in such a way as to disabuse the world hat an outsider could act to prevent crime better'n a policenan. Mother Superior merely sniffed and said that she was orry she had given in and allowed herself to be talked into alowing outsiders entry into the grounds.

But the kitchen nuns, who knew it is never enough to be intelligent, and that it is important to have brains, too, knew the truth. That the sister, newly arrived in their midst, had prevented the sacred altar cloths, all the sacred altar cloths, from being stolen. They were sitting over a cup of well-brewed tea, these nuns, while the rest were at their prayers.

'Nothing's been said about how you knew. Didn't make a pass at you, did he?' asked Sister Ursula, who still enjoyed shocking the others. 'Is that why Sister Teresa wouldn't listen to your warning? She doesn't like to hear such things?'

'Och, but it was a joke my father used to tell,' said Sister Brona, 'about how a man was discovered in a nunnery.'

The kitchen nuns laughed.

'Some of the places I've been to,' said Sister Ursula, 'and in saying this I shall be admitting to you the most secret, intimate action of my private life, some places I've been to, where men are admitted, I've . . .' she made a polishing motion with one hand. 'It wasn't fit to sit on.'

'Back home we polish it like a mirror when the bishop comes callin',' said Sister Brona in a tone of pure one-upmanship, 'and I gave it a special shine two days runnin' to make sure,' she added, and outshocked even Sister Ursula.

TURNING POINT

★

ANTHEA FRASER

IF I HADN'T BEEN so vulnerable it wouldn't have happened; but Clive and I'd been having one of our periodic bad patches, and to add to my misery Jamie, our youngest, had just started boarding-school. It seemed I was at one of life's turning points, and needed to stop and consider what lay ahead.

On the face of it, it didn't seem promising. I'd given up my job when we married; Clive's income was more than adequate, and as I'd always been a mother-hen rather than a career girl I was only too happy to stay home. In any case we'd started a family almost at once. Now, though, with all three children away at school and Clive busy with trips abroad and business entertaining, time would hang heavy. I needed an interest of my own.

And then, coming out of the library, I saw the poster. In a blaze of red and gold, it announced an exhibition in a nearby town by the artist whose biography I'd just finished reading.

Fate! I told myself, little realising the danger in submitting to it. For here was a chance to get away for a few days and sort myself out. My mind raced eagerly ahead. I'd find myself a b. & b., visit the exhibition, and, since Sandham was on the coast, perhaps spend an hour or two on the beach. And maybe by the time I came home I'd have some idea what I wanted to do.

'I'm going away for a few days,' I said casually over dinner that night.

Clive looked up in surprise. 'To your mother's, you mean?'

'No, to Sandham, actually. There's an exhibition on by a Mexican artist, Sancho Perez. I've just read his biography, and I'd like to see it.'

He regarded me suspiciously. 'Is this tit-for-tat? Because I'm off to Brussels?'

'Nothing so childish. I simply need a break and you're not free to come with me. And you're not interested in art, so it wouldn't appeal to you anyway.'

'When are you going?'

'Tomorrow; it's only on this week.'

'So you'll be back at the weekend?'

'I don't know; I might stay on a few days, since you'll be away.'

Clive shrugged, losing interest. 'Fine, if that's what you want.' And he reached for the cheese.

So the next morning, quite excited at the prospect, I packed swimming things, jeans, an assortment of shirts and sweaters, and a solitary dress in case I visited a restaurant. I also tucked in some paperbacks as insurance against loneliness. Thus provisioned, I reckoned I could last up to a week in Sandham if it took my fancy. And if I didn't like it, I'd come home.

BUT I DID: I liked it very much. It was a pretty, grey little town tucked into the shelter of some cliffs to protect it from the strong east winds, and at the end of the summer it had a clean, fresh feel about it.

Most of the holiday-makers had left with the start of the school term, and already beach cafés and amusement arcades were boarded up. But the inhabitants of the town, who had been skulking in their gardens during the summer invasion, were beginning to reappear, breathe a sigh of relief, and take up their normal lives again.

There was a long promenade, with old-fashioned shelters positioned along it where, doubtless, the local youth conducted their love affairs. Bordering it were colourful gardens, bright now with chrysanthemums and dahlias and late-blooming roses, and seats where you could sit and look at the view, or read, or doze in the still-warm sunshine. The art gallery, smug behind its stone façade, overlooked a square boasting a variety of shops, some selling buckets, spades and cheap souvenirs, others dealing in designer clothes. And on one of the headlands an imposing hotel stood sentinel, its grounds sweeping in a series of terraces down to the sea.

'Why in heaven's name don't you stay at the Grand in comfort?' Clive had asked, when I'd mentioned my intention of a b. & b.

'Because I don't want to have to dress for dinner and sit in solitary splendour.'

Again he'd shrugged, as though despairing of me, and said no more.

Though it was late September, there were still plenty of bed-&-breakfast signs in evidence. I selected a tall, whitewashed house on the front, with a long path lined by seashells. It proved a good choice. Its owner, a Mrs Carlisle, was delighted to welcome a guest at the end of the season, and her home was spotless—brass shining, furniture gleaming with polish, linen crisp and smelling of the salt winds that had dried it. I felt immediately at home.

The next morning, refreshed after the best night's sleep I'd had in months, I set off to view the exhibition—and it was all I hoped it would be. The large, rather austere rooms leading out of each other were exploding with colour—hot pinks and purples, acid greens and yellows, deep shadows and blazing sunshine such as this grey English town could never have known. Peasants dozed in doorways under large-brimmed hats, naked children played on white sand, girls clapped their hands, buildings shimmered in the heat. All the vividness, the vibrant life of Mexico was pulsating in the canvases, reaching out to ensnare the passer-by and fill him with undefined yearning.

I spent the morning alternately wandering round or sitting in a bemused, colour-washed daze consulting my catalogue and trying to get my tongue round the titles of the paintings. And when I finally left, satiated for the moment, it was with the intention of returning when I was ready to take in more.

Outside on the pavement I stood for a moment, drawing a deep breath and reacclimatising myself to the muted tones of an English autumn. Then, unbelievably, I heard my name called.

'Melanie—as I live and breathe!'

I spun round as the voice echoed down the years, rekindling in that first instant all the forgotten hopes and dreams of my romantic teens. It couldn't be—but it was.

'Philip!'' I said, glad of the support of the warm stone wall behind me. With the sun in my eyes it was hard to see the blurred figure striding towards me, which added to the unreality.

'What a fantastic coincidence!' he was exclaiming. 'Whatever brings you here?'

He had reached me now, and, with his hands on my shoulders, was staring down at me with a wonderment matching my own. And now that he was between me and the sun, I could see the face I'd thought never to see again: older, of course, than I remembered, but as strong, as ruggedly good-looking as it had ever been, and the eyes as piercingly blue.

'God, it's been years! I can't believe it, running into you like this. Let's have a coffee, and you can tell me what you've been doing with yourself.' He took my arm and led me down the road to one of the few cafés that remained open, where, seated opposite each other, we exchanged cautious smiles.

'It's really great to see you,' he said. 'Do you live round here?'

'No, I came to see the art exhibition.'

He glanced at my wedding ring. 'Your husband with you?'

I shook my head. 'He's not interested in art.' I added hesitantly, 'And you—are you married?' As I asked the question, I remembered that I'd once hoped he would marry me. My face grew hot, but Philip didn't notice. His eyes were on the coffee as he swirled his spoon in his cup.

'No; I tried it briefly but it didn't work. I'm not the marrying kind, Mel, as you might remember!' He grinned at me ruefully, and I weakly forgave him all those nights of heartbreak.

'So my mother warned me!'

He laughed. 'Mothers always know best. So—what have you been up to for the last fifteen years?'

'Bringing up children for most of them—twins of thirteen and a boy of ten. He's just started boarding-school.'

'Poor little devil,' Philip said carelessly.

Since he was obviously not interested, I didn't elaborate. 'And what about you?' I asked instead. 'What have you been doing?'

'Oh this and that. Making a fast buck when the chance offered.'

As footloose, apparently, as he'd been at twenty. 'No staying power, that lad,' my father had observed. 'Don't get involved with him, Mellie, he'd only bring you heartache.' Perhaps fathers also knew best.

'How long are you here for?' Philip was asking, possibly to forestall further questions.

'It depends on the weather, really. My husband's away so there's no rush to go home.'

'You're at the Grand, I suppose?'

'No, just a boarding-house; I wanted somewhere informal. Are you on holiday?' It seemed an odd choice for someone as restless and mercurial as Philip.

'Sort of, a short break.'

I wasn't sure I believed him. 'I'd have thought you'd have gone for the bright lights,' I remarked.

He looked up then, and there was an expression in his eyes that I couldn't fathom. 'Sometimes I prefer the shadows,' he said. Then he smiled quickly. 'Specially when I'm with a pretty woman! What do you say, Mel? You've no immediate plans, have you? Shall we spend the day together, for old times' sake?'

I could hardly have declined, could I, when he knew I was alone in a strange town. And to be honest, I didn't want to. There was a touch of the old magic about Philip—perhaps, for me, there always would be. So coffee stretched into lunch, and afterwards we went for a long, exhilarating walk over the cliffs, where the gulls were screaming and where, out on the headland, the wind tore at our hair and clothes, catching our words and flinging them to the wide blue sky.

We talked constantly, not of personal matters but of the world in general: art, music, politics. Whatever his lifestyle,

Philip proved knowledgeable on a variety of topics and was an entertaining companion.

We stopped for tea at a village along the coast and caught the local bus back to Sandham. Philip proposed dinner at an Italian restaurant he'd discovered.

'No need to dress up, it's quite informal,' he assured me. 'I'll meet you outside the art gallery at eight and we'll have a drink somewhere first.'

IT WAS DUSK when I closed the front door of Bay View behind me and set off down the path. The first stars were pricking through and a gold sickle of moon hung over the sea. But there was a hint of chill in the air; the wind we'd encountered on the cliffs had, in diminished form, followed us back to town and I pulled my jacket closer as my thin dress swirled round my legs. I should have followed Philip's advice, and kept on my jeans and sweater.

As I turned the corner by the gallery I saw him under a street lamp, his hands deep in his pockets. He looked up at the sound of my footsteps and, straightening, came towards me with a smile.

'Let's see about that drink,' he said, slipping my hand through his arm. We walked quickly, heads down against the wind, and turned into the lighted doorway of the Three Pigs. Loud laughter came from the public bar but Philip guided me to the saloon, where more subdued customers sat at tables and talked in quiet voices.

He brought the drinks over and sat down. 'Here's to old times,' he said, raising his glass. It was not the toast I'd have chosen, but I nodded and drank, the cold liquid making me shiver.

The two-hour break had, I realised, dissipated our ease with each other and we were constrained, strangers again. It would have been wiser not to have met this evening; an afternoon together was all that was called for in the circumstances. Perhaps, though, he'd thought I expected it. The idea made me uncomfortable.

Philip was frowning into his glass, his face withdrawn and older than it had seemed earlier. Then, suddenly conscious of my gaze, he looked up and smiled.

'Sorry, Mel!' he said, with a swift return to his easy manner. 'I'd some business to attend to after leaving you, and my mind was still on it.'

I smiled back, reassured. Another fast buck, no doubt. My eyes drifted past him to the bar. It was L-shaped, and in the mirror I could see the reflections of the men in the public bar on the far side; and of one man in particular, tall and red-haired, who was staring intently at my own reflection. As our eyes met in the mirror he moved quickly back out of sight.

Philip was saying, 'You do like Italian food, I hope? If you'd rather go somewhere else—'

'I love it,' I answered, turning back to him.

'Good. Drink up, then, and we'll be on our way.'

The wind was waiting for us, undeniably cold now, sending leaves scuttering in the gutters and unlatched gates banging. Scraps of paper swirled through the air like birds, swooping and dipping above our heads as we hurried up the road.

'And it's only September!' Philip commented. 'Imagine it in winter.'

I was glad to reach the shelter of the restaurant, warm and welcoming with its candles and lamps. Philip ordered a bottle of Chianti and we settled down to study the menu, relaxed and at ease again.

The meal was delicious, a mouth-watering concoction of lamb, garlic and olives. The waiter kept refilling my glass and the empty bottle of wine was replaced. I could feel my inhibitions slowly dissolving, all the restrictions, disappointments and responsibilities of everyday life slipping away until I was a different person entirely from the rather dull woman Clive would have recognised. In short, I felt young again.

Over coffee, Philip unwrapped a handful of amaretti and put a match to each flimsy paper in turn, watching as it curled into a spiral and took off to float up to the ceiling. Like children, we made bets with each other as to which colour would rise the highest.

I was laughing at the game when I happened to glance towards the window. The lower half was covered by net curtains, but above them darkness pressed against the glass. And as I looked, I could have sworn that someone moved swiftly aside, someone who had been standing looking into the lighted room. Briefly I wondered if it was the man from the bar, but dismissed the idea as ludicrous. My senses, blurred by good food and wine, were playing tricks on me.

It was time to go, and reluctantly, not wanting the evening to end, we went once more into the cold darkness. I clung to Philip's arm as the wind leapt on us, buffeting and intrusive as we battled our way along the narrow pavements back towards the seafront. Once, I thought I heard footsteps behind us, but the wind distorted sounds, and when I turned there was no one there.

'What are you doing tomorrow?' Philip was asking.

'I want another look at the exhibition. I couldn't take it all in at once.'

'If it's as good as that perhaps I should see it myself. How about meeting there about eleven?'

'Fine,' I agreed, glad of the prospect of his company.

'We can have lunch afterwards and then, unfortunately, I must be on my way.'

'You're leaving?'

'Afraid so. I did say it was only a short break.'

So once again he was going to walk out of my life. Yet what did I expect, a married woman with three children? The Melanie who had loved Philip, I reminded myself, was long gone.

The wind gusted suddenly, throwing a handful of sand into our faces. Philip reached for a handkerchief, but when he withdrew his hand he was holding a buff-coloured envelope. 'Damn! It's the final demand for my gas bill. I meant to buy a stamp for it.'

'I have some in my room,' I said, 'and there's a pillarbox at the gate. I'll post it for you.'

'Are you sure?' He felt in his pocket again. 'I can give you—'

'Twenty-four pence? Don't be ridiculous. Think what you've spent on me today—coffee, lunch, tea *and* dinner.'

He laughed. 'Put like that, we seem to have spent most of our time eating. Well, if you're sure, thank you. I don't want them turning the gas off, with cold weather on the way.' He handed me the envelope and I slipped it into my handbag. We had now reached the gate of Bay View, but although we came to a halt, he did not release my hand.

'I wish you were staying at that nice, anonymous hotel,' he said wryly, 'instead of a boarding-house where every movement is noted.'

'What if I were?' I asked, my mouth dry.

'I'd suggest a nightcap in your room, and no doubt one thing would lead to another.'

'You're very sure of yourself,' I said.

'Oh, Mel!' He pulled me suddenly against him, and for long moments we clung together, while the wind tore at our clothes as though trying to separate us.

'Why the hell did I let you go?' he said against my hair.

With an effort I pulled myself free. 'Good night, Philip. And—thank you.'

He sighed and, lifting my hand to his lips, kissed the base of each finger in turn. 'Till tomorrow morning, then.'

'Eleven o'clock at the gallery,' I confirmed.

'I'll be there.'

As I walked alone up the path, I knew—and the knowledge filled me with shame—that had I been at that 'anonymous hotel', I should happily have spent the night with Philip.

I awoke with a headache, and at first thought the low, persistent humming was in my head. Then I identified it as a lawnmower. At this hour? I thought grumpily. I reached for my dressing gown and went to the window with some half-formed intention of complaining. But my view of the garden was obscured by the fire escape, and while I waited for the perpetrator to come into sight my annoyance evaporated and, abandoning the hope of further sleep, I went for my bath.

'You start work early round here,' I commented to Mrs Carlisle, when she brought the tea and toast which was all I could face for breakfast.

'The grass, you mean? My son cuts it before he goes to work. I hope he didn't wake you, but it's the only chance he gets.'

After breakfast I went to the pillarbox with Philip's letter. It was still early but, feeling in need of fresh air, I continued walking along the promenade. In the cold light of morning, the memory of my behaviour the previous evening was deeply embarrassing and again I doubted the wisdom of another meeting with Philip. But there would be no chance of amorous dalliance today. We'd look at the exhibition, have lunch, and then he would go.

And I? I'd be guided by the weather, as I'd told him. If it became warm enough to sit on the beach, I'd stay on a few days. The wind had dropped this morning, and the air felt as sluggish as I did.

I walked as far as the boating pool, stood for a while watching small boys sailing their yachts, then made my way slowly back to town. The library clock was striking eleven as I turned the corner by the gallery, but this time Philip was not there. Nor, though I stood waiting with increasing impatience, did he appear.

Perhaps, I thought eventually, he'd meant us to meet inside? I bought a ticket and hurried in, but a quick search proved he wasn't there either. Disconsolately I began my solo round of the paintings.

But though I was looking at the same pictures as the day before, my reactions were very different. The sizzling colours no longer seemed joyous but discordant, violent even, and the stinging yellows and throbbing reds hurt my eyes. Every few minutes I went back to the door, from which I had a clear view of the steps and the lamp-post outside. But Philip did not appear.

By twelve o'clock I had to accept he wasn't coming. He could at least have phoned, I thought irritably; the staff would have passed on a message. But as I knew to my cost, Philip had never been considerate. No, something else must have come up and he'd abandoned me without a second thought.

Because it was the only place I knew, I went to the café we'd visited the previous day. He'd mentioned lunch, and there was a faint hope he might be there. He was not. I was served a leathery omelette and a tepid cup of coffee. Had the fare been as poor yesterday? I'd been too engrossed in Philip to notice. Well, that was what I got by behaving as though I were eighteen again.

Annoyed, humiliated, and with a by this time blinding headache, I returned to the boarding-house. Mrs Carlisle was out, but she'd provided me with a front door key. As I went up the stairs I was composing a withering speech to Philip, though I knew I'd never have the chance to deliver it. But the moment I entered my room, it went out of my head.

Someone had been there, I knew it instinctively—someone other than Mrs Carlisle, who'd made the bed and cleaned the basin. I stood stock still, looking for proof to back up intuition. And found it. One of the dressing-table drawers, which I'd noticed shut crookedly, was not quite straight, though I'd left it so.

Swiftly I checked my belongings, though fortunately I'd nothing of value with me. The intruder, whoever he was, must have reached the same conclusion, for though some items were out of place, nothing seemed to be missing.

I straightened, looking round the outwardly undisturbed room, and with a shiver realised belatedly that no burglar would have left things so tidy. It had been a search rather than a robbery, which I found even more disquieting.

Uneasy and bewildered, I walked to the window and stood staring down at the newly mown lawn. Then something closer at hand caught my eye. On both the windowsill and the top step of the fire escape were several blades of freshly cut grass. Altogether too easy a means of entry.

I began to pack, and by the time Mrs Carlisle returned, was waiting to pay the bill. I didn't mention the intruder; there seemed little point.

Well, my bid for independence had not been a success, I reflected in the taxi on the way to the station. Not only had I made a fool of myself over a man I'd not seen for years, but I'd attracted enough attention for someone to think it worth searching my room. In retrospect, the whole venture had been sordid and degrading. I should have stayed meekly at home, as I'd always done before. My only consolation was that I could now put Philip out of my head once and for all.

But in that I was mistaken, as I discovered the next morning when I opened the newspaper.
MURDER AT RESORT, I read. Then, with increasing horror:

> *The body of a man in his late thirties was discovered yesterday morning in the seaside town of Sandham. Death had been caused by a stab wound and probably occurred overnight.*
>
> *Identification has not yet been established, but a bus ticket from Lee to Sandham dated the previous day was found in his pocket. An incident room has been set up at Sandham Police Station, and police are asking anyone who might have any information to contact them there. The telephone number is—*

The print swam before my eyes. Philip was dead. All the time I'd been seething at his non-appearance, he'd been lying murdered. But by whom? The red-haired man who'd watched us in the bar, and probably also through the restaurant window?

Then something occurred to me with the impact of a douche of cold water. The police were appealing for information: suppose someone reported seeing him with *me*? On the bus back from Lee, for instance—mention of the ticket might jog someone's memory—in the café, the pub or the restaurant? Looking back, we'd hardly kept a low profile.

Should I forestall any informer and go to the police myself? But there was nothing I could tell them—and how would Clive react to my involvement in a murder case? I shivered. Though deeply shocked by Philip's death, I had no wish to be dragged into its aftermath.

Philip's death, my brain repeated numbly. Philip, who had been so alive, so vital, was dead. In God's name, why? I remembered the footsteps I'd heard and our embrace at the gate. The watcher in the shadows would have seen that, and known where to look the next day. But for what?

The envelope. It had to be. Anyone following us would have seen Philip hand it to me. Whatever he'd imagined it contained, it seemed likely Philip had died because of an unpaid gas bill.

Somehow the days crawled past. The murder, which had made the regional news headlines that first evening, was unaccountably dropped from subsequent bulletins, nor could I find any follow-up to the newspaper story. The clamp-down struck me as ominous; such items usually ran for days. Perhaps they'd caught the killer? But if so, why not announce it?

My conscience remained uneasy and I still felt I should contact the police. Yet even if I did, I argued with myself, I had little to report—I'd not even known where Philip was staying. No, I decided finally, I'd made enough mistakes in the last few days. Better to sit tight and volunteer nothing.

CLIVE ARRIVED HOME at last, and I was overwhelmingly glad to see him. He looked tired, I thought, the few days apart lending an added perception.

'And how was your trip?' he asked, accepting my fervent kiss with some surprise.

'Not an unqualified success,' I admitted.

'But you saw the exhibition?'

'Oh yes. It was—' How was it? Joyous and exuberant or stridently threatening? Which of my visits was the more discerning? But he wasn't really listening.

'I gather there was a bit of excitement while you were there,' he said, tossing his briefcase on a chair. 'Murder, no less. If I'd known where you were staying, I'd have phoned to check you were all right.'

'You surely didn't think I was involved?' I hoped he wouldn't hear the tremor in my voice.

'Hardly. Though oddly enough, *I* was, in a way.'

I stared at him, a pulse beginning to throb in my temple. 'How do you mean?'

'By a freak chance one of our chaps was in the thick of it. It seems the man had been stalking him all week and suddenly sprang out and attacked him. He was lucky—the outcome could have been very different.'

I felt I was floundering in a foggy sea. 'One of your chaps?' I repeated blankly. 'But—you're in electronics!'

Clive gave a tired smile. 'You've never been interested in my work, have you, Melanie? If you had, you'd have realised that electronics covers a multitude of things. Listening devices, for example, and other bugging equipment, the use of which can be quite controversial. Sometimes we do odd jobs for the government and at others we're caught up in industrial espionage. Every now and then it backfires, which was what happened this time. One of our devices picked up some sensitive material which could net several big fish. Let's say they weren't anxious for it to be passed on.'

I gazed at him speechlessly. My conventional, dull-seeming husband had been leading a double life which I'd never even suspected. How could I have lived with him all these years and not known? It wasn't that he'd deliberately kept it from me, just, as he'd said, that I'd never been interested.

Hot with shame, I remembered all the times he'd come home, full of the day's events, and started to tell me of something that had happened, only to be interrupted by a request to do and say goodnight to the children, or the announcement that dinner was ready.

Clive had been watching me, reading without difficulty the emotions crossing my face. 'Don't look so stricken, love,' he said gently. 'It wasn't meant as criticism.'

I said shakily, 'How could I have been so—so blinkered and self-centred?'

'Well, you were involved with the children, weren't you? There's no harm done. I only mentioned it because of the coincidence of your being there and because the chap concerned is calling round any minute to put me in the picture.'

The nightmare, it seemed, was not over. I said with difficulty, 'So it was he who killed—that man?'

'In self-defence, yes. I gather he made a grab at the knife, and in the struggle the other man fell on it.'

'Who—who was he, do you know?'

'Not specifically, but his outfit had been under surveillance for some time. They sell information to the highest bidder.'

Making a fast buck when the chance offered. Tearing my mind from Philip, I realised with horror that Clive's colleague must be the red-haired man I'd cast as villain. He'd seen me with Philip—how would he react if I were introduced as Clive's wife? The sound of the doorbell cut into my panic.

'That'll be him now,' Clive said.

'I'll go upstairs, then, so you can talk.' I started frantically for the door.

'No, stay here,' Clive said over his shoulder. 'I'd like you to meet him.'

Heart hammering, I stood immobile in the centre of the room. Because of that one reckless day with Philip, my marriage, my whole future hung in the balance and there was nothing I could do to salvage it.

There were voices in the hall, and they were coming closer. Like a rabbit caught in car headlights, I fixed my eyes on the door. And as the visitor came into sight, felt myself jerk and sway. For there, regarding me across the room with an expression of disbelief, was Philip.

Dizzily I tried yet again to adjust. Ironic that I'd gone to Sandham to consider the turning point in my life; ever since my return I'd been spinning like a top, unsure from one moment to the next which way I was facing, while Philip, the red-haired stranger, even Clive, shifted and changed places in my perceptions, as though performing the intricate steps of a *danse macabre*. And yet, I thought, as the faintness passed, the only constant was, and had always been, Clive.

Over Philip's shoulder, he was saying, 'Darling, this is Philip Barr, whom I was telling you about. My wife, Melanie. By an odd coincidence she was in Sandham herself last week.'

Philip's eyes still held mine, and it wasn't difficult to read their message. 'Really?' he said, and came forward to take my hand. 'I'm delighted to meet you, Mrs Roper. I hope our little melodrama didn't spoil your holiday.'

I smiled back, sure of myself at last. 'Not in the slightest. I knew nothing about it until I got home,' I said.

PROFESSOR KAA'S DOORWAY

★

PETER O'DONNELL

'THIS ONE'S DEAD all right,' said Superintendent Kobold. He looked up from the body of the man with curly black hair who lay on the stateroom floor in pyjamas. 'Close that port-hole, Gazpacho, it's damn cold.'

Inspector Augustus Patch smiled to hide his hatred. 'With respect, sir, I prefer to be called Patch. Or Gus if you wish to be informal. Not Gazpacho.'

Kobold ignored the request. He was a small man with the face of an angry gnome, and had invented the nickname for a subordinate he detested. 'Bit different from old Dew's trip,' he said.

'I beg your pardon, sir?'

Kobold sighed and spoke with heavy patience. 'In 1910 Chief Inspector Dew was sent to Quebec to collect *Crippen*. You remember the case, I hope? It was only two years ago.'

Patch flushed. 'Of course, sir.'

'Good. Well, you may recall that we are now on our way to *New York* to pick up a wanted man, but four days out from Southampton we run into murder on the high seas. Murder by *snake*, so the murderer tells us. Different from old Dew's trip, see?'

Patch, burly and square-faced, closed the port-hole and its cover, shutting out the night sky. 'A double murder,' he said.

'Don't correct me, Gazpacho,' Kobold said wearily. 'If one person kills two, that's a double murder. Here we have two persons killing each other, which doesn't qualify.'

Patch put his hands behind his back so that he could clench his fists unseen. 'Quite so, sir. And in fact one of the persons is not yet dead. The Indian rajah chap.'

'He's not a rajah, he's a professor according to the passenger list,' said Kobold. 'Perhaps he just likes dressing up. Anyway, we'd better hear what he's got to say before he snuffs it.'

They returned to Professor Kaa in the adjoining stateroom. He was sitting in an armchair with eyes closed, just as they had left him two minutes earlier, wearing a pale blue silk jacket and trousers, and a single gold earring. Lying flat on the table was a device the size and shape of a small suitcase, fashioned from grey metal with several dials on the upper surface. In one of the long sides was an opening eighteen inches long and three inches deep giving access to the dark interior.

Beside the device was a bulky folder tied with white ribbon, an oriental flute, and an earring which matched the one Professor Kaa already wore. Superintendent Kobold sat down and said, 'How are you feeling, Professor?'

The Indian opened his eyes. 'The cold has now reached my thighs,' he said calmly. 'It will reach my heart in the next few minutes.'

'But you refuse to see the ship's doctor?'

The professor smiled wanly. 'He cannot save me, Superintendent. When I sent a note asking you to attend me secretly here, I knew I had little time left. My colleague, the late Mr Borgier, used a truly fatal poison.'

Kobold glanced at the table. 'In that earring, you say?'

'Yes. He substituted it for one of the pair I wear when dressed in traditional apparel. Being a skilled craftsman, Mr Borgier constructed it so that in preparing to attach same to my ear I caused poison to be vigorously injected into my finger via the small hollow needle now apparent.'

Patch looked about the stateroom warily. 'I suppose the snake would be equally fatal, sir?'

'That has gone,' said Professor Kaa. 'I brought it abroad in a basket, and when its work was done I disposed of it via Mr Borgier's porthole.'

'Its work?' Kobold prompted.

'To cause my colleague's departure from life, Superintendent. I placed the reptile in Mr Borgier's bed, and to keep it quiescent until disturbed I induced somnolence by playing a funeral march—in fact Handel's "Death March" in *Saul*.' He smiled sadly. 'A small courtesy to an esteemed colleague. This procedure was most effective, as also was the venom of the reptile, a taipan whose bite produces paralysis followed rapidly by death.'

Kobold said, 'But you were able to avoid the reptile's fatal bite yourself when disposing of it, sir?'

Professor Kaa nodded slowly. 'Some humans have an affinity with reptiles, Superintendent. I have that gift. It was my intention, after the event, to put on traditional dress, as is my custom following dinner, and join my fellow passengers in the Palm Court lounge, leaving Mr Borgier to be discovered in due course, deceased from some cause difficult to elucidate. I did not know, until I prepared to attach the second earring, that he also had implemented a carefully devised plan.'

Kobold said, 'Why did you seek to dispose of each other?'

'Ah, that is an important question. Kindly peruse the magazine on the chair to your right, Superintendent.'

Kobold picked it up. Watching him, Patch saw a look of surprise appear as he studied the cover before starting to turn the pages. Five minutes later he thrust the magazine towards Patch and said in a croaking voice, 'What in God's name...?'

Patch looked at the cover and was astonished, for it was in colour and the printing was of a quality he would not have thought possible. The title was *Focus*, and the date of issue was, absurdly, 21 December 1988. The cover bore a portrait photograph of a young man wearing a Father Christmas hat, and in one corner were the words: *Royal Family Album*.

Clearly the magazine was a hoax, thought Patch, but the remarkable quality of photograph reproduction in colour stopped him announcing that immediate judgement. He began to turn the pages, and caught his breath. Here was an advertisement with a photograph of a motor car, but a machine of such strange beauty that it could exist only in imagination.

And here was another advertisement—women in underwear! Legs exposed to the *hips*! Kobold's hand reached out,

urning some pages to reveal a supplement. 'The Royal Fam-
y Album, nineteen eighty-eight,' he said throatily. 'Look at
hem!'

Patch looked. Here was a young woman, declared to be the
Duchess of York, trying to prevent the wind billowing her
hort skirt above her already exposed thighs! And here an
lder woman—the Queen *Mother*, it said?—with some Irish
Guards in bearskins. On another page was a younger woman
1 yellow coat and hat, arms outflung. The caption read: *The
Queen is carried away by the excitement of this year's Derby.*
The *Queen*?

Kobold took back the magazine. 'Nobody in the world
ould have imagined all that's in here,' he said in a voice that
hook. 'Nobody could have concocted such photographs, and
o technology exists that could print them like this.'

Both men looked at Professor Kaa.

'I assure you gentlemen that it is genuine.' His manner was
deprecating. 'I happen to have genius in mathematics, a qual-
ty not unknown in my country's history. It was an Indian who
devised the symbol for zero, and thus revolutionised the numerical system—but I digress. The magazine was obtained
rom 1988, seventy-six years hence, via the machine designed
y myself and constructed by the late Mr Borgier, a mechani-
al genius without peer.' He indicated the device. 'As yet it can
orm only a small, slot-shaped penetration of Time for up to
bout eighty years, as registered on the simple time-control
etting. The focus for location is also limited at present, and
ppears to be in the area of a newsagent's shop or a bookstall
n central London. This is suggested by early editions of
ewspapers I have received.'

'How—?' Kobold began.

Professor Kaa lifted a feeble hand. 'The cold has now
eached my upper abdomen. It is my dying duty to mankind
o tell you that Time and Space are integral, and may be con-
quered by mathematics applied to the forces of electromag-
netism and gravity. All my formulae are in the file there,
hough perhaps young Einstein is the only man alive at pres-
nt who will fully understand them. The device is powered by
ight, natural or artificial. When it acquires sufficient power

to operate, the green light will show. The time-dial may the be set, and the device switched on. It will seek any artefact c suitable size, weight and material within its focus, and exer attraction upon it. The artefact will appear in the cavity be tween the upper and lower sections.'

Sweat broke out on Professor Kaa's brow, and he hurrie on. 'In a few years Mr Borgier and I would surely have openee a Doorway to the Future, and to the Past, through which hu man beings would be able to pass. Now that task must fall t others, but have no doubt, gentlemen, that it will be achieved His chest began to heave, and his eyes closed.

Kobold said urgently, 'Professor! *Why* did you kill eacl other?'

The reply came faintly. 'I insisted...the whole world shoul benefit from our work. Mr Borgier insisted...we must kee it a secret for personal gain. It seems we both had strong feel ings...and felt there could be no compromise...so it wa necessary that the other should go.'

The voice faded, and his head fell forward as he died.

After a few seconds Patch said, 'Do you believe it, sir?'

Kobold glared and held up the magazine. 'You can't *disbe lieve* this—unless you're a damn fool, Gazpacho.'

AN HOUR LATER the two detectives stood leaning on the rail o the upper promenade deck, wearing topcoats and hats agains the cold wind. This was a secure place to talk unheard.

Professor Kaa's device and formulae were now in the third class cabin they shared. The captain had been told only tha according to Professor Kaa's dying confession the two mer were dead by each other's hand from motives of professiona jealousy.

Now Inspector Patch was saying, 'The dial that sets the fu ture year, sir...if we set it for *next* year we might get a news paper with information that would make our fortunes Winners on the racecourses, shares on the stockmarket, se crets of the next budget—there's no end to it!'

Kobold glared up at him. 'When we reach New York,' he said grimly, 'I shall deliver the machine, the formulae, and i full report to our ambassador there. This discovery will now benefit the British Empire—or possibly the whole world. And I shall certainly report your disgraceful suggestion that we should steal it for ourselves, Inspector!'

Patch looked down at the sea. 'What's that?' he said sharply.

'Eh?' Kobold leant over the rail, peering at the phosphorescence along the waterline. Patch bent to seize him by the ankles and tipped him neatly over the rail. For a moment the phosphorescence was disturbed, then all was normal again.

Most of the passengers were in the various lounges or in their cabins, and Inspector Gus Patch was unseen as he made his way down the companionway to his own cabin, aft on the port side. '... and when I woke this morning,' he rehearsed mentally, 'Superintendent Kobold's bed was empty.'

Taking off topcoat and cap he sat gazing at the device for a while, then picked up the magazine and spent ten minutes studying some of the astonishing items in it.

'Another world,' he murmured at last, wonderment in his voice. 'And the British Empire can have it with pleasure. I'm a true patriot. I just want to get rich first, that's all.'

A thought struck him. Professor Kaa had said this device would be developed by others to become a doorway into the future and the past. If so, Patch reasoned, there would surely be movement through it both ways, and probably not just within the present limits of eighty years or so. In that event, why was there no word in this magazine about such travelling through time? He would have expected to find advertisements for holidays in the past or future—a day trip to Queen Victoria's coronation, for example, or to the relief of Mafeking.

Why had nobody ever met anyone who had come back on a visit through Professor Kaa's doorway? Why had it never happened? Or why *would* it never happen? With the device itself and that file of formulae to work on, what could possibly go wrong? Or have gone wrong?

Patch was so immersed in speculation that he scarcely felt the long tremor that ran through the ship as an iceberg tore a 300-foot gash in the starboard hull of the *Titanic*.

THE LAST KISS

★

SUSAN KELLY

October wind is sweeping
Garrulous leaves across gravelled pathways
On to the gravestones, death-date deep.

Autumn is creeping
In tarnished gullies
As I crouch to read a weather-eaten stone:
One Florence Mary Perkins—housemaid—
Eighteen-fifty; nineteen years of age.
The pious legend:
And so He giveth His beloved sleep.

I am the interloper—peeping
Into sorrow generations dead.
Across the years I hear the ancient questions:
*'Are you sure? How long? It is mine, is it?
Trust me, Florrie.'*

      Then the final kiss.
She drank the draught he gave her later—
The work of some wise woman, so he said.
And so he gave his beloved sleep.

His grave—for he lived, was rich, was reaping
His reward for eighty-something years—
Stands beside his wife, his sons, his brothers,

Preserved in limesoil till the Judgement Day.

Father, in Thy gracious keeping
Leave we now Thy servant sleeping.

And close beside me, in the half light,
No, on the very bench where I now sit,
Is the sound of a woman, weeping.

THE MOOD CUCKOO

★

JONATHAN GASH

HONG KONG slammed at her, just like the old days.

The man next to her on the economy flight had been a pest. All through that interminable Cathay Pacific CX 260 he'd been 'amusing' with the garrulous impertinence of the unwelcome. What hotel was she at, why Hong Kong and not Bangkok. He resorted to whining, he'd been surcharged £54 a day at the Mandarin, some late-booking thing. Helen thought, what was Morris's dictum, Great Britain exports her best menfolk, her worst women?

The slam was the assault of the subtropics. The colony hadn't lost the knack. So many changes! The heat was the same, the traffic, verve, the gain-driven pandemonium the norm. She looked for similarities with the Hong Kong she had known over twenty years before, but that first day she was defeated.

Kai Tak's size! The cleaning amahs appearing from holes in runways to crouch endearingly in the aeroplane's shade. A quarter of a century back, the aerodrome had been a stone strip in the harbour. She didn't recognise a thing. The beautiful travel courier fizzed with energy. Hong Kong girls still had perfect bottoms, first-class honours degrees in sociology, meagre breasts, and were fervent about money. Use the Hang Seng Bank, no commission and a good exchange rate; street money-changers charged over 10 percent, do avoid them. Helen listened dutifully to the girl's prattle on the coach, managed not to smile when the girl said to the driver in Cantonese, 'This lot will be broke by Monday.'

Quite the worst of it was that Helen had no bearings. It was ridiculous. She wandered from the hotel, sun-blinded. What was Kellet Island doing among traffic? St John's Cathedral once dominated the skyline; she finally found it huddled below impossible flyovers and filled with Filipinos. She had picked a hotel right on the Star Ferry; except she no longer recognised the pier. And goodness, if anybody knew Wanchai, she did, had. But now you *drove underneath* the harbour, a choice of tunnels. You didn't need to catch the bus for Sham Shui Po; you got the Tube.

Everything was gone, altered. Even the Kowloon-Canton Railway clock tower had been moved; it stood forlornly on the waterfront, a posh ectopic wart.

So she almost wept with joy when, walking south from those impossible waterfront high-rises, she heard a familiar whirring. She ran, unmanageable heels and in that heat, blundering among crowds, apologising reflexly in regenerating Cantonese—and beheld a real live tram! Calamitously discoloured instead of sap green and shamefully covered in adverts, but there it undoubtedly was: old, noisy, exasperating, and not altered in the slightest. Deliriously happy, she fumbled in her handbag, buffeted by pedestrians. The hotel's transport pass worked for the tram, she discovered. You still got on at the rear, alighted from the front.

To orientate, she decided to go the dear tram's whole journey, Shau Ki Wan (maddeningly spelled six different ways) to Kennedy Town. She had always loved Hong Kong's trams. This moved as ever like a great indifferent whale among shoals of fish. Standing was still allowed on the top deck, compulsory even. The impossible standing hurled you about, yes, but the tram gave her points of reference and proved she was right to come. Hong Kong was the place.

To a stranger, she thought, getting a seat at Pedder Street, these points might not seem much. To Helen, they were a lifeline. She scored yet more successes on the clamorous swaying run out of Sheung Wan: a wicker tray of fish sun-drying on top of a tram stop; traffic signs obscured by dangles of flattened ducks draped to desiccate. She began to list them, for there might be no time when she confronted Evadne. Of *course* there were differences, bound to be. The absence of junks in the harbour, you simply couldn't lose 20,000, each one galleon-size with families, goats, chickens, garden boxes. And the harbour was clean; where was the floating dross? (She remembered bad oranges bobbing in an oily slick of planks and plastic.) Then she spotted a familiar doorway god by an offal shop, with his red light glowing on his tribute of four piled oranges, so the colony had not altered altogether beneath its tumult.

Irritation, her hallmark of well-being, returned. She became quite optimistic, sure now that she was right to fight here. She concentrated on letting herself be annoyed. It was patently absurd for the tram route to make that absurd loop. Western Market was simply no excuse. And why did the terminus skulk in a side street near a tatty godown? Twenty-five years ago she had written sternly to the Tramways Authority, still nothing done!

She cooled on the return journey, confidently noting more unchanges. Murder was a stupid, pretentious word, so, quickly, make memory use its DEL key with its reverse arrow. Only foreigners resorted to such exaggerations. She thought of her decision, six months old now, instead as 'that M word'. Teutons, psychotics all, would say 'murder' outright; and gormless Gauls; and carping Celts awash in self-pity pretending to love their slithery P and Q languages none of them could speak. Plus Americans, to whom life was code for death as merriment. No, she thought, proudly riding the crowded tram, we English are above it all. Helen knew her attitude was not nationalism; no, it was there like Royal Doulton, to be brought out on the right occasion. English murderers like Jack the Ripper were probably throwbacks, Levantines cloned from an Armada wreck, who knew?

FOR TWO DAYS Helen excavated *her* Hong Kong. Statue Square, such as it was; the Supreme Court building, minute and chasmed; the old temple in Hollywood Road above Cat Street. It was duty, something she never shirked. The cuckoo survives by conviction; host fledglings die for lack of it. Mood was everything, morale to a warrior. She had trained herself for half a year to be a cuckoo of mood. The intolerable alternative was to suffer yet more defeat at Evadne's hands.

To her astonishment, her language came back with thrilling slickness. She bartered for sandals with aplomb. Only occasionally did she falter, stricken, as when explaining her circumstances to a Des Voeux Road shopkeeper, *My husband, who passed away a few months since*... remembering in the nick of time ohmyGod there's no relative pronoun in Cantonese. A narrow squeak. Helen resorted to terse unconvolutions and took the stand-up comedian's oath: *Stick to one-liners!*

By the third day her points of reference formed a veritable library. It included surprising minutiae like, the Hakka women road-diggers wore jeans now instead of black cotton trousers; and, my goodness, *thousand* dollar notes? The cadres of exhausted suited youths on the *Shining Star* now dozed clutching portable phones. And so on.

Her mood just right, she rang Evadne.

'NO, EVADNE, I wouldn't have dreamt of coming a second sooner.' Helen was firm. 'Jet-lag conversation? I endured enough of those when we lived here, thank you very much!'

'I began to worry!' Evadne told Helen. 'Flying tomorrow and everything!' Evadne gave one of her troubled falsetto laughs, supervising supper. Helen wondered how on earth George had managed to stand those insane giggles, seeing the middle-aged bitch on sly holidays year after year, but gave an approving smile of innocence. 'I wouldn't have been able to introduce Rol, show you the flat!'

Helen's apologetic smile included Rol Groombridge, Evadne's nearly famous writer. Out of his depth, poor man, what with two women and vexed his tame typist was leaving for a month. 'You forget I know these flats, Evadne. Cape Mansions are the only place Hong Kong hasn't obliterated.'

Evadne was determined to spot possible gloom, her prophylactic proving her irreplaceable qualities. 'Jenny has her foibles, Helen!'

Evadne's Filipino live-out amah (but now you said maid) was bickering in the kitchen with Rol's Hong Kong Cantonese live-in amah Ah Fung (you still said amah). Helen's spirits rose.

'Oh, I'll manage.' She bided her time. Then, when Evadne simply had to go and see what was delaying the blueberry tart, Helen started her campaign with quiet humour. 'It's the oldest things I *do* manage.'

'What things?' Rol said, with the politeness that just avoids silence.

'It sounds silly. I'd quite forgotten it's proper to join others' conversations. I had a high old time on the tram, two old *fokis* about water bills.'

Rol showed a flicker of interest. 'You speak Cantonese?'

'I did,' with a trace of rue. 'It's coming back.'

It better had be. The revision course at London's School of Oriental Studies cost the earth and was riddled with neurotic linguists. It was the first of her weapons, honed over five hard months. She laughed shyly, better than Evadne's mad cackle any day. 'Hong Kong's street puppeteers had the oddest speech mannerisms. Do they still perform near Cleverly Street, sort of Punch and Judy? Such wondrous stories! I loved *The White-Haired Girl*. No wonder that legend dominated all China throughout the sixties. And every *shroff* used the abacus, not now. And *cheong-saams* were everywhere. I haven't seen a one... But I'm sorry, you'll know all that. Am I talking too much?'

'No—'

She coursed on, preventing his excuses. Of course he didn't know. You had to have lived in the colony through that murderous Red Guard mayhem, the curfews, bombs, the droughts, the lunatic ideologies of those days. And hadn't Evadne's friendly letters to her explained how her beloved nearly famous writer wanted to create the last great colonial novel—and failed, and failed, and failed?

Helen spoke urbanely of the festivals, Cantonese jokes ('Don't they simply love puns...?') and so on, until it was, 'Oh, here comes Evadne!'

Evadne was followed by the two sulky servants. The blueberry thing was fine. Their row was all about cream, Jenny battling to add sugar, Manila style, Ah Fung ginger. Helen made a timely postponement of using weapon two. She ascertained, by canny eavesdropping, that Jenny, Catholic sureness translated to ethnic disdain, had virtually no Cantonese; Ah Fung's muttered blame proved it. The minute Helen got the chance—Jenny triumphant in the kitchen, Ah Fung siding away, Evadne doling out her last drop of Macau Portuguese red—she managed with quiet amiability to tell the amah to make less noise. Ah Fung was so astonished hearing correct tonal Cantonese that she almost dropped the plates with a delighted 'Waaaiiii'. Helen instantly knew she had an ally: tenacious, opinionated, and utterly reliable.

Helen decided not to mention her word-processing proficiency until Rol escorted her to the bus. It was a short walk down Mount Davis Road, past his house at Felix Villas. He showed the colonist's relief at not having to drive a guest to some hotel. Helen insisted, no, the bus was fine. Gracious, she'd lived here years!

She could tell Rol was glad the evening was over, meeting Evadne's middle-aged friend. The only reason he'd agreed to come was that he would need access to his manuscripts. Evadne stored them, her air-conditioned flat saving his papers from Hong Kong's corrosive summer moulds. Impossible to air-condition his antique four-storeyed house; those grey flappy fans always had been a waste of time, Helen agreed. She bade Evadne a teary goodbye, which was really marvellous of her, seeing the bitch was only leaving to rake in the profits—holiday home at Scratby-on-Sea, time shares in Tuscany, Spain, some trust fund—from two decades of illicit consorting with Helen's George, deceased. Poor George, hoarding Evadne's explicit letters. Thank God it was she, Helen, and not one of the children who had found Evadne's filed letters ('Tax: Valued-Added'; 'Private: Confidential'). She had brooded a fortnight, then decided to rid herself of Evadne. The traitorous cow had earned sanctions, along with real estate. Fair's fair.

Strolling in the hot humid night with Evadne's nearly-made-it writer, Helen used weapon two.

'I miss the bauhinias, Rol,' she said after the have-a-nice-flight goodbyes. 'Their roots practically held the mountainside up! And the Wall-Building Ghost—it lived along this stretch—never lifted a finger to prevent landslides.' She was speaking humorously.

Rol coughed, hesitant. 'You know the colony well.'

'Nothing of the kind! I *knew* it *almost* well. Now I'm quite lost. If they rebuild the Gloucester Tea Rooms I might just get my bearings!' She let his unamused chuckle go. 'The colony's ladies used to congregate in such splendour! I called them The Ladies Who Tea! Not so ritzy as these Samsonite executives in the five-stars in Central, but immeasurably grander!'

They waited to let a car go by, dragged by its cone of headlights.

'I'm interested in the colony as it was,' Rol said. 'I've only been here five years.'

'Oh, then I'm the one for you!' She masked her elation with a little sadness. 'Hardly a commendation, is it, to be valued for reminiscence!' He said nothing. There was enough light to walk by, gateway lamps and the sky glowing with monetary heat. 'The apple lady used to come up here. Cantonese, looked a Hakka but was a true Punti, people said. Such a chatterbox! Not at all like these young salesmen you suffer now. They really aren't up to scratch, not even in word-processing.'

'You do word-processing?'

Helen knew he wrote longhand, revising on Evadne's laboured typescripts, three months each draft. Evadne's letters to Helen had explained that Rol held strong views against composing on electronics.

'Mhhh? Oh, yes. I do my brother's manuscripts.' She didn't, of course. She gave a light non-Evadne laugh, to reassure Rol that her brother was no threat to a nearly-famous writer like himself. 'Every Friday, a hundred thousand words, clockwork.'

'A week?'

'Edited script, the rate Bernard goes. Four weeks from autograph; takes longer, you see. He's in administration,' she invented, safely deleting her non-writing gardener sibling. 'Bores for England—was that Muggeridge's phrase?'

'Autograph manuscript typed in a month, edited in a week?'

'Fortnight and four days respectively, *if* you please! Unless I have something else on.' She made herself sound dismissive, for an instrument is innocent. She asked with a hint of awe, 'Do you compose on a PC?'

'No.'

'Oh. Well, if there *is* anything I can do...' She tutted as they reached the main road to Kennedy Town. 'What a pity they've built that terrible wall! I used to run to this very spot to see the typhoon signal on Green Island. It was quite an occasion, the amahs relaying my shout up to the squatter shacks, scores of thousands of refugees in lean-to shelters up the hillside *nullahs*.'

The 5B bus was predictably but annoyingly punctual. She hurriedly squeezed in shy envy at Evadne's superb luck at helping a 'real writer'. She also got in one or two last zingers: 'Oh, do please tell your amah—Ah Fung, isn't it?—that cobra is $63 a catty in Causeway Bay. Scandalous! And deer tails are cheapest in Wanchai. Do you let her cook Cantonese? How rare street opium smokers are now along Hollywood Road! And I've hardly seen a single one in Tsim Sha Tsui; the influence of the Tube, do you suppose...?' Et babblingly cetera.

Then she was on the bus, making the driver grin by betting him a dollar he couldn't take the bus via the Wanchai Star Ferry, making sure Rol heard her oven-ready speech.

Her goodbye smile was as casual as she could make it.

She felt she had got it right, at least made a start on Evadne's downfall. A writer wanting to break the colonial perception barrier needed the local language, indigenous folklore, and docile non-creativity among all others. Hitherto, Rol Groombridge had enjoyed only the last, in Evadne. Helen convincingly offered him all three.

After which Evadne could resume her suicidal gestures, in her cramped little nest in Cape Mansions. Cyclical depressions had been Evadne's speciality until three years ago when she had 'found'—her execrable term—Rol, whose literary demands cured her of 'all that nonsense'. Helen had analysed this before coming to flat-sit for Evadne. The bitch's depressions had possibly been worsened by George's inability to cut free from Helen and marry the cow. George could never have done it; too orthodox, too addicted to his surreptitious holidays with his breathy plump Chanel-scented mare. The cache of letters had formed a decisional matrix. (Helen had heard the term at night school: computers, Intensive Unit Three-C. She had excelled.)

The 5B dropped her off in Central District, which cartographers still tried to con everybody into calling Victoria. She told the concierge she would be leaving in the morning.

She took up residence in Evadne's flat in Cape Mansions as arranged.

EVADNE FLEW ON TIME, thank goodness, leaving the colony ethnically cleansed. Helen began war instantly. Jenny seemed willing to put up with the situation. A month was not long.

Three days of Helen's vigorous sweetness put paid to the Filipino. It was easy. Evadne's letters to Helen—all camouflage, year after year, cloaking the real correspondence with Hoarder George—had detailed Evadne's perennial bribes that kept the invaluable Jenny from leaving her. Helen picked at Jenny, found fault with everything. She was joyously matter of fact, seeing her off when the crunch came then, satisfyingly alone, got down to business.

She surveyed the flat, wasting no time gloating. Those Third World Catholics learned guilt well, par for the course, but could never come to grips with hate. That required true English constancy. Another word for propriety, perhaps, once so evident in the Gloucester Tea Rooms? Helen smiled, enjoying the increased elbow room.

Rol's manuscripts were heaped in boxes, neatly labelled and stacked on two shelves in the spare bedroom Helen was to use. So as not to be taken by surprise, she immediately perused several, and was disappointed. Did Rol Groombridge really have the makings of a latter-day Somerset Maugham? Firmly she laid the question aside. Rol's literary excellence was irrelevant. She had to be about her task, which was to keep her image clear in Rol's nearly-famous mind. Humble Mrs Blake type helper, language fluency, super manuscript: he would summon her before long, as if slavery was an unearned

knighthood for which one ought to be grovellingly grateful.
The call would come.

Making breakfast, Helen found she was actually enjoying
herself. She admired the lovely view over the Lamma Channel almost as much as she admired herself. As reward, she re-
arranged all the furniture, and got rid of two of Evadne's
pictures. (One drained all possible colour from the walls, the
other looked a nasty spillage). The curtains were eminently
swappable. One pair had to go.

For two days more she made satisfying judgements of this
kind. Then she went across to ask Ah Fung's help in making
a Chiu Chow dish. She reduced the amah to helpless laughter
at her ineptitude, Swatow fried chicken with cheunjew sauce.
With humility, she deferred to the amah's bullying instruction and left a large deposit of gossip about Visit-Missie's cu-
linary mistakes and exploration of the island. She knew Ah
Fung would recount them to Rol in her limited English. He
would—should—be impressed by Helen's search for old
villages and departed people. She had included remembered
disasters—mudslides, droughts, riots, famous financial collapses, typhoons, scandals, folklore. Of course, back home she
had sweated blood over her old diaries, phoned half-forgotten
acquaintants on the thinnest pretexts, really slogged.

Watching the sun set—you could just see it going down over
the Pearl River if you stretched—she felt gratified. If she had
Rol's ambitions right, he would find her irresistible. Just
across the road, for God's sake, the 'research' a writer craved.
She would seem a window on the colony's past, his chance. He
must take it.

He reviewed books, examined local school Eng. Lit., taught
part-time in a couple of drossy academies. She had delved, was
confident nothing about him would take her by surprise. The
two newspapers—*South China Morning Post*, the old *Standard*—advertised jobs she could have walked into. If nothing
came of this before Evadne got back from cashing in on
George's death, well it might be necessary to think again.

The phone rang. It was Rol inviting her to supper: would tomorrow be all right? nothing special, seeing she was on her own.

Helen said diffidently, 'Why, how kind! Are you sure? I don't want to interrupt . . .' Effortless, in how many days?

FROM THERE, she found it surprisingly hard going. Ah Fung was as valuable as Helen had predicted. Rol himself proved the problem. She wondered if she had overdone it, that first supper, inserting her gems to quite good effect, she thought. It came to her that she had not fathomed the creative writer's paranoia.

She changed her tactic when, on guard, Rol said the language was beyond him. He had tried.

'I don't know anyone who hasn't tried and given up.' It was said in self-defence. 'Those tones finish you.'

'I was just lucky,' Helen apologised quickly, shaking her hair, done that very day at the New Scholar Hairdresser in Bonham Road, still there, like Government House. 'Some quirk in me caught the Cantonese tonality. Two hard years. Then it became a hobby. I'm so uncreative,' she said, paper-trailing for him like mad. God, what a *dawdler*. 'Little oddities, like one syllable having several meanings, according to the pitch. And the use of opposite meanings! Yesterday I used the original word for tongue instead of a mutated verb!' She laughed, fanning herself in mock relief.

He watched her warily, impressed but not following. She hoped her altered course didn't show and went on, 'I've kept it up, bits at a time. But you'd think I'd have found some way to use it, over two decades. Except it's going to be obsolete in what, three years and China takes Hong Kong back? Everybody'll have to speak Mandarin, all that *shir-bu-shir* business. Ugh!' She shivered, smiled. 'Then I *shall* be an anachronism.'

'There will be a resurgence of interest. As now for the fifties.'

'Will there?' she asked, being bovine.

'Literature goes in cycles,' he pronounced. Ah Fung flopped in with the sweet millet soup, finish of her grand little meal.

Any moment now she'd bring out an orange in a brown paper bag for Missie to take home, the traditional one for the road.

'Does it?' Helen asked, round of eye.

'It seems to.' He nodded pontifically, shadows whipping across his face in synchrony with the beating fan. 'There are various theories, none successful.'

'Really?' She was humble, intent.

He began to expound, very much as she supposed he must to students in his seminars along Caine Road, Wednesdays. She listened, very adoration of the magus. As she left that evening (bagged orange at the door, Ah Fung laughing making the presentation) Rol cleared his throat and made the concession she needed.

'Look, Helen. If you really are at a loose end, you could do me a couple of pages . . .'

Helen gasped in awe, delight, amazement, sheer grovelling exultation at being so favoured. She cried out that her luck was in and that she hoped she was up to his standards . . .

That night she did not sleep. Her excitement at landing him was less than she'd expected, for Rol the nearly-made-it creative writer was a dud. He would never make it in a million years. The pieces she'd read were derivatively mundane. She made tea about three o'clock and looked out at the sheen of the South China Sea, and the ugly coal-fired power station some lunatic planners had built near Yung Shue Wan to mar paradise.

Rol could write for ever, he'd be ninth-rate. As somebody famous once said, 'Writing? That's *typing*.' Rol had the academic's disease of yardage and replication. Helen had assembled a file of writers' Ten Commandments, Robert McKee to Mario Puzo, and believed not a single line.

By dawn, she realised Evadne would now be Home and taking possession of the Scratby pavilion, the time share properties, milking George's probate. She seethed, deliberately broke one of Evadne's best cups, saying 'Whoops!' as she flung the saucer after it. She swept up and binned the fragments with relish.

SHE REPORTED FOR DUTY on time, collected Rol's two chapters, not mere pages, and whacked them off on her PC, working through the next day. It was a brilliant job, a tabulated list of spellings, flagged stickers to show where she queried his accuracy—the colony's folklore, speech idioms. She was exhausted, but chattering brightly with Ah Fung about weird Fukienese sauces when Rol returned home. She made a breathlessly deferential exit.

He rang, casual, about eight o'clock, donated airy thanks and asked her over for a drink. She did her giddy are-you-sure act, and sprinted across before he changed his mind. Seen as human endeavour, of course, she was throwing good time after bad. But seen as part of the Destroy-Evadne campaign it was loading the guns.

The evening was dire. Rol started worriedly over his story word by weary word. Had Helen been a man she'd have called Rol's masterpiece utter crap, but convent schooling had been convent schooling in her day and she had to live with it. His balderdash concerned a prim Hong Kong Cantonese girl dragged into a Customs fraud and heading for perdition possibly by Chapter Seven. Helen pretended to be enthralled by Rol's imagination, ecstatic at his grasp of 'Hong Kong's inner self'. His book, she guessed tiredly as ten o'clock chimed from his copy-Swiss hall clock (Haiphong Road, $40 HK), would be some recycled metaphor for the demise of colonial life in a changing new world order, if you please.

'Tremendous!' she exclaimed when Rol modestly outlined exactly that about half-eleven. 'I want to know what happens! Does she survive . . . ?'

Released at one a.m., she went back to Evadne's flat and to bed, knowing that soon she would be indispensable, and Evadne superfluous. Tit for tat, really, was her goodnight thought, for hadn't that sow displaced me, George's wife? The fact is, you can *not* be a half-hearted cuckoo. You had not merely to supplant but throw out the enemy fledgling to certain death. Evadne's long history of teetering on the edge of depression, from which entering Rol's service had clearly rescued her, would provide the final topple. It was eminently satisfying. Half-measures were repellent. She slept, and awoke refreshed and singing.

THE MONTH PASSED with intolerable swiftness. Rol's creation progressed apace. Helen settled his romanisation problems, finally going for a miserable concoction of the ugly Meyer-Wempe system without those grotesque accents. He of course worried what academic linguists might say. She cheerily got on with his novel, saying to herself what did Yale University know anyway. Unless some easy-touch publisher had a rush of blood to the head Rol's tripe would never see the light of printed day anyhow.

Two cards had come from Evadne, claptrap about relatives cluttering up the Cotswolds, hasn't Home changed and all that. Helen used them to line the kitchen waste bin. Two others, filled with worship, arrived at Rol's. Helen read them before Rol arrived home—she mostly worked at Felix Villas now, having brought a compatible laptop. This had the benefits of conscripting Ah Fung, who was dismayed by the prospect of losing her Cantonese-speaking Missie, and of reducing the pile of typescripts in Evadne's flat. Helen presented Rol with the first disc, containing a dozen old review articles. 'You see, Rol,' she lied gravely, 'discs last for ever, and are a permanent record for posterity.'

He saw the wisdom of that, and wrote and wrote.

His story got worse. The man had very little imagination; his mundanities and fourth-form metaphors were driving her to screaming pitch. But war is war, and she'd come too far, with Evadne's third card promising she'd return on time. Meanwhile Rol's heroine was involved in a shoot-out near Stonecutter's Island between two Pearl River Junks while a Royal Navy minesweeper, Christ, stood off helplessly in deeper water symbolising Western inadequacy. Helen was too sickened to correct that particular chapter. Rol was clearly a moron.

Later, she was to wonder if it was her growing contempt for the man that led to his taking her into his bed in that last week. She was utterly astonished. She had of course vaguely wondered if he and Evadne had ever 'taken steps', as she mentally classified sexual activities. Wholly unprepared, she went through the carnalities with a sort of anxious preoccupation rather than anything approaching passion, though he entered into it with the male's usual efficient abandon. There was very little manoeuvre, no gradual seduction. It was almost matter of fact. Rol seemed gratified—she had always checked with George immediately after, at least in the first few years, after which it had fallen off as an event.

She urgently wanted to know if dear Evadne had brought Rol to this pitch of activity, but wisely forbore asking. It was the night Ah Fung slept out—she had a child in Hung Hom, bus from Robinson Road then the ferry direct from Wanchai, dollar-twenty—so presumably Rol had decided on his move well beforehand. It took some moments to plot her response. She finally opted, more from doubt than conviction, to be mistily gratified. It worked well. To her further surprise she found herself making love a second time, not without positional difficulty and a few bruises that might need Max Factor pancake. Eventually when he was quiet she dozed, wondering if Whiteway's Store was still on the harbourside; they always stocked that invaluable Leichner heavy-duty make-up in the old days. But even such worries were superfluous, for who was to accuse her? George was gone. Rol seemed replete, and men, in her limited experience, always declined responsibility for damage. Except, a bruise and an air of repletion might prove a telling opportunistic weapon when Evadne arrived, displayed with a welcome-home-guess-what innocence.

With two days to go—Helen evasively humble, Rol not mentioning That Night—he asked what she was going to do when Evadne returned. Helen showed quite good sadness and said she would go Home, just as the really interesting Chinese festivals were approaching and—she did a really sincere blush—she had more reasons than ever for wanting to stay.

Rol said she could always lodge in Felix Villas, he had plenty of room, and his book was reaching a critical juncture.

Helen hesitated. 'Won't Evadne mind, Rol? I'd hate to seem, well, *pushy* . . .'

When Evadne's flight declined at that strange angle behind the *MOTOROLA* sign on Kowloon side into Kai Tak, Helen wasn't there to meet her, and she made certain the phone was unanswered. She strolled in an hour after Evadne reached the flat, and made minimal fuss. Evadne, tired, was taken aback by the disposition of the furniture.

Helen assumed an abstracted air, several times saying, 'Mmmmh?' as if thinking of something else. She explained Jenny's departure: some Filipino tantrum she couldn't quite understand, no forwarding address but it was probably all to the good. Then, with Evadne still reeling, Helen sweetly said she was staying with Rol, because his writing must come first. She asked absently after Evadne's friends at Home, but was unable to resist getting their names wrong.

She left Evadne to her own devices after thirty minutes. As she left, she called instructions over her shoulder about milk in the fridge, the small air-conditioner being on the blink, and so forth.

Pleased, she told Rol that Evadne was too tired to call; the flight had aged her. She thought she'd been quite superb.

THE LONELINESS of Hong Kong, Helen knew, is not the enervating Middle East kind. It does one of two things. It prods the expatriate into being an entrepreneur of breathtaking flair, or it dooms. Mix in sports, zoom into the Hong Kong Singers' next *Iolanthe*, or stay alone and rot. The suicide rate is prodigious among certain segments.

As time went by, Evadne's withdrawal into the predictable depression became increasingly evident. Helen grew impatient. The woman was clearly superfluous, so what on earth was the delay, for heaven's sake? She should leave Planet Earth without more ado. The round of coffee mornings, a narrow circuit, quickly dried up for the stupid mare, and her desperate forays into social events only exposed her as a lonely woman craving company in a confined place that, rushing from hour to dollar-driven hour, showed no compassion. Helen made sure she saw her once or twice, simply to remind Evadne of her inadequacies.

Incredibly it took an amazing four months for Evadne to do the necessary. Helen wondered if she should persuade Rol to incorporate Evadne's tumble from her Cape Mansions balcony into his manuscript, but his brain was too set in its ways.

She had to face it, when at last Ah Fung flapped in, horrified, just as Helen arrived back, the amah calling that a Missie had fallen from a flat across the road and ambulances and the police were already... The terrible truth was that Rol was simply not up to it. His novel was rubbish—who'd believe the worn symbolism of a train entering a tunnel to conclude *three* chapters? His characters were wooden. She had slaved to make him see sense about prostitution—it was no shame to Hong Kong, never had been. The stupid man simply couldn't leave Edwardian Hampstead. She sent flowers for Evadne: the colonial cemetery in Happy Valley, a race day.

She slept with Rol regularly now. They made love. She became Missie at Number Four, Felix Villas. Ah Fung was delighted with her as long as she made regular mistakes in buying or ordering, that the amah could laugh about with other Chinese amahs on the terraces. She did his word-processing, translated his Cantonese, explained festival ceremonies, told how the colony really was a quarter of a century before.

Hopeless, all terrifyingly hopeless. In short, a complete waste of time.

The book was rejected eight months later, naturally. Rol was almost suicidal, a spin-off she disliked. He faced her over supper, haggard. 'What's wrong Helen? Nine publishers! I did everything right. All the ingredients: history, social details language!'

Darling, she should have said, *your themes are undergraduate, like Cambridge Fringe on telly; Campus Capers, in Dickie Henderson's damning phrase.*

Instead, 'There's nothing wrong, darling!' she cried loyally. 'It's wonderful, the great colonial novel, Booker material!'

'I'm lost, Helen!'

'I have an idea, darling.' She found the right words after rather fetching supportive smiles across the tureen of black faced carp congee. 'Could it be that you are...well, stale. Look how you've positively *slogged*, ever since whatsername Evadne Thing, proved so useless.'

'I can't stop now!'

She said firmly, 'Of course you can't. But you deserve a rest. Recharge your batteries!' She winced at that, but the idiot's brow cleared.

'And not rewrite?'

She smiled at the sacrilege. 'Not you, darling. *Me*!'

'You?' His paranoia resurfaced, but she was as disarming as ever.

'Of course, darling! Who else? Then you could come back to the redraft refreshed!'

'You think so?'

She smiled endearingly through the candle flames at his anxious face. 'Solved? I promise I'll have it organised in a month's time.'

Which was how they left it that night.

THE TROUBLE WAS, Helen thought, in her—well, in Rol's so far—elegant old house, looking out over the quiet waters to Lamma Island, that she had fallen for Hong Kong all over again. Just as when she was young, the children at Glenealey School, George in his Government accounts job. Hong Kong had recaptured her heart. Yet she'd accomplished her task; shouldn't she simply go?

The whole colony seemed silent tonight. Rol was late, revision classes at Sai Ying Pun. Traffic had dwindled. The buses to Aberdeen on the lower road ran muted, hardly a gear change. The ships glided in the sunset, the huge black butterflies and the birds stuporous, hardly making it to the next hibiscus.

There was something else, though. She had not touched Rol's manuscript lately. There was no need. Her own colonial novel, offered under her maiden name, was already accepted. The question was whether Rol was superfluous. He suspected nothing about Evadne's death, of course. Helen could share her success with him, just as creatures shared a living space in the wild, got along, made the best of things. She could tell the publishers it was a joint authorship.

But the more she thought the more Rol seemed impedimenta, not needed on voyage. Or was he? This, after all, might actually *be* her destined voyage. He was acceptable, served. If

she decided on partnership, they might wed. He was already
dependent on her. Think of Ah Fung's excitement at a marriage feast, the 'face' the amah would gain! It would be worth
it for that. But how would Rol view a wife/lover who was a
successful creative writer? Somebody threatening his space, in
the modern phrase?

Or she could convince Rol that her book was simply a re-
hash of his . . . Hong Kong was destined to vanish off the map
in three years; worth batting out time, surely?

In the twilight she looked down the steep hillside, down
among the bauhinia trees with their gentle pastel flowers, the
hibiscus, the bougainvillaeas, and the unceasing loyal lanta-
nas. Hong Kong's picturesque heights were paradise. So
beautiful, so serene, but such a long way for somebody to fall.

CLEWSEY'S CLICHÉS

CONRA:AN GLORVM EXER

QUICK, CHAPS! THE SWINE HAVE GOT PHYLLIS AGAIN.

DISHONOURABLE MEMBERS

★

CAROLE RAWCLIFFE

Distinguished historian, Carole Rawcliffe, shows us that true-life crime in high places surpasses even the most fevered imagination of the crime writer.

CONTRARY TO EXPECTATIONS, the readiness of publicity-hungry MPs to admit first microphones and then television cameras into the chamber of the House of Commons has done little to improve their collective image. Far from being impressed at the sight of democracy at work, listeners and viewers have been deeply disillusioned by the conduct of their elected representatives. The hooting and braying of Tory backwoodsmen, fresh from the hunting field or the stands at Twickenham, combine with the jeers and cheers of their opponents to create an atmosphere not unlike that of a cross-Channel ferry loaded to the gunwales with inebriated football hooligans.

Just occasionally, during a lull in the hubbub, some mordant (almost *sotto voce*) aside about the mental capacities or personal attributes of an Honourable Member may be heard in the ranks of the militant left, but this merely serves to confirm the impression that when they are not being uncouth or loutish, MPs delight in malice and vituperation. Of course, as social commentators never cease to tell us, the dramatic decline from the days when Members were *gentlemen*, and behaved as such, is symptomatic of a general collapse in national

standards. With such an example before them is it surprising
that the young have nothing but contempt for authority?

But historians take a rather different view. Indeed, to those
familiar with Parliament's 700 or more years of stormy (and
sometimes uncertain) progress, today's MPs seem a tame and
unusually law-abiding bunch, models of seemly conduct with
barely a criminal record between them. A few convictions for
dangerous driving, perhaps, and maybe even the occasional
whisper of fraud or insider dealing, but what are these com-
pared with the histories of murder, arson, rape, mayhem and
even mutiny which characterised so many of their predeces-
sors?

A recent study of the 3,173 individuals who entered the
House of Commons during the late fourteenth and early fifteenth centuries[1] enables us for the first time to take a close
look at the activities of the early forerunners of such contemporary heroes as Michael Heseltine and Dennis Skinner, men
to whom a brief flurry with the mace or outburst of unparlia-
mentary language would seem a poor substitute for serious
action with a double-headed axe or broadsword.

The career of the Cornish knight, Sir Henry Ilcombe, pro-
vides a case in point, being marked from the start by a singu-
larly underdeveloped sense of *meum* and *teum*, which involved
him in frequent poaching expeditions on neighbouring estates. In order to finance an extravagant lifestyle and pay off
some of his mounting debts, he hit upon the idea of abduct-
ing a wealthy widow, although things went badly wrong from
the outset.

Never one for the subtle approach, Ilcombe led a raiding
party of armed men to her manor house, sacked it and carried off all her possessions. The widow herself was allegedly
raped and held captive, but she proved more than a match for
her assailant by escaping and taking him to law. By the time
the case came before the courts, in 1381, Sir Henry had com-

---

[1] *The House of Commons 1386-1421*, ed J.S. Roskell, L.S. Clark and C.
Rawcliffe (4 vols, Alan Sutton, 1993). All material cited in the text appears in these volumes, in the biographies of individual MPs, who are listed
in alphabetical order.

pounded his offence by forging a papal bull (to prove a legal marriage had taken place), and then made matters worse by attempting to murder his reluctant bride on the quayside at Westminster.

This homicidal attack, launched on her and her protector, Guy, Lord Brian, within the purlieus of the Court of King's Bench, caused some concern to the authorities (who generally accepted the abduction of rich heiresses as an unpalatable but inescapable fact of life), so Ilcombe decided to make himself scarce for a while until the fuss died down. King Richard's uncle, the Earl of Cambridge, was just about to lead a military expedition to Portugal, and seemed glad to recruit a man of Sir Henry's experience, however ingloriously obtained, although he soon had cause to regret his decision once the knight and his brothers, who had accompanied him, began plotting a mutiny.

The expedition proved a total fiasco, largely as a result of the Ilcombes' duplicitous behaviour, and on their return to England they took to the Welsh hills, where they and their gang of ruffians survived by banditry and cattle-stealing for the next couple of years. Even so, since the English medieval state possessed a conveniently short memory so far as all but the most heinous cases of treason were concerned, it was only a matter of time before Sir Henry managed to inveigle his way back into polite society.

The award of a royal pardon, forgiving him all his past excesses, and, no doubt even more surprising to modern day readers, the subsequent formalisation of his marriage to the unfortunate widow (whose opinion of the proceedings is not recorded) marked a process of rehabilitation, culminating, in 1388, in his election to Parliament as Member for Cornwall. Given the circumstances of his early life, Ilcombe's appointment as county coroner seems particularly ironic, but contemporaries were rarely disposed to make much of a connection between private morality and public office, regarding the two as quite separate and unrelated spheres of human endeavour.

Although remarkable for the diversity of his criminal activities, Sir Henry was by no means the only adventurer to take a seat in the late fourteenth-century House of Commons. His colleague, Sir John Thornbury, who, in his youth had belonged to the notorious 'White Company' of international mercenaries, appears, if anything, to have been even more colourful. By the date of his return to Parliament, in 1391, he could look back on a long and highly profitable career as a *condottiere* in Italy, where he had amassed a fortune while commanding the papal armies in Gregory XI's war against the Visconti.

Not all the vast store of booty with which Sir John bought his way into the ranks of the English country gentry had, however, been honourably or legally come by: at all events, he considered it expedient to mark his transition from freebooter to landowner by purchasing a royal pardon for

> all seditions, adhesions to the King's enemies and favour shown them in England and abroad, captures or deliveries of towns, castles and fortresses without licence, breaches of truces and safe-conducts, sales of castles and cities in England, Brittany and Gascony, violations and forgeries of the King's seal…and all captures of ships or piracy on the high seas and in port in times of truce.

Far from passing judgement on this remarkable catalogue of felonies, Sir John's parliamentary associates seem to have held him in considerable awe, tinged with envy. Few, indeed, were in any position to criticize him at all, since the great majority were either already what we would describe as hardened offenders, or were later to become implicated in serious crime. For, in each of the Parliaments which met between 1380 and 1420, *at least* a third of the 250 or so elected Members are known at some point in their careers to have faced charges of murder, arson, rape, piracy, mayhem, robbery with violence, embezzlement, fraud or forgery or to have been a party to other illegal acts largely to do with the upkeep of armed retinues and the intimidation of anyone rash enough to stand in their way.

Unlike today, these men were elected by only a small proportion of the male population, made up of freeholders in the counties and enfranchised residents in the towns, so they inevitably came from the upper reaches of both urban and rural society. With rare exceptions, the most brutal and spectacularly criminous among them were the gentry, many of whom achieved notoriety as practitioners of what one historian has perceptively dubbed 'fur collar crime'.

Just as journalists nowadays tend to report the most sensational crimes at the expense of routine but less newsworthy stories of ordinary life, so medieval chroniclers concentrated on exciting and often gory anecdotes, enthusiastically embroidering them to suit their own moral or political purposes. Contemporary legal records, from which historians derive a substantial part of their information, are also less than impartial, and present the reader with a confusing mixture of wild exaggeration and unsubstantiated charges.

It is now impossible to establish the truth of accusations levelled against the Yorkshire MP Sir Thomas Wensley, who was said to have attacked a neighbour with a gang of 200 ruffians (a nice round figure), robbed him of goods worth 200 marks (which is highly unlikely in view of the plaintiff's modest income), kept him hostage for a week without food or water and then cut off his right hand. Obviously, the aggrieved party could display his mutilated arm in court, but without Sir Thomas's version of events we should not rush to judgement, or necessarily assume that he was the unprovoked aggressor.

Yet even allowing for these words of caution with regard to our use of evidence, there can be no doubt at all that late medieval England was, by modern Western standards, an extremely violent place. Nobody would have been particularly surprised if Sir Thomas Wensley *had* behaved in such a sadistic fashion, especially during a time of intense political and social upheaval, which saw the outbreak of the Peasants' Revolt, the deposition and murder of Richard II and a series of bloody rebellions almost on the scale of civil war. Furthermore, a number of long-term factors combined, on the one hand to encourage open displays of lawlessness, and on the other to limit any effective means of discipline or punishment.

First, we should remember that national stereotypes change: just as it is hard to recognise the stoical, empire-building Roman in today's Armani-clad Italian youth, so the fifteenth-century English gentleman seems a totally different animal from his modern counterpart, famous in legend, if not in fact, for the stiffness of his upper lip and rigidity of his self-control. Foreigners arriving here 500 years ago found us excitable, prone to embarrassing displays of emotion and easily moved to wrath. Not surprisingly, the hot-tempered English needed little in the way of provocation before swords were drawn and blood was spilt.

Meetings of the Mercers' Company, to which some of the richest and most powerful merchants of the day belonged, frequently deteriorated into unseemly brawls, and even the King was known to resort to fisticuffs. Admittedly during a period of acute stress, Richard II struck one of his disaffected noblemen across the face before a crowd of bemused onlookers, and later avenged himself properly on the victim by having his head cut off. A disagreement between members of the Bedfordshire bench, in 1428, saw one justice of the peace (who was also an MP) leap across the table and hold a dagger to the throat of his associate, Lord Fanhope, sparking off a full-scale brawl which erupted down the steps of the court house into the streets of Bedford and lasted for several days.

Not even in Parliament itself could men be relied upon to curb their feelings. In 1426, when the struggle between the infant Henry VI's relatives for control of the government had reached crisis point, the threat of violence was such that Parliament had to be summoned to Leicester, well away from the London mob. Yet the rival gangs still turned up, armed to the teeth, and as the MPs also seemed in a confrontational mood

everybody was warned and ordered through the town that they should leave their weapons in their hostels, that is to say swords and shields, bows and arrows, axes, pikes and the like. But then the people took great bats [of wood] on their shoulders, and so they went. The next day they were told that they should leave their bats at their hostels: and so they took great stones in their shirts and up their sleeves. And so they went to Parliament.

For obvious reasons, this particular assembly has gone down in history as the Parliament of Bats, although in the event bloodshed was narrowly averted.

Late medieval painting and sculpture furnish us with innumerable depictions of death in all its gruesome manifestations, and serve as a reminder that life was, indeed, both uncertain and cheap. High levels of infant mortality, the grim toll of childbirth, repeated epidemics, poor levels of nutrition and the inability of the medical profession to cure quite minor diseases made the business of survival a very hit and miss affair.

In the early fifteenth century the average Florentine did not reach the age of thirty, and thus grew, as did his contemporaries throughout Europe, to regard this world as a temporary staging post on the way to better things. It was a relatively short step from the doctrine of contempt for the body as preached by the Church to the general disregard for human suffering shown by the likes of Sir Henry Ilcombe. Certainly, the mood of ingrained pessimism and resignation which followed the Black Death led men and women to expect little and fear the worst, pinning all their hopes on heavenly joys to come.

The readiness of the government to overlook, if not actually condone, homicides and other serious crimes (at least when committed by those with enough money or influence to secure royal pardons) compounded the problem. Misguided acts of clemency undermined the law and encouraged others to behave as they liked without fear of reprisals. The effect upon the wrongdoers of Westmorland, for example, of official letters excusing Sir John Lancaster MP 'diverse dissensions, unlawful assemblies, subsequent murders, insurrections and riots in breach of the peace', all perpetrated while he was responsible, as deputy sheriff, for the enforcement of order in the county, may easily be imagined.

Several of those slain in hot blood were as much the victims of medical ignorance or incompetence as they were of actual physical assault, which may have inflicted comparatively little damage. It is astonishing that so many men survived the wanton acts of mutilation which are quite regularly reported in contemporary sources. Within the space of a few years quite a number of MPs, including Richard Cheddar, Sampson Erdeswyk and Sir Henry Pierrepont, were themselves badly maimed: Cheddar losing his nose in a fight, Erdeswyk sustaining irreparable damage to his legs and feet (his severed toes were actually forced down his throat) and Pierrepont having his thumbs hacked off in Chesterfield parish church. Yet they all lived on, nourished no doubt by an all-consuming desire for revenge.

Along with many of their associates in Parliament, each of these far from innocent victims had been embroiled in a personal vendetta which rapidly got out of hand. Erdeswyk and his brother, Hugh, who himself represented both Staffordshire and Derbyshire in the House of Commons, were notorious even by fifteenth-century standards for the tenacity and vindictiveness with which they harassed their enemies. Although due allowance should be made for the evident bias of the surviving legal records, Hugh appears to have taken early to crime, gleefully embarking on such quintessentially 'fur-collar' pursuits as cattle-stealing and illegal hunting on nearby estates.

In 1407 things took a more serious turn, with the first of at least two attempts to murder another MP, Sir John Bagot, who was then active in local government as an agent of the increasingly unpopular Lancastrian regime. Dislike and jealousy of Henry IV's placemen in the north Midlands almost certainly caused the Erdeswyks' protracted feud with a group of officials at Newcastle under Lyme, against whom they waged a virtual war of attrition, laying siege to the town and burning down valuable property.

So great was the alarm felt at the collapse of order in the area that the Parliament of 1410 (which contained the usual quota of hooligans and desperadoes) took the extreme step of petitioning for the arrest of the brothers and their henchmen. The Erdeswyks were duly indicted on several charges of murder, arson, riot, trespass, the illegal recruitment of a private army and other terrorist activities, but Hugh, the chief culprit, chose to ignore successive writs of summons, appearing in court only after the award of a royal pardon, which made a complete mockery of the proceedings.

If King Henry felt that the mere threat of justice was enough to bring such hardened malefactors to heel he was sadly mistaken: within a matter of months the brothers had assembled an even larger following of armed men, this time for support in their long and bloody quarrel with the young Lord Ferrers, whose entry into his inheritance posed a threat to their local hegemony.

Once again a damning list of charges was laid against them, and once again they escaped punishment by producing the inevitable pardons. Just possibly, the newly crowned Henry V, a much stronger character than his father, may have managed by sheer force of personality to reconcile the warring factions. His decision to resume hostilities with France at this time provided an ingenious, if temporary, solution to the problem of regional violence: the worst offenders could be shipped overseas and let loose on the unsuspecting enemy.

The proliferation of gentry gangs in outlying areas of England was partly due to the unsettled way of life along the Welsh and Scottish borders, where the Crown was obliged to rely heavily upon local landowners for help in maintaining a military presence. Since the country possessed neither a standing army nor anything remotely resembling the royal navy of Nelson's day, responsibility for national defence fell upon men whose sense of patriotism sometimes lagged far behind their less honourable instincts. Mobilisation against Welsh or Scottish invaders presented a splendid pretext for settling old scores with rivals nearer home as the MP Richard Lacon discovered in the early years of the fifteenth century.

Although retained to fight Owen Glendower's Welsh rebels, Lacon was far more interested in pursuing a private vendetta against John Talbot, Lord Furnival. Such was his loathing of Talbot that he deliberately shut the gates of Shrewsbury against him as he was trying to escape the clutches of Glendower's men, and thought nothing of attacking his roops, even though they were ostensibly his own comrades in arms.

Clearly, Lacon reserved his most bitter animosity for other Englishmen, such as the Prior of Wenlock, who had slighted him in the past. He was, indeed, not only prepared to supplement his income by selling forged safe conducts to the Welsh (at 6s. 8d. each), but actually to recruit them into his service. A large contingent of rebels made up the force which he led, with clarions and trumpets', in a full-scale military operation against the priory, just before taking his seat in the House of Commons.

Lacon's conduct was remarkably similar to that of Sir Robert Ogle, a Northumbrian MP, who treacherously hired a rabble of Scots to besiege his own brother's castle at Bothal. Long before their father's death, in 1409, the two men had been at odds over the partition of the family estates, and the old knight's body still lay unburied when Sir Robert rode out at the head of a gang of mercenaries to seize by force what he felt to be rightly his.

Ignoring appeals from two local justices of the peace, Ogle destroyed the buildings and made off with large quantities of booty, provoking yet another series of protests about 'common larceny, terrible thieves and their protectors'. By a nice irony, which can hardly have been lost on those present, he was one of the northern Members who subsequently urged Parliament to take more seriously the question of law enforcement on the border.

At the best of times these areas were difficult to govern: distance and inaccessibility from Westminster, the poverty of all but a small proportion of the population, endemic disease and malnutrition, and, worst of all, the anarchic conduct of the major landowners conspired to promote a permanent state of upheaval. In such a traditionally warlike society property disputes soon got out of hand, resulting in wholesale depredation and general instability.

In 1421, the sessions of the peace at Appleby in Westmorland were disrupted by a mob under the leadership of the borough's parliamentary representative, William Thornburgh, four of whose sons then stood charged with trying to murder

the above-mentioned Sir John Lancaster. (Sir John had re
cently married into this unruly clan, but far from being wel
comed into the bosom of the family he was branded as an
unscrupulous fortune-hunter for ensnaring their wealthies
widow.) Thornburgh intended to stall the proceedings by in
timidating the justices and jury and terrorising the townsfolk
but he underestimated his adversary, who refused to be cowed
into submission.

As was often the case in the complex and constantly shift
ing world of gentry politics, Lancaster and the Thornburgh
eventually settled their differences, and together launched a
murderous assault on none other than Lancaster's own son-in
law, John Crackenthorpe MP, while he too was president ove
a judicial inquiry in the town. (This particular investigation
into 'great and outrageous riots, disturbances, quarrels and
affrays' laid the blame fairly and squarely at the door of his
turbulent relatives, many of whom had served on the county
bench as well as sitting in parliament.) Crackenthorpe man
aged to escape, but was killed in 1436 by one of the Thorn
burghs, being the second MP for Appleby to meet a violen
death within a matter of decades. The other, a lawyer named
William Soulby, had been murdered by a parliamentary col
league from Yorkshire, following a disagreement over prop
erty.

Just as the government had little choice but to allow what
now seems an unacceptable degree of licence to the gentry and
noblemen upon whom it relied for armed support in times of
crisis, so too it was obliged to tolerate insubordination, if no
open defiance, on the part of merchants and shipowners
commissioned to protect English waters. Although theoreti
cally charged with the task of keeping the seas safe for native
and friendly shipping, and attacking enemy vessels in times of
war, the captains involved showed scant regard for the nice
ties of maritime law.

Confusion or lack of up-to-date information about change
in foreign policy obviously made life difficult for the medi
eval mariner, who could easily mistake a friend for a foe at sea
In many cases, however, owners and masters alike were sim
ply out for plunder and had no compunction in attacking the

rst craft to sail into view, especially if it seemed to be laden
ith valuable merchandise. Since the machinery for punish-
g offenders and obtaining compensation was so inade-
uate, the victims of piracy were themselves often driven to
cover their losses in the same way, thus intensifying the
roblem.

Of the many medieval MPs to stand accused of piracy on a
rand international scale, William Long, the representative for
ye in Sussex, was by far the most shameless, flagrantly de-
ving the royal council, wrecking years of careful diplomacy
etween England and Flanders, and bringing the country to
e verge of war. As the leader of a squadron of intrepid sea-
en from the Cinque Ports, Long had already made a small
rtune by seizing 'enemy' cargoes at sea when, in 1405, he
lped himself to goods worth the enormous sum of £210 from
Spanish vessel travelling under letters of safe conduct.

Furious at yet another slight to his authority, the King or-
ered Long's immediate arrest, only to discover that the free-
ooters had evaded capture and were still at large. Having
ntravened the commercial treaty between England and
russia by commandeering a German ship *en route* from the
altic, Long's men, who probably felt they had nothing to
se, did even more damage to international relations as a re-
lt of their unprovoked attack on two Flemish vessels in the
hannel. Since the truce with Flanders was then only two
onths old and seemed likely to collapse at any minute, the
uthorities redoubled their efforts to place Long under lock
nd key. But all to no avail.

Far from surrendering to the warden of the Cinque Ports
whom King Henry had made personally answerable to the
raged Flemings), Long joined up with a second squadron of
rates from the West Country led by his old friend and par-
amentary colleague, John Hawley. Between them they
unched several highly successful raids on Breton shipping,
though after a while Long returned to his preferred hunting
round in the Channel, where he could more easily prey upon
e Flemish merchant fleet. By now the Duke of Burgundy's
atience was wearing thin, and in 1411 he confiscated the
oods of all Englishmen trading in Flanders, partly as com-

pensation for his subjects' losses at sea but also as a means o
forcing King Henry to stop wringing his hands and take posi
tive steps against the miscreants.

Heedless of the diplomatic consequences of his actions
Long now began openly recruiting mariners in the Cinqu
Ports, where he was regarded as a national hero rather than ar
international menace. In conjunction with the pirate fleet fron
Devon, he captured two Flemish ships with cargoes valued a
almost £600, and also seized a Florentine carrack carrying win
and iron. By the time that the English and French ambassa
dors came, in April 1411, to consider renewing the ill-fate
truce another fourteen Flemish vessels (worth over £3,000) ha
fallen into his hands, making the prospect of war all too real

One of the main reasons for Long's success lay in the en
thusiastic support he enjoyed along the Kent and Sussex coast
often from those who had been ordered to arrest him. Whe
his ships, stuffed with plunder, put into the Camber loca
landowners, magistrates and clergymen were among the firs
to join the scramble for stolen salt, wine and exotic merchan
dise. The vicar of Lydd offered him comfortable (and safe
accommodation, the Bishop of Chichester stocked his cellar
from the pirate ships and one of the Rye MPs provided much
needed storage facilities in return for cut-price booty. In th
circumstances, Long might have pursued his dubious callin
indefinitely, secure in the knowledge that none of his friend
would betray him, but the threat of hostilities from Flander
and the ensuing disruption of commerce forced the govern
ment's hand.

Reckless to the last, Long's only response was to sail up th
Rother and make off with the *Juliane*, a ship belonging t
Henry, Prince of Wales, from its moorings six miles inland i
dry dock. His fate was sealed. It is hard not to feel som
sneaking admiration for this foolhardy but audacious se
captain, who was finally captured by the Admiral of Englan
and a large fleet, especially mobilised at vast expense for th
purpose. After nineteen months of imprisonment in the Tow
he was released, evidently on the grounds that he had seen th
error of his ways and would not break the law again. True t
his word, he committed no further acts of piracy, trying h

hand at smuggling instead. Yet he was still returned to five Parliaments, where it may be assumed he spoke with considerable authority on naval affairs.

To many of his contemporaries Long was not a criminal but a patriot, even though he repeatedly and knowingly broke the law. And although their actions could not by any stretch of the imagination be justified, countless among them felt that they too were personally exempt from the norms of civilised behaviour. One of the great ironies of the medieval House of Commons lies in the fact that men who collectively spent their time petitioning for higher standards of law enforcement and bemoaning the government's inability to deal with a growing crime wave were individually responsible for causing the problem in the first place.

This notorious double standard was by no means confined to MPs: civil servants, for example, were *expected* to take bribes as a means of supplementing their wages, and customs officers to arrange preferential rates for themselves and their friends. One judge, the notorious John Penrose, inflicted a reign of terror on his native Cornwall and used his position to avenge himself on his enemies. Despite serious allegations of corruption and misconduct made against him while he was serving as a royal justice in Ireland, he was promoted to the King's Bench at Westminster, where he survived an even graver scandal.

Charges of conspiracy to murder, perjury and the falsification of evidence, all supported by the sworn testimony of witnesses, had little immediate effect on Penrose's career, although after three years' maladministration of justice he was eventually obliged to retire. The fate of another judge of the period, who was publicly disgraced after attempting to ambush and kill one of his neighbours, suggests that occasional efforts were made to weed out the worst offenders, but he would probably have escaped censure had his victim been of humble birth: his real crime lay in assaulting a member of the aristocracy rather than breaking the law.

Anyone hoping to understand the workings of medieval society has to come to terms with a completely different and often disturbing set of values. Men who assuredly believed in hell

fire and the damnation of sinners repeatedly risked their im-
mortal souls by committing acts which they knew would lead
to perdition. Perhaps they hoped to purchase a speedy trip
through purgatory by spending lavishly on good works, and
redeem themselves at the last moment through deathbed re-
pentance. Quite evidently, little or no stigma attached itself to
the very worst of their crimes while they lived.

Distinguished parliamentarians of the stamp of Sir Philip
Courtenay, a son of the Earl of Devon and staunch supporter
of the church, did not scruple to torture those who held important political secrets, even if they enjoyed the protection of
holy orders. The awful fate of a Carmelite friar, who had informed King Richard about a conspiracy implicating his uncle, makes terrible reading, not least because his tormentors
were all prominent in government circles.

They passed a rope over a beam, tied the friar's hands
behind him, and, hanging from his feet a stone weighing
as much as two bushels of wheat, hauled him up by the
rope so as to make him dangle, suffering torturing pain,
in mid air... They proceeded to yet crazier excesses and
brutally swung him to every corner of the room, alternately bearing him down and tossing him high and adding no little to the distress of his frail body... They went
on to light a big fire beneath him [and] in stubborn con-
tinuation of their vicious conduct they added outrage to
outrage, suspending from his genitals a second stone, as
heavy as a bushel of wheat, upon which Sir Philip Courtenay afterwards climbed and stood; and the weight of his
body, coupled with the stamping of his feet, violently
wrenched sinews and veins to such an extent that the stone
he stood on dipped low enough to collide with the [other]
one attached to the friar's feet... They now took him
down and forced his feet and the whole length of his shins
up to the knees to rest for some time on the fire... Finally they made him lie on his back and poured over his
face, which they covered with a sheet, three gallons of hot
water, pressing him repeatedly to confess.

'ar from suffering any pangs of remorse when news reached hem of their victim's death, Sir Philip and his cronies in-licted further indignities upon his body.

Although Courtenay's conduct was far from typical, mur-'er or attempted murder seems to have been something of a ite of passage for medieval MPs. Several of them had similar areers to that of Sir Henry Retford, who was twice charged vith homicide and repeatedly involved in violent affrays be-ore being returned to the House of Commons. Once elected, hese unrepentant, but not necessarily sadistic, individuals ound themselves in the company of cold-blooded killers, such s Sir Nicholas Harryngton, an accessory to the murder of Ralph, Lord Dacre, by the latter's brother and next of kin. The uthorities had been forced to view this particular crime with everity because of the rank and wealth of the victim, yet nei-her culprit was ever punished. Indeed, the brother actually nherited the title (as he had planned) and Sir Nicholas went on o do away with his own wife so that he could make a more rofitable marriage.

In the light of all this evidence, and of the scores, if not undreds, of other cases of insolent lawlessness on the part of he medieval gentry which have been documented in recent ears, the works of today's historical novelists often seem to ffer a pale and sanitised reflection of real life. Perhaps one ay we will encounter Sir Henry Ilcombe or William Long in he pages of a novel, but it is unlikely that their fictional ex-loits will ever be as outrageous or as reckless as the real thing. On the other hand, we can rest assured that, however badly ney may behave, our own parliamentary representatives could e a great deal worse.

SLIGHT OF HAND

★

CATHERINE AIRD

THE PREMISES of the Mordaunt Club were situated in one o
the quieter streets of London's district of St James's. It wa
thus easily accessible from the higher reaches of Whitehall (i
both senses), the Admirality, the headquarters of certain fa
mous regiments and New—or rather New, New—Scotlan
Yard.

Membership of the Club was open to all those of a simila
cast of mind to Sir John Mordaunt, fifth baronet (1650-1721
except for active politicians of any—or, indeed, of no—party
This is because Sir John, although an assiduous Member o
Parliament himself in his day, had promised to vote in th
House according to the promptings of reason and good sense
in the 'publick good' rather than with selfish 'interest' as it ha
been put in the early-day equivalent of an election address.

Henry Tyler was wont to drift in to have luncheon at th
Mordaunt Club at least once a week. Whilst it was perfectl
possible to reserve a table there when hosting guests or eve
when dining unaccompanied it was the happy custom of th
club that members themselves, if lunching alone, joined thos
eating at the long refectory table at the far end of the pannelle
dining-room.

This was how it was that Henry Tyler came to be sitting nex
to Commander Alan Howkins, a senior policeman with muc
on his mind. It was a Monday morning and they were so fa
alone at the communal luncheon table.

'Good weekend?' enquired Henry Tyler politely. He was
little stiff himself from an excess of gardening at his home i

the country and he was glad that the week ahead back at his desk at the Foreign Office promised to be less taxing—physically, at least.

The Commander shook his head. 'Rather disappointing, actually.'

'Sorry about that.'

'Can't expect to win them all, I suppose,' said the policeman.

'True,' observed Henry, projecting the proper sympathy due from a member of one of Her Majesty's Offices of State to another. Lessons about not always winning had been learned at the Foreign and Commonwealth Office a long time ago and had been regularly reinforced by international events over the years.

'But I don't like being beaten,' said Howkins with unexpected savagery.

'Who does?' said Tyler. Not that the Foreign Office ever admitted to being beaten—something which, quite typically there, they saw as completely different from 'not winning'. What they did when it happened—for instance, in 1776—was to use another expression altogether. The Foreign Office was great on euphemisms.

'Outwitted,' said Howkins, tearing a bread roll apart with unnecessary vigour. 'That's what we were.'

'Ah,' said Tyler. So Scotland Yard, then, didn't go in for euphemisms . . .

'Lost Mr Big,' said Howkins briefly, turning to the hovering waiter. 'I'll have the whitebait, please, and the beef. Underdone.'

'Tough,' said Henry Tyler. 'No, no,' he said hastily to the waiter, 'I wasn't talking about the beef. I'll have that, too.'

(The letters between Sir John Mordaunt and his wife had frequently dwelt on game, brawn, pickled bacon and such-like country fare and a tradition of good cooking was maintained at the club.)

'I suppose it's always the big fish that get away,' resumed the policeman, more philosophically.

'No,' said Henry kindly, 'but you miss them more than the little ones when you do lose them and you remember them for longer.'

'True.'

'Better luck next time, anyway,' said the Foreign Office man.

'That's what the Assistant Commissioner said after the first time,' said Howkins.

'Like that, is it?'

'And after the second time,' murmured the Commander into his drink, 'he said he hoped it would be a case of third time lucky.'

'And it wasn't?' divined Henry Tyler without too much difficulty.

'Slipped through our fingers again on Saturday night.'

'Bad luck.'

'Oh, it can't be luck,' said Howkins at once. 'He must have a system. The only trouble is that we can't break it.'

'His luck may run out, though.' Henry Tyler felt he ought to make a pitch for Lady Luck, who had come to the aid of the Foreign Office more often than he liked to think about.

'I'd rather ours held,' said Howkins, demonstrating that policemen could play with words too. 'I shouldn't think we'll get many more chances with this fellow.'

'Slippery customer, eh?'

'Let me tell you this much, Tyler...'

Henry bent his head forward attentively although there were no guests within earshot. The Mordaunt Club members themselves had an unbroken history of total discretion which was implicit and not enjoined upon them. It was in the tradition of the seventeenth-century country gentleman after whom the Club was named: and was one of the many points which figured in the thinking—if not in the Minutes—of the committee during its deliberations on the ticklish question of the admission of women to the Club.

The Commander said, 'It's not every day we get a chance of picking up the real brains behind a drug racket right here in the middle of London, I can tell you.'

'If criminals have got brains, then they use them,' agreed Henry Tyler.

'Let alone three chances,' said the Commander, lapsing back into melancholy.

It wasn't a question of brains that was making the question of the admission of women to the Mordaunt Club so tricky. Diehards were insisting that the question was academic (since women *per se* were seldom of a sufficiently Mordaunt cast of mind to qualify for Membership) and the views of Sir John Mordaunt himself on the subject unknown (but not too difficult to conjecture).

'Ah,' said Henry Tyler, himself cast in the mould of Dreier's celebrated dictum of a diplomat being a man who thought twice before saying nothing. 'Shall you get a fourth chance, do you think?'

Howkins still looked depressed. 'Well, so far we've always known where to find him the weekend after a shipment comes in, which is something that doesn't happen in every case.'

'And do you always know when that is going to be?' enquired Tyler pertinently.

'Oh, yes, that's no trouble. Thanks to your people, actually. The local Brit-bod in Lasserta usually tips us off in good time.'

Something in Henry's expression caused the Commander to rephrase this. 'Sorry,' he grinned. 'That's shortspeak for Her Britannic Majesty's Ambassador to the Sheikhdom of Lasserta.'

'Anthony Heber Hibbs?'

'That's him. He's got a pretty good intelligence system going out there where they make the stuff so that's no problem.'

'So what is?' Identifying the problem was always important. Even if nothing could be done about it. That was part of the working credo in Henry's department.

'Evidence, lack of, and need for,' said Howkins cogently. 'It's got to be stone-cold, straight-up and irrefutable evidence before we blow our cover or we've lost everything and then we'll never catch him.'

'You want him red-handed,' said Henry, falling back on an earlier phrasing. It was one which Sir John Mordaunt would have understood.

'We do.' The Commander started on his whitebait. 'And we want him rather badly.'

'I can see you don't want just small fry either,' agreed Henry Tyler, who had opted for hors-d'oeuvres rather than whitebait. 'Small fry aren't worth losing your set-up for.'

'Let's face it,' said Howkins. 'Our cover can't be all that good or someone wouldn't be giving him the nod every time we close in, but for what it's worth we'd like to try to keep our cover and nobble whoever's doing the Sister Ann act.'

'What Sherlock Holmes would have called a three pipe problem . . .'

'More like half a dozen hookahs,' said Howkins, getting pessimistic again. 'I've been racking my brains all weekend.'

'He—your chappie—can't be too worried about walking into a trap then, can he?'

The Foreign Office man didn't get a direct answer. 'Have you ever heard, Tyler, of a famous restaurant in Manlow Street?'

'Mother Carey's Chickens? Oh, yes . . .'

'Well, we established first of all that our man has regular meetings there at "Les Poulets de la Mère Carey" the week after a shipment of heroin comes in from the sheikhdom.'

'Then he is doing well, your drugs baron,' said Henry. 'It must be one of the most expensive eating places in town.'

'That's what our auditors say, too,' said Howkins. 'They've even suggested we weren't nobbling our suspect too soon because we liked eating there too.'

'Men without souls, auditors,' observed Henry.

'If I could only work out how he knows when to walk out of Mère Carey's empty-handed and when not to, then I'd be a happy man.'

'Because you could then catch him dealing,' agreed Henry.

'Which he would only do if he didn't know we were there.' The Commander sounded injured. 'It's not only that. It's the cocking a snook aspect that gets me, too.'

'He's doing a Queen Anne's Fan on you,' said Henry Tyler calmly.

The Commander looked mystified. 'I know she's dead, Tyler, but...'

'Putting your thumb to your nose with your fingers spread out is pure Queen Anne.'

'Queen Anne?'

'None other. Her reign was a time of much politicking and snook-cocking, as our revered namesake Mordaunt found out.'

'Really? Well, as far as I'm concerned the farther police are from politics the better.'

'There weren't any police then.'

'No heroin either, though,' said the Commander, still licking his wounds.

The arrival of an ashet of rare beef temporarily put paid to conversation.

'This man of yours...' resumed Henry presently.

'Sharp as a barrel-load of monkeys and the mentality of a buccaneer...'

Yes, it would be the latter that rankled, thought Tyler.

'... Carrying on his business in one of the best restaurants in London before our very eyes.'

'Which means he has a high-class clientele.'

'That's part of the problem,' said the Commander. 'Before we know where we are, Tyler, we'll be getting questions asked in the House. And you don't need me to tell you where that can lead to.'

'No.' Howkins was talking to a man with whom the phrase struck home hard. Tyler glanced up at a portrait of Sir John hanging on the wall. Politics had been simpler in Mordaunt's day. In the words of his biographer, 'As a country squire, John must automatically have supported the one established Church, agricultural rather than commercial interests, and peace rather than war.' Parliamentary life wasn't as uncomplicated as that any more.

'We just can't fathom who tips chummie the wink,' said Howkins, pushing his plate away.

'The head waiter?' suggested Henry, sometimes—but not always—a believer in going straight to the top.

'Believe you me, Caesar's wife is nothing in comparison,' responded Howkins. 'Hippolyte Chatout's been with Mother Carey's man and boy, and as far as we can make out he's as honest as they come. Well,' the Commander amended this thoughtfully, 'as far as head waiters come.'

'One of the other waiters then . . .'

Howkins sighed. 'We've had a couple of those fancy microphones under the tablecloth of our laddie's reserved table and never once picked up anything in the way of warning.'

'A message in the menu?'

'Not that our cipher people can find,' said the policeman wearily.

'A message in a bottle then?' suggested Tyler. 'By the way, will you have a spot more yourself?'

The Commander shook his head. 'Thank you, no. The sommelier's French, too, and as clean as a whistle.'

Henry Tyler, though a Foreign Office man through and through, let that pass. 'He could have brought wine "a" when wine "b" had been ordered,' he said.

'We know it isn't him,' said Howkins, 'because our chappie got away twice while the sommelier was off sick so he's in the clear anyway.'

'The hat check girl?'

'Our villain's always already on his way before he gets near Monique.'

'Madame herself?'

Commander Howkins looked properly shocked. 'Madame Thérèse de l'Aubigny-Febeaux feels very strongly the pleasures of the table to be superior to those of any drugs and in any case she insists that she has first of all her reputation to think of.'

'Quite so,' murmured Henry.

'She has been most accommodating,' said Howkins warmly, 'and very cooperative with the Force . . .'

'I'm glad to hear it,' said Henry, whose whole training was to prefer *entente to détente*.

'Most accommodating—except, naturally, in the matter of expenses.'

'Naturally,' agreed Henry Tyler who, in his day, had served time on the Paris desk in the Foreign Office. 'Well, Howkins, then in my view that only leaves us, too, going the way of all flesh . . .'

'What was that, Tyler?'

'The way of all flesh,' quoted Henry, 'is to the kitchen.'

'Pudding, gentlemen?' The waiter at the Mordaunt had appeared at their elbows. The terms 'sweet' and 'dessert' were not used at the Club. 'There's plum duff, raisin sponge and a very good blackberry and apple tart . . .'

As soon as important decisions in this matter had been taken, the Commander returned to worry at his own private bone. 'We've been over the kitchen staff of course, but we just can't see how they could get a message to chummie anyway. They never go into the dining-room.'

'But they know when you're there?'

The Commander nodded as he leant a little to one side to allow a piece of raisin sponge to be placed before him. 'Bound to. It's the only place from which we can watch him without him seeing us. We have a couple of our people dining at the next table to him, too, but the kitchen's a line of escape we just have to keep covered.'

Henry Tyler's choice of pudding was an old-fashioned plum duff. 'Tell me about the food at Mother Carey's.'

'Very good, unless you go in for the fancy stuff. You know what I mean—half an ounce of fish in a pretty sauce, five shavings of carrot, three peas and a tomato all looking more like a painting than a proper meal.'

'Nouvelle cuisine.' His dining companion, no lightweight, nodded sadly.

'And what you might call "afters" is a slurp of syrup with three strawberries on a plate the size of your hand.' The Commander was tucking into his raisin sponge with purpose.

'So your man has a watcher in the kitchen, then?'

'Seems like it,' said the Commander, 'but we can't arrest the lot and anyway we need to know how the message is got across to catch our quarry. It's him we want, don't forget, and before he sees the writing on the wall.'

'And who's doing the cooking out there at the back?'

'Four chefs, three assistants, a couple of vegetable cooks and a slip of a girl who does the sweet course and nothing else.'

Henry considered his plum duff thoughtfully. Then he lifted his face, a seraphic smile on his countenance. 'The writing isn't on the wall, old man.'

'No?'

'It's on the *pavé de pastille* or something very like it.'

'What?'

'I'm prepared to wager ten ecus to a brass farthing,' said Henry grandly, 'that your drug dealer got his warning in cream.'

'Cream?'

'Written with a little stick across the blackcurrant coulis or whatever. It's not difficult . . .'

'But—' Howkins's spoon was suspended over the last of his raisin sponge.

'It would be something very simple, of course. Probably a word like "scram" or "flee" or even,' he added unkindly, 'seeing that it's a French restaurant, "cochons".'

'And no one except the waiter would see it,' said the Commander, slapping his thigh. 'I've got you. Nouvelle, indeed! I'll make mincemeat of him next time. That's not French, is it, Tyler?'

INCIDENT AT MILLIONAIRES' ROW

★

H R F KEATING

THE PRIVATE ROAD, called officially Kensington Palace Gardens, that runs down the west side of one of London's royal parks, is more commonly known as Millionaires' Row. It is lined by a number of huge houses with their backs looking out on the stretches of grass and towering old trees. In their time these mansions—they are nothing less—have belonged to fabulously wealthy maharajahs, have housed the ultra-secret Embassy of the Soyuz Sovetskikh Sotsialistichesikh Respublik, have numbered among them even the residence of a television mogul.

So perhaps it should be a matter of no surprise that early one morning in the late winter of the year 199- two police motorcyclists should come at full speed, sirens yowling, one after another along the Bayswater Road and turn with squealing tyres through the mildly crumbling stone gateway that leads into this most discreet of discreet thoroughfares. Or that, minutes later, they were followed by a police car, flashing its blue lamp with equal urgency.

Outside the residence of the Ambassador of a certain Arab state, which had better be nameless, they halted. The enormous front door of the building opened. Giving each other fractionally nervous glances, the helmeted, yellow-jerkined motorcyclists, outriders of a team from the Diplomatic Protection Group, entered the building. To be greeted in the high marbled hallway by the sight of the Ambassador himself, apoplectic with fury, striding back and forth, brandishing even a small camel-whip and apparently incapable, in the enormity of the crisis he was experiencing—whatever it was—of bringing himself to use the barbarous language of his host nation.

In the background, distinctly subdued, hardly daring to look at one another, a dozen members of the Ambassador's staff, ranging from secretaries to cooks, watched in terrified helplessness.

With the arrival a minute or two later of the car bringing the group's night-duty officer, Detective Inspector Greenmoor, however, His Excellency contrived to abate his fury enough to communicate at least an outline of the monstrous trouble that had befallen him.

'He is in there. There.'

The little camel-whip was pointed, quivering, at a stout gleamingly polished tall door towards the back of the hall.

'I see, sir. Yes. But may I—er—enquire whom you are referring to?'

'No. Yes. No. Mr Inspector, these policemen, do they understand Arabic?'

Inspector Greenmoor peered at the faces under the ballooning yellow helmets.

'No, sir. Unfortunately neither of them speak any of your language, as far as I am aware.'

'Good, good, Mr Inspector. And you? Do you speak Arabic?'

'Well, sir, I can manage a word or two, part of my duties as you might say.'

There followed from the ambassadorial mouth a stream of language, from which the two motorcycle men, hands resting lightly on their revolver holsters, were able to make out that the Ambassador was still in an almighty rage.

Inspector Greenmoor, though a good deal foxed by the speed and volume of the outpouring, thought he had grasped at least the essentials of the situation.

The Ambassador, a Prince of the royal blood, had, it appeared, been entertaining for the night at this his private residence an envoy from a neighbouring Arab country usually at daggers drawn with his own.

A piece of vigorous involuntary mime had helped the Inspector here.

Negotiations, he had gathered then, were taking place. A huge change of alliances was in the air. No one must know. Most secret, Mr Inspector, 10,000 per cent.'

The Ambassador had fallen into English for that. The rest of his explanation was in even faster, more furious Arabic, and Inspector Greenmoor's scanty knowledge of the tongue almost failed him.

But, it seemed, earlier that morning the visitor, a distant relation in fact of his host—'cousin, cousin, just, just, you understand?'—had kidnapped the Ambassador's small daughter and was holding her, perhaps to ransom, in the room with the heavy, well-polished door.

'Well, sir,' the Inspector said, descending to his own language, 'Commander Holsworthy, HODGP, that is,—er—Head of the Diplomatic Protection Group, is on his way, I am pleased to say. But perhaps it would be worthwhile, just now, be trying the door of the room.'

'As you wish, as you wish.'

Inspector Greenmoor went over to the door, gently turned the massive brass handle, gently pushed. Locked. He ventured a polite tap on one of the gleaming panels.

'Go away,' said a childish voice in Arabic.

'Are you well and happy?' Inspector Greenmoor ventured in the same language.

'Go away.'

'It looks as if the poor little girl may be under some sort of threat, sir. I think perhaps we had better wait till Commander Holsworthy arrives.'

'Wait, wait, wait. All the time it is waiting, waiting. Never acting, acting. I must speak to my cousin. Now, now. And not through any door.'

'Yes, sir.'

At that moment, much to Inspector Greenmoor's relief, his superior arrived, in a suitably superior motor vehicle. And in full, braid-sparkling uniform.

A quick word at the door and he was put in the picture.

'Your Excellency, this is a most unfortunate business However, I am reasonably fluent in your language, and perhaps I may be able to persuade your cousin to release your little daughter.'

This provoked a yet more torrential and enraged outpouring. But when comparative calm had descended at last, Commander Holsworthy, who had succeeded only in interjecting a very occasional question, went over and had a quiet word with his deputy.

'Seems you got the wrong end of the stick a bit, John What's happened here apparently, if you can believe it, is no that the Ambassador's cousin has kidnapped his daughter, bu that the little girl, who's aged just eleven, has kidnapped him She's got him locked in the dining-room there, and nothing he father can say will make her open the door.'

'But why, sir? What on earth's the idea?'

'Nobody seems to know. Least of all her father. Still, he' agreed to let me have a go. So perhaps a rather more diplomatic approach... But what I want you to do is talk to th Ambassador.'

'Yes, sir. Er— What about?'

'Oh, come on, John. About anything. Anything. So long a he doesn't come barging in, cracking that whip of his, whil I'm doing my stuff.'

Inspector Greenmoor gulped. Once. And marched over t the Ambassador.

'This-er— Well, Your Excellency, I believe this is the firs time you've had occasion to call on our services.'

'What? What is that? That man—your Head of whatever i is—what is he saying?'

Greenmoor had heard two quiet taps on the heavy, locke door followed at once by an indignant squeaked 'Go away' i Arabic. And now there was a stream of gently inflected Ara bic, Egyptian variation, in reply. But luckily too far away fo the words to be made out.

The Ambassador started out in its direction. Inspecto Greenmoor went so far as to put a hand on his arm.

'As I was saying, Your Excellency... That is, what was saying? Oh, yes, I was about to ask you—about to ask yo if... if you had any recommendations about our work? Yes. I mean, are you satisfied with the guard we keep at the embassy itself? We're always ready to listen to the people we have the—er—pleasure of serving. Any ideas of—er—that sort?'

'No.'

'I see, Your Excellency. Then—then we must be doing all right. Yes. Well, I'm pleased to hear that. But—'

A tug at the hand on the ambassadorial arm.

'One moment more, Your Excellency, if I may. We don't often get an opportunity of hearing whether our services...'

Then, at last, the sound of a small female voice speaking in what seemed to be an altogether reasonable manner from directly on the other side of the tall door.

More Egyptian Arabic.

Was there a wheedling note in it? Or was it just that genuine Arabic sounded like that?

'As I was saying, your Excellency...'

And, unbounded relief, the click of a heavy door being unlocked.

Inspector Greenmoor whirled round.

A small, and very pretty girl came out, leading by the hand an impeccably distinguished young man in white jellaba and white headdress. She was smiling up at her captive in a manner that, in two or three years' time, would be nothing short of open invitation.

'Uncle is very, very nice,' she said in clear, if slightly childish English, addressing the assembled representatives of the Metropolitan Police as much as the still cringing members of the Ambassador's household at the far end of the hall. 'I had to have him for myself, just for a bit. There was too much talking and talking all the time.'

The sound that emanated from her father at this could only be described as a snarl of pure rage.

'Come here,' he shouted in a voice that reverberated and reverberated from the marble walls all around.

'No, Your Excellency,' Commander Holsworthy snapped. 'I very much regret to inform you that it is my duty to place your daughter under arrest.'

'Under arrest? Under arrest? Mr Policeman, have you gone mad?'

'No. Your Excellency. A crime has been committed, the serious offence of kidnap. The culprit must be brought to justice.'

'Mr Policeman, this is my house, my country's territory. I shall exercise whatever justice is to be done.'

And the little camel-whip was brought down with an almighty thwack on the top of a conveniently placed buhl chiffonier.

'Well, no, Your Excellency, that's not quite the situation,' Commander Holsworthy replied. 'Perhaps it has slipped your memory that this is not your country's embassy, which of course is out of our jurisdiction, but simply your private house. So I am afraid I have no alternative but to take this young lady into custody.'

Before the Ambassador had quite finished drawing himself up to his full height Commander Holsworthy had ushered his 'collar' out of the wide front door.

Inspector Greenmoor, at a nod of command, got into the back of the commander's car, sliding the young criminal in beside him.

'The Yard, Jenkins,' Commander Holsworthy said to his driver, slipping inside in his turn.

Smoothly the car took off. Only when they had turned into the Bayswater Road did Inspector Greenmoor venture to lean across the small figure between them.

'With respect, sir,' he said. 'Wasn't that a bit—well, high-handed? Not exactly diplomatic, you might say?'

'Yes, John. In one way it was. On the other, you could say I was exercising to the full the duties of the Diplomatic Protection Group. Using what you might call a little adroit diplomacy to protect this young lady's backside.'

WORKING WITH SUZIE

★

JEAN McCONNELL

I COULD HARDLY believe my ears when Vincent, my agent, rang me. First, that he had rung at all, since I had neither seen nor heard of him for months. Second, that he should dare to voice this outrageous suggestion to one who had lined his pockets so richly from such a distinguished dramatic career.

Third, that he had the audacity to remark that the experience would *stretch me*. True, he quickly corrected this to *prove a challenge*. Either way it was a ludicrous proposition to present to *me*. I, who had played all the great classic roles in my time. Whose Medea, Mrs Danvers, Lady Bracknell were already legends in theatre history. I, whose Lady Macbeth was said to have curdled blood! Whose Lucretia Borgia had occasioned several members of the audience to require the St John's first-aider! The enormity of it!

Here he was asking me to entertain conjecture of a part so trivial as to be beyond contempt. What was he saying now? Impudence! That I had not worked in two years? Well, whose fault was that? Had he pressed the National when they were casting Electra? Had he pursued the RSC about the Duchess of Malfi? Judi couldn't play *everything* surely!

He was interrupting me again. He was talking about money. Naming a sum. For one day's work. *How* much?

'Because they do appreciate it's quite out of your usual sphere, Dame Alice. That's precisely why they want *you*. An actress of stature. Of reputation. Well known to the public. To make their point.'

'Which is?'

'That their product is in a class of its own.'

'But a *commercial*, Vincent.'

'Did you hear what I said they're offering?'

'That's all very well . . .'

'Will you look at the script?'

'There is a script?'

'A short one. In the very best of taste. Let me send it round. *Bring* it round. Everyone would be so—honoured. And wouldn't it be sort of a lark? Like Larry playing the Entertainer?'

'I'm not attracted to larks, Vincent. And the example you quote does not inspirit me.'

I put down the receiver. However, as I rose from the telephone, I caught my heel in a strand of carpet and it occurred to me that the London apartment could use a little refurbishment. And as for my cottage in Dorset . . .

I rang back.

Vincent brought the script round that afternoon, and I settled on my chaise longue as he read it to me.

'Vincent, who is this Suzie character?'

'That's the other part. But you have all the lines, Dame Alice. All of them. She just sits there while you serve her tea in a charming garden setting.'

I was a trifle mollified. At least my status was recognised. But I remained suspicious. I insisted on scanning the script for 'business'—action that might change the emphasis away from me to her. It was all very well to have the lines, but if the other character was doing distracting things with the sandwiches, say, . . .

But it looked harmless enough on the page. Bland, in fact. Clearly, the very fact of a doyenne of the drama such as myself being seen to endorse the product would be considered sufficient. As well it should.

Then Vincent mentioned the name of the director. 'He's one of the very best. International reputation. They can afford them on these commercials, you know. And he especially asked for you. He'll ring himself if I can just tell him you're mulling it over.'

'Well . . .'

'Everyone's doing them these days.' Vincent ran off a string of names for me. And I confess I had recognised several famous colleagues on voice-overs.

So I accepted. The contract was signed. And I ordered a hundred-per-cent wool close-carpeting for the whole apartment.

Then on the first day I feared I had made the mistake of my life.

I rang Vincent immediately. 'What have you done to me! This will be the end of my career. Get me out of this at once!'

His voice sounded icy. 'What's the matter? Are you afraid of working with Suzie? Worried she'll steal the scene?'

'Steal it! If she could *play* it. The whole prospect is ghastly!'

Ghastly it was. It had been bad enough when Suzie had first appeared on the set. I took an instant dislike to her. She had a smile that never reached her eyes. In fact her eyes not only showed no respect to one of my years and experience, but even seemed unbelievably calculating.

I could see at once that keeping her in her place might be difficult. Though she had with her a personal coach, here again I felt a distinct lack of deference. Certainly the man sought to guide her at all times, but he showed no sign of controlling her excessively high spirits.

She seemed to delight in playing to the gallery, clowning about when I was trying to rehearse my lines, reacting to everything I did with silly expressions in order to gain the attention of the technical crew. They are true professionals and seldom distracted from their business, but several times Suzie had everyone in fits of laughter at some impromptu antic of her own inventing.

I myself was not amused. I was becoming quite dis̲t̲r̲a̲u̲g̲h̲t̲, in fact. Yet determined not to lose my dignity. Th̲i̲s̲ ̲s̲e̲e̲m̲e̲d̲ ̲t̲o̲ entertain everyone even more. I had the disti̲n̲c̲t̲ ̲f̲e̲e̲l̲i̲n̲g̲ ̲t̲h̲e̲y̲ were secretly rolling the cameras in the hop̲e̲ ̲o̲f̲ ̲c̲a̲t̲c̲h̲i̲n̲g̲ out-takes for that Norden fellow.

I had more than one heated exchang̲e̲

'You may think you've prepared̲ me for this, but you've clearly fallen down on you̲r̲

'At least she's not fluffing her lines!'

'How do you imagine I can concentrate! Just make her sit down and pay heed!'

As he turned away I overheard him utter to the PA that Suzie could act me off the stage any day.

At this point I appealed to the director.

'Perhaps if you could stick to the precise wording of the script, Dame Alice.'

I was astounded. The insolence!

'The advertisers are very particular about these things,' he added.

He then proceeded to run the scene again and again. Only the old trouper in me kept me going, determined not to be beaten, though I was getting more and more confused and weary. Like Eliza, I longed for one of those cups of tea I kept pouring.

'I think we'll *try* for a take.'

It was music to my ears. At last we'd get it over and done with. I was all geared up ready.

'Set up the tea-things again will you, Props!'

'Just a minute, please, Suzie has to have a snack now or she gets overtired.'

'OK. Take five.'

She gets overtired. I could give her sixty years and probably more. I strode briskly to my dressing-room.

I could see that whatever I did, however the scene was shot, this Suzie was intent on ruining it for me. A thing that had never happened in all my years in the profession. Time was when an *ingénue* once tried to upstage me and I had her gown nailed to the boards. And there had been a few others who had aimed to steal my limelight. And had found their contracts unexpectedly severed.

If they imagined I'd allow Suzie to get the better of me... I had not risen to the pinnacle of my craft without breaking a few spirits.

In my dressing-room I took a last look at my words and ⎯llowed a single nerve-quietening pill from the bag of as- ⎯dications that always travelled with me. Made cer- ⎯rations. Then rested on my couch.

Our call came and everyone resumed their places. The Props girl clucked at me as I deftly adjusted the cups to my personal convenience.

Action! The studio manager signalled me. The cameras were running. I began to serve the tea and to say my lines, first holding up the packet towards camera one.

The branches of the realistic-looking silver birch stirred in the breeze from the wind-machine. A twitter of birds would be dubbed in later, I knew. An idyllic scene. It was going flawlessly. I said the words correctly, took up the pot on the exact syllable, holding it precisely three inches above Suzie's cup for a close-up.

'There is simply nothing to compare with an old-fashioned dish of tea in the garden,' I said.

Suzie made a horrible face at me. I sensed the laughter all around. I went on. I filled Suzie's cup.

She drank it.

She made another dreadful grimace. I actually heard a titter now.

Then suddenly she clutched her stomach and screeched. She jumped down from her chair and rolled round the floor. Then she ran up the birch tree. From the top, giving ear-splitting howls she leapt across to the sound boom, swung on it for a second, gibbering ferociously, then dropped to the floor and lay there still as an old rug.

Her trainer ran to her side. 'She's upped and died!' he shouted.

'Well, I think we can use what we've got,' said the director. 'I can cut away to a close-up on Dame Alice at the end.'

I had to get my make-up freshened.

'Props! Strike that monkey out of the way,' called the director.

'One of my cleverest chimps!' grumbled Suzie's coach.

'Acting can be very stressful sometimes,' I said, touching his arm sympathetically. 'Calls for a quality of *resolve* that not everyone possesses.'

And I made one of my best exits ever.

A VACANCE EN CAMPAGNE

★

TIM HEALD

---

1 August

I CAN'T THINK what possessed Jill to agree to a holiday with Brian and Lulu. They're perfectly OK in Putney in small doses but the idea of being holed up with them in a barn in Brittany for two whole weeks is frankly unspeakable.

The ferry was bloody and not made any easier by Brian's attitude. It doesn't help to bang on and on about it being 'a Frog boat'. We're all in the EC now so we might as well muck in and even though the fellows on the car deck were absolute swine the food is a sight better than on those ghastly British boats. Entrecôte and frites. Crème brûlée. Very decent little Nuits-Saint-Georges. Café filtre and a large Armagnac. But Lulu just had to send her steak back because it was pas bien cuit. Brian put away an alarming quantity of Armagnac because, he said, it stopped him getting seasick. As the Channel was flat as a mill pond this seemed a pretty feeble excuse.

Mercifully the boys were absent. We gave them enough cash to get a self-serve supper in the cafeteria along with the backpackers and the train passengers and the rest of the great unwashed. I think they spent most of it on the fruit machines. Richard came in at some unearthly hour and snored till I threw a shoe at him.

1 August

THIS IS GOING to be a bloody nightmare unless Mum and Dad sort it. Gary's parents are pigs too. Actually his mum's not too bad but his dad's like weird. And if anything he's even more of a fascist than Dad. The way he was talking to the French was really really embarrassing.

Mum and Dad had their usual map-reading row getting to the ferry-port and then Dad stalled on the car deck and this big French bloke in overalls started shouting and it was well funny only Dad didn't think so and his ears went all pink like they do when he knows he's done something pathetic.

After we'd found the cabins they all wanted to go off to the posh restaurants only they didn't want us around which I don't mind because the food's all muck in there and Mum and Dad always get in a great thing about table manners and not eating with your fingers and chugga-lugging and that so Gary and I played the machines which were well wicked. Then we had a frankfurter and some fries and met these French girls who'd been hitching round Angleterre and we had some drinks with them. Gary bought me some stuff called Pernod which is sort of like water only when you mix it with lemonade it goes all cloudy and tastes like Liquorice Allsorts. Terrific kick. I got quite a high. In fact I didn't think I'd be able to find the cabin only Véronique didn't think my idea of sharing her sleeping bag on deck was a very good one, so she helped me find the cabin. Then just when I got to sleep Dad started shouting and throwing things. Still Gary and I have got our own room at this 'jeet' thing. Gary's dad Brian keeps going on about the 'jeet' but I don't think he knows what it is any more than anyone else. Gary says it's all been fixed up with some bloke they met in Putney whose dad is a French Count.

2 August

SOME BLOODY GÎTE! Why in God's name we couldn't have fixed it through Chris at Vacances en Campagne like we usually do I cannot think. I mean what can one expect of someone at a party in Putney who claims to be some sort of French aristo? He was pure Maurice Chevalier atte Bowe. Probably born under the family barrow in the Old Kent Road! It's not as if it's cheap either—in fact it's outrageously expensive. And everything's extra. You get charged for the electricity—what there is of it—and the Calor gas—and the wood for the 'open' fires (actually they're more like 'closed' fires because it's quite obvious that the chimneys haven't been swept since the Revolution). There's no phone so he can't charge for that. Even the water's on a meter and the bedlinen is ten francs a pillowcase and twenty a sheet. Brian and Lulu, naturally, are putting a brave face on it. No more talk about 'bloody Frogs' just endless, 'Oh isn't it charming?' and 'It's too enchantingly typical' and—worst of all—'Not like home, eh Gordon?' I could have belted him when he said that. I could have done him a serious mischief. Still, even though she is a silly cow you can't help fancying Lulu. For a woman of her age she's got terrific legs.

Oh Jesus, where to begin?!

First of all the house is in the middle of absolutely nothing and miles from nowhere. The nearest village is a place called Tréguerpoul-le-Grand. I'd like to know what Tréguerpoul-le-Petit is like. Le Grand has a 'Bar des Sports' with a pool table and a handful of chaps in blue overalls puffing away on filthy unfiltered cigarettes and drinking cider out of mugs. Then there's a village shop which is run by an old bag with one tooth. It sells gumboots, chocolate biscuits and gallon containers of vin ordinaire. There was a 'crêperie', but that's closed for summer. The church has a steeple with holes in it. Apparently this is to stop it being blown over by the prevailing gale—though at the moment there is no wind at all, just a light drizzle and a thin blanket of fog.

T. le Grand is about a kilometre away if you walk over the artichoke fields but by car it's about five. The 'gîte' as Brian and Lulu will keep calling it is entirely surrounded by artichokes. 'Well, we won't starve,' said Brian. 'Ho, ho, ho.' I had never noticed before how Brian signals his jokes with this thigh-slapping 'Ho, ho, ho' as if he were one of the seven dwarfs.

Anyway, Brian's 'gîte'. Barn is putting it kindly. Yes it's true there are three double bedrooms in the sense that there are three bedrooms into which it is possible to insert two average-sized human beings. And if you don't mind sleeping on horsehair there is not a lot wrong with the beds. Provided you get on all right with your partner and go easy on the garlic. The bathroom has a bidet but no bath—only a shower which has two temperatures: scalding or freezing.

The living-room is at least big but it leaks and there are draughts everywhere. Some musty old prints on the walls, exposed beams, threadbare rugs on the floor. There are mice too. The armchairs are uncomfortable and the dining table wobbles even when you stick folded newspaper under the legs. The kitchen has a fridge with mould in the ice compartment—which doesn't freeze—and a stove with a one-speed oven. There is one frying pan, two saucepans and a job lot of spoons, knives and forks and the whole thing smells of gas.

Thank God we stocked up on duty-free. At least a few stiff Scotches kept out the worst of the damp and cold. Sally and Lulu cooked spaghetti with a tinned Bolognese sauce which we'd brought with us. There were, naturally, no shops open apart from the one in T.-le-grand which is effectively useless unless you want roast gumboot. Christ, Gary's table manners are dreadful—even worse than Richard's. He seems completely unable to keep his mouth shut while eating. He and Richard went out after supper while we played bridge. God knows what they got up to. They didn't get back till after we'd gone to bed. We should have left them at home or sent them to some kind of summer camp. Borstal, preferably. I never realised what a constant provocation teenage boys could be.

2 August

I HATE OLD PEOPLE. If anything Gary's old people are worse than my old people but there's not much to choose between them. Luckily we were able to escape after supper. Mum and Gary's mum did a spag bol which was like well revolting only none of them seemed to notice. They'd bought some massive bottles of booze on the boat so they were all too pissed to taste anything. They're horrible when they're drunk. All laughing at each other's feeble jokes all the time. I think Dad fancies Gary's mum. He's always eyeing her up.

Gary and me played pool in the village. Gary has a torch so we made it through the fields. I think I like Pernod. Also we bought some Gauloise cigarettes which are well smoky.

When we got back they were all snoring and the walls are so thin the whole jeet shakes.

3 August

TO THE SEASIDE at Perros-Guirec. A sort of Bognor-sur-mer. They have scrabble tournaments every Monday and when we arrived there were a whole lot of people in track suits prancing about on exercise mats under the leadership of a rather fanciable gamine brunette. Brian and I swam briefly before the fog rolled in; the girls found a café and drank kirs; and bloody Gary and Richard buggered off and did God knows what in the casino. I slipped Richard a 50-franc note, which was worth it just to get them out of our hair. Lunched on langoustes and Muscadet then a supermarché shop, back to base, slurped some duty-free, supper, bridge and bed. Could be worse, I suppose. The boys sloped off after the evening meal griping about not having anything to do, not having enough cash etc. etc. I told them they were extremely privileged to be enjoying the sort of holiday most of their friends would give their eye teeth for. They didn't seem convinced.

3 August

CHRIST, another twelve days of this. We went to the seaside which was just like the seaside in England except there were all these French people hitting balls at each other on the beach. Sort of ping-pong without a table or a net. Dad and Gary's dad ogled some middle-aged women wobbling about in time to continental house music—not very heavy metal. Mum and Lulu went off to start getting pissed—which is all the oldies seem to think about—and Dad and Brian went swimming which was pretty pathetic. They've both got dreadful beer bellies but they strutted down the beach sucking their breath in and sticking their chests out and trying to look like they were well smart but they just looked white and pathetic and English and old. I hope I never look like that.

The evenings are really dreadful. The jeet is cold and miserable and they just sit about talking crap and then they have supper and then they play cards and the only time they like notice us is to complain about what we're wearing or what we're doing or not doing. Like, 'Why don't you read a good book?' or, 'Why don't you go for a walk?'

Tomorrow night Gary and me are going to cook supper. We might slip in some really poisonous berries. One of the old blokes in the bar tried chatting us up, which was a bit spooky. Good pool table though and I do like Pernod. When we got back they'd left one of the burners on in the kitchen. Dad had made Breton coffee—Nescafé and calvados which is some sort of apple brandy. Also they'd left some money lying around on the sideboard. Not much but we nicked it anyway. Hope they won't notice.

4 August

RAINED AGAIN. Sally and Brian both said they were feeling a bit hung over so they stayed home while Lulu and I drove in to do a shop in Tréguier. We took the boys and dumped them outside the cathedral. For once they didn't ask us for money. After the shopping we adjourned to the bar at the Hôtel Estuaire and sank a couple of beers. I must say Lulu *has* got bloody good legs and actually once she's away from Brian she's not nearly as insular and stupid as I'd thought.

Brian and Sally seemed a bit peeved that we were so late getting back. Actually we weren't that late and anyhow I blamed it on the boys. At least they have *some* uses.

We've practically finished the duty-free but we bought some calvados (excellent) and some Breton whisky (doubtful) at the supermarché. Richard and Gary cooked supper, which, I have to admit, wasn't too bad. They did a spaghetti carbonara which was really bacon and scrambled egg with pasta, but it was properly cooked which you can't always say about the girls' offerings. Afterwards, however, we tried teaching them how to play bridge. Not a success. Gary swore, unforgivably, at his father. Actually I was inclined to side with the boy. Brian had taken far too much of the Breton whisky and it's just not practical to order a sixteen-year-old to go to his room. The pair of them buggered off out and didn't come in till the small hours. God knows where they'd been but for once I'm not sticking my head above the parapet.

Incidentally, I made some Breton coffee with some of the whisky when we'd finished the bridge but everybody dozed off before I'd finished. So I'm afraid I slurped the lot—and then nodded off myself. I only woke when the boys came in, by which time the others seemed to have gone to bed. Maddening. Naturally I pretended I'd stayed up late reading, had a long day, just nodded off for a second or two but I could see the little beasts smirking. I shall have to talk to the others about their coming in so late. We really can't have them lager-louting round the French countryside at all hours of the night.

4 August

I HADN'T REALISED old people were so like, well, pathetic really. All they want to do is play cards and get pissed and take it out on us. We found a wicked pool table in Tréguier in the morning. Then in the evening after Gary and I cooked this brill carbonara they decided they'd teach us to play cards. Honestly, it was *so* boring and then Gary did something he shouldn't have done with his ace of clubs—I think—and his dad got well mad and started having a right go at him and told him to go to his room as if he was a baby so Gary was well gutted and told his dad to get stuffed and his dad went an amazing colour and his eyes all sort of shrunk and piggy and Gary's mum looked as if she was going to start blubbing and Mum and Dad just looked at their cards and pretended noth-ing was happened.

So we went out and instead of going to the village we went to the end of the road and managed to hitch a lift into Tré-guier and went and played pool in this bar and hung around and there were some French kids who spoke a bit of English and it was quite nice really and one of them had this really beaten up sort of van and he gave us a lift almost all the way home and when we got in there was this terrible smell of gas because they'd forgotten to turn the stove off and Dad was asleep on the sofa and snoring, so we woke him up only he was really too smashed to know what was going on.

5 August

RICHARD ASKED for money again. I don't know what to do about him and his bloody money. He spends it like water and seems to think it grows on trees. We compromised in the end and I gave him half what he'd asked for. It's not as if he does anything to earn it. Neither of them even make their beds and their room's like a pigsty. More rain and fog. An interesting tête-à-tête with Lulu when Sally and Brian went to investigate the architectural pleasures of the local château. I get the distinct impression that all is not as well as it might be between her and Brian. The boys disappeared around lunch and didn't get back till about midnight. Brian and I agree that we must have serious words with them both. We should never have brought them.

5 August

I DON'T KNOW why Gary and I have to have parents as naff and disgusting as ours. You'd think they'd be glad to pay us to keep out of their way so they can get drunk and have it off with each other—there's definitely something funny going on between Dad and Gary's mum and if you ask me Mum and Gary's dad have sussed it and are going to pay them back by getting up to something themselves. If it wasn't so pathetic it would be well disgusting. Gary says it's like something out of *Eldorado*. Anyway we both asked for money and you'd think we'd asked for cocaine or snuff movies or something. Both dads were the same, like really really angry and lots of stuff about how all we ever did was complain about not having anything to do and going out and money money money. I mean if we were home I could get a job even if only a paper round but I can't see us getting a paper round in Tréguerpoul-le-Grand. Gary says we could try and get work in the supermarché at Tréguier but I don't think our French is up to it even if we were just humping boxes around. We certainly couldn't do the checkout. So I don't know what Dad's problem is. I didn't ask to come to Brittany with them, I'd much rather stay home, but now he's blaming me for everything—even the freezing fog.

Still we got another lift into Tréguier and met Philippe and he's lent us like serious money—well 200 francs. We'll have to try and nick some from one of the old people's wallets. They always leave them lying around.

6 August

SUN. Absolute bliss. We went to the beach at Tregastel and lay in the sun and swam and had a heavenly assiette de fruits de mer in a bar overlooking the sea. Considering her age, Lulu looked bloody marvellous in her swimsuit—plain black, one-piece. The boys scarpered but who knows where or what they did. The main thing is they weren't in our hair. We even bought a pair of those curious oversized ping-pong bats and balls. There doesn't seem to be any scoring system but I have to say I'm a great deal better at it than Brian.

Picked up some tuna steaks in a pêcherie plus stacks of Muscadet. The boys failed to make our rendezvous by the Grand Hotel so after a while we went home. They're old enough to fend for themselves and they know where the gîte is. If they want to be independent then let them be independent.

6 August

GOD, PARENTS ARE like well shitty! They were all in a terrific mood in the morning because the fog had gone and you could actually see the sky. Hello sky! Hello sun! Hello birds! Hello flowers! So we all went off to the beach again. You'd think we were in a tropical heat wave the way the oldies were all carrying on but actually it was still pretty freezing.

No way were we going to join in being silly like them so we went off and tried to find where it was like at and actually it wasn't that bad. We met these English kids and had a great time with them playing the machines in the casino and eating frites and glacés and complaining about parents. They all have the same problem. What *is* it with old people?

We got to our meeting place outside the Grand Hotel and they didn't show. We waited and waited but eventually we decided they'd given us up. Quelle horreur! comme on dit en France. So we went back to hanging out and having a good time, then like hitched back and walked the last mile or so through the artichokes. Got in at about 1 a.m. and they're all snoring fit to bust. Horrible smell of gas. Hardly dared have a fag in case we blew the whole place sky high. So smoked in the garden.

7 August

BRIAN AND I have had serious words with the boys. I explained very patiently in my view that going on holiday together was a team effort and that therefore everybody bloody well had to pull together and if we, for example, made a rendezvous then the rendezvous had to be kept otherwise the whole shooting-match collapses, no one knows where anyone is, the gendarmes have to be alerted and it's all utter confusion.

Richard said, 'But you didn't call the gendarmes Dad. You didn't give a fuck!' which caused Brian to lose his temper and shout, 'Don't get smart with your father, sunshine. If you were my son I'd lay you across my knee and give you a right thrashing.' Which was understandable but not altogether sensible. So I said, 'I think perhaps you'd better leave this to me, Brian.' Which seemed to make him even madder, though he didn't say anything coherent, just spluttered, but there was an almost understandable sentence which sounded suspiciously like, 'If you spent less time chasing other men's wives and more time disciplining your offspring . . .'

I ignored this, of course.

'I wish you wouldn't swear,' I said to Richard, and I did think he looked embarrassed. He's not a bad boy, really. Just absolutely maddening. But maybe it's his age.

And that was about it really. Reading it through I can see it looks rather weedy and wimpish but what was I supposed to do? I told the boys that they weren't helping, that, like it or not, we had another whole bloody week in Brittany and if they went on behaving in this ridiculous selfish way they would make life an absolute misery and even if they didn't care about us they owed it to their mothers to behave in a less mean-spirited way and attempt to be a little more grown up. Gary, I'm sorry to say, said something to the effect that if being grown up was what we were doing then he didn't ever want to grow up thank you very much, which made his father even more apoplectic. I thought he was going to have a cardiac arrest then.

Anyway, Richard said he had a proposal, which was that if we gave them enough money they would, as he put it, 'stay out of our hair' until the end of the holiday. Brian said that was blackmail and Richard said that it wasn't blackmail it was a business proposition and I'm afraid I said, 'How much?' And in the end I agreed. So did Brian, sort of, though he wasn't really capable of speech. It was more than we could really afford, but it seemed worth it and off they went to God knows where.

Brian said I shouldn't have given in and he'd get even with the little bastards. I said something flippant about the one thing they weren't was little bastards. That didn't go down very well, and Oh shit, I'm going to have a drink. I don't like writing this down. It's demeaning.

7 August

WELL, WE FINALLY had the big bust up. Gary's dad is a complete jerk and real bully or he would be if he had the guts. He's like well violent except now we're big enough to smack him back he daren't do it. Gary says he used to hit him well hard with a leather belt and with hairbrushes. Anything he could get his hands on. He says he used to beat his mum sometimes too, especially when he'd had a few.

Dad on the other hand is just pathetic, a real wimp. I knew the one thing he didn't want was serious trouble, like he's frightened of a bad argument and scared of getting hurt and especially of upsetting Mum. Mum's much stronger than he is.

In fact she completely dominates him. She's just sort of the one who wears the trousers and tells him to shut up when he says something stupid and pig-ignorant which is most of the time.

Anyway I screwed some money out of him by being like dead reasonable. Gary was going to make a big fight out of it because he's like his dad, sort of well violent. He can do a vicious head-butt.

So after we got the money we went down Tréguier and met Philippe and some English kids in the 'Irish Bar' which is this mean place with a pool table and a whole lot of Irish stuff like Irish flags and Pogue tapes and Guinness and paddy whiskey. It's all because they're like Celts or something and talk the same language. Don't ask me what it's all about but it's a great place to hang out and there were some kids from Cork who said there'd been this wicked accident on their camp-site. This caravan like just blew up because there was something wrong with the gas cylinder. Apparently this bloke just went to make himself a mug of Nescafé and he lit a match and the whole place went Poof! They said you could hear the explosion all over the camp-site and there was a helicopter to take the bloke and his wife to the hospital in St Brieuc. All the windows got blown out. Gary said it sounded like the sort of gas gear we have back at the jeet and he gave me a funny look and said, 'Makes you think dunnit?'

8 August

SUN SHONE. To the beach. Dropped the boys who said they'd be back around midnight. Swam. Muscadet and langoustines for lunch. Sunbathed. Played bridge. Cooked some magret de canard which I picked up at the market in Lannion. Peaches. Some gungy Livarot also from a farmer's stall in the marché.

If I say it myself I think we've sorted out our domestic troubles quite successfully. The boys didn't say much. In fact they didn't say anything at all. But at least they weren't rude or particularly hostile. Lulu was impressed with the way I handled things. She says Brian is so violent. She likes quiet, civilised people.

8 August

WELL HOT DAY. Hung out. Philippe was impressed by the
dosh. He wanted to know whether our parents were rich which
Gary and I didn't really know how to deal with. I meant there's
always enough. We're not exactly skint but if we were really
rich we'd be down the south of France in a smart hotel not
freezing to death in a crummy jeet in Brittany. Even though it
was hot today.

He is a funny bloke, Philippe. He wants to come and have
a look at the jeet when the old people are out. Says it might be
embarrassing if they were there. Which is right. I mean they
wouldn't like Philippe on account of they're not into pigtails
and tattoos. He's got one on his bum of this naked woman and
a snake. It's dead rude.

9 August

THIS IS MORE LIKE IT. Another fine day weatherwise. Food,
drink, sea, sand though alas no sex. Just as well there isn't
much more of the holiday because I think both Lulu and
I...well let's just say that we've agreed to meet for a little lunch
soon after we get back. I don't think Brian and Sally suspect
anything. In fact they seem quite engrossed in each other,
which is a relief. The guys slept here last night but that's about
it. They go their way and we go ours.

9 August

WE SHOWED PHILIPPE the jeet. He couldn't believe the rent we
were paying. He thought it was a real rip-off. He said no self-
respecting Frog would think of living in a place like it, especially not in the middle of an artichoke field.

This is really weird coming from him because the place he
lives in is just a shed—all corrugated iron and an outside bog.
He says his parents kicked him out when he was fifteen. Gary
thought this was well cool. At least that's what he said later.
Only he did say that even though he'd rather not have to live

with his boring parents he wouldn't like to live in a dump like Philippe's. There's not even a TV.

Gary really really hates his mum and dad. I mean I like think mine are dead boring, and embarrassing and irritating but Gary really hates his. I mean hates. He thinks we should do something clever with the gas cylinder to teach them a lesson for being so shitty. I thought he was joking and he said yes he was joking because it wouldn't be like the explosion in the caravan because the jeet's so big and draughty. It would just be a little joke. Nothing serious. He really meant it. No one would ever know we had anything to do with it, it would look like an accident. All we had to do was make sure the gas was leaking well good, then go down the bar and leave them to light up later.

10 August

QUELLE DRAME! Another quiet day with the boys out of our hair. I thought as they were behaving so relatively well etc. etc that it might be an opportunity to extend the proverbial olive branch. To my surprise Gary suggested we all have a drink together. So we piled off to Tréguier and for once there were no rows. To my relief Brian and Gary didn't come to blows for once. Afterwards the boys went off to do whatever it is they do while we went home to cook supper.

Then lo and behold we were just driving back down the drive all feeling rather jolly when there was a bloody great explosion from the gîte. Well, of course we charged off and arrived to find the kitchen completely wrecked and a bloke in jeans and pigtail lying face down on the floor. Dead, I'm afraid. A burglar I suppose. Presumably he struck a light so he could see and the gas must have been left on—and Poof! Quelle palaver! Had to summon the gendarmes and God knows what. Oddly enough when the boys came home, Richard seemed much more upset than the rest of us. More sensitive than we thought, perhaps. The girls were pretty devastated and I have to say I was a bit shaken. Gary and Brian, however, appeared completely unmoved. They both took the attitude that the burglar got what he deserved. Maybe Gary has more in common with his father than he'd like to think.

10 August

OH GOD I can't wait to get out of this place. I mean suddenly Gary gives me the creeps. There's something really sinister about him. He seems to think it's all some sort of joke. He says it was nothing to do with him but I don't believe him. He says I've gone soft and I daren't say I think he's gone mad because he frightens me, he really does. He even laughed about it. Actually laughed out loud only it wasn't the sort of laugh you get when someone tells a funny story it was sort of, well, different. All his dad thinks about is the insurance. And the mums and Dad are all being wet about it but only in a sort of sentimental selfish way. Like, 'How could such a horrible thing happen to *us*. On *our* holiday.' They don't seem to think of Philippe being a human being. When I saw him lying all dead on the kitchen floor I just thought of how we'd had some good times together. I mean he wasn't what you'd call normal but he was sort of a friend even if he was Frog and I don't understand how Gary can just say 'he blew it' and then do that horrible laugh of his.

Mind you, if Philippe hadn't blown himself up then...

WELL SHOT
A John Rebus Story

★

IAN RANKIN

A TERRIFIED WOMAN was on the telephone to the police.

'My husband's got a gun. He's going to—'

'What's the address?'

'Eighteen Shettle Street. I'm Janis Fordle.'

'And you say your husband's got a gun, Mrs Fordle?'

'He's holding us hostage. That's what he says. I'm scared to death he'll do something. He's...'

There was the sound of a masculine roar, and the receiver went dead.

IT WAS THE HOTTEST DAY of the year. You could hear an ice-cream van chiming its way around the pebbledash estate. The houses were terraced SSHA jobs, built in the early 1960s. The Shettle Estate used to have a bit of a reputation for its teenage gangs, vandalism, drugs. But it had lost that reputation these last half-dozen years. The garages might still be spray-painted with nicknames, half the front gardens might still be over-grown or have been transformed into outdoor workshops for rusting Ford Capris and countless gutted motorbikes, but the place still felt safer. New front doors had been fitted to all the houses, in a mix of six colour schemes, and new windows had been fitted where necessary. Today these windows had been angled open to allow in any chance of a breeze. Doors were mostly open too, with kids playing on the front steps, squeal-ing their way down echoing closes, marking out with stones on hot pavements the rudiments of a game of 'paldies'.

They heard the ice-cream van, and headed indoors to ask their mothers for money. A good day to be in the ice-cream business.

'He'd do a fortune over here,' commented Detective Inspector John Rebus. 'Plenty of roasting coppers needing cooled down.'

But of course the ice-cream van would not come near Shettle Street. The street had been cordoned off at both ends, and families had been ordered to stay indoors. Not that many of them were heeding this instruction. They stood in clusters at this or that garden gate, watching idly and smoking cigarettes. They were women mostly, their men still out at work this Thursday afternoon. They didn't all have a good view of the siege, for the simple reason that halfway down its length Shettle Street contained a cul-de-sac, and at the end of this cul-de-sac was No. 18, the home of Craig and Janis Fordle and their seventeen-year-old son Bryan.

The neighbours either side of the Fordles had been moved out of their houses, where police officers now roamed. There were police too in the house which backed on to the Fordles' overgrown back garden. Three marked patrol cars were parked across the opening to the cul-de-sac, and behind these milled yet more sweating shiny-faced policemen, including Rebus and Chief Inspector Frank Lauderdale.

They were taking the siege seriously: they couldn't afford not to. When the message of Mrs Fordle's initial phone call had been passed to CID, a detective constable had called her back. She had managed to screech something into the receiver before it had gone dead again. So CID had come out to Shettle Street, where neighbours already knew something was wrong. The roller-blinds had been pulled down beneath the Fordles' net curtains in the living-room windows, front and back. Noises of an argument had been heard behind the rollerblinds, male roars and a woman's high-pitched pleading. It had happened before, and often.

Craig Fordle was in his early forties and had been unemployed for three years. His wife too was unemployed, as was their son Bryan. This in itself wasn't unusual: unemployment

on the housing scheme ran at over 30 per cent. But Craig Fordle had a furious temper, and his wife often sported facial
bruises which even her clever use of make-up—she had been a
beautician and hairdresser—could not mask. Once or twice,
Fordle and his son had even had punch-ups on the street outside the house, usually around midnight as both were returning drunk (or 'half shot' as the neighbours put it) from the
local pub. Fordle thought his son should try harder to get a
job. Bryan thought this was the pot calling the kettle black;
after all, *he*'d only been unemployed for a year.

All of this the police learned from questioning the neighbours, none of whom, however, knew anything about a gun.
Fordle didn't own a gun licence, though he had been in the
army for two years back in the early seventies. He was not well
liked on the estate. Several times, Janis Fordle had sought the
safety of neighbours' houses when her husband's temper
peaked. She had left him twice, going to her mother's in
Oxgangs. But both times she had returned after a week. There
would be calm at No. 18 for a week or two . . . never longer.

All in all, thought Rebus, Fordle was a nutter. But did he
have a gun? It seemed so, from his wife's phone call. It seemed
that Fordle's son was in the house too, also at the mercy of his
father. Rebus stared at the house. It looked quiet enough, almost funereal with its closed blinds. Upstairs, the two bedroom windows were net-curtained, showing no signs of life. At
the back of the house, no movements had been reported from
the bathroom or the back bedroom, or from the kitchen
downstairs. A close separated No. 18 from No. 16, and four
officers were positioned in the close, two to the front and two
to the back. From time to time, they had peered into the small
kitchen window, seeing nothing. And they'd tried windows
and the back door—locked, as was the front door.

Chief Inspector Lauderdale was holding a portable telephone. From time to time he would push the last-number re-
dial button, and there would be a pause before he heard the
steady whine which told him that inside 18 Shettle Street the
telephone was either off the hook or had been disconnected.
Lauderdale looked worried. This was his show, and he didn't

know what to do. Firearms had been issued, but nobody was keen to use them. As long as the blinds remained closed, there was no chance of a shot picking off Craig Fordle. More than this, there was no way of knowing what was going on inside the house. Were people already dead? Did Fordle have a *real* gun? They had evidence only of Janis Fordle's terror and her husband's fury, both heard over the telephone and by the neighbours. But no one had yet seen anything. This made things difficult for Lauderdale, difficult to make a decision. They could take a chance and rush the place, or they could wait it out. Official policy was to wait out a siege, but then this was no ordinary siege. They didn't know what Fordle's grievance was. He'd made no demands. There was no link-up between police and the living-room. They could wait it out, but they couldn't quite know *what* they were waiting out.

And all the time, the sun was burning Lauderdale's neck, his damp clothes chafing him. John Rebus loved it. He hoped things would go on like this for hours. After all, *he* was free to wander away from the scene. Maybe he'd even seek out the ice-cream van and come sauntering back as he finished off a '99' cone. He could nip into one of the nearby houses for a cool drink. He could come and go. Lauderdale couldn't. Lauderdale was in charge. He had to stand behind one patrol car and grit his teeth, like the old sweat he was, now and again shouting in a furious whisper at some child who had come out of his house to play on a tricycle.

'Where's his mum? Doesn't she know what's going on here?'

And so on. Yes, Rebus was thoroughly enjoying himself. He approached his superior again with the same question.

'What should we do now, sir?'

'Fuck off, John,' hissed Lauderdale.

'Right you are, sir,' said Rebus, turning away. Never one to disobey an order, he decided to go and find the ice-cream van. He was ten yards into his mission when he heard the commotion behind him.

'Sir, look! At the window!'

Rebus got back to the patrol car in time to watch what the others were watching. The blind in the living-room window had been pushed aside, and a woman was standing there. She lifted the net curtain, giving the police a better view of her.

'That's her,' said Lauderdale, remembering the description offered by several of the neighbours. 'That's Mrs Fordle.'

Suddenly an arm appeared in the window. In its hand there was a handgun, and the gun was pointing at Mrs Fordle's head. Rebus sucked in a breath and held it. Janis Fordle had screwed shut her eyes, but now she opened them again, and opened the window. A man's yelled voice sounded from the living-room.

'Try anything, she gets it!'

'Mr Fordle!' Lauderdale yelled back. 'We'd like to talk to you! We'd like to know what it is you want!'

But Janis Fordle was already closing the window again, and locking it, the gun still pointed at her head.

'Mr Fordle!' Lauderdale repeated.

Now the net curtain swung down, and Janis Fordle disappeared from view as the roller-blind fell back into place.

'Damn,' said Lauderdale. 'Someone get me a megaphone. If I can't speak to him by phone, I'll just have to shout the odds at him.' He turned to Rebus. 'Did you see the gun?'

'I saw it.'

'Was it real?'

Rebus shrugged. 'Hard to tell from this distance. I wouldn't take a chance of kicking the door down, that's for sure.'

'Thanks for the advice,' snapped Lauderdale. Then he spoke into his radio, informing the other officers in the vicinity that Fordle was carrying a handgun of some kind. Rebus kept his own ideas to himself. If he were in charge, he'd have someone pick the lock on the back door. The kitchen and living-room were separated by only a small front hall, but connecting kitchen to living-room was a large serving-hatch, just like in the neighbouring houses. Get Lauderdale busy on the megaphone, offering anything that would keep Fordle listening, then have two men go in through the living-room door while a third opened the serving-hatch. Fordle was desperate about something, and he'd a record of violence, but he'd never come even close to murder. Rebus doubted the man would shoot either his wife or his son. Maybe he'd offer no resistance at all. Maybe he'd raise his gun. If he did, they'd shoot him, aiming to wound. Bang.

Bang.

The sound of a single gunshot from inside the house collided with Rebus's thoughts. Lauderdale froze. Rebus could see that the armed officers in the close were staring towards their superiors, itching for instructions. Now someone was screaming from inside No. 18: a woman.

'We've got to go in!' Rebus cried.

'Yes,' said Lauderdale. He raised the radio to his mouth, but still gave no orders, simply staring at the house. The officers ducked back into the close as the front door flew wide open. Those at the patrol cars ducked instinctively, peering over the hot bodywork. As though through a haze of desert heat, Janis Fordle came running out of her house, collapsing on the front lawn.

'Christ.'

Still nobody moved towards her. One question was uppermost: where was Fordle? Now another figure was staggering out of the house. Guns were raised then lowered again. It was the son, Bryan.

'He's shot himself!' he cried. 'Get an ambulance!'

There was one waiting just around the corner. A DC ran off to fetch it. The others ran towards the house. As he got closer, Rebus could see that both mother and son were spattered with a fine spray of glittering red, almost like freckles. Almost.

The officers from the close had already entered the living-room by the time Lauderdale and Rebus reached it. Rebus was amazed by the change in Lauderdale which took place between the patrol car and the house.

'We got him,' Lauderdale kept saying quietly to himself. 'We got him.' He was relieved now, and confident, and he was ready to accept all credit for the outcome of the siege. The only casualty, it appeared, had been the one they could afford . . .

He sat slumped on the sofa, still holding the gun in his hand.
The bullet's trajectory was easy to trace. All you had to do was
follow the red spray along and up the wall behind the sofa,
where it crossed a cheap reproduction painting and continued
to the ceiling. It wasn't just the blood that made Craig Fordle
look a mess. He was wearing a grubby T-shirt, distended over
a fat stomach. His trousers had what looked like grease stains
on them, and he wore tattered tartan slippers. He hadn't
shaved for a few days, and his eyes were dark against his pallid skin. On the floor in front of him lay two empty whisky
bottles. The wall unit's drinks cabinet was open, now boasting only a bottle of Malibu and one of advocaat.

It was the advocaat that did it for Rebus. Suddenly he felt
he could see Craig Fordle's whole life. There had always been
advocaat, too, in Rebus's parents' pantry, in the days before
wall units. As a boy, Rebus loved the colour of the drink, and
would open the bottle merely to sniff it. It was only ever drunk
at New Year, by maiden aunts or female cousins, who would
share with the boy the rich flavour of the Dutch drink mixed
with Barr's lemonade. Rebus and Craig Fordle were from the
same working-class stock, tight-knit families, cramped living-
rooms made even more cramped by their oversized sofas and
armchairs, the cabinet for the best china, dining table against
the back window. He could imagine Fordle's despair: no job,
no prospects, everything sinking so slowly you could hardly
perceive it—like the level in an advocaat bottle opened for just
one day each year.

Lauderdale stared down at the dead body for a moment,
then smiled. 'Got you, you bastard,' he said, before moving
off again. He did not notice John Rebus's hands curling into
fists. Neither did John Rebus. This is just a job, he kept telling himself. It's not personal, never personal. It's just a way
of paying the supermarket for Friday night's trolleyfull of
shopping . . .

IT WAS FRIDAY before Dr Curt got round to doing the post-
mortem on the body of Craig Douglas Fordle. By which time
Janis and Bryan Fordle had been interviewed by the police and

then left to get on with the funeral arrangements and redeco-
rating the living-room. Rebus sat on Friday morning reading
through the interview transcripts. The story was pathetically
simple. Fordle had been on a bender lasting several days, and
had come home in a fouler temper even than usual, ready to
start on what whisky there was in the house, aided by another
bottle he'd bought in an off-licence. He was, as his wife—now
widow—put it, 'absolutely steaming'.

On the sofa, he started complaining about things: life in
general, his good-for-nothing son, his lazy slut of a wife, the
shite-hole they lived in, the muck they had to eat, the crap on
the telly, their snooty selfish neighbours, the money they had
to live on . . .

Yes, Janis Fordle knew that her husband had a gun. He kept
it in a shoebox in the bottom of the wardrobe. He'd bought it
somewhere abroad while serving in the army, and told her he
kept it for 'sentimental reasons' though she'd no idea what
these reasons could be. He kept one box of ammo for it
alongside the gun in the shoebox, the whole lot wrapped in an
oiled cloth and two polythene bags. Still, she took him seriously enough when he came downstairs carrying the revolver.
By this time he had become maudlin, mumbling that it all had
to end some day. When he'd pointed the gun at her, she'd been
able to see the bullets in at least three of its chambers. Shortly
afterwards, he'd told her she should phone the police . . .

It was never satisfactorily explained exactly what Fordle had
hoped to gain from any of this, except perhaps a notorious end
to his anonymous life. Rebus had read the account of the
tragedy in the evening paper, and had heard about it on the
radio. Bryan Fordle was said to be 'shocked and grief-stricken'.
He had been able to add little to his mother's statement. The
media had featured another character in the drama too: Chief
Inspector Frank Lauderdale, smugly defending his decision to
wait out the siege. He'd popped up on the local radio station
just before midnight, shattering Rebus's bedtime tranquillity,
as now the telephone shattered the early morning peace of the
CID room. Rebus lifted the receiver.

'CID.'

'Inspector Rebus, good morning.'

'Hello, Dr Curt. You're an early bird.'

'Then you must be the captured worm, Inspector. I'm informed that your Chief Inspector isn't available today. I just thought I'd let you know the first results from the Fordle post-mortem. I'm teaching today, so I thought I'd wrap this one up early . . . so to speak.'

Rebus smiled. 'Go ahead,' he said.

'Interesting,' said Dr Curt. 'Yes, quite interesting. Maybe you should come down to the mortuary.'

Now Rebus winced. 'I've just had breakfast.'

'We can always lend you a bucket if you're squeamish.'

Rebus sighed. 'Half an hour?'

'Better make it twenty minutes. I'm due in the lecture theatre in an hour.'

'Twenty minutes it is. Are you going to give me a clue what this is about?'

'I'll answer that with another question, Inspector: which wrist was Mr Fordle's watch on? Goodbye now.'

DR CURT being Dr Curt, however, he was going to lead John Rebus all round the houses before pointing to the right door. They sat either side of the desk in the cramped mortuary office, the preliminary report in front of Curt. As the doctor's fingers turned the pages of the report, Rebus could smell soap, the soap with which Curt had scrubbed himself clean after the post-mortem. Soap, that normally pleasant and acceptable smell, hinting at cleanliness and freshness. But in this room, it made Rebus's stomach swill.

'The swollen liver, of course, was the real indicator of how much alcohol this man had consumed.'

'Two bottles at least,' said Rebus.

'At the very least, Inspector. It surprised me that a man who had drunk so much would even be conscious, never mind able to brandish a gun . . .'

'And by implication,' added Rebus, 'able to point the gun at his own head and fire.'

Curt shrugged. 'Speculations only, of course.'

'Of course.'

'But then we found something else. Traces of drugs, sleeping pills to be precise.'

'Oh?'

'And according to the deceased's medical records, he was never prescribed sleeping pills.'

Rebus thought about Bryan Fordle's statement. His father had been in a much worse state than usual, slurring his speech, stumbling . . . : 'mental' was the young man's own word for it. Which had made police ask, couldn't you have disarmed him if he was in such a state? Bryan had shaken his head. His father's state, added to the fact that he was holding the gun, made any such move more dangerous. The police had agreed with this.

'All in all,' Dr Curt was saying, 'I'm surprised he wasn't comatose. Some men can take this sort of bodily abuse, but men of greater stature than Fordle.'

Rebus nodded thoughtfully, then noticed Curt smiling at him.

'What's this got to do with his wristwatch?' Rebus asked on cue.

'Inspector Rebus, I thought you'd never ask. Think back.'

Rebus thought back, repressing a shudder. He saw the advocaat bottle first, then the body on the sofa. Left arm flung out over the arm on the sofa. Right arm lying in the body's lap, still holding the gun. The head jarred back by the force of the blast. The spray sweeping from left to right across and up the wall. He tried to see Craig Fordle's wristwatch. The arm stretched out over the sofa's edge was bare.

'The watch was on his right wrist?' Rebus guessed.

Curt nodded 'While yours I see is on your left wrist. I take it you're right-handed.' It was Rebus's turn to nod, then he saw what Curt was getting at. The watch was on Fordle's right wrist, the gun in his right hand . . .

'He was left-handed, but he shot himself with his right hand.'

'Well done, Inspector. I can't think why you didn't see it sooner.'

Because, thought Rebus, I was too busy with a bloody advocaat bottle.

'Can I just say something, between the two of us?' asked Curt.

'Go on.'

'Having read about Mr Fordle last night and this morning, I'm tempted to sympathise with the wife and son.' He paused. 'Whatever they did.'

Rebus shook his head slowly. 'That's not our job,' he said.

THERE WAS NO ONE at home at 18 Shettle Street. All the blinds were down, the doors firmly locked. Rebus asked a neighbour, who confirmed that Janis and Bryan were staying with her mother in Oxgangs.

'I doubt she'll ever come back,' judged the neighbour, arms folded across her chest, adding, as Rebus turned away, 'She's well shot of him.'

Indeed she was. He walked through the close to the back of the house. A tethered dog barked at him from across a fence, setting off a chain reaction in other dogs on the estate. Rebus ignored the noise, as he ignored the twitching net curtains around him. By the side of the back door stood a large black rubbish bin, set on two wheels so it could be manoeuvred out to the front of the house for collection. He lifted its lid and peered in, finding what he was looking for. He brought out a polythene bag from his pocket and folded it inside out, then placed it over the empty whisky bottles, wrapping it around them without touching them with his fingers.

She's well shot of him. The words reverberated in his head as they had done since the neighbour had spoken them.

THEY WERE STICKING to their story.

And meantime, Rebus had to explain himself to Chief Superintendent Watson and Chief Inspector Lauderdale. Rebus would like nothing better than to put Lauderdale's gas at a very low peep, but it wasn't turning out like that.

Drinkers at Craig Fordle's local hadn't been able to confirm that he was left-handed. Some said he used his left hand to lift a glass, others said his right.

'He was a whisky man?' Rebus had asked.

'Oh aye. Except when he had an advocaat.' There were smiles of reminiscence at this.

'He drank *advocaat*?'

'Ach, only now and again. It was a bit of a joke. If he was on top form about something, he'd have an advocaat and lemonade. He said he'd always liked it as a laddie...'

Meantime, from the lab had come news that though Fordle's stomach had contained traces of Mogadon, the whisky bottles had been clean—too scrupulously clean, in fact. They had been washed and rinsed.

'Why would anyone rinse empty bottles before chucking them out?' This was Rebus's question. It was one he didn't bother to ask Janis Fordle, knowing she'd have a ready answer, something to do with being confused in her grief... washing the bottles before realising what she was doing. She did though admit that she had renewed her prescription for Mogadon only the previous week, adding that Craig used to take a couple of her tablets now and again, though she'd warned him against it. More, she was able to tell CID that her husband had been 'a bit ambidextrous'.

All in all, it wasn't looking good for John Rebus. Lauderdale was still looking the relaxed man on the media.

'So,' said Chief Superintendent Watson, 'as I see it, John, you're saying her husband started waving this gun around, so she crushed up some sleeping pills into his drink, then when he was unconscious she took the gun from him and shot him. Is that it?'

Rebus shook his head. 'Not quite. I think they planned the whole thing from the start—both Mrs Fordle and her son. They knew Fordle was on a bender, so they laced the bottle of whisky and waited for him to come reeling home. Once he was unconscious, she phoned us.'

'And the shouting in the background?'

'Bryan. It was him at the window too, holding the gun. They wanted to reinforce the idea that they were being held at gunpoint. As soon as they'd done that, they shot Fordle.'

'A messy way to get rid of someone,' complained Lauderdale.

'But plausible, Frank,' Watson added.

'So where's your evidence, John?'

'If I'm right,' Rebus said nonchalantly, 'we look at the six-shooter. It'll have the son's prints all over it, unless he wiped it.'

'And supposing he did wipe it?'

Rebus shrugged. 'We offer what we've got to the Procurator-fiscal, let him decide.'

Watson shook his head. 'There's nothing like enough proof for that, none at all in fact. If the gun's clean, we drop it.' It was Rebus's turn almost to say something.

'Ok?' Watson persisted.

'Yes, sir,' said Rebus.

THE GUN WAS CLEAN, the only smudged prints on it belonging to Craig Fordle. Even Dr Curt, asked by Rebus if there was anything, any other clue he could add, shook his head.

'Drop it, Inspector. It's not worth the grief.'

'It is to me,' said Rebus.

He brooded on it most of the sweltering weekend, walking along the Water of Leith, meandering his way through the quiet parts of the city and the busy parts. Even when he took Dr Patience Aitken out to dinner, he talked his suspicions over with her, and she played along, bouncing questions and ideas at him. All to no effect, which was perhaps why he found himself back in Shettle Street on the Monday morning, squeezing his car past a dustbin lorry and parking in the cul-de-sac. The police had a set of keys for No. 18, which were due to be handed back later that day. A neighbour was wheeling her dustbin out towards the pavement as Rebus opened the door.

'She's at her mum's,' the neighbour called. Rebus smiled and nodded towards the woman. He knew that: it was why he was here. 'She was here earlier,' the neighbour continued, 'but she's not here now.'

Here earlier? Rebus wondered why. Inside the house, he made for the living-room. It was much as it had been on the Thursday, excepting the missing corpse. The blood on the wall had dried the colour of the rust on Rebus's car's door-panels. The whisky bottles were gone of course, and the cocktail cabinet had been closed. Outside, the dustbin lorry had stopped with a hiss of air-brakes at the end of the cul-de-sac. Now, with a buzzer sounding the warning, it was reversing in. He could hear the dustbin men collecting the bins, yelling greetings to some of the neighbours. Life went on. Idly, he pulled open the door of the cocktail cabinet, and saw that the advocaat bottle was no longer there. He stared for a moment at the space where it should have been, then flew to the door.

Thoughtfully, a binman had wheeled No. 18's dustbin out to the kerb, ready to dump its contents into the back of the lorry.

'Stop!' Rebus shouted. 'Hold it a minute!'

The binmen looked at him as though he were a ghost. Certainly, they hadn't been expecting anyone to be at home at No. 18. They were even more surprised when he flung off the lid of the bin and gazed down, a grin spreading across his face. The advocaat bottle had been pushed deep down into the rubbish, but even so Rebus could see that this time no one had bothered to rinse it out...

KNOWING HER HUSBAND occasionally drank advocaat with lemonade, Janis Fordle had taken no risks: she'd crushed a good lot of sleeping pills into that bottle as well as into the whisky. But afterwards, in shock, she hadn't remembered to dump the bottle, and neither had Bryan, though he'd rinsed out the whisky bottles. When the police had come back to her on Friday with more questions, she'd begun to worry, and had eventually remembered the advocaat. Knowing the bins were emptied first thing Monday morning, she'd hurried back to Shettle Street and dumped the advocaat bottle into her bin.

There was enough now, enough so that when Janis Fordle found out they were going to tie both her and her son to the murder, she didn't give them the chance. Instead, she changed her story, taking all of the blame. As John Rebus saw it, it was yet another triumph for Scottish justice and in particular for the City of Edinburgh Police. Dr Curt wasn't so sure. He wondered what would have happened if he hadn't said anything to Rebus in the first place. John Rebus himself had an answer for him.

'That bugger Lauderdale would still be like the cat that got the cream. Instead of which, last time I saw him he looked like the vet had given him his balls as a souvenir.'

Rebus began to laugh, but he laughed alone. There were times when Dr Curt not only didn't understand John Rebus but thought that maybe he didn't much like the man either . . .

WHERE'S STACEY?

★

LIZA CODY

'WHERE'S STACEY?' I asked, looking round. I don't go to
Manatee Key often, and while I am away I like to think that it
remains, as it does in my memory, static: a little world waiting for me to reinhabit it. I am always disappointed. Manatee
Key may look like a quiet, subtropical resort, a place designed for well-heeled Americans to retire to, but it has a sublife all of its own. Behind every sunny, welcoming door is a
snake-pit of writhing ambition and discontent. The café you
love changes hands. The tennis coach you swapped stories with
becomes bored with his crop of lessons and leaves to rejoin the
professional circuit. Paradise is a frustrating place for those
who work there. It is only paradise for those of us who go there
to play.

If it weren't for Elaine I wouldn't know much more about
what went on behind the sunny, welcoming doors than any
other tourist. Elaine runs the pro shop at the Manatee Key
tennis club. She will sell you your Reeboks, your Fila shirt,
your Head skirt, your Wilson Hammer System. She will get
your racquet strung to exactly the right tension, she will book
your lessons, arrange a fill-in when one of your foursome
drops out. She will even tell you the best place to eat if you like
Italian. She does most of this all by herself, in perpetual motion between the phone, the clothes racks and the long white
counter, but sometimes she hires part-time help. Last year it
was Stacey.

This year, although I have been coming in every day for a
week, I haven't seen Stacey, so I ask, 'Where's Stacey?'

Elaine is folding sweatshirts and packing them into cellophane bags. She doesn't stop, but her bright eyes brighten.

'Din't I tell you about Stacey?' she says.

My eyes brighten too. Elaine is about to tell me a story.

'You haven't heard?' she asks. She knows I haven't.

'Well, Liza,' she says. 'I had some trouble with that girl, a lotta trouble.'

I lean my arms on the counter and settle in. But Elaine isn't ready yet.

'Have you seen Keith?' she asks. 'Only I don't want Keith walking in thinking I'm talking about him behind his back. He liked Stacey, see.'

Keith is the maintenance man. They have clay courts at Manatee tennis club. Clay is a beautiful surface to play on, but it takes a lot of looking after. Keith is an artist when it comes to looking after the courts but he is a touchy man.

I look out of the window.

'Keith's busy,' I say. 'He's talking to Lew.'

'Well, I sure hope he's apologising,' Elaine says. ''Cos, Liza, Lew and me, we been having problems with Keith 'cos he's like this sorta Dr Jekyll and Mr Hyde character. One day he's nice as pie and then the next day you ask him to do sump'n and he just blows up in your face. Like, this morning I asked him to string a racquet for a lady. This lady needed it for her two o'clock game, and Keith, he snaps at me and says he'll do it when he gets round to it. But he didn't, so this lady never got her racquet and Lew had to lend her one, and she was pissed and I was pissed and Lew was pissed. And Keith, he thinks he can get away with murder, but he can't, see, because Lew and me employ him, not the other way round.'

'Well, they seem to be getting on all right now,' I say. I can see them talking quite amiably, their eyes screwed up against the late afternoon glare.

'Yeah? Well Lew's too soft on him. Just 'cos he's great with the courts.'

'Stacey,' I say, to remind Elaine.

'Yeah, Stacey,' she says. 'I had a lotta trouble with that girl, Liza. You remember Stacey? She was young, right?'

'Yes.'

'And pretty. Right?'

'Yes.'

'Well, some of the older guys thought she was pretty. Older guys go for those little blonde girls, don't they, Liza? But Stacey wasn't real smart. So it was like this, see, she got to running around with a funny crowd. She'd tell Keith all about it, see, and he'd tell Lew, and Lew'd tell me. But, see, I din't believe it. "Nah," I said to Lew. "Stacey's a sensible girl." I mean, I knew she wasn't real smart but I thought she was sensible.

'But one day, right here in the shop, I got a cheque back from the bank marked "insufficient funds". That's what they write on them here, Liza, when a cheque bounces—"insufficient funds". The name on the cheque was Madder Tungate, and I didn't know the name. Which surprised me 'cos I know everyone who comes in here.'

This is true. Elaine knows everyone.

'I din't know this Madder Tungate, but there was a phone number on the back of the cheque so I wasn't worried. I call the number, y'know, to tell him about the "insufficient funds", 'cos he'll want to make good, right? But when I call, this little kid answers, and I ask for Madder Tungate, and the kid says he isn't in and puts the phone down real quick. I think nothing of it. I mean, what do little kids know?

'Anyway, I call again an hour later, and this time a woman answers, and I ask for this Madder Tungate, and she says he isn't home. But I say, "Tell him to call Elaine at the Manatee tennis club." And she says, "Sure," and puts the phone down.

'Well, Liza, later in the afternoon, that same afternoon, I just happened to be looking at the paper, y'know, the *Manatee Observer*. I was looking at the paper, and I saw this name— Madder Tungate! Yeah. Well, he's wanted for murder. Murder, Liza.'

Elaine's bright eyes are brilliant because if there is one thing which really turns her on it is real-life crime. Not fictional crime, not fictional cops. It has to be real to satisfy Elaine. She tolerates me, even though I only write fiction, because she knows I like true stories too. Real voices telling true stories.

'Madder Tungate,' she goes on, 'this name on my cheque marked "insufficient funds" is wanted for murder. See, he used to work at some hotel down the beach a way, and he got fired for stealing, and he went back and strangled the manager. He, and this other guy, Mick, they rented a room at the hotel. Mick said he went to the bathroom, and when he came out this Madder Tungate was strangling the hotel manager. Then, he said, Madder intimidated him into driving him to Tampa airport 'cos he wanted to get out of the state. That's what it said in the paper.

'So I looked at the cheque again. And two days before the hotel manager got strangled Madder Tungate was right here at the Manatee Key tennis club buying a sweatshirt! Can you believe that?'

'Astonishing,' I say. I know there is more.

'Astonishing. Right,' says Elaine, nodding. 'So what do I do? Well, I start goin' through all the sales dockets. 'Cos where there's a cheque, Liza, there's gotta be a sales docket. Right?'

'Yes.'

'Right. And here was the funny part, Liza—when I found it, half the sales docket was written up in Stacey's writing, and half of it, I didn't know the writing but it looked like the writing on the cheque.

'Well, Stacey knows, 'cos I told her and told her, she knows no one's supposed to write on a sales docket but her. So I thought, "This Madder Tungate is one of Stacey's friends."

'And I asked around, and Keith told me—yeah, this Madder Tungate is one of the guys Stacey's running around with, and what's more, she spent the night at his place a couple days before. But she said nothing happened. "Like hell nothing happened," I said, but Keith swears she said nothing happened.

'Anyway, Liza, about this time, there was a cop working here at the club. Cleaning houses. Moonlighting, 'cos his wife runs the cleaning agency that was taking care of the condos. So this cop was in here and I showed him the sales docket, and he said, "Well, don't you be too surprised if a detective comes in to talk to you."

'And I said, "Why would a detective want to talk to me?"'

'And he said, "'Cos you know Madder Tungate."'

'And I said, "But I don't know Madder Tungate. He's one of the guys Stacey runs around with. In fact, she spent the night at his place but she swears nothing happened."'

'And he said, "Too right nothing happened. The guy's a confirmed gay."'

'So I says to Keith, "If the guy's a confirmed gay, what's Stacey doin' runnin' round with him?"'

'And Keith says, "She said he was changing."'

'And I said, "If she believes that she'll believe anything." I said, "A leopard does *not* change his spots." Ain't that the truth, Liza?

'But, see, I was worried, and what was worrying me was that Stacey's parents had this rented Winnebago and the whole family had gone up north to Pittsburgh on a vacation. And I thought this Madder Tungate had taken a plane out of Tampa and gone to Pittsburgh. And Stacey's parents wouldn't know about the hotel manager getting strangled, see, and they'd take him in.

'So I said to the detective, I said, "Y'know, you should go look for this Madder Tungate in Pittsburgh 'cos that's where Stacey's at."'

'And was he?' I asked. 'In Pittsburgh?'

'He'd went to San Francisco,' Elaine said, shaking her head regretfully.

'And Stacey?'

'Stacey was in Pittsburgh all right, and when she got back I called her up and I said, "What was this Madder Tungate doing out at the Manatee tennis club?"

'And she lied to me. She said, "I don't know no Madder Tungate."'

'"Don't lie to me, my girl," I said. "I've got his cheque marked 'insufficient funds', and that's his writing on the sales docket where it shouldn't be because you're the only one supposed to write on the sales docket."'

'And she said, "You don't trust me any more. You're going to can me."'

'I said, "You got your job. I trust you, Stacey, but I don't trust your friends."

'And then a coupla weeks later, one of the members here comes up to me and says, "Who's that dark-haired little girl working here Sunday?"

'And I said, "What dark-haired little gal? I don't know any dark-haired gal." Because Stacey's blonde, as you know, Liza, and she was the only one working for me on Sunday.

'So I asked around, see, and Keith told me one of Stacey's friends had been in the club all day. And Stacey let her behind the counter. So I called Stacey to ask her what was goin' on. And she lied to me. She said there'd been no one there Sunday but her. But too many people had told me about the dark-haired little gal, see. So I caught Stacey out.

'Then, Liza, then I had this run-around with Stacey's mother. 'Cos you see, Liza, remember I told you our apartment on Cortez was broken into?'

'I remember,' I say.

'Well, the woman downstairs saw someone running away carrying something. Remember I said that?'

'Yes.'

'Well, when all this about the hotel manager getting strangled happened I remembered what the woman downstairs said. And I thought the guy she described matched the description of Madder Tungate. So I asked Stacey's mother if she had a picture of him I could show the woman downstairs. But you know what, Liza, she got real uptight. Sure she had a picture but she said I couldn't have it. Which made me think.

'So then I said to Stacey, "Listen, Stacey, is there any way this Madder Tungate coulda got Lew's and my address?"

'And she said, "No way at all."

'But she made a mistake, see. She asked what was taken in the break-in, and I told her, "The VCR, the video camera, all that electrical stuff." And all of Lew's tennis trophies, Liza, which was real mean. They even took his Wimbledon medal and that medal meant a lot to Lew.'

'I know,' I say. 'I remember him telling me.'

'Yeah, right,' Elaine says. 'Well, when I told Stacey about the VCR and stuff going in the break-in, she made this mistake. Y'know what she said? She said, "Oh, Madder doesn't take electrical goods and that sort of stuff. He takes furniture and paintings."

'I mean she *knew* he stole! And she still ran around with him! She said he drove a black car with tinted glass, and he wore black clothes and dressed real funny so he wouldn't be seen at night. She knew all of that and she *still* ran around with him!

'Then Stacey said, "You're going to let me go, aren't you? You don't trust me any more."

'And I said, "I trust you. It's your friends I don't trust."

'But she came in here the next day when I wasn't expecting her, and told me she was quitting. See, Liza, she was bored with the job.'

'Bored?' I say.

'Yeah. She said it was boring and I guess maybe if she was so bored that was why she ran around with Madder Tungate.'

'What happened to him?' I ask. 'Was he caught?'

'Nah,' Elaine says. 'The cops tracked him as far as a motel in Palm Springs and then they lost him.'

'And where's Stacey now?'

'Well, Liza, that is kinda funny. Coupla months ago I got this letter from the hotel down the beach. Y'know, the one where Madder Tungate strangled the manager. Well, the new manager there wrote to me saying Stacey wanted to work there in reception. She gave him my name for a reference.'

Elaine grins at me, and I grin at her.

'I lost the letter,' Elaine says. 'I lost it before I could write the reference. But I heard Stacey got the job anyway. Nothing I woulda said coulda made much difference. They're not real careful who they hire down there.'

KEEP TAKING THE TABLOIDS

★

ROBERT BARNARD

'You know who Sam Sprutt is, I suppose?' Inspector Carling asked of Sergeant Haggard, who was new to the area. He liked the newcomer, but the fact that he came from London made him almost by definition an unknowable quantity. Of course it was not unknown for policemen from the metropolitan area to opt for the quieter life; but there were rumours about Haggard, and Carling had seen two or three of the young PCs at the station whispering by the coffee dispenser, and pointing.

'Oh, I know who he *is*,' said Haggard, keeping his eyes on the road towards Marleigh Towers. 'What I can't work out is why they've sent us. Or rather why they've sent *you*. As far as I can make out it's a perfectly straightforward case of affray. A uniformed PC would be perfectly adequate.'

'Oh, Sam Sprutt is a very important man in this part of Lincolnshire.'

Haggard raised eloquent bushy eyebrows.

'It's coming to something when a sleaze merchant like Sam Sprutt is described as a very important man.'

'I'd agree every time. But don't tell me you haven't seen the boys reading the *Sunday Sensation* in the canteen.'

And of course he couldn't. Policemen read the *Sunday Sensation*, as housewives and navvies, schoolkids and secretaries read it. It had started five years before, with the undeclared aim of making the other British tabloids look respectable. Now when people talked about newspapers going downmarket, Sam Sprutt's was the market they were go-

ing down to. The *Sensation* specialised in pictures of bimbo
and hunks; its letterpress was almost entirely tales of the bed
room, the jacuzzi and the massage parlour. It slavered whe
it caught a whisper of politicians with their trousers down
actresses surprised *in flagrante*, or any story that suggeste
Britain was a nation of rutters and bitches on heat, rather tha
the sexually torpid nation everyone knows it to be. It also ha
a nice line in totally fabricated or fantastic stories of the w
FIND IRAQI SETTLEMENT ON MARS type, as well as interview
with the famous or temporarily notorious which never in fac
took place. Interviews with the *Sensation* hardly ever did tak
place: no one in their senses would talk to it.

'Of course you've got to admit its headlines sometimes d
grab you,' said Carling. Haggard was slowing down as the
approached two magnificent gateposts, and his mouth wa
twisted into a grimace 'You may sneer, but they do. You know
GRANNIES ON THE GAME, or TV STAR'S LESBIAN LOVE-NEST I
HACKNEY, or STUDENT STREETWORKERS—A Quick Poke in th
Interests of Learning, or I WAS A TEENAGE VAMPIRE.'

Haggard was silent as they drove up the imposing tree-line
drive towards the Georgian mansion. Then he said: 'If we ha
a proper education system people wouldn't *want* to read gar
bage like that. People in other countries don't.'

'Maybe you're right.' Carling surveyed the splendours o
eighteenth-century architecture spread out before them
'Meanwhile it means that people like Sam Sprutt are raking i
in. I wonder if this is a straight domestic, or whether it's on
of his scoops that has got him into trouble.'

'I expect there's a woman in it somewhere. He never make
any secret of how straight and basic his interests are. We wer
told to go round the back. Tradesman's Entrance, I expect.'

But the imposing porticoed front, with only a narrow
sanded path leading to it, was hardly a place to leave a car, the
had to admit. The path led naturally round to the side, wher
there was a small tarmacked area. Looking towards the back
of the house they could see an expanse of lawns and flow
erbeds that eventually gave way to a wooded area sloping dow
to the river. Sleaze paid, all right! As they got out of their ca
they could hear from the back of the house male and femal

voices raised in furious altercation. They ran on to the lawns, and headed towards a handsome, blue-papered drawing-room with open french windows, but they were diverted by a butler who emerged from the modest back entrance and pointed to the far end of the house.

'A spot of bother in the study,' he said with a smirk as they ran up to him. He barely attempted to conceal his contempt for his employer. Whatever happened to the impenetrability of butlers, Carling wondered? But then, critics of Sam Sprutt's papers were always asked, 'Do you think we're living in the nineteenth century?' A leering butler was perhaps a true manifestation of Sam Sprutt's twenty-first-century Britain.

The study windows were open too, and as they charged through they were confronted by a yelling pair so close they looked as if they were swapping halitoses. Watching them, sitting on the arm of a sofa and calmly chewing bubble-gum, was a well-developed girl in a dress that started just above her nipples and finished just below her crotch.

'I'm going to sue you for breach of contract!' screamed the woman.

'There was no fucking contract!'

'Breach of promise then! You promised to make my Sandra a page three girl!'

'So she didn't have what it takes.'

'She didn't let you take it, more like!'

They seemed about to resort to violence, from which, judging by the scratches that went all the way down Sam Sprutt's cheeks, they had only just desisted. Haggard went and grabbed Sprutt. He was short, fat and fiftyish, with a few stray hairs flattened over a balding pate. He had little piggy eyes blazing out of fat cheeks, and chins all the way down his neck. When Haggard threw him unceremoniously down on to a heavily padded armchair he sat there puffing and snorting as if he'd just done the hundred metres.

'Bloody women—who needs 'em?' he asked, which was rich coming from someone who had done pretty well out of their more obvious physical features.

Carling kept a hold on the woman's arms, which ended in blood-red talons that had obviously already done their share of damage. Her face was caked with make-up so thick that Carling, an asthmatic, was already breathing short. The hair was brazen red and the body chunky and top-heavy.

'Now, what's all this about?' Carling asked. The woman turned to him and pointed a melodramatic claw in Sprutt's direction.

'He's a filthy rotten cheat, that's what it's about. He promised to make my Sandra a star. Samantha Fox's successor, that's what he promised—said he'd get her pin-up in every locker-room. Don't make me laugh! One measly page three, and since then not a dicky-bird!'

'I see. And why do you think that was?'

'I know why it was. It was because he started to paw our Sandra and she kicked him in the groin.'

Our Sandra suddenly became more interesting and sympathetic. However she just sat there on the sofa imperturbably, apparently concentrating on chewing and blowing pink bubbles.

'And how old is Sandra?'

'Eighteen,' said Sprutt.

'Seventeen,' said her mother.

'Ahhh ... Well, that can be checked later. And had anything been said about ... about what she might give in return for all this ... exposure?'

' 'Course I expected her to show willing!' yelled Sprutt. 'What's the matter with you? You live in the nineteenth century or something?'

'Dirty old sod!' yelled Sandra's mum.

'And you knew!' yelled Sprutt back at her, trying to struggle to his feet. Haggard pushed him back into the chair's embrace, and Sprutt hissed: 'Your Chief Constable will hear about this!'

'Sandra, what have you got to say to all this?' Carling asked, turning to her. She shrugged and went on chewing.

'How old are you, Sandra?'

'Fourteen.'

'And Mr Sprutt made advances to you?'

She grinned derisively.

'You could call it that. It was after the second photographic session. He took me into a room at the back and started groping me as if he owned me. Nobody owns me. I kneed him in the groin and told him to lay off.'

'You didn't know of any...agreement between your mother and him?'

She shrugged again. It showed off her shoulders, but made the dress look perilously unsuspended.

'So what? She'd never asked me. She doesn't own me either. I didn't fancy him. I mean—look at him! Who would? I don't do it with guys I don't fancy.'

That didn't seem likely to limit Sandra's career as a page three girl, but Carling didn't think it advisable to say so.

'And did he say anything after you'd...kneed him?'

'Not for a bit. I did it good and hard. Then he said, "Right, little lady, that's your lot. Career over and done with at fourteen. Finished—get me?"'

'So he knew your age?'

'I did not know her age! She's lying!'

Sandra sneered up at Carling.

'Sure he knew my age. So what? Do you think I'm the only one who's doing it at fourteen? Go and talk to a few schoolkids, Granddad!'

Carling took a deep breath.

'Right. Well, I think I've got the picture. You two had better come out to the car, and we'll take a statement from you both at the station. And I may well want to talk to you later, sir.'

This time Sam Sprutt pushed aside Haggard's restraining hand and struggled to his feet.

'Take them off my back by all means, in fact I bloody insist on it, but if you start believing anything that slag tells you, or her nymphet daughter, I'll see that you and the whole police force of Lincolnshire are publicly crucified. You get my meaning? I don't have to spell it out, do I?'

'No, sir, you don't have to spell it out. Come along Mrs—'

'Slattery.'

'Sluttery, more like,' yelled Sprutt as a Parthian shot. 'And it's not Mrs.'

They emerged from the great man's study and into the hall, which was hung with what looked like copies of Kneller portraits of beauties of Charlies II's day, perhaps chosen to show that toplessness was not a modern invention. They heard the door locked behind them. But they had no sooner started towards the front entrance than an eruption of violent noise there disturbed the temporary calm.

'Let me get at him! You're not stopping me this time. I'm going to spill the bastard's guts.'

The butler had been rudely pushed aside—though he had made no more than token resistance—by a heavy-set man of forty or so who ran shouting threats into the hall.

'Where are you, Sprutt? You're not going to be able to hide this time!'

He ran in the direction of the study, screaming hoarsely, and it took a rugby tackle by Haggard to bring him to the floor. A minute later, his arm behind his back in a half-nelson, the man was still shouting threats.

'I'll get you, Sprutt! You can hire a private army and it still won't protect you from me!'

Carling very much resented the implication that the police were Sprutt's private army. The butler came towards him, sliding over the tiled flooring, smiling conspiratorially.

'Normally Bates would have been here,' he murmured with the utmost composure. 'Charming character, Bates. Built like a buffalo. Ex-wrestler with a record as long as your arm. Footman, we called him. In fact he was His Nibs's minder. Employed for situations like this one.'

'Why's he not here?'

'Snitched one thing too many. Got the boot yesterday. We hadn't got around to interviewing a successor. It was Bates brought this laddie down last time he was here.'

'Who is he?'

The butler shrugged. 'Wife had a baby last year—late baby, much wanted. It was snatched from its pram in a supermarket. Police got the woman who took her within an hour or two, but in the scuffle the baby fell and its brain was damaged. It was largely hushed up, but the *Sunday Sensation* ran a we

NAME THE CARELESS MUM story—a whole page. Our laddie never blames the police unless they refuse to dance to his tune.'

'I think I'd prefer a different sort of supporter. What happened?'

'Wife committed suicide. Coroner attributed it to the brain damage the baby suffered. Husband doesn't agree—as you can see.'

The man on the floor had been watching him. Now he started struggling with Haggard.

'You're talking about her! That bastard in there killed her as sure as if he'd put a knife into her. I'm going to get you, Sprutt! You can't keep me out!'

'Oh, for God's sake lock him up somewhere,' said Carling. 'I'm going to radio for more help.'

Haggard frog-marched the bellowing man across the hall, pitched him into a room which left a momentary impression of blue elegance on his retina, then took the key from inside the door and locked it. He quickly went back to the group, where Carling was murmuring into his walkie-talkie.

'I'm bringing in a mother and daughter. I wouldn't rule out charges against Sprutt... Yes, I mean it: charges against Sprutt. The law of the land applies to Sprutt as well as anyone else, whatever he may think. Meanwhile I need a couple of men to bring in a maniac we've got here—'

But he was interrupted by the sound of breaking glass and crunching wood, and then by a howl—a terrible scream, rising in pitch to an agonised squeak and then subsiding into thick, choking coughs. It sounded like an animal being killed in some savage piece of peasant barbarity.

'It wasn't the blue drawing-room you put him into, was it?' asked the butler of Haggard.

When they got to the study Sprutt was dying, his fat cheeks red and blotchy, his pudgy body spouting blood. His killer was watching, now almost dispassionate, noting rather than gloating, and making no effort to escape or hide the bloodstained knife in his hand. Somehow the scene presented itself to Carling in the form of newspaper headlines: PORN KING SLAIN BY VICTIM'S HUBBY. Or perhaps simply: STUCK PIG.

It was several hours before they were driving back to police headquarters. There didn't seem much point in taking the mother and daughter in for questioning now. Carling had given the mother a long lecture, which he knew would be ignored. One could only hope that the daughter would stick to her quaint habit of only going with men she fancied.

'There'll be a black mark against your name,' Carling said to Haggard. 'You should have thought about checking the windows. Mind you, I should have told you to search him for any weapons...' The Sergeant merely nodded, and kept his eyes on the road. Carling was puzzled by the stolid man's negligence, as well as by his apparent unconcern. This wasn't at all the sort of thorough police work he would have expected from him. As they sat silently speeding towards town Carling did begin to wonder.

But only Haggard would *know*. They might find out it was a picture of his daughter, in costume, on her way to perform in a student production of *The Threepenny Opera*, that had illustrated the STUDENT STREETWALKERS story. He rather suspected some version of this story was already current at the station. But he could point out that although she had felt bruised and angry and degraded, the story had hardly ruined her life.

Only he could *know* that, as he had held the man on the floor in a half-nelson, he had crouched there counting the doors in the hall, and trying to calculate which would lead to the blue room with the french windows open on to the lawn.

A LITTLE MISSIONARY WORK
A Kinsey Millhone Short Story

★

SUE GRAFTON

SOMETIMES YOU HAVE to take on a job that constitutes pure missionary work. You accept an assignment not for pay, or for any hope of tangible reward, but simply to help another human being in distress. My name is Kinsey Millhone. I'm a licensed private eye—in business for myself—so I can't really afford professional charity, but now and then somebody gets into trouble and I just can't turn my back.

I was standing in line one Friday at the bank, waiting to make a deposit. It was almost lunchtime and there were eleven people in front of me, so I had some time to kill. As usual, in the teller's line, I was thinking about Harry Hovey, my bank robber friend, who'd once been arrested for holding up this very branch. I'd met him when I was investigating a bad cheque case. He was introduced to me by another crook as an unofficial 'expert' and ended up giving me a crash course in the methods and practices of passing bad paper. Poor Harry. I couldn't remember how many times he'd been in the can. He was skilled enough for a life of crime, but given to self-sabotage. Harry was always trying to go straight, always trying to clean up his act, but honest employment never seemed to have much appeal. He'd get out of prison, find a job, and be doing pretty well for himself. Then something would come along and he'd succumb to temptation...forge a cheque, rob a bank, God only knows what. Harry was hooked on crime the way some people are addicted to cocaine, alcohol, chocolate and unrequited love. He was currently doing time in the Federal Correctional Institution in Lompoc, California, with all

the other racketeers, bank robbers, counterfeiters, and form
er White House staff bad boys...

I had reached the teller's window and was finishing m
transaction when Lucy Alisal, the assistant bank manager ap
proached. 'Miss Millhone? I wonder if you could step this way
Mr Chamberlain would like a word with you.'

'Who?'

'The branch vice-president,' she said. 'It shouldn't tak
long.'

'Oh. Sure.'

I followed the woman toward Mr Chamberlain's glass
walled enclosure, wondering the whole time what I'd done t
deserve this. Well, OK. Let's be honest. I'd been thinkin
about switching my account to First Interstate for the fre
chequing privileges, but I didn't see how he could have foun
out about *that*. As for my balances, I'd only been overdraw
by the teensiest amount and what's a line of credit for?

I was introduced to Jack Chamberlain, who turned out t
be someone I recognised from the gym, a tall, lanky fellow i
his early forties, whose work-outs overlapped mine thre
mornings a week. We'd exchange occasional small talk if w
happened to be doing reps on adjacent machines. It was od
to see him here in a conservative business suit after months c
sweat-darkened shorts and T-shirts. His hair was croppe
close, the colour a dirty mixture of copper and silver. He wo
steel-rimmed glasses and his teeth were endearingly crooked i
front. Somehow, he looked more like a high school baske
ball coach than a banking exec. A trophy sitting on his des
attested to his athletic achievements, but the engraving wa
small and I couldn't quite make out the print from where
was. He caught my look and a smile creased his face. 'Varsit
basketball. We were state champs,' he said, as he shook m
hand formally and invited me to take a seat.

He sat down himself and picked up a fountain pen, whic
he capped and recapped as he talked. 'I appreciate your time
I know you do your banking on Fridays and I took the li
erty,' he said. 'Someone told me at the gym that you're a pr
vate investigator.'

'That's right. Are you in the market for one?'

'This is for an old friend of mine. My former high school sweetheart, if you want the truth,' he said. 'I probably could have called you at your office, but the circumstances are unusual and this seemed more discreet. Are you free tonight by any chance?'

'Tonight? That depends,' I said. 'What's going on?'

'I'd rather have her explain it. This is probably going to seem paranoid, but she insists on secrecy, which is why she didn't want to make contact herself. She has reason to believe her phone is tapped. I hope you can bear with us. Believe me, I don't ordinarily do business this way.'

'Glad to hear that,' I said. 'Can you be a bit more specific? So far, I haven't really heard what I'm being asked to do.'

Jack set the pen aside. 'She'll explain the situation as soon as it seems wise. She and her husband are having a big party tonight and she asked me to bring you. They don't want you appearing in any professional capacity. Time is of the essence, or we might go about this some other way. You'll understand when you meet her.'

I studied him briefly, trying to figure out what was going on. If this was a dating ploy, it was the weirdest one I'd ever heard. 'Are you married?'

He smiled slightly. 'Divorced. I understand you are, too. I assure you, this is not a hustle.'

'What kind of party?'

'Oh, yes. Glad you reminded me.' He removed an envelope from his top drawer and pushed it across the desk. 'Cocktails. Five to seven. Black tie, I'm afraid. This cheque should cover your expenses in the way of formal dress. If you try the rental shop around the corner, Roberta Linderman will see that you're outfitted properly. She knows these people well.'

'What people? You haven't even told me their names.'

'Karen Waterston and Kevin McCall. They have a little weekend retreat up here.'

'Ah,' I said, nodding. This was beginning to make more sense. Karen Waterson and Kevin McCall were actors, who'd just experienced a resurgence in their careers, starring in a new television series called 'Shamus, PI,' an hour-long spoof of every detective series that's ever aired. I don't watch much TV,

but I'd heard about the show and after seeing it once, I'e
found myself hooked. The stories were fresh, the writing wa
superb, and the format was perfect for their considerable act
ing talents. Possibly because they were married in 'real' life
the two brought a wicked chemistry to the screen. As witl
many new shows, the ratings hadn't yet caught up with the rav
reviews, but things looked promising. Whatever their prob
lem, I could understand the desire to keep their difficultie
hidden from public scrutiny.

Jack was saying, 'You're in no way obligated, but I hop
you'll say yes. She really needs your help.'

'Well. I guess I've had stranger requests in my day. I bette
give you my address.'

He held up the signature card I'd completed when I opene
my account. 'I have that.'

I soon learned what 'cocktails-five-to-seven' means to th
very rich. Everybody showed up at seven and stayed until the
were dead drunk. Jack Chamberlain, in a tux, picked me u
at my apartment at six forty-five. I was decked out in a slink
beaded black dress with long sleeves, a high collar and n
back; not my usual apparel of choice. When Jack helped m
into the front seat of his Mercedes, I shrieked at the shock c
cold leather against my bare skin.

Once at the party, I regained my composure and manage
to conduct myself (for the most part) without embarrassmer
or disgrace. The 'little weekend retreat' turned out to be
sprawling six-bedroomed estate, decorated with a confiden
blend of the avant-garde and the minimalist: unadorned whit
walls, wide, bare, gleaming expanses of polished hardwoo
floor. The few pieces of furniture were draped with whi
canvas, like those in a palatial summer residence being close
up for the season. Aside from a dazzling crystal chandelier, a
the dining-room contained was a plant, a mirror, and a ben
wood chair covered with an antique paisley shawl. *Très chi*
They'd probably paid thousands for some interior designer
come in and haul all the knickknacks away.

As the party picked up momentum, the noise level ros
people spilling out on to all the terraces. Six young men, i
black pants and pleated white shirts, circulated with silv

latters of tasty hot and cold morsels. The champagne was exquisite, the supply apparently endless so that I was fairly iddy by the time Jack took me by the arm and eased me out f the living-room. 'Karen wants to see you upstairs,' he murmured.

'Great,' I said. I'd hardly laid eyes on her except as a glittering wraith along the party's perimeters. I hadn't seen Kevin t all, but I'd overheard someone say he was off scouting locations for the show coming up. Jack and I drifted up the spiral stairs together, me hoping that in my half-inebriated state, I wouldn't pitch over the railing and land with a splat. As I reached the landing, I looked down and was startled to see my iend Vera in the foyer below. She caught sight of me and did a double-take, apparently surprised to see me in such elegant surroundings, especially dressed to the teeth. We exchanged a uick wave.

The nearly darkened master suite was carpeted to a hush, ut again, it was nearly empty. The room was probably fifty et by thirty, furnished dead-centre with a king-sized bed, a icker hamper, two ficus trees, and a silver lamp with a wenty-five-watt bulb on a long, curving neck.

As Jack ushered me into the master bathroom where the eeting was to take place, he flicked me an apologetic look. I hope this doesn't seem too odd.'

'Not at all,' I said, politely... like a lot of my business eetings take place in the WC.

Candles flickered from every surface. Sound was dampened by thick white carpeting and a profusion of plants. Karen Waterston sat on the middle riser of three wide, beige, marble eps leading up to the Jacuzzi. Beside her, chocolate-brown ath towels were rolled and stacked like a cord of firewood. he was wearing a halter-style dress of white chiffon, which mphasised the dark, even tan of her slender shoulders and rms. Her hair was silver-blonde, coiled around her head in a wist of satin ropes. She was probably forty-two, but her face ad been cosmetically backdated to the age of twenty-five, a rocess that would require ever more surgical ingenuity as the ears went by. Jack introduced us and we shook hands. Hers

were ice cold and I could have sworn she wasn't happy to have
me there.

Jack pulled out a wicker stool and sat down with his back to
Karen's make-up table, his eyes never leaving her face. My
guess was that being an ex-high-school sweetheart of hers was
as much a part of his identity as being a former basketball
champ. I leant a hip against the marble counter. There was a
silver-framed photograph of Kevin McCall propped up beside
me, the mirror reflecting endless reproductions of his perfect
profile. To all appearances, he'd been allowed to retain the face
he was born with, but the uniform darkness of his hair, with
its picturesque dusting of silver at the temples, suggested that
nature was being tampered with, at least superficially. Still, it
was hard to imagine that either he or Karen had a problem
more pressing than an occasional loose dental cap.

'I appreciate your coming, Miss Millhone. It means a lot to
us under the circumstances.' Her voice was throaty and low,
with the merest hint of tremolo. Even by candlelight, I could
see the tension in her face. 'I wasn't in favour of bringing
anyone else into this, but Jack insisted. Has he explained the
situation?' She glanced from me to Jack, who said, 'I told her
you preferred to do that yourself.'

She seemed to hug herself for warmth and her mouth suddenly looked pinched. Tears welled in her eyes and she placed
two fingers on the bridge of her nose as if to quell their flow.
'You'll have to forgive me...'

I didn't think she'd be able to continue, but she managed to
collect herself.

'Kevin's been kidnapped...' Her voice cracked with emotion and she lifted her dark eyes to mine. I'd never seen such
a depth of pain and suffering.

At first, I didn't even know what to say to her. 'When was
this?'

'Last night. We're very private people. We've never let anyone get remotely close to us...' She broke off again.

'Take your time,' I said.

Jack moved over to the stair and sat down beside her, putting am arm protectively around her shoulders. The smile she
offered him was wan and she couldn't sustain it.

He handed her his handkerchief and I waited while she blew her nose and dabbed at her eyes. 'Sorry. I'm just so frightened. This is horrible.'

'I hope you've called the police,' I said.

'She doesn't want to take the risk,' Jack said.

Karen shook her head. 'They said they'd kill him if I called in the police.'

'Who said?'

'The bastards who snatched him. I was given this note. Here. You can see for yourself. It's too much like the Bender case to take any chances.' She extracted a piece of paper from the folds of her long dress and held it out to me.

I took the note by one corner so I wouldn't smudge any prints, probably a useless precaution. If this was truly like the Bender case, there wouldn't be any prints to smudge. The paper was plain, the printing in ballpoint pen and done with a ruler.

Five hundred thou in small bills buys your husband back. Go to the cops or the feds and he's dead meat for sure. We'll call soon with instructions. Keep your mouth shut or you'll regret it. That's a promise, baby cakes.

SHE WAS RIGHT. Both the format and the use of language bore an uncanny similarity to the note delivered to a woman named Corey Bender, whose husband had been kidnapped about a year ago. Dan Bender was the CEO of a local manufacturing company, a man who'd made millions with a line of auto parts called Fender-Benders. In that situation, the kidnappers had asked for $500,000 in tens and twenties. Mrs Bender had contacted both the police and the FBI, who had stage-managed the whole transaction, arranging for a suitcase full of blank paper to be dropped according to the kidnappers' elaborate telephone instructions. The drop site had been staked out, everyone assuring Mrs Bender that nothing could possibly go wrong. The drop went as planned except the suitcase was never picked up and Dan Bender was never seen alive again. His body—or what was left of it—washed up on the Santa Teresa beach two months later.

'Tell me what happened,' I said.

She got up and began to pace, describing in halting detail the circumstances of Kevin McCall's abduction. The couple had been working on a four-day shooting schedule at the studio down in Hollywood. They'd been picked up from the set by limousine at 7 p.m. on Thursday and had been driven straight to Santa Teresa, arriving for the long weekend at nine o'clock that night. The housekeeper usually fixed supper for them and left it in the oven, departing shortly before they were due home. At the end of a week of shooting, the couple preferred all the solitude they could get.

Nothing seemed amiss when they arrived at the house. Both interior and exterior lights were on as usual. Karen emerged from the limo with Kevin right behind her. She chatted briefly with the driver and then waved goodbye while Kevin unlocked the front door and disarmed the alarm system. The limo driver had already turned out of the gate when two men in ski masks stepped from the shadows armed with automatics. Neither Karen nor Kevin had much opportunity to react. A second limousine pulled into the driveway and Kevin was hustled into the back seat at gunpoint. Not a word was said. The note was thrust into Karen's hand as the gunmen left. She raced after the limo as it sped away, but no licence plates were visible. She had no real hope of catching up and no clear idea what she meant to do anyway. In a panic, she returned to the house and locked herself in. Once the shock wore off, she called Jack Chamberlain, their local banker, a former high school classmate—the only person in Santa Teresa she felt she could trust. Her first thought was to cancel tonight's party altogether, but Jack suggested she proceed.

'I thought it would look more natural,' he filled in. 'Especially if she's being watched.'

'They did call with instructions?' I asked.

Again she nodded, her face pale. 'They want the money by midnight tomorrow or that's the last I'll see of him.'

'Can you *raise* 500,000 on such short notice?'

'Not without help,' she said and turned a pleading look to Jack.

He was already shaking his head and I gathered this was a subject they'd already discussed at length. 'The bank doesn't keep large reservoirs of cash on hand,' he said to me. 'There's no way I'd have access to a sum like that, particularly on a weekend. The best I can do is bleed the cash from all the branch ATMs...'

'Surely you can do better than that,' she said. 'You're a bank vice-president.'

He turned to her, with a faintly defensive air, trying to persuade her the failing wasn't his. 'I might be able to put together the full amount by Monday, but even then, you'd have to fill out an application and go through the loan committee...'

She said, 'Oh for God's sake, Jack. Don't give me that bureaucratic bullshit when Kevin's life is at stake! There has to be a way.'

'Karen, be reasonable...'

'Forget it. This is hopeless. I'm sorry I ever brought you into this...'

I watched them bicker for a moment and then broke in. 'All right, wait a minute. Hold on. Let's back off the money question, for the time being.'

'Back *off*?'

'Look. Let's assume there's a way to get the ransom money. Now what?'

Her brow was furrowed and she seemed to have trouble concentrating on the question at hand. 'I'm sorry. What?'

'Fill me in on the rest of it. I need to know what happened last night after you got in touch with Jack.'

'Oh. I see, yes. He came over to the house and we sat here for hours, waiting for the phone to ring. The kidnappers... one of them... finally called at 2 a.m.'

'You didn't recognise the voice?'

'Not at all.'

'Did the guy seem to know Jack was with you?'

'He didn't mention it, but he swore they were watching the house and he said the phone was tapped.'

'I wouldn't bet on it, but it's probably smart to proceed as though it's true. It's possible they didn't have the house staked out last night, but they may have put a man on it since. Hard to know. Did they tell you how to deliver the cash once you got it?'

'That part was simple. I'm to pack the money in a big canvas duffel. At eleven-thirty tomorrow night, they want me to leave the house on my bicycle with the duffel in the basket.'

'On a bike? That's a new one.'

'Kev and I often bike together on weekends, which they seemed aware of. As a matter of fact, they seemed to know quite a lot. It was very creepy.'

Jack spoke up. 'They must have cased the place to begin with. They knew the whole routine, from what she's told me.'

'Stands to reason,' I remarked. And then to her, 'Go on.'

'They told me to wear my yellow jumpsuit—I guess so they can identify me—and that's all there was.'

'They didn't tell you which way to ride?'

'I asked about that and they told me I could head in any direction I wanted. They said they'd follow at a distance and intercept me when it suited them. Obviously, they want to make sure I'm unaccompanied.'

'Then what?'

'When they blink the car lights, I'm to toss the canvas duffel to the side of the road and ride on. They'll release Kevin as soon as the money's been picked up and counted.'

'Shoot. It rules out any fudging if they count the money first. Did they let you talk to Kevin?'

'Briefly. He sounded fine. Worried about me...'

'And you're sure it was him.'

'Positive. I'm so scared...'

The whole time we'd been talking, my mind was racing ahead. She had to call the cops. There was no doubt in my mind she was a fool to tackle this without the experts, but she was dead set against it. I said, 'Karen, you can't handle something like this without the cops. You'd be crazy to try to manage on your own.'

She was adamant.

Jack and I took turns arguing the point and I could see his frustration surface. 'For God's sake, you've got to listen to us. You're way out of your element. If these guys are the same ones who kidnapped Dan Bender, you're putting Kevin's life at risk. They're absolutely ruthless.'

'Jack, I'm not the one putting Kevin's life at risk. *You* are. That's exactly what you're doing when you propose calling the police.'

'How are you going to get the money?' he said, exasperated.

'Goddamn it, how do I know? You're the banker. You tell me.'

'Karen, I'm telling you. There's no way to do this. You're making a big mistake.'

'Corey Bender was the one who made a mistake,' she snapped.

We were getting nowhere. Time was short and the pressures were mounting every minute. If Jack and I didn't come up with *some* plan, Kevin McCall was going to end up dead. If the cash could be assembled, the obvious move was to have me take Karen's place during the actual delivery, which would at least eliminate the possibility of her being picked up as well. Oddly enough, I thought I had an inkling how to get the bucks, though it might well take me the better part of the next day.

'All right,' I said, breaking in for the umpeteenth time. 'We can argue this all night and it's not going to get us any place. Suppose I find a way to get the money, will you at least consent to my taking your place for the drop?'

She studied me for a moment. 'That's awfully risky, isn't it? What if they realise the substitution?'

'How could they? They'll be following in a car. In the dark and at a distance, I can easily pass for you. A wig and a jumpsuit and who'd know the difference?'

She hesitated. 'I do have a wig, but why not just do what they say? I don't like the idea of disobeying their instructions.'

'Because these guys are way too dangerous for you to deal with yourself. Suppose you deliver the money as specified.

What's to prevent them picking you up and making Kevin pay additional ransom for *your* return?'

I could see her debate the point. Her uneasiness was obvious, but she finally agreed. 'I don't understand what you intend to do about the ransom. If Jack can't manage to get the money, how can you?'

'I know a guy who has access to a large sum of cash. I can't promise anything, but I can always ask.'

Karen's gaze came to rest on my face with puzzlement.

'Look,' I said in response to her unspoken question. 'I'll explain if I get it. And if not, you have to promise me you'll call the police.'

Jack prodded. 'It's your only chance.'

She was silent for a moment and then spoke slowly. 'All right. Maybe so. We'll do it your way. What other choice do I have?'

Before we left, we made arrangements for her to leave a wig, the yellow jumpsuit and the bicycle on the service porch the next night. I'd return to the house on foot some time after dark, leaving my car parked a few discreet blocks away. At eleven-thirty, as instructed, I'd pedal down the drive with the canvas duffel and ride around until the kidnappers caught up with me. While I was gone, Jack could swing by and pick Karen up in his car. I wanted her off the premises in the event anything went wrong. If I were snatched and the kidnappers realised they had the wrong person, at least they couldn't storm back to the house and get her. We went over the details until we were all in accord. In the end, she seemed satisfied with the plan and so did Jack. I was the only one with any lingering doubts. I thought she was a fool, but kept that to myself.

I HIT THE ROAD the next morning early and headed north on 101. Visiting hours at the Federal Correctional Institution at Lompoc run from eight to four on Saturdays. The drive took about an hour with a brief stop at a supermarket in Buelltown where I picked up an assortment of picnic supplies. By ten, I was seated at one of the four sheltered picnic tables with my friend, Harry Hovey. If Harry was surprised to see me, he didn't complain. 'It's not like my social calendar's all that full,' he said. 'To what do I owe the pleasure?'

'Let's eat first,' I said. 'Then I got something I need to talk to you about.'

I'd brought cold chicken and potato salad, assorted cheeses, fruit and cookies, anything I could grab that didn't look like institutional fare. Personally, I wasn't hungry, but it was gratifying to watch Harry chow down with such enthusiasm. He was not looking well. He was a man in his fifties, maybe five-foot five, heavy-set, with thinning grey hair and glasses cloudy with fingerprints. He didn't take good care of himself under the best of circumstances, and the stress of prison living had aged him ten years. His colour was bad. He was smoking way too much. He'd lost weight in a manner that looked neither healthful nor flattering.

'How're you doing?' I asked. 'You look tired.'

'I'm OK, I guess. I been better in my day, but what the hell,' he said. He'd paused in the middle of his meal for a cigarette. He seemed distracted, his attention flicking from the other tables to the playground equipment where a noisy batch of kids were twirling round and round on the swings. It was November and the sun was shining, but the air was chilly and the grass was dead.

'How much time you have to serve yet?'

'Sixteen months,' he said. 'You ever been in the can?'

I shook my head.

He pointed at me with his cigarette. 'Word of advice. Never admit nothin'. Always claim you're innocent. I learned that from the politicians. You ever watch those guys? They get caught takin' bribes and they assume this injured air. Like it's all a mistake, but the truth will out. They're confident they'll be vindicated and bullshit like that. They welcome the investigation so their names can be cleared. They always say that, you know? Whole time I'm in prison, I been saying that myself. I was framed. It's all a set-up. I don't know nothing about the money. I was just doing a favour for an old friend, a big wig. A very Big Wig. Like I'm implying the Governor or the Chief of Police.'

'Has it done you any good?'

'Well, not yet, but who knows? My lawyer's still trying to find a basis for appeal. If I get outta this one, I'm going into therapy, get my head straight, I swear to God. Speaking of which, I may get "born again", you know? It looks good. Lends a little credibility, which is something all the money in the world can't buy...'

I took a deep breath. 'Actually, it's the money I need to talk to you about.' I took a few minutes to fill him in on the kidnapping without mentioning any names. Some of Karen Waterston's paranoia had filtered into my psyche and I thought the less I said about the 'victim', the better off he'd be. 'I know you've got a big cache of money somewhere. I'm hoping you'll contribute some of it to pay the ransom demands.'

His look was blank with disbelief. 'Ransom?'

'Harry, don't put me through this. You know what ransom is.'

'Yeah, it's money you give to guys you never see again. Why not throw it out of the window? Why not blow it at the track...'

'Are you finished yet?'

He smiled and a dimple formed. 'How much you talking about?'

'Five hundred thousand.'

His eyebrows went up. 'What makes you think I got money like that?'

'Harry,' I said patiently, 'an informant told the cops you had over a million bucks. That's how you got caught.'

Harry slapped the table. 'Bobby Urquhart. That fuck. I should have known it was him. I run into the guy in a bar settin' at this table full of bums. He buys a round of tequila shooters. Next thing I know, everybody else is gone. I'm drunk as a skunk and flappin' my mouth.' He dropped his cigarette butt on the concrete and crushed it underfoot. 'Word of warning. Never confide in a guy wearing Brut. I must have been nuts to give that little faggot the time of day. The money's gone. I blew it. I got nothin' left.'

'I don't believe you. That's bullshit. You didn't have time to blow that much. When you were busted, all you had were a few lousy bucks. Where's the rest of it?'

'Un-uhn. No way.'

'Come on, Harry. It isn't going to do you any good in here. Why not help these people out? They got tons of money. They can pay you back.'

'They got money, how come they don't pay the shit themselves?'

'Because it's Saturday and the banks are closed. The branch VP couldn't even come up with the cash that fast. A man's life is at stake.'

'Hey, so's mine and so what? You ever try life in the pen? I worked hard for that money so why should I do for some guy I never seen before?'

'Once in a while you just gotta help people out.'

'Maybe you do. I don't.'

'Harry, please. Be a prince...'

I could see him begin to waver. Who can resist a good deed now and then?

He put his hand on his chest. 'This is giving me angina pains...' He wagged his head back and forth. 'Jesus. What if the cops get wind of it? How's it gonna look?'

'The cops are never going to know. Believe me, this woman's never going to breathe a word of it. If she trusted the cops, she'd have called them in the first place.'

'Who are these people? At least tell me that. I'm not giving up half a million bucks without some ID.'

I thought about it swiftly. I was reluctant to trade on their celebrity status. On the other hand, she was desperate and there wasn't time to spare. 'Swear you won't tell.'

'Who'm I gonna tell? I'm a con. Nobody believes me anyway,' he said.

'Kevin McCall and Karen Waterston.'

He seemed startled at first. 'You're kidding me. No shit? You're talking, *Shamus, PI*? Them two?'

'That's right.'

'Whyn't you say so? That's my favourite show. All the guys watch that. What a gas. Karen Waterston is a fox.'

'Then you'll help?'

'For that chick, of course,' he said. He gave me a stern look. 'Get me her autograph or the deal's off.'

'Trust me. You'll have it. You're a doll. I owe you one.'

We took a walk around the yard while he told me where the money was. Harry had nearly two million in cash hidden in a canvas duffel of his own, concealed in the false back of a big upholstered sofa, which was locked up, with a lot of other furniture, in a commercial self-storage facility.

I headed back to Santa Teresa with the key in my hand. Unearthing the money took the balance of the afternoon. The couch was at the bottom of an eight-by-eight-foot storage locker crammed with goods. Tables, chairs, cardboard boxes, a desk, a hundred or more items which I removed one by one, stacking them behind me in the narrow aisle between bins. The facility was hot and airless and I could hardly ask for help. By the time I laid my hands on the canvas tote hidden in the couch, there was hardly room in the passageway to turn around. By six o'clock, feeling harried, I had taken all but half a million out of Harry's tote. The rest of the stash I stuffed back into the couch, piling furniture and boxes helter-skelter on top of it. I'd have to return at some point—when the whole ordeal was over—and pack the bin properly...

THE DROP PLAYED OUT according to the numbers, without the slightest hitch. At ten that night, I eased through a gap in the hedge on the north side of the Waterston/McCall property and made my way to the house with Harry's canvas bag in tow. I slipped into the darkened service entry where Karen was waiting. Once the door shut behind me, I shoved Harry's canvas tote into the large duffel she provided. We chatted nervously while I changed into the wig and yellow jumpsuit. It was just then ten-thirty and the remaining wait was long and tense. By eleven-thirty, both of us were strung out on pure adrenalin and I was glad to be on the move.

Before I took off on the bicycle, Karen gave me a quick hug. 'You're wonderful. I can't believe you did this.'

'I'm not as wonderful as all that,' I said, uncomfortably. 'We need to talk the minute Kevin's home safe. Be sure to call me.'

'Of course. Absolutely. We'll call you first thing.'

I pedalled down the drive and took a right on West Glen. The cash-heavy duffel threw the bike out of balance, but I corrected and rode on. It was chilly at that hour and traffic was almost non-existent. For two miles, almost randomly, I bicycled through the dark, cursing my own foolishness for thinking I could pull it off. Eventually, I became aware that a sedan had fallen in behind me. In the glare of the headlights, I couldn't tell the make or the model; only that the licence plate was missing. The sedan followed me for what felt like an hour, while I pedalled on, feeling anxious, winded, and frightened beyond belief. Finally, the headlights blinked twice. Front wheel wobbling, I hauled the duffel from the basket and tossed it out on to the shoulder of the road. It landed with a thump near a cluster of bushes and I pedalled away. I glanced back only once as the vehicle behind me slowed to a stop.

I returned to the big house, left the bicycle in the service porch and made my way back across the blackness of the rear lawn to my car. My heart was still thudding as I pulled away. Home again, in my apartment, I changed into a nightie and robe, and huddled on the couch with a cup of brandy-laced hot tea. I knew I should try to sleep, but I was too wired to bother. I glanced at my watch. It was nearly 2 a.m. I figured I probably wouldn't get a word from Karen for another hour best. It takes time to count half a million dollars in small bills. I flipped on the TV and watched a mind-numbing rerun of an old black-and-white film.

I waited through the night, but the phone didn't ring. Around five, I must have dozed because the next thing I knew, it was eight thirty-five. What was going on? The kidnappers had had ample time to effect Kevin's release. *If* he's getting out alive, I thought. I stared at the phone, afraid to call Karen in case the line was still tapped. I pulled out the phone book, looked up Jack Chamberlain, and tried his home number. The phone rang five times and his machine picked up. I left a cryptic message and then tried Karen at the house. No answer there. I was stumped. Mixed with my uneasiness was a touch of irritation. Even if they'd heard nothing, they could have let me know.

Without much hope of success, I called the bank and asked for Jack. Surprisingly, Lucy Alisal put me through.

'Jack Chamberlain,' he said.

'Jack? This is Kinsey. Have you heard from Karen Waterston?'

'Of course. Haven't you?'

'Not a word,' I said. 'Is Kevin OK?'

'He's fine. Everything's terrific.'

'Would you kindly tell me what's going on?'

'Well, sure. I can tell you as much as I know. I drove her back over to the house about two this morning and we waited it out. Kevin got home at six. He's shaken up, as you might imagine, but otherwise he's in good shape. I talked to both of them again a little while ago. She said she was going to call you as soon as we hung up. She didn't get in touch?'

'Jack, that's what I just said. I've been sitting here for hours without a word from anyone. I tried the house and got no answer...'

'Hey, relax. Don't worry. I can see where you'd be ticked, but everything's fine. I know they were going back to Los Angeles. She might just have forgotten.'

I could hear a little warning. Something was off here. 'What about the kidnappers? Does Kevin have any way to identify them?'

'That's what I asked. He says, not a chance. He was tied up and blindfolded while they had him in the car. He says they drove into a garage and kept him there until the ransom money was picked up and brought back. Next thing he knew, someone got in the car, backed out of the garage, drove him around for a while, and finally set him out in his own driveway. He's going to see a doctor once they get to Los Angeles, but they never really laid a hand on him.'

'I can't believe they didn't call to let me know he was safe. I need to talk to her.' I knew I was being repetitive, but I was really bugged. I'd promised Harry her autograph, among other things, and while he'd pretended to make a joke of it, I knew he was serious.

'Maybe they thought I'd be doing that. I know they were both very grateful for your help. Maybe she's planning to drop you a note.'

'Well, I guess I'll just wait until I hear from them,' I said and hung up.

I showered and got dressed, sucked down some coffee and drove over to my office in downtown Santa Teresa. My irritation was beginning to wear off and exhaustion was trickling into my body in its wake. I went through my mail, paid a bill, tidied up my desk. I found myself laying my little head down, catching a quick nap while I drooled on my Month-At-A-Glance. There was a knock on the door and I woke with a start.

Vera Lipton, the claims manager for the insurance company next door, was standing on my threshold. 'You must have had a better time than I did Friday night. You hung-over or still drunk?' she said.

'Neither. I got a lousy night's sleep.'

She lifted her right brow. 'Sounds like fun. You and that guy from the bank?'

'Not exactly.'

'So what'd you think of the glitzy twosome...Karen and Kev.'

'I don't even want to talk about them,' I said. I then proceeded to pour out the whole harrowing tale, including a big dose of outrage at the way I'd been treated.

Vera started smirking about halfway through. By the end of my recital, she was shaking her head.

'What's the matter?' I asked.

'Well, that's the biggest bunch of horsepucky I ever heard. You've been taken, Kinsey. Most royally had.'

'*I* have?'

'They're flat broke. They don't have a dime...'

'They do, too!'

She shook her head emphatically. 'Dead broke. They're busted.'

'They couldn't be,' I said.

'Yes, they are,' she said. 'I bet you dollars to donuts they put the whole scam together to pick up some cash.'

'How could they be broke with a house like that? They have a hot new series on the air!'

'The show was cancelled. It hasn't hit the papers yet, but the network decided to yank 'em after six episodes. They sank everything they had into the house up here when they first heard they'd been picked up...'

I squinted at her. 'How do you know all this stuff?'

'Neil and I have been looking for a house for months. Our real estate agent's the one who sold 'em that place.'

'They don't have *any* money?' I asked.

'Not a dime,' she said. 'Why do you think the house is so empty? They had to sell the furniture to make the mortgage payment this month.'

'But what about the party? That must have cost a mint!'

'I'm sure it did. Their attorney advised them to max out their credit cards and then file for bankruptcy.'

'Are you sure?'

'Sure I'm sure.'

I looked at Vera blankly, doing an instant reply of events. I knew she was right because it suddenly made perfect sense. Karen Waterston and Kevin McCall had run a scam, that's all it was. No wonder the drop had gone without a hitch. I wasn't being followed by kidnappers...it was him. Those two had just successfully pocketed half a million bucks. And what was I going to do? At this point, even if I called the cops, all they had to do was maintain the kidnapping fiction and swear the bad guys were for real. They'd be very convincing. That's what acting is all about. The 'kidnappers', meanwhile, would have disappeared without a trace and they'd make out like bandits, quite literally.

Vera watched me process the revelation. 'You don't seem all that upset. I thought you'd be apoplectic, jumping up and down. Don't you feel like an ass?'

'I don't know yet. Maybe not.'

She moved towards the door. 'I gotta get back to work. Let me know when it hits. It's always entertaining to watch you blow your stack.'

I sat down at my desk and thought about the situation and then put a call through to Harry Hovey at the prison.

'This is rare,' Harry said when he'd heard me out. 'I think we got a winner with this one. Holy shit.'

'I thought you'd see the possibilities,' I said.

'Holy shit!' he said again.

The rest of what I now refer to as my missionary work I can only guess at until I see Harry again. According to the newspapers, Kevin McCall and Karen Waterston were arrested two days after they returned to Los Angeles. Allegedly (as they say) the two entered a bank and tried to open an account with $9,000 in counterfeit tens and twenties. Amazingly, Harry Hovey saw God and had a crisis of conscience shortly before this in his prison cell up in Lompoc. Recanting his claims of innocence, he felt compelled to confess . . . he'd been working for the two celebrities for years, he said. In return, for immunity, he told the feds where to find the counterfeit plates, hiding in the bottom of a canvas tote, which turned up in their possession just as he said it would.

SOLUTION TO
THE CRYPTIC CRIME ACROSTIC

The quotation is:

She was competent with the razor. Years before when she
had first come out of the desert and worked for Louche in
Tangier she had spent part of each day as an assistant in a
barber's shop attached to a high class brothel. It was a place
where men talked and the gossip she picked up had been
valuable.

Peter O'Donnell, *Modesty Blaise*

The clues are:

A	Pith	N	Modus operandi
B	Eunuch	O	Oath
C	The lesser of two evils	P	Damask
D	Ellis Peters	Q	Earthenware
E	Rash	R	Sue Grafton
F	Orphan	S	Thatched Cottage
G	Deathbed	T	Ypres
H	On the sabbath	U	Bathsheba
I	Newspeak	V	Laird
J	Nephew	W	Afghan
K	Echo chamber	X	Identification
L	Last straw	Y	Shakespeare
M	Liza Cody	Z	Edward the Confessor

THE CRIME WRITERS' ASSOCIATION

In the 1850s, crime fiction sprang fully formed out of the dark genius of one man—Edgar Allan Poe—and he did it with a handful of short stories; forty years later, again principally in short story form, Arthur Conan Doyle established the genre apparently for ever. Subsequently, some of the best examples of the short form in the English language—G. K. Chesterton's Father Brown tales, Somerset Maugham's Ashenden series—were crime stories, or their near neighbours, espionage adventures.

2nd Culprit, the latest in an annual collection by members of the Crime Writers' Association, follows in this tradition. The contributors include, as has long been the case, novelists of the first order who can adapt their talents to the disciplines of brevity, encapsulating drama, tension and wit in concentrated doses.

It is exactly forty years since John Creasey founded the CWA, with the aim of promoting crime fiction. It is particularly appropriate that we have now added to our Gold, Silver and Diamond Daggers a special short story prize, which will be presented at our annual awards dinner on our anniversary, 5 November 1993. By coincidence, Ellis Peters, this year's Diamond Dagger winner, is among those whose work enhances this book.

To all who helped prepare *2nd Culprit*, our thanks: to all who wrote for it, our admiration; to all who read it, our hopes that they will enjoy and return for more.

ROBERT RICHARDSON
CWA Chairman, 1993-94

Clewsey's drawings appear regularly in the CWA's monthly newsletter, *Red Herrings*.

Born in London, **Liza Cody** is the author of six Anna Lee mysteries, most recently *Backhand*, and a new novel, *Bucket Nut* (Chatto & Windus/Arrow).

Madelaine Duke, of Dutch-Russian origin, has written forty books from biography and historical novels to crime and (under Alex Duncan) humour. She was chairman of the CWA and the first winner of *The Times*-Veuve Clicquot short story competition.

Anthea Fraser has written twenty-six novels, some about the paranormal, some mystery suspense and the last ten straight crime novels. She also enjoys writing occasional short stories, with which she began her career at the age of five!

Antonia Fraser has written seven full-length mystery novels featuring Jemima Shore Investigator and has had two books of short stories published: *Jemima Shore's First Case* and *Jemima Shore and the Sunny Grave*.

Sue Grafton is the author of ten novels, from *'A' is for Alibi* to *'J' is for Judgment*, all available in Great Britain (Pan-Macmillan). She lives in Southern California where she is currently at work on *'K' is for...*, the latest in her Kinsey Millhone series.

Jonathan Gash Creator of 'Lovejoy' (Arrow); writes also as Jonathan Grant (The 'Sealandings' historical trilogy), etc. Doctor, with quite a family. Terrible musician. Lazy.

Tim Heald, born in 1944 has a wife and four children, none of them as tiresome as those in his short story. He is an ex-chairman of the CWA and the creator of Simon Bognor of the Board of Trade.

Reginald Hill has written more than thirty books, including the well-known Dalziel/Pascoe series. His latest novel *Blood Sympathy* (HarperCollins) introduces a new series character, Joe Sixmith, redundant lathe operator and serendipic p.i. who lives in Luton. Hill lives in Cumbria.

Tony Hillerman, a former farm boy, journalist and college professor, is best known for his novels involving the Navajo Tribal Police and crimes in the Indian Country of the US Southwest. He is now published in fourteen languages.

HRF Keating gets up every day, 6.59 a.m. (like one of the characters in Inspector Ghote's sixteenth dilemma, *Dead on Time*) and goes for a briskish walk. Approaching Kensington Gardens one morning, he saw two speeding police motorcyclists, and fell into a train of thought...

Susan Kelly's latest novel—*The Seventh Victim*—will be published in January 1994 (Hodder Headline). Her poetry has appeared widely in magazines and anthologies and been broadcast on BBC Radio 4.

Michael Z Lewin's latest Albert Samson mystery is *Called by a Panther*, a call Samson regrets anthering. A new Indianapolis book, *Underdog*, introduces the eponymous Jan Moro.

Nancy Livingston was born in Stockton-on-Tees, worked as an actress, secretary, air stewardess and TV production assistant before settling down thankfully to be a full-time writer. Her historical sagas and whodunnits are all in paperback, currently *Two Sisters* (Warner) and *Mayhem in Parga* (Gollancz).

Peter Lovesey's novels and short stories have been adapted for radio, TV and film. His detective 'memoirs' of the Prince of Wales now run to three volumes, of which the latest is *Bertie and the Crime of Passion*.

Carole Rawcliffe is a medieval historian at the University of East Anglia. She is joint editor of *The History of Parliament, 1386-1421* (4 volumes, Alan Sutton, 1993), and has written widely on medieval society and medicine.

Jean McConnell began as an actress then turned to writing drama and comedy for the stage, radio and television. As well as documentaries and books on true cases, she has written innumerable short crime stories.

Susan Moody, former Chairman of the CWA, is the author of the Penny Wanawake series, featuring a black female sleuth. Her three suspense novels are: *Playing with Fire*, *Hush-a-Bye* and *House of Moons*. Her most recent book is *Takeout Double*, starring amateur detective Cassandra Swann, professional bridge player and weight watcher.

Peter O'Donnell has written for all media except radio. Created Modesty Blaise for strip cartoon in 1963, and subsequently featured her in eleven novels and a book of short stories. Also produced nine novels under the pen-name Madeleine Brent.

Ellis Peters, who is also Edith Pargeter, has scored up 57 years of novel-writing, under both names, but burst into the wider world's notice only with the launch of Brother Cadfael in 1977. She has enjoyed every moment of it.

Ian Rankin is the author of five Inspector Rebus novels, the latest of which is *The Black Book* (Orion Books), and a collection of Inspector Rebus short stories. He was born in Fife but now lives.

Eric Wright was born in England and emigrated to Canada as a young man. He has written ten Charlie Salter novels (Collins Crime Club) and a number of short stories. He now lives in Toronto.

Margaret Yorke is a past chairman of the CWA. She lives in Buckinghamshire and is the author of thirty-five novels, the most recent being *Dangerous to Know*. She has also published many short stories in various anthologies.

ACKNOWLEDGEMENTS

PREVIOUSLY UNPUBLISHED works in this collection are: 'Slight of Hand' by Catherine Aird; 'Sister Brona and the Sacred Altar Cloth' by Alex Auswaks; 'Keep Taking the Tabloids' by Robert Barnard; 'Where's Stacey?' by Liza Cody; 'The Image of Innocence' by Madelaine Duke; 'Jemima Shore and the Frightened Girl' by Antonia Fraser; 'Turning Point' by Anthea Fraser; 'The Mood Cuckoo' by Jonathan Gash; 'A Vacance en Campagne' by Tim Heald; 'True Thomas' by Reginald Hill; 'Incident on Millionaires' Row' by HRF Keating; 'The Last Kiss' by Susan Kelly; 'Boss' by Michael Z Lewin; 'Betrayal' by Nancy Livingston; 'Working with Suzie' by Jean McConnell; 'Better to Forget' by Susan Moody; 'Professor Kaa's Doorway' by Peter O'Donnell; 'The Frustration Dream' by Ellis Peters; 'Well Shot' by Ian Rankin; 'Dishonourable Members' by Carole Rawcliffe; 'The Duke' by Eric Wright; 'The Last Resort' by Margaret Yorke.

Acknowledgements are due for those works which have been previously published, as follows:
'Exquisitely Gowned' by Eric Ambler was published as the introduction to the first American edition of *The Dark Frontier* (Mysterious Press, New York, 1990); 'A Little Missionary Work' by Sue Grafton was published in *Deadly Allies* (Doubleday, New York, 1992); 'First Lead Gasser' by Tony Hillerman was published in *Ellery Queen Mystery Magazine* (New York, April 1993); 'The Curious Computer' by Peter Lovesey was published in *The New Adventures of Sherlock Holmes* (Carroll & Graf, New York, 1987); the Clewsey cartoons first appeared in *Red Herrings*, the newsletter of the CWA.

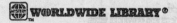

MURDER ONCE REMOVED
Kathleen Kunz
A Terry Girard Mystery

First Time in Paperback

FAMILY SECRETS TO DIE FOR

Terry Girard returns from a weekend of research to find her adored aunt Cecile dead—a victim, apparently, of suicide. But Terry is convinced CeCe was murdered.

She and her aunt were partners in an expensive genealogy research service, catering to St. Louis's most prominent families. In constructing someone's exclusive family tree, had CeCe stumbled upon an ancient scandal?

Convincing the investigating detective that there is a killer loose is an uphill battle. But when another body surfaces, it's clear that someone among the city's historic elite will stop at nothing—not even murder—to keep secrets buried.

"An invigorating tale."

—Publishers Weekly

Available in August at your favorite retail stores.

ONCE